W9-BYA-905

great barracuda

spotted drum

jew fish

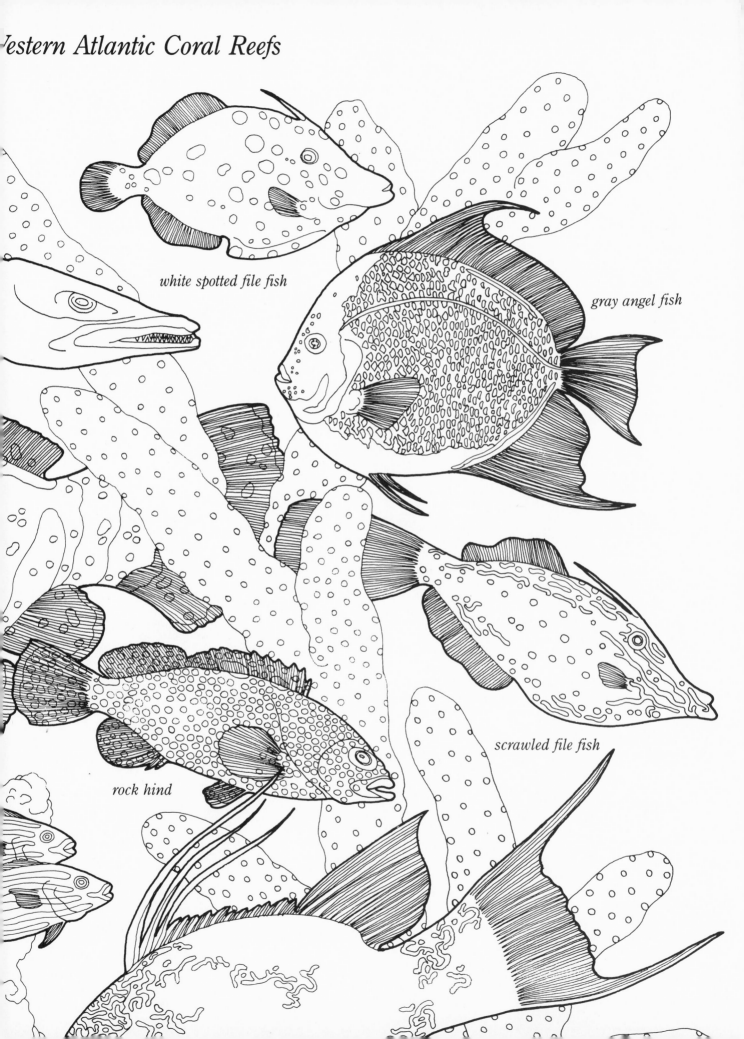

white spotted file fish

gray angel fish

scrawled file fish

rock hind

OCEANS

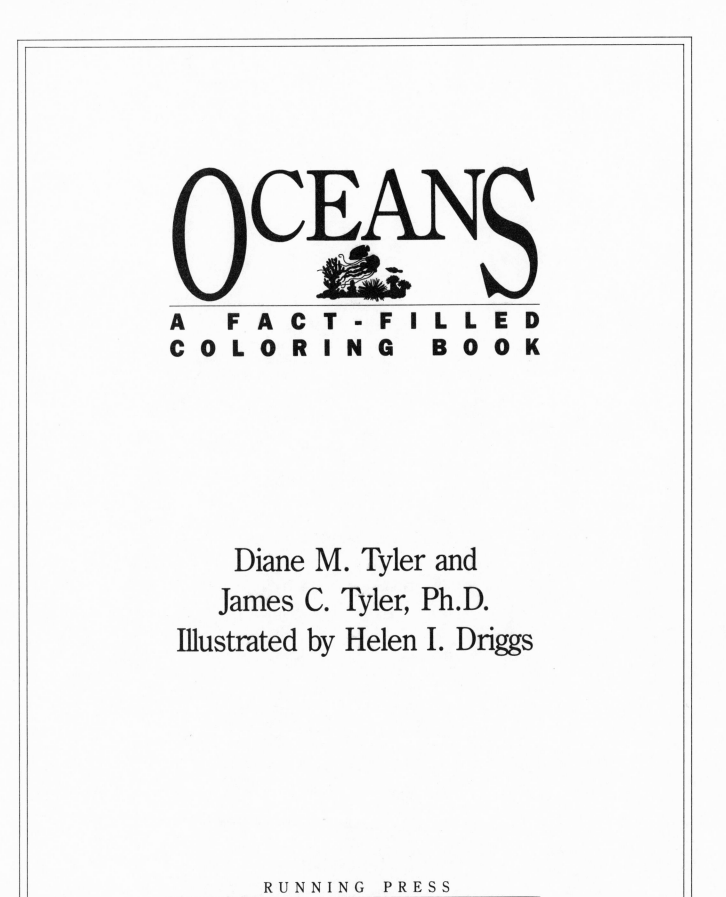

A FACT-FILLED COLORING BOOK

Diane M. Tyler and
James C. Tyler, Ph.D.
Illustrated by Helen I. Driggs

RUNNING PRESS
PHILADELPHIA, PENNSYLVANIA

Copyright © 1990 by Running Press.
Printed in the United States of America. All rights reserved
under the Pan-American and International Copyright Conventions.

*This book may not be reproduced in whole or in part in any form or by any
means, electronic or mechanical, including photocopying, recording, or by any
information storage and retrieval system now known or hereafter invented, without written permission from the publisher.*

Canadian representatives: General Publishing Co., Ltd.,
30 Lesmill Road, Don Mills, Ontario M3B 2T6.

International representatives: Worldwide Media Services, Inc.,
115 East Twenty-third Street, New York, NY 10010.

9 8 7 6 5 4 3 2 1

Digit on the right indicates the number of this printing.

ISBN 0-89471-759-6

Editorial Director: Nancy Steele
Editor: Chris Bittenbender
Cover design: Toby Schmidt
Interior design: Liz Vogdes
Cover illustrations: Helen I. Driggs
Interior illustrations: Helen I. Driggs
Poster illustration: Helen I. Driggs
Poster copyright © 1990 Running Press Book Publishers
Printed by Chernay Printing, Inc., Coopersburg, Pennsylvania
Typography by Commcor Communications Corporation,
Philadelphia, Pennsylvania

This book may be ordered by mail from the publisher.
Please add $2.50 for postage and handling.
But try your bookstore first!
Running Press Book Publishers
125 South Twenty-second Street
Philadelphia, Pennsylvania 19103

CONTENTS

INTRODUCTION
The Seven Seas

The first ocean explorers probably were fishermen who used boats to fish in waters deeper than they could wade. When fishermen learned to sail miles from their homes, they discovered a vast world beyond their own villages.

As the first explorers sailed to other settlements, they began to trade food and materials with the people they met. This led to more exploration to find new marketplaces and new people with whom to trade. In this way, ocean trade routes became established.

Little did the passengers of the Mayflower know what lay before them as they sailed from Holland on their long voyage across the Atlantic Ocean to a new world. As they began their journey across a vast ocean, they must have wondered what sorts of creatures existed in the waters beneath the creaking hull of their ship.

Early explorers and sailors told tales of sea monsters and mermaids. Today's scientists have discovered real animals and plants that are every bit as mysterious and fascinating. From microscopic life to majestic, spouting whales, the oceans offer living treasures whose future depends on our help and respect.

When you look at the surface of the ocean, all you see are waves. Though it may be hard to believe, there are as many different types of scenery underneath those waves as you might see on land.

The shallowest part of the ocean floor, nearest the land, is called the *continental shelf*. This is the part of the ocean that we know the most about and which contains the greatest wealth of oil, minerals, fishes, and other food resources. The continental shelf starts at sea level at the coastline, and gradually slopes down to about 300 to 400 feet deep.

Introduction: The Seven Seas

Further offshore, the ocean quickly becomes deeper, sloping off steeply to about 10,000 to 15,000 feet. This area is called the *continental slope*. Most of the deepest part of the ocean lies beyond the slope on the somewhat flatter *abyssal plain*. The vast expanse of that area is broken up by underwater mountain chains as majestic as any of those on land, and by trenches longer and deeper than the deepest pits and canyons on any continent.

All the oceans of the world are interconnected, but they are divided by the continents. For that reason, it is easiest for us to talk about them as the Pacific, Atlantic, and Indian Oceans. The northern parts of the Pacific and Atlantic Oceans around the North Pole are called the Arctic Ocean. The southern parts of all three of the main oceans extend to surround the Antarctic Continent. All of these and the larger bodies of salt water that are more closely surrounded by land, such as the Mediterranean and Caribbean Seas, are what we call the Seven Seas.

PART ONE

EXPLORING THE OCEANS

The Pacific Ocean

The largest of all the oceans is the Pacific Ocean. It's a huge, rounded basin that stretches from the Americas on the east to China, Indonesia, and Australia on the west, and from the Arctic Sea near Alaska and Siberia on the north all the way south to Antarctica.

Thousands of exotic tropical island groups are scattered across the surface of the Pacific Ocean. Many of these islands are actually the tops of otherwise sunken volcanic mountain chains. One such group makes up the islands of Hawaii. Another is the Galapagos Islands. This group has been of great interest to scientists since the time of Charles Darwin in the mid-1800s, because each island in the group contains many different kinds of plants and animals unique to that island but closely related to the plants and animals on nearby islands. Many of these plants and animals are found nowhere else on Earth. Other Pacific Ocean islands are parts of coral reefs, such as Australia's Great Barrier Reef, the largest coral reef in the world.

Many volcanoes can be found where the great plates of the Pacific Ocean floor shift and slide. Volcanoes erupt so often in these areas that the edges of the Pacific are called the ''Ring of Fire.'' Over the course of millions of years, underwater volcanoes have erupted many times. Sometimes a volcano on an existing island erupts with such force that the entire island is blown away. This happened at Krakatoa (Krak-uh-TO-uh) in 1883.

The Pacific is home to more kinds of sea creatures than any other ocean.

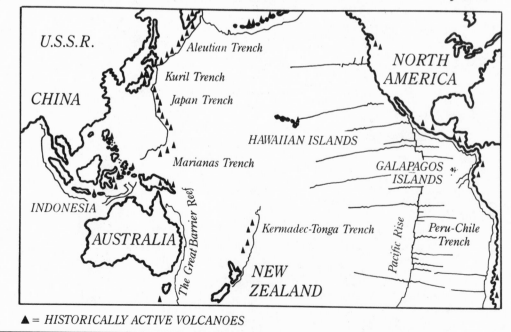

▲ = HISTORICALLY ACTIVE VOLCANOES

Volcanoes erupt above and beneath the water all around the rim of the Pacific Ocean—an area where volcanoes erupt so often that it's called the "Ring of Fire."

Early Explorers of the Pacific Ocean

In 1513, Vasco de Balboa of Spain hacked a path from the Atlantic coast of Panama through its rain forest and became the first European explorer to see the Pacific coast. Next came the exploration of the Pacific by Ferdinand Magellan of Portugal. During the years 1520 to 1521, he sailed from the Atlantic Ocean around the southern tip of South America (called ''the Horn'') into the Pacific Ocean and across the Pacific to the Philippine Islands.

Being an explorer was a risky business. Magellan left Spain (for whose king he was working) and sailed west with five ships and about 270 men, but only two ships made it as far as the Moluccas in the Indian Ocean. Only one of those ships returned home to Spain in 1522, and there were only 17 survivors. Magellan himself was killed in 1521 in the Philippines in a fight with islanders. After Magellan's death, the expedition continued under the command of Juan Elcano. By continuing to sail west in his return to Spain, Elcano became one of the first explorers to give proof that the earth is round.

Another great explorer of the Pacific Ocean was Captain James Cook of England, who charted the east coast of Australia, and many islands including New Zealand, New Guinea, and Hawaii. Between 1768 and 1779, Captain Cook made three great voyages of exploration in the north and south Pacific. His discoveries led to the colonization of Australia and New Zealand by the British.

WATER, WATER EVERYWHERE

Seventy-one percent of the earth's surface is covered with water—and most of that is the salty water of the oceans.

The oceans are deep. Their average depth is 2½ miles. But the deepest parts of the ocean, called trenches, *are nearly 7 miles deep. The deepest place on earth, the Challenger Deep in the Marianas Trench in the western Pacific Ocean south of Japan, is 36,200 feet deep. By comparison, the tallest mountain in the world, Mount Everest in the Himalayas of Asia, is 29,000 feet high. If Mount Everest were turned upside down and put into the Marianas Trench, it would be covered by water more than one mile deep.*

European explorers crossed the paths of many other civilizations in their voyages throughout the Pacific Ocean.

The Atlantic Ocean

The Atlantic Ocean is the second largest of the oceans. It is more clearly divided into several areas than the others.

The North and South Atlantic are separated at the equator where the ocean is narrowed by the hump of Brazil and the bulge of West Africa. In fact, in ancient times, these parts of South America and Africa were one piece of land.

The great seas of the Gulf of Mexico and the Caribbean are located in the western Atlantic. In the eastern Atlantic, the Mediterranean Sea separates Europe from Africa. The British Isles are separated from Scandinavia by the North Sea. An underwater mountain chain curves along the middle part of the North and South Atlantic and is called the Mid-Atlantic Ridge. The ocean floor is slowly spreading apart along this ridge.

Currents in the North Atlantic—such as the Gulf Stream off Florida—flow clockwise. In the South Atlantic, currents flow counterclockwise. The northernmost and southernmost points of the Atlantic are filled with huge glaciers and ice floes, but its middle regions are tropical, and there are coral reefs in the Caribbean. In the area east of Florida is a great expanse of fairly calm water, called the *Sargasso Sea*. It abounds with the floating brown seaweed called sargassum.

The shallow continental shelf off New England and Newfoundland has rich commercial fisheries on the Georges Bank and Grand Banks. Oil and fisheries are found in the Gulf of Mexico and in the North Sea between England and Scandinavia.

Sargassum, a floating brown seaweed

The currents that flow throughout the Atlantic Ocean affect the weather in the surrounding countries.

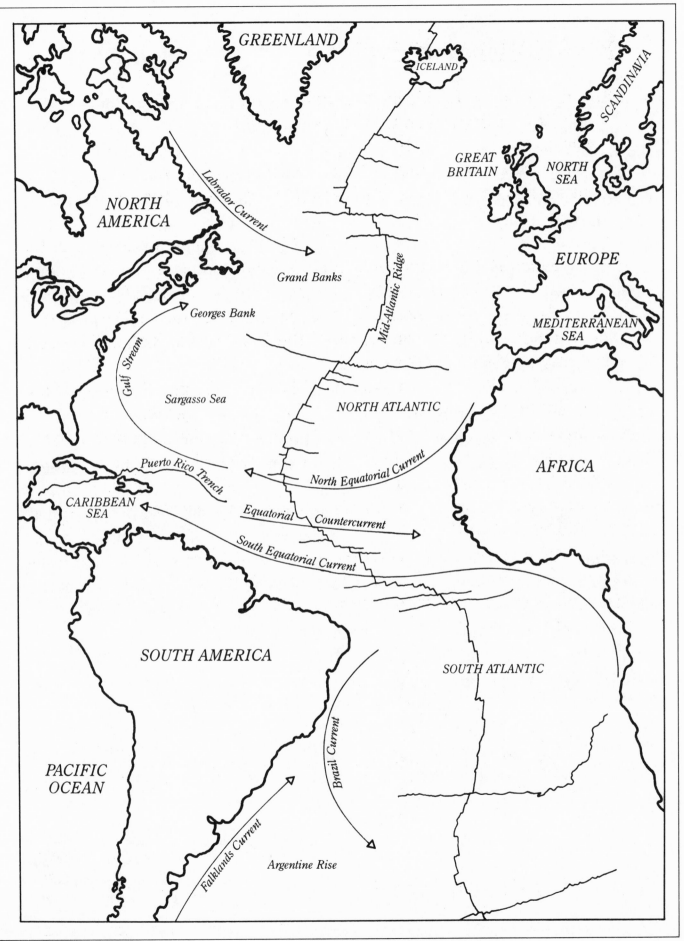

GREENLAND

ICELAND

SCANDINAVIA

NORTH AMERICA

Labrador Current

Grand Banks

GREAT BRITAIN

NORTH SEA

Mid-Atlantic Ridge

EUROPE

Georges Bank

Gulf Stream

Sargasso Sea

NORTH ATLANTIC

MEDITERRANEAN SEA

AFRICA

Puerto Rico Trench

North Equatorial Current

CARIBBEAN SEA

Equatorial Countercurrent

South Equatorial Current

SOUTH AMERICA

SOUTH ATLANTIC

PACIFIC OCEAN

Brazil Current

Falklands Current

Argentine Rise

Early Explorers of the Atlantic Ocean

The Atlantic Ocean has been especially important to the history of exploration. Europeans had to learn to sail across it before they could get to the Indian and Pacific Oceans.

Vikings from Scandinavia, such as Leif Erikson, explored Iceland, Greenland, and the New England coast of the United States between the years 1000 and 1400. The Vikings founded temporary colonies along these coasts at least as far south as Massachusetts. They called these areas *Vineland* for the grapes that they grew in those regions.

Discoveries by Christopher Columbus of Italy led to the colonization of the Americas and changed the course of history. Columbus made four great voyages of exploration from 1492 to 1504 for King Ferdinand and Queen Isabella of Spain. On his first voyage in 1492 to 1493, Columbus sailed in his flagship, *Santa Maria*, along with the *Pinta* and *Niña*. The *Santa Maria* was 117 feet long, but the other two ships were each only 50 feet long.

On August 3, 1492, they left Spain for the Canary Islands, the most distant civilized area in the Atlantic. On September 6 they left the Canaries sailing west, not knowing what they would find. After just over a month at sea, they sighted their first land, the island of San Salvador in the Bahamas.

Columbus sailed on to Cuba and Hispaniola. On Christmas Day, the *Santa Maria* ran aground in a strong wind and sank off the northern coast of Haiti. Columbus took command of the *Niña* and returned safely to Spain on March 25, 1493.

On his next three voyages, Columbus discovered much of the rest of the Antilles (Guadalupe and Martinique), Trinidad, the northern coast of South America (Venezuela), and the Caribbean coast of Central America (Panama to Honduras). But Columbus never landed or even came within sight of what is now the United States.

Later in 1564, the Spaniards colonized Florida at St. Augustine. In 1620, the *Mayflower* landed at Plymouth, Massachusetts, with a handful of English settlers.

Christopher Columbus was one of the first explorers to visit the Americas. He discovered many of the islands in the Caribbean Sea.

The Indian Ocean

The smallest of the three major oceans is the Indian Ocean. It is bounded on the north by Asia and Arabia. India divides the ocean into the Arabian Sea to the west, toward Africa, and the Bay of Bengal to the east, toward southeast Asia and Indonesia.

Two of the greatest rivers of Asia pour into the Indian Ocean at the north. They are the Indus, through Pakistan, and the Ganges, through India and Bangladesh.

Around the shores of Saudi Arabia, the Indian Ocean extends into the oil-rich Persian Gulf and the Red Sea. It leads through the Suez Canal to the Mediterranean. To the south, the Indian Ocean reaches Antarctica.

Most of this ocean is in the tropics or subtropics. Its weather is dominated by fierce winds, known as *monsoons,* that change directions with the season. In summer, they blow toward the Asian mainland, bringing heavy rains. In the winter, they blow from the mainland toward the sea, arriving in India as hot, dry wind. Violent tropical storms called *cyclones* (what are called hurricanes in the Atlantic) often occur in monsoon season.

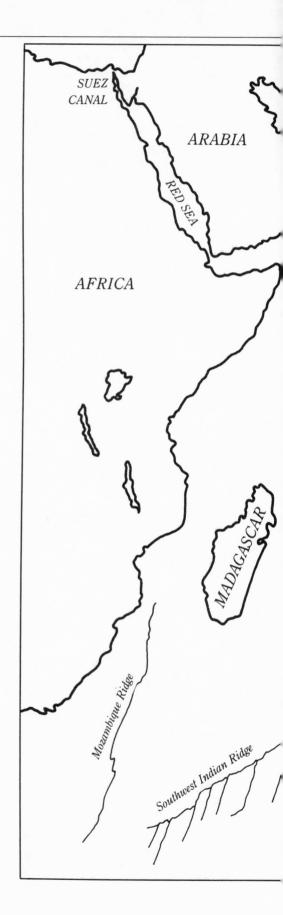

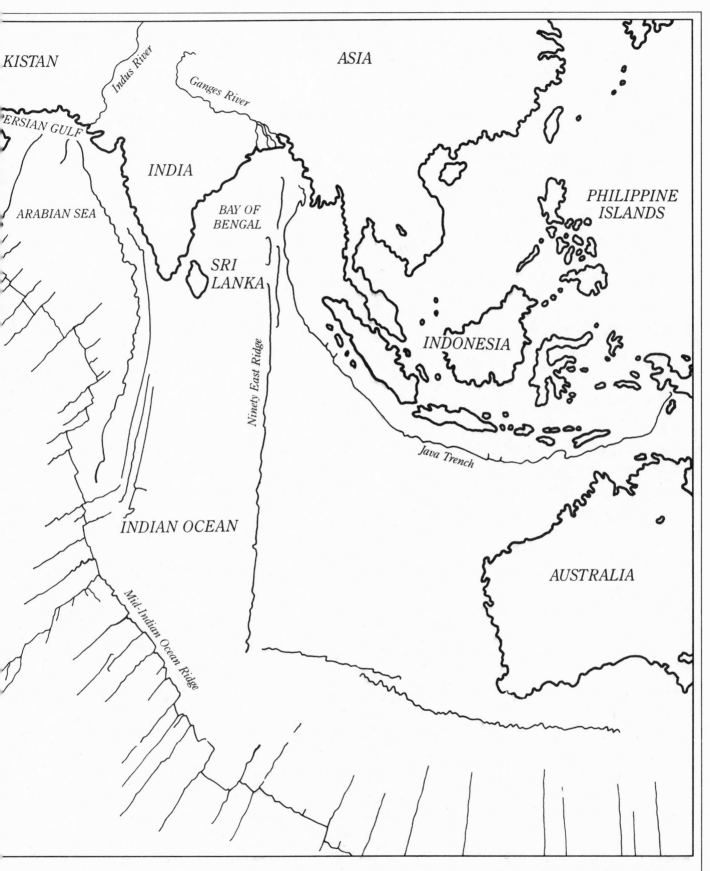

KISTAN

Indus River

ASIA

Ganges River

ERSIAN GULF

INDIA

ARABIAN SEA

BAY OF
BENGAL

SRI
LANKA

Ninety East Ridge

PHILIPPINE
ISLANDS

INDONESIA

Java Trench

INDIAN OCEAN

Mid-Indian Ocean Ridge

AUSTRALIA

*The Indian Ocean is huge—but it is the smallest
of the world's three major oceans.*

Early Explorers of the Indian Ocean

The Indian Ocean was the first ocean extensively traveled for trade.

The ancient Egyptians explored the Arabian Sea through the Red Sea. Long before Europeans ever saw the Indian Ocean, Arabs and Chinese traded tea, spices, and silk with one another along the coast of southeast Asia. In the 13th century, Marco Polo, the Italian explorer, returned from his expedition to China partially by way of the Bay of Bengal.

The first European to sail far from land through the Indian Ocean was Vasco da Gama. He reached India in 1498, after sailing with four vessels down the west coast of Africa, all the way around the Cape of Good Hope, and then to southern India. By doing this, Vasco da Gama opened up a new sea route for European trade with Asia.

Da Gama devoted much of his life to the Indies. He made a second voyage from 1502 to 1503, with a fleet of 13 ships. Da Gama sailed to the east coast of Africa and Arabia and then on to India, where disputes with Arab traders led to terrible fights and even deaths. Later, Da Gama returned to India as its Portuguese ruler in 1524. He died there after helping make Portugal a major sea power during the years of great exploration and discovery.

The great explorers of the Pacific Ocean were also important to the Indian Ocean, as they usually sailed through it on their way to or from the Pacific. Captain James Cook, on his second and third voyages between 1772–1775 and 1776–1779, became the first to explore the southern part of the Indian Ocean when he sailed the frigid waters along the Antarctic, south of Australia and Africa.

European traders risked long voyages across the Indian Ocean to buy silks and spices in India and China.

The Arctic and Antarctic

Think of the Arctic and Antarctic. Can't you almost feel the bitter, freezing temperatures and frigid wind? Winter nights are long in the polar regions. During the middle of winter it is dark the entire day. But then, summer days are long, too. During the summer months, daylight lasts for 24 hours.

Though it is never warm in the polar regions, days can be bright and pleasant when the sun is out and the winds are calm. The scenery along the shore is spectacular almost everywhere. The landscape is filled with floating glaciers, walls of solid ice that hug the coast, and steep, mountainous peninsulas projecting into the sea.

Fewer kinds of animals and plants live in the polar regions than in the tropics. But the creatures that do live there often can be found in huge numbers. Shrimp-like crustaceans called *krill* flourish in polar regions in such enormous numbers that baleen whales migrate to those areas to feed upon them. Sea birds and some fishes also feed on krill, as well as several kinds of penguins and seals. In the Antarctic, krill are probably the most important animal in the food chain.

Wild animals are not the only ones that fish in polar waters. These regions are also home to some important commercial fisheries for humans. The harvesting of *Alaskan king crab* is a major industry in the Arctic waters off Alaska. Some fishes, such as certain cod fishes, have huge populations and live together in groups of millions of individuals. As a result, fishermen can catch large numbers at one time.

Some marine mammals, such as seals, sea lions, walruses, and penguins, gather at a certain time of year to give birth to their babies. An area where they gather is called a *rookery*. In the early 1900s, hunters took advantage of this seasonal event to kill these animals for their skins and blubber. So many were killed that some groups nearly became extinct. Now there are laws to protect marine mammals. Other laws limit the number of certain fishes that a fisherman may catch during a season, and may prevent fishermen from taking these fishes when they are spawning.

The Arctic and Antarctic may seem to be very similar, but there are many differences. For example, polar bears and walruses live only in the Arctic, while penguins are found in the Antarctic. Whales and seals are found in both the Arctic and Antarctic.

A polar bear looks for fish as walruses swim in icy Arctic waters.

Ships that Study the Seas

Modern ocean research began more than 100 years ago with the British sailing ship *Challenger*. This full-rigged ship, called a corvette, also had a steam engine.

Between the years 1872 and 1876, *Challenger* traveled the world, exploring the sea—its plants and animals, its currents and temperature, its bottom, and the chemical composition of its water. It traveled 68,000 miles in its explorations and began the modern age of ocean research.

From 1889 to the early 1900s, the United States hosted many year-long research expeditions on its first oceangoing research vessel, the *Albatross*. Scientists aboard the *Albatross* discovered thousands of new kinds of sea creatures. They also brought back information on the waters in which these animals lived and the types of places where they rested or burrowed.

Today, many countries of the world have research vessels that study the oceans. Scientists on board collect information about the chemistry and biology of the oceans, the patterns of their currents, and about the plants and animals that live in the oceans.

This work gives us more knowledge of the world in which we live, and helps us appreciate and enjoy our environment. It also tells us more about how we can protect the oceans while also wisely using the mineral and fishery resources of the sea.

Some of the world's major research vessels are the German *Meteor*, the English *Discovery II*, and the Russian *Vitiaz*. In the United States, some of the most famous of the oceangoing research vessels are the *Knorr*, *Oceanus*, and *Atlantis II* from the Woods Hole Oceanographic Institution in Massachusetts; the *Melville* and *New Horizon* of the Scripps Institute of Oceanography in California; the *Albatross IV* and *Oregon II* fishery research vessels of the National Marine Fisheries Service in Mississippi; and the *Seward Johnson* of the Harbor Branch Oceanographic Institution in Florida.

These boats have many complex pieces of equipment to gather information. For example, water is collected at many ocean depths in order

Sailors aboard the early exploring ship Challenger *helped scientists bring up nets filled with plants and animals from the ocean floor.*

Ships that Study the Seas

to learn more about the chemicals and animals that are in it. Rocks and sediment are collected from the bottom of the ocean, using instruments that grab a chunk of the ocean floor or drill core samples. Scientists study these samples to learn more about what they're made of and how they might have been formed. Samples of living creatures are collected with plankton nets, trawls, and dredges.

Oceanographic research is a worldwide, cooperative adventure in sharing information. The collected samples of marine creatures and the ocean floor are studied by scientists all over the world. Samples collected by a German vessel may be sent to a marine biologist at a university in Los Angeles, and shellfishes collected by a Virginia researcher may be shipped to a colleague in Tokyo.

The United States has an Oceanographic Sorting Center at the Smithsonian Institution in Washington, D.C. This center brings in marine biological collections from all over the world. The Center then sorts the collections into groups of similar kinds of plants and animals. It sends these samples all over the world, to researchers who specialize in studying those groups.

FROM Sea to Sky

Humans have been interested in the oceans since ancient times.

One of the first persons to study the sea was Aristotle, the Greek philosopher who lived more than 2,000 years ago. He discovered that the level of seawater usually stays the same. Why is this? It's because the ocean loses water by evaporation, but the same amount of water is added by rainfall. Aristotle explained that this is why the ocean doesn't dry up or overflow its boundaries.

Aristotle

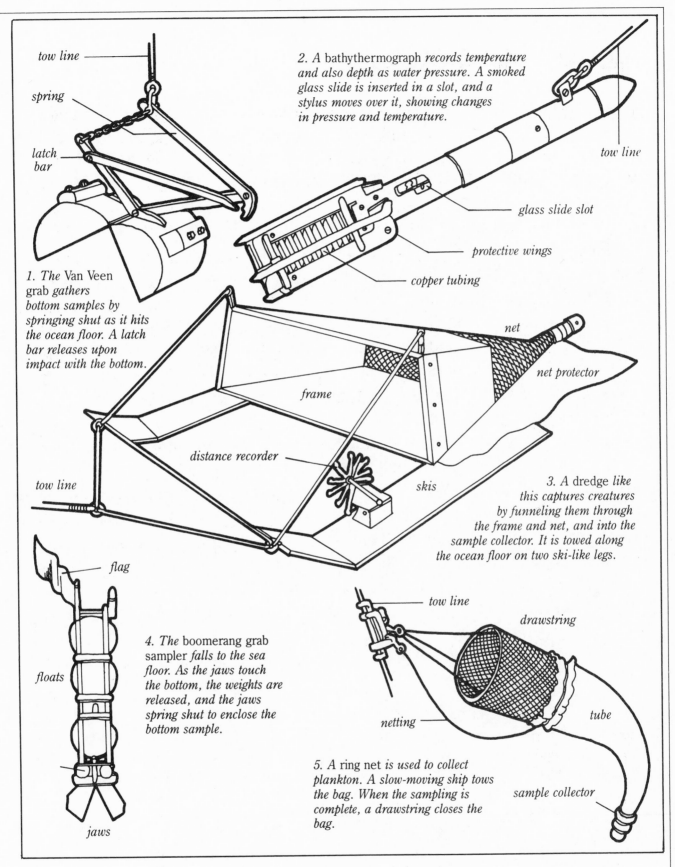

tow line

spring

latch
bar

1. The Van Veen
grab *gathers
bottom samples by
springing shut as it hits
the ocean floor. A latch
bar releases upon
impact with the bottom.*

2. A bathythermograph *records temperature
and also depth as water pressure. A smoked
glass slide is inserted in a slot, and a
stylus moves over it, showing changes
in pressure and temperature.*

tow line

glass slide slot

protective wings

copper tubing

net

net protector

frame

distance recorder

skis

3. A dredge *like
this captures creatures
by funneling them through
the frame and net, and into the
sample collector. It is towed along
the ocean floor on two ski-like legs.*

tow line

flag

4. The boomerang grab
sampler *falls to the sea
floor. As the jaws touch
the bottom, the weights are
released, and the jaws
spring shut to enclose the
bottom sample.*

floats

tow line

drawstring

netting

tube

jaws

5. A ring net *is used to collect
plankton. A slow-moving ship tows
the bag. When the sampling is
complete, a drawstring closes the
bag.*

sample collector

Modern research ships use many devices to explore the ocean.

Jacques Cousteau and the *Calypso*

Imagine what it must feel like to be a fish. Though you must watch out for predators, you can scoot through the water in any direction you choose. You can swim to the surface. You can dive to the ocean floor. You don't have to worry about coming to the surface for air. If you're a filter feeder, you don't even have to worry about hunting for food!

We humans can have a sense of this freedom, thanks to the invention of SCUBA (Self-Contained Underwater Breathing Apparatus) diving. Scuba gear was invented by French engineers and perfected by the Frenchmen Jacques Cousteau and Emile Gagnan.

Cousteau became the world's best-known underwater explorer as captain of the *Calypso*. He staffed the ship with a crew of highly trained divers, technicians, photographers, and visiting naturalists. The underwater films that Captain Cousteau and the *Calypso* crew have produced have been seen on television by millions of people.

Cousteau's TV work helps us understand the oceans and their many forms of life. This work also helps us understand the importance of protecting the oceans. When Captain Cousteau states that he has seen signs of pollution from the Antarctic to the middle of the Pacific, no matter how far out at sea, people take notice. They may be less likely to throw trash into the sea. They also may try to see to it that other people, businesses, and their governments follow commonsense practices to keep our oceans clean.

Captain Cousteau's message is simple. He wants everyone to realize that the oceans are an enormously important and beautiful feature of the Earth. He hopes we'll all work to conserve the oceans, for our use and enjoyment, and to keep the oceans alive for our own children to explore. That means we must all work hard to prevent pollution and to solve other problems that threaten our seas.

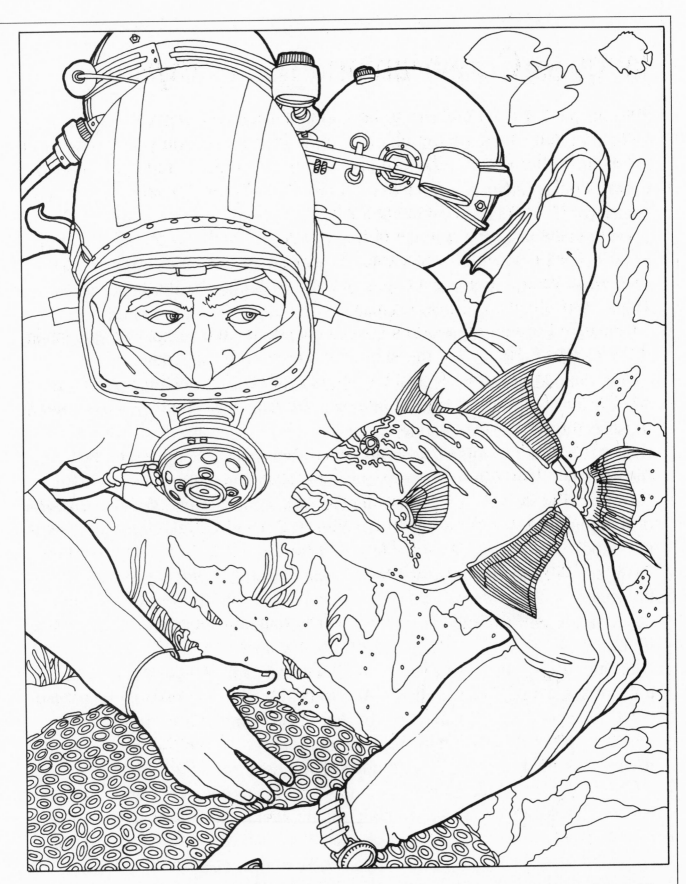

Jacques Cousteau and a greenish-blue queen trigger fish (with bright blue bands) observe one another.

Subs for Science

Deep below the ocean's surface—8,200 feet down—all is dark, except for a beacon of light coming from the tiny submarine in which we travel. We are off the west coast of South America, near the Galapagos Islands, in an area known as the *Galapagos Rift*. This is part of a long underwater mountain chain where the ocean floor is slowly spreading apart and where molten lava rises from deep within the earth.

We hover in our submersible, *Alvin*, over an area where plumes of super-hot, mineral-laden water spew from cracks in the sea floor. Clustered around these thermal vents are tube-shaped worms eight feet long; clumps of foot-long, white-shelled clams whose flesh is scarlet red; strange-looking crabs; and beautiful, delicate creatures that look like dandelions! These creatures had never been seen by humans until they were discovered in 1977 by John Corliss, Robert Ballard, and other scientists. But that is not the only reason these creatures are interesting. Until they were discovered, scientists thought that only plants could make their own food. Plants do this by using the energy of the sun to convert carbon dioxide and water into food. But these newly discovered creatures feed on bacteria that use *sulphur* (instead of the sun) as a source of energy to convert carbon dioxide and hydrogen into food!

We are here to videotape with underwater cameras the communities of unusual plants and animals that live near the vents of hot water, and to collect a few of the exotic animals so that scientists can learn more about them.

Sitting inside *Alvin*, we operate a mechanical arm with a claw that can pick up samples from the ocean floor. We direct the claw to pick up a huge clam. Next, we scoop up a small chunk of the ocean floor so that we can learn what chemicals and minerals are in it. Without a submersible vessel such as *Alvin*, we would not be able to study these deep, hot-water vents.

The idea of a submersible is as old as the *diving bell*. This was a big bucket, turned upside down over a person's head, into which air was

Submersible Alvin *studies the ocean floor near a thermal vent. The strange-looking creatures near the vents are red tube worms.*

Subs for Science

pumped. Diving bells were used in ancient times in the Mediterranean Sea, but only in shallow water.

The first underwater trip very far beneath the surface was made in 1934 by William Beebe and Otis Barton of New York. Lowered from the side of a ship and travelling in a hollow steel ball, called a *bathysphere*, they sank to the then-record depth of 3,000 feet.

By 1960, the Swiss scientist Auguste Piccard had constructed for the U.S. Navy a much larger cylinder for underwater research. It was 60 feet long and weighed 50 tons. It was called the *bathyscaphe* (deep boat) *Trieste*. *Trieste* could descend to the deepest part of the ocean floor at about 36,000 feet. There it could move around on the bottom for up to a mile before coming back to the surface to be picked up by the mother ship.

Alvin, launched for the U.S. Navy in 1964 by the Woods Hole Oceanographic Institution in Woods Hole, Massachusetts, has been one of the most used submersibles. *Alvin* can carry three persons to depths of about 13,000 feet, and can freely move around for many hours at a time.

Another excellent research submersible is the *Johnson Sea-Link* of the Harbor Branch Oceanographic Institution in Ft. Pierce, Florida. *Sea-Link* carries a pilot and one scientist in a forward sphere made of 4-inch-thick plexiglass, and two more persons in a rear chamber of 3-inch-thick aluminum. A one-person submersible called *Deep-Rover*, developed by Deep Ocean Engineering in San Leandro, California, can travel to a depth of about 3,000 feet to collect specimens. *Deep-Rover* has a manipulator arm so sensitive that you could use it to pick up a pencil and draw pictures underwater!

Science subs such as *Alvin* and *Sea-Link* have cameras, lights, traps, buckets, and mechanical arms with claws that can pick up almost anything a scientist wants to collect. They also have instruments that record information about the environment. Most dives last no more than five to ten hours, but the subs could stay down for several days, if necessary.

Rattail fishes have large heads and whip-like tails. They are among the most common deep-sea fishes.

The bathyscaphe Trieste *explored some of the deepest areas of the ocean floor.*

Research Labs on the Ocean Floor

Imagine waking up in the morning and then, instead of dressing, putting on a jacket, and walking to school or catching the bus, you get up, pull on a swimsuit and a wetsuit, step through a hole in the floor of your room, and drop into the cool, crystal-clear waters of the ocean.

You and your partner swim over to a rack of scuba tanks, and each of you turn on a tank, put it on your back and away you go, off to the day's classroom—a coral reef. Instead of a breeze blowing through your hair, you feel the gentle tug of the current. You don't have to look both ways for cars down here, but do watch out for that clump of fire coral just ahead!

Once at the reef your assignment is to observe, photograph, and collect exciting and exotic sea creatures. You can even set up experiments and record the results while the marine creatures all around you go about their business of making a living.

After a while you check the pressure gauge attached to your scuba tank. It tells you that the air in the tank is getting low, so you'd better head back home to your underwater habitat. Besides, after being in the water for a long time, you're beginning to get cold.

You and your buddy return to the habitat by climbing a ladder through the hole in the lab's floor. Two other scientists are there

Divers take photographs and collect samples outside their underwater habitat.

Research Labs on the Ocean Floor

talking, planning their next night of work on the reef. The work goes on around the clock, usually with time out only for eating and sleeping. The average length of stay in the habitat is about two weeks. But these two weeks have given you many hours to study the nearby reef without going to the surface!

Listening to the others talk, you still laugh at how funny their voices sound—it's like listening to Donald Duck. That's because the air in the habitat is compressed and has a different mixture of gases than we breathe on land. Someone calls out "The water is hot, if you want hot chocolate." You reach for the kettle, but something looks wrong—the water is not boiling. The air pressure is so great in the habitat that water will not boil.

Does all this sound like science fiction, or a dream? The truth is, scientists have been working and living in underwater habitats for about 35 years! French explorer Jacques Cousteau and his team experimented with an early habitat called *Conshelf*. So did the U.S. Navy, with its 200-foot deep *Sea Lab*. Habitats first became available to most marine biologists during the 1969–1970 *Tektite* habitat program of the U.S. Navy. *Tektite* was placed in water 50 feet deep off the Virgin Islands. *Tektite* had two large rooms welded together, and housed four scientists and one engineer.

The next big U.S. habitat program was *Hydrolab*, also in the Virgin Islands. More scientists used the *Hydrolab* than any other habitat. It housed four scientists, but had only three bunk beds. That was because one scientist always had to be awake to watch the life support systems of air, temperature, pressure, and electricity. *Hydrolab* had such a distinguished history that when it was retired from service in 1986 it was donated to the Smithsonian Institution, where it is now on display at the National Museum of Natural History in Washington, D.C.

The newest and largest underwater habitat is the *Aquarius*. It soon will replace *Hydrolab* somewhere in the Caribbean. It has more state-of-the-art instruments than any habitat ever built. *Aquarius* will hold four scientists and one engineer to run the life-support instruments. Maybe one day you will have a chance to live and work in an underwater habitat.

Amid a school of jacks, a diver explores the area around the underwater habitat Hydrolab.

The Shore

To see fascinating sea creatures, you don't have to go scuba diving or join an expedition in a sub. You only have to wade along the shore.

The shore is a rich part of the ocean. Plants can grow there abundantly, bathed in the full sunlight that shines through the shallow waters. Nutrients are washed into the sea from the land or are brought up by currents from the deeper parts of the ocean. The seashore's many types of rocks, sand, and grass beds provide nooks and crannies in which sea animals can grow, reproduce, and hide from predators.

On the shore you can usually see many kinds of sea birds—such as *sea gulls, sandpipers, ospreys, frigate birds,* and *herons*. You can often see land crabs scurrying about just above the high-water mark. But be careful if you try to pick one up—it will defend itself with its pincer claws.

Most shore creatures live in the area between the high-tide and low-tide marks. This area is called the *intertidal zone*. Many small animals live below the surface of the sand, in the first few feet of water just below the low-tide mark. When you walk in the intertidal zone with the waves lapping at your ankles, you may be walking over thousands of animals hidden in the sand. Some of these sand-dwellers may be several inches wide, such as *clams* and *scallops*. But most of them are tiny mollusks, crabs, worms, and crab-like animals so small that they can live between the grains of sand. In fact, there's a whole world of miniature animals buried in the sand that we can see only by using a magnifying glass or a microscope. But these animals are worth trying to see because many of them have strange, interesting shapes that can be quite beautiful.

The arrowhead sand dollar is a flat sea urchin.

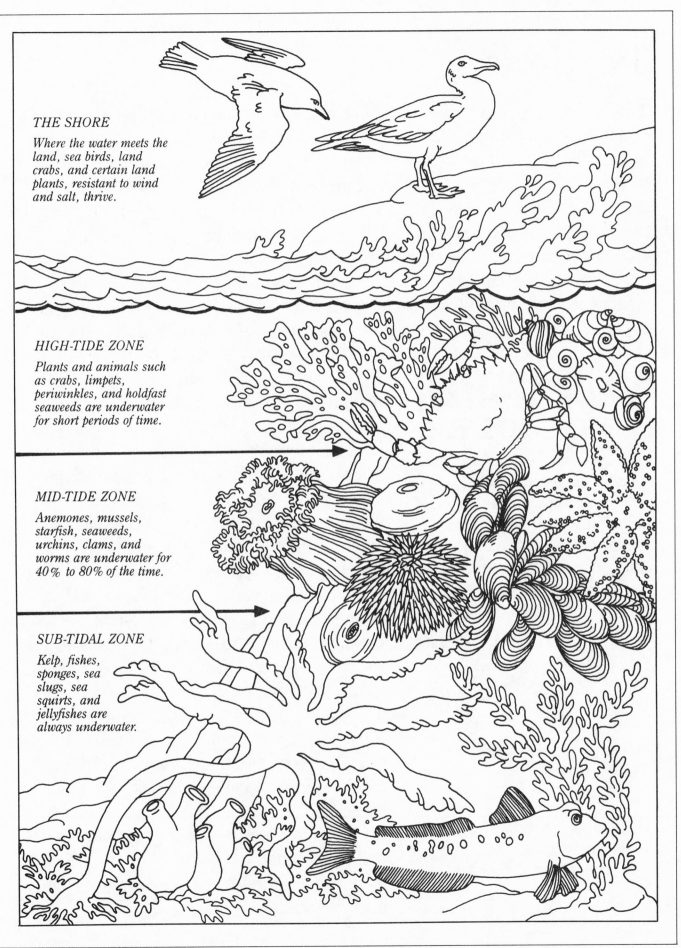

THE SHORE

Where the water meets the land, sea birds, land crabs, and certain land plants, resistant to wind and salt, thrive.

HIGH-TIDE ZONE

Plants and animals such as crabs, limpets, periwinkles, and holdfast seaweeds are underwater for short periods of time.

MID-TIDE ZONE

Anemones, mussels, starfish, seaweeds, urchins, clams, and worms are underwater for 40% to 80% of the time.

SUB-TIDAL ZONE

Kelp, fishes, sponges, sea slugs, sea squirts, and jellyfishes are always underwater.

Tide Pools

Waves beat against a rocky stretch of shore. Over and over they crash, their rhythm constant for thousands and thousands of years. The waves wear away some parts of the rock more quickly than others, leaving deep pockets. Water collects in those pockets and remains there, even when the tide goes out. These pockets are called *tide pools*. Tide pools also are created when shoreline rocks shift and slide, or when powerful geological processes shatter the earth's crust at the ocean's edge.

Tide pools are alive with plants and animals. The animals have a constantly renewed supply of food and clean water. The plants have a good supply of nutrients and sunlight. But a tide pool is a changing world. Waves constantly splash over the pools. Twice a day, the tide comes in to flood them. To withstand the force of the water pounding against them, many animals have developed ways of clinging to the rocks.

Two kinds of mollusks that have adapted to life in the tide pool are limpets and chitons. *Limpets* have low, cone-shaped shells, sometimes with a keyhole-like opening at the top. A *chiton* (KYE-tun) has eight plates across its back. Each of these mollusks has a large, muscular foot beneath its shell, which it uses to cling firmly to the rocky bottom and sides of the tide pool.

Other creatures to look for in tide pools are *sea anemones* (uh-NEM-uh-neez), with their soft, fleshy tentacles, and little fishes called *gobies*, with belly fins that are joined together into a sucker-like disk. Gobies use these fins to stick to the bottom to keep from being swept out of the tide pool by the pull of the outgoing waves. The belly fins of *cling fishes* are even better developed into suction cups.

UNDERWATER FOSSILS

The most ancient and primitive of all living mollusks are chitons. Fossilized chitons have been found that are thought to be more than 500 million years old.

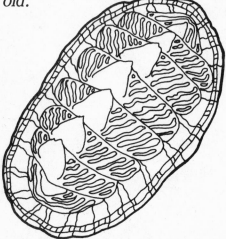

A chiton *can cling to the bottom and sides of a tide pool using the muscular foot beneath its shell.*

A lot is happening in a tide pool both above and below the water. Above the water:
*1. bladder wrack (upper left); 2. Japanese sargassum (upper right); 3. sea anemones (lower left);
4. keyhole limpets (lower middle); 5. blue mussels (lower right).* Beneath the water: *1. sugar kelp
(left); 2. cling fish (middle); 3. sea vases (lower middle); 4. common sea star (lower right).*

Mangroves

Mangroves are among the few kinds of trees that can grow in sea water. They grow in tropical regions throughout the world and even in warmer areas such as Florida. They reach about 20 feet tall and are densely packed, forming a forest of interlaced branches and "prop roots." Prop roots grow down from the base of the tree trunk above the high-water mark. They make a strong supporting structure around the trunk which helps it to withstand heavy storms and even hurricanes and typhoons.

Mangrove forests play a very important role in protecting the shoreline. The churning seas created by storms hurl much of their energy against the mangrove forest, rather than wearing away the land. This limits erosion and conserves the shoreline.

Sometimes, mangroves actually help to create new land, because their large root systems trap sediment draining off the soil. They also make new land by trapping their own falling leaves. As the leaves decay, they are packed down, and become new soil in the form of dense peat.

The water in mangrove forests is low and still. That makes it an ideal breeding place for insects, including mosquitoes and "no-see-ums." People sometimes cut down the mangroves to get rid of the insects. While this may solve one problem, it creates another, far more serious problem. It leaves the shore exposed to the sea and almost guarantees the loss of land through wave action wearing away the unprotected shore.

Mangroves are important breeding and nursery grounds for many fishes and small sea creatures. The mangroves' elaborate underwater root systems offer shelter and safe hiding places for young animals trying to avoid predators during their most tender stages of life. Many commercially important fishes, such as grunts and snappers, make their homes among mangrove roots while they are young. Other animals, including many kinds of sponges and sea anemones, live attached to prop roots and spend all their lives in the mangroves.

Mangroves also provide homes for many types of birds, such as frigates and warblers. So, under the water line and in the branches, a lot is happening in a mangrove forest.

Mangrove forests are homes for:
1. *shore crabs (upper left and middle);* 2. *common whelks (center middle);* 3. *young herrings (middle right);* 4. *sea vases (lower right); and* 5. *mussels (lower left).*

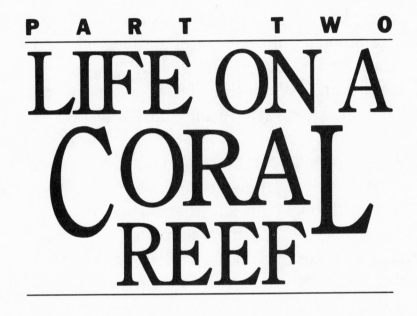

PART TWO

LIFE ON A CORAL REEF

Fringing Reefs, Barrier Reefs, and Atolls

The magical world of a coral reef can be found only in certain places. The water must be clear, because the tiny plants that live within the tissues of coral animals need sunlight to grow. The seawater around a coral reef must not be diluted by large amounts of fresh water running off the land. The water temperature must be 68 degrees Fahrenheit or warmer. For these reasons, coral reefs are found only in the shallow waters of tropical oceans, and around islands and continents where they have a platform on which to grow.

There are three basic types of coral formations: *fringing reefs, barrier reefs,* and *oceanic atolls*. Fringing reefs grow close to the shore around continents and islands, with only a shallow, narrow channel of water to separate them from the land. As ocean waves batter a fringing reef, pieces of it break off. Gradually, these broken pieces help build a platform on which new coral can grow and expand the reef. Other broken coral may be washed ashore and build up the shoreline.

Barrier reefs are formed in the same way as fringing reefs, but they are located miles offshore on the continental shelf. The channel between the reef and shore may be well over 100 feet deep. The Great Barrier Reef, off the east coast of Australia, is a classic example of a huge barrier reef. It stretches 1,200 miles long and is 10 to 14 miles wide. Another large barrier reef is located off the coast of the Central American country of Belize in the western Caribbean.

A chambered nautilus shell

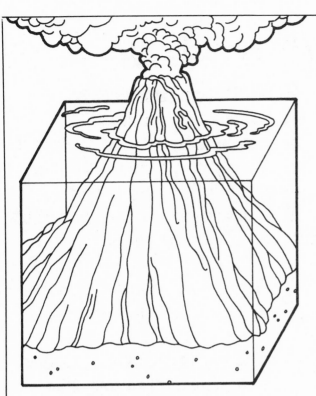

1. *An active volcano rises from the sea floor, forming a mountainous island.*

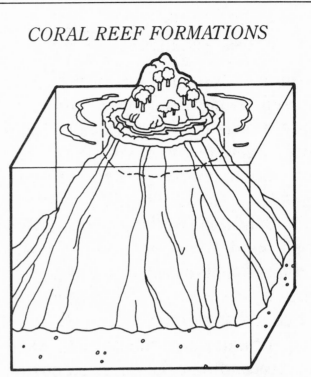

2. *A fringing reef forms when coral grows around the shores of the island. A narrow channel of shallow water is left between the island and the reef.*

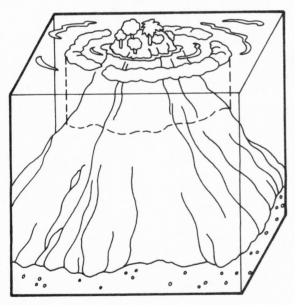

3. *A barrier reef is formed as the island is eroded by weather, or as the core of the original volcano begins to sink into the seabed. The corals of the barrier reef continue to grow upward as the volcano sinks.*

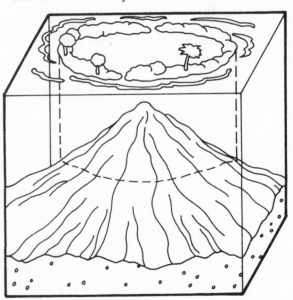

4. *An atoll is a circular reef that surrounds a lagoon. The original island peak around which the reef formed has sunk below the ocean's surface, leaving a calm lagoon surrounded by narrow islands.*

Fringing Reefs, Barrier Reefs, and Atolls

An *atoll* (A-tuhl) is a circular reef, enclosing a lagoon. Atolls are often found far from land in the Pacific and Indian Oceans. The naturalist Charles Darwin believed that atolls were formed around the edges of the peaks of underwater volcanoes. As the volcanoes became inactive, they slowly sank beneath the surface, while the fringing reefs around them grew upward at the same rate. Finally, all that was left at the surface were the circular reefs, with no land inside them. Darwin's theory was proven correct when scientists drilled deep cores in Eniwetok (en-i-WEE-tuk) Atoll in the Pacific, and found a 60-million-year-old extinct volcano about a mile below the surface.

Reefs change in size according to changes in sea level and temperature. During the ice ages, so much water froze that the sea level dropped. Most of the ocean water became too cold for corals to grow. During that time, corals were able to live only close to the Equator. After the ice ages, when the ocean waters warmed again, the reefs were able to spread further north and south.

Some tropical shorelines depend on coral reefs to protect them from erosion. Without a protective wall of reef in front of it, the shore would wash away from wave action much more rapidly.

At low tide, many coral formations can be seen poking above the surface of the ocean.

Coral Polyps

Corals form massive limestone reefs of great strength. But if you were to look closely at a coral head, you would see that it is made up of millions of tiny animals called *polyps* (POL-ups).

Each polyp is a delicate creature. For their homes, polyps secrete a limestone framework. When we look at a coral reef we are seeing the limestone structures produced by billions of coral polyps over thousands of years.

Thousands of different kinds of plants and animals find homes on the surfaces of coral colonies and in their nooks and crannies. More than 2,000 types of corals are alive today. An even greater number have been found as fossils from as far back as 500 million years ago.

Most corals—such as *brain coral, staghorn coral,* and *elkhorn coral*—have tiny polyps, usually about a tenth of an inch across. A few, such as the *mushroom coral*, have much larger polyps that are many inches wide.

Each coral polyp is like a tube closed at the bottom, with an open mouth surrounded by tentacles at the other end. Individual polyps usually keep some connection with each other. Touching one part of a colony will make other regions react, the way ripples form when you throw a stone into water.

A polyp feeds on microscopic animals called *zooplankton* (zoe-PLANK-tun) that the ocean currents carry by it. The tentacles filter the animals from the water, often by stinging them, and then the tentacles move the food to the mouth. In most corals, the polyps stay inside their stony capsules during the day, but extend their tentacles at night when the tentacles most actively capture food. At night, the otherwise hard coral looks as if it has a soft coat of fuzz.

Each little reef coral polyp contains thousands of microscopic, single-celled plants called *zooanthallae* (ZO-an-tha-lay). These plants and the coral polyps help each other. Zooanthallae make oxygen that polyps need to live. They also make a substance that, in some way not yet fully understood, helps the coral to build its limestone skeleton. Zooanthallae also consume some of the coral's waste products, such as the chemicals nitrogen and phosphorus. In return, the coral polyps protect the zooanthallae. Much of the color of corals comes from the color of the zooanthallae.

collumnar coral

massive coral

tier-forming coral

branching coral

encrusting coral

whorl-forming coral

solitary free-living coral

flexible coral

CORAL
GROWTH
FORMS

*Coral polyps are the main builders of coral reefs.
A single coral formation contains millions of coral polyps.*

Reef Plants and Animals

Dozens of different kinds of corals may make up the framework of a reef, from massive brain corals to branching staghorns. But those few dozen types provide homes for hundreds of other kinds of marine creatures as well.

Although coral polyps are the main builders of the reef, many other organisms, especially *algae* (AL-jee), help with the task. One type of plant that is very important to the structure of a coral reef is *coralline* (KOR-a-linn) *algae*. These plants are very small. They deposit lime around themselves to help cement the algae and the reef together. Some of these lime-secreting algae are better able to withstand the pounding of the waves than are the corals. They are very important in building and holding the ocean side of a reef together, where the breaking waves first hit.

Some corals don't secrete limestone around their polyps. Called *soft corals*, these are more flexible than hard corals. The flattened, lacy network of the *sea fan* is one kind of soft coral found growing on hard coral reefs. Long, soft *sea whips* are another. The sea fan itself becomes the place of attachment for other reef organisms, like *flamingo tongue sea shells* and *basket starfish*. During the day the basket starfish curls up in a ball. But at night the branches of its five arms unfold into a gorgeous lacy network that filters food from the passing current.

Many kinds of marine worms, such as the beautiful *feather duster worm,* make their home on coral reefs. Most marine worms secrete a tube around their long bodies for protection or dig a hole in the reef, which becomes their burrow. When the worms die, their tubes and burrows are recycled as homes for other invertebrates and small fishes.

The giant clam is a spectacular example of a large reef mollusk. It can grow to over four feet long and weigh over 500 pounds! Its chalky white shell is rather plain, but its fleshy tissue has colors ranging from green and blue to reddish yellow to tan, with spots and wavy lines of lighter colors.

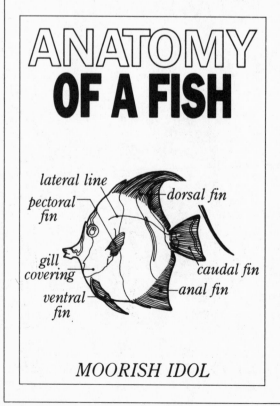

ANATOMY OF A FISH

lateral line
pectoral fin
dorsal fin
gill covering
caudal fin
anal fin
ventral fin

MOORISH IDOL

Some plants and animals you might see on a coral reef are: 1. a sea fan (left); 2. flamingo tongue sea shell (on the sea fan); 3. copper banded butterfly fish (right); 4. red-lined cleaner shrimp (lower right); and 5. plumed sea slug (lower left).

Reef Plants and Animals

Crabs of many colors, shapes, and sizes crawl around the reef using their mighty pincer claws to break open or tear apart food while scavenging and cleaning up the reef.

There are always a variety of sponges on a coral reef. The sizes and shapes vary from low, hard-to-spot sponges that cling to the surface of the reef to long, tubular, or vase-shaped ones many feet in length. Some sponges secrete a chemical that eats away a pit in the coral to give the sponge a nice hole in which to live. The tubular sponges are flexible and sway gently in the currents. Skeletons of sponges are strengthened by microscopic rods and plates. When a sponge dies, these pieces of its skeleton contribute to the construction of the reef and sand.

Moray eels hide in small caves of the reef, waiting to slither out to prey on other fishes. Damsel fishes hover about the surface of the reef guarding their eggs and feeding places, dashing out and fighting with other fishes that get too close. Parrot fishes with huge jaws come by and scrape off algae that grows on the reef surface. Their scraping action also scrapes off pieces of coral, helping to create sand around the reef. There are often more than 100 different kinds of fishes living within a few hundred feet of a reef.

Many plants, such as sea grasses, are found around the base of the reef and its sandy bottom, rather than on the reef itself. These grass beds are important habitats for many types of invertebrates (animals without backbones), such as shrimps, sea slugs, starfishes, and sea cucumbers. They are also home to fishes, such as file fishes and wrasses, and they serve as a nursery ground for the young stages of many bottom-dwelling fishes. The grass flats also are a place where many reef fishes and invertebrates feed during the day. Within a distance of 20 to 30 feet from the base of the reef, the grass and algae that grow on the white sand bottom is so eaten away by feeders that the bottom is pale in color. When viewed from above the reef, these heavily grazed areas look like a halo around the reef.

A large assortment of creatures live on a coral reef. Top, *left to right: 1. grunts; 2. spotted eagle ray; 3. grouper.* Upper middle, *left to right: 4. lookdown fish; 5. butterfly fish; 6. jellyfish.* Center, *left to right: 7. clown wrasse; 8. hog fish; 9. spotted moray eel 10. sea anemone.* Lower middle, *left to right: 11. sea pen; 12. brain coral; 13. pork fish; 14. spiny lobster; 15. honeycomb cow fish.* Bottom, *left to right: 16. porcupine fish; 17. spiny brittle star.*

Gardens of Eels

One hundred feet beneath the surface of the Caribbean Sea at Carrie Bow Cay in Central America, a television camera points at what looks like a huge underwater garden with thousands of thin, straight stalks swaying gently in the current. A scientist in scuba gear who is studying this ''garden'' swims up to adjust the camera. Instantly, the ''stalks'' sink down into the sand and disappear, all but their tips. After the scientist swims away, the creatures come out again.

These ''stalks'' are *garden eels*. They live near coral reefs, in colonies of hundreds or even thousands. Each eel lives in the sand in a curved burrow that is two or three times as long as itself. Most eels are active at night, but garden eels are active during the day. They spend the day with the front part of their bodies sticking out of their burrows. The garden eels peck at the tiny living things floating in the current that flows by their homes.

A garden eel has just one way to defend itself. If it senses danger, such as a scuba diver, or an eel-eating fish such as a snapper or grouper, a garden eel disappears into its burrow. A garden eel's eyes are close to the tip of its snout, so it only needs to raise the tip of its head above the surface to see if the danger has passed. At sunset, every member of the colony settles down deep in its burrow for safety. At dawn the next day, they come out to start feeding again.

If divers approach slowly, they may be able to see garden eels outside their burrows.

Night and Day on a Coral Reef

Coral reefs are homes to many living things. Reefs are full of crevices, holes, caves, and overhangs which offer safe shelter for fishes and other sea creatures. These shelter spaces are so valuable on the reef that many of them are used twice a day.

Some fishes make their homes in these crevices during the daytime. When darkness falls, they leave their safe retreats to feed in the nearby grass beds and sand flats. The places they have just vacated then can become the night-time resting places for fishes that have been feeding along the sand flats in daylight.

Three groups of fishes often seen on the reef during the day are red *cardinal fishes*, red *squirrel fishes*, and purplish-colored fishes called *glassy big eyes*. These three types of fish hover around the reef during the day, seeking shelter from predators. At nightfall, they leave the reef and use their keen night-time vision and the light of the moon to find food. These are nocturnal fishes—active at night. Red is a hard color to see at night, and many nocturnal fishes are red. They usually have large eyes, which let them absorb what little light comes from the moon. Other nocturnal reef animals include fishes called *grunts* (because of the sounds they make), *moray eels*, long spiny *black sea urchins*, and a number of mollusks.

Many other groups of fishes feed during the day—*wrasses* and *puffer fishes* that feed over the sand flats and grass beds; *butterfly fishes* that pluck polyps from the corals; *blue chromis damsel fishes* that swim around in schools above the top of a reef, feeding on zooplankton; and brightly colored parrot fishes that browse along the surface of the coral. As the sun goes down, all these fishes return to the reef and get ready to settle into the nooks and crannies that will soon be vacated by fishes such as the cardinal and squirrel fishes.

This changeover of occupancy happens within about a half hour, at dawn and at dusk, every day, like clockwork. For the few minutes when the ''night shift'' is on its way out and the ''day shift'' hasn't settled in yet, the reef looks deserted.

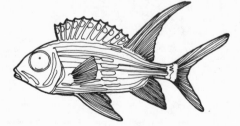

The squirrel fish is usually silvery-red and about one foot long.

*The spotted moray eel (top) and the purple-colored glassy big eye (bottom) are
nocturnal hunters. During the day, to protect themselves from predators,
moray eels hide in crevices while the glassy big eye hovers close to the reef.*

Protecting the Reefs

We receive many benefits from coral reefs, in addition to their beauty.

Coral reefs protect tropical shores from erosion. Fishes, lobsters, and other animals that live around reefs are important as food for people who live on tropical islands and coasts. Reefs also shelter tiny animals that commercially important fishes, such as sardines, mackerel, and tunas, feed upon. Some chemicals found in soft corals are helpful in treating heart disease, asthma, ulcers, and in easing the difficulty of childbirth. The limestone skeletons of corals are the source of building materials for houses. Ground-up lime also is used as fertilizer. The thrill of snorkeling and diving on coral reefs attracts tourists and helps poor countries improve their standard of living.

Unless we are very careful, the benefits of coral reefs will be lost. Coral reefs are endangered in many parts of the world, especially where there are large human populations. The main threat to reefs is pollution. Corals are very sensitive to water quality, and must have pure, clear ocean water. Sewage from cities and factories, even those far inland on rivers, eventually makes its way to the sea. There, many chemicals in the sewage travel on ocean currents to coral reefs, which can harm the growth of polyps.

Oil spills from tankers in tropical waters can destroy reefs. The floating crude oil tends not to do too much damage—that's because it doesn't coat the submerged corals as it does beach areas. But some chemicals found in oil can be deadly. Marine biologists are alarmed at the thought of drilling oil wells in areas rich in coral reefs such as the Arabian and Red Seas, the Central American coast of the Caribbean, the Great Barrier Reef off Australia, and in the Indian Ocean.

Just as harmful is the sediment washed to sea from farmlands and from tropical forests that are being cut down. Suspended silt blocks the sunlight that the coral polyps need to grow. Pesticides, fertilizers, and other chemicals used on farms are deadly to corals.

Sailors, fishermen, and other boaters can thoughtlessly destroy coral by anchoring on the reef itself rather than the sandy bottom around it. An anchor digging into the reef is bad enough, but worse yet is dragging an anchor through a reef. Hundreds of years of growth can be destroyed by one carelessly-placed anchor.

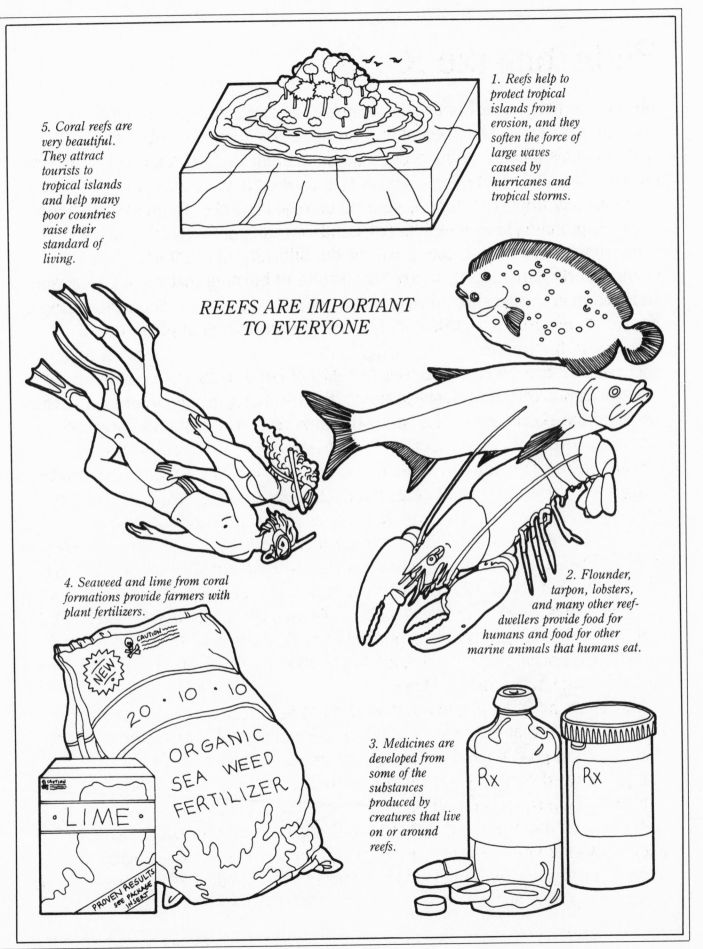

5. Coral reefs are very beautiful. They attract tourists to tropical islands and help many poor countries raise their standard of living.

1. Reefs help to protect tropical islands from erosion, and they soften the force of large waves caused by hurricanes and tropical storms.

REEFS ARE IMPORTANT TO EVERYONE

4. Seaweed and lime from coral formations provide farmers with plant fertilizers.

2. Flounder, tarpon, lobsters, and many other reef-dwellers provide food for humans and food for other marine animals that humans eat.

3. Medicines are developed from some of the substances produced by creatures that live on or around reefs.

NEW

CAUTION

20 · 10 · 10

ORGANIC SEA WEED FERTILIZER

CAUTION

·LIME·

PROVEN RESULTS SEE PACKAGE INSERT

Rx

Rx

Protecting the Reefs

Fishermen in some Pacific islands now use laundry bleach to kill fishes on reefs, and that also kills the coral in that patch of reef. Some island fishermen even blast the fishes out with dynamite, destroying great chunks of reef.

Even though tourists should know better, too many of them cannot resist the temptation to break off a piece of coral to take home as a souvenir. People even throw trash and garbage overboard on reefs. In several countries in Southeast Asia, coral is allowed to be collected to be exported and sold in souvenir shops. That is the source of the coral sold in the Florida Keys.

We must try to reduce these threats to our coral reefs if we wish to continue to enjoy their benefits and pass the reefs on in good condition to our children and to future generations. To protect these beautiful formations we need to educate everyone about the importance of coral reef survival.

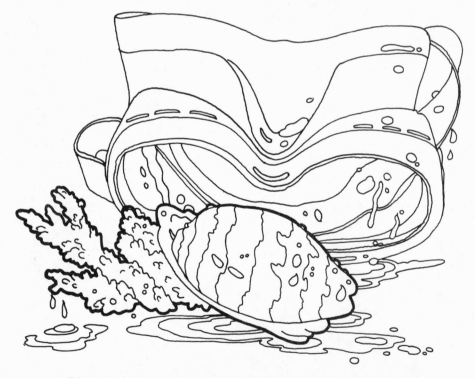

If you're lucky enough to visit a reef, be careful not to damage coral, and never take a living plant or animal from its home.

Aluminum cans, plastic rings, and broken fishing line can harm wildlife. Never litter!

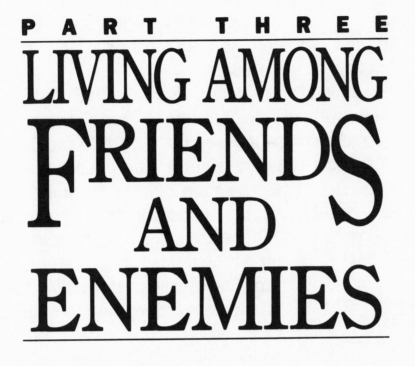

PART THREE
LIVING AMONG FRIENDS AND ENEMIES

Plant Eaters

Plants can live without animals. They use the sun's energy to convert carbon dioxide and water into food. This process is called *photosynthesis* (fo-to-SIN-thuh-sis). But animals can't live without plants. Fishes and most other animals cannot make their own food, so they must eat plants, or they must eat other animals that have eaten plants.

The most common plants in the sea are: *diatoms* (DYE-uh-toms), which are too small to be seen without a microscope; *algae*, which can be microscopic or very large; and *sea grasses* that attach to the ocean floor. Because plants need sunlight to grow, none can live deeper than about 250 feet. That's as deep as sunlight penetrates with enough strength for photosynthesis.

In general, the largest meat-eating fishes tend to eat smaller meat eaters. These, in turn, eat smaller, plant-eating animals. When animals feed on other animals that have eaten plants, we describe these relationships as a *food chain*. But not all large sea creatures are meat eaters. Some of the biggest whales and sharks eat some of the tiniest plants and animals.

All members of the large and colorful group of fishes called *parrot fishes* have huge jaws with fused teeth to scrape plants off coral and rocky reefs. Sometimes a parrot fish will bite right through the limestone that makes up a reef. If you go snorkeling near a coral reef where parrot fishes are feeding, and you float quietly on the surface so that you don't startle them, you may be able to hear them crunching noisily on coral. When a parrot fish spits out pieces of coral, a shower of sandy rubble drifts to the ocean floor.

ARISTOTLE'S LANTERN

Many marine plant eaters have special teeth and mouth parts.

Animals called sea urchins *have a mouth that is called* Aristotle's lantern *(named after the ancient Greek philosopher who first described it, because it reminded him of the lanterns used at that time).*

Aristotle's lantern is a circular mouth with five tooth plates around it. The tooth plates scrape plants off sand or gravel as the urchin slowly moves around on the ocean floor.

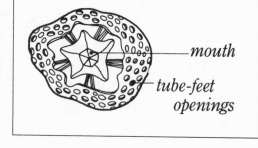

—mouth

—tube-feet openings

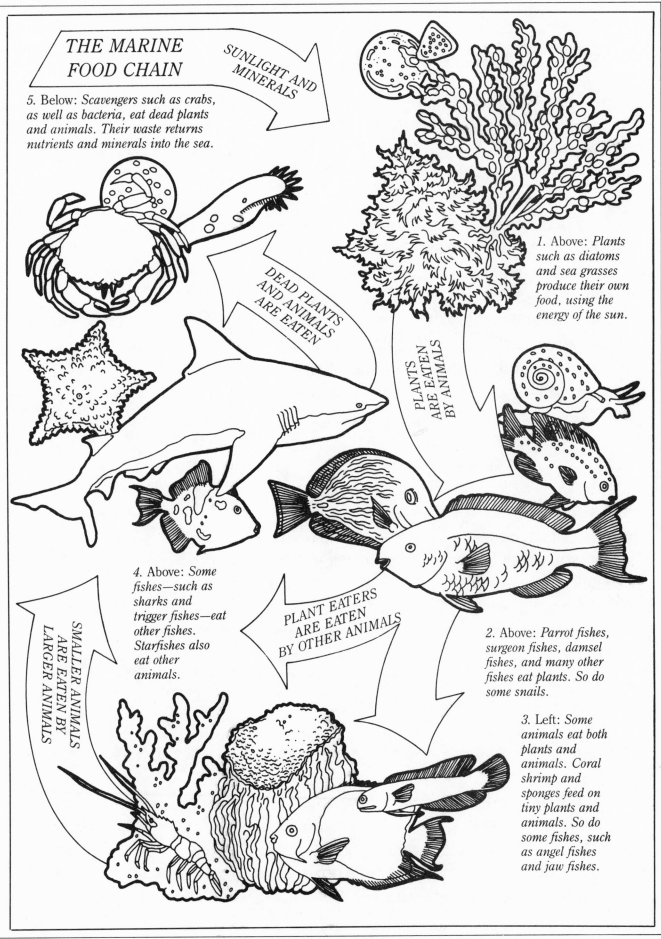

THE MARINE FOOD CHAIN

SUNLIGHT AND MINERALS

5. Below: *Scavengers such as crabs, as well as bacteria, eat dead plants and animals. Their waste returns nutrients and minerals into the sea.*

DEAD PLANTS AND ANIMALS ARE EATEN

PLANTS ARE EATEN BY ANIMALS

1. Above: *Plants such as diatoms and sea grasses produce their own food, using the energy of the sun.*

4. Above: *Some fishes—such as sharks and trigger fishes—eat other fishes. Starfishes also eat other animals.*

PLANT EATERS ARE EATEN BY OTHER ANIMALS

2. Above: *Parrot fishes, surgeon fishes, damsel fishes, and many other fishes eat plants. So do some snails.*

SMALLER ANIMALS ARE EATEN BY LARGER ANIMALS

3. Left: *Some animals eat both plants and animals. Coral shrimp and sponges feed on tiny plants and animals. So do some fishes, such as angel fishes and jaw fishes.*

Meat Eaters

A large *grouper* waits quietly in a crevice. A small fish swims closely by. Suddenly, the grouper darts forward and gulps the fish into its mouth. Then it retreats to its crevice, to await another meal.

Many ocean animals eat other animals to stay alive. *Starfishes* are another example. Most starfish have five arms. Under each arm are hundreds of "suction cups"—actually, tiny, tube-shaped feet. When a starfish finds a clam or an oyster, it wraps its arms firmly around the creature's shell. Using its "suction cups" to get a good grip, the starfish slowly pries open the shell, drawing the soft clam or oyster to its mouth.

Octopuses eat shellfish, too. When an octopus finds a clam, it drills a little hole in the clam's shell with its ribbon of teeth. Then it sends a poison into the shell through the hole. The poison paralyzes the clam's muscles, and the shell opens easily.

Thousands of kinds of fishes are meat eaters. A *barracuda* glides through the ocean until it finds a small fish. Then it darts out and snatches the fish in its long, toothy jaws.

The most feared meat-eating shark is the *great white shark,* but not all sharks are so ferocious. Some sharks are scavengers—they eat only the remains of dead creatures. Others are filter feeders, sucking in water over their gills and filtering out tiny animals and plants.

Many seals and whales are meat eaters, and another marine mammal, the *sea otter,* eats abalone, a type of shellfish.

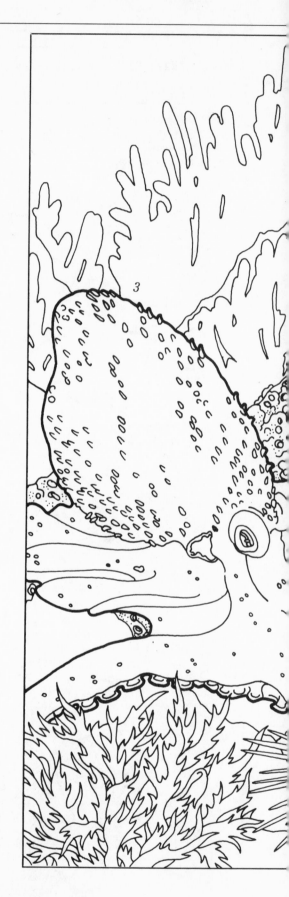

Some meat eaters of the sea—1. *in the distance at top, a sand tiger shark;* 2. *below the shark, a barracuda;* 3. *at front, a closeup view of an octopus, and* 4. *a queen trigger fish eating a sea urchin;* 5. *at right, a starfish.*

Filter Feeders

A school of thousands of herrings swim slowly through the ocean, their mouths open as water flows over their gills. Though it may be hard to believe, these fish are eating. Long, comb-like structures in their gills, called *rakers,* filter tiny animals from the sea. This way of collecting food is called *filter-feeding.*

The ocean is full of tiny plants and animals and the young stages of larger animals. These creatures float in the water or swim weakly as they are carried along by the currents. Animals that can filter these tiny creatures out of the water have a plentiful supply of food.

Sponges are filter feeders. There are sponges of almost every possible shape and color, from long tubes with hollow centers to great rounded masses several feet thick. Their color may be a drab gray or black, or a bright yellow, red, or vibrant lavender.

Sponges eat by taking water through pores or openings on the surface of their bodies. As water passes through a sponge, certain cells inside the sponge's body eat the tiny plants and animals. Then the water is expelled, and new water is taken in.

Clams, scallops, and oysters are filter feeders, too. They eat by pumping water through their bodies to remove the plants and animals in the water. These shellfishes can live in beds of enormous numbers—proof that sea water is filled with a wonderful richness of tiny plants and animals that can be eaten.

Many marine worms are filter feeders. The *feather duster worm* has long, delicate feeding tentacles that stick out of its tube. Not surprisingly, it looks just like a feather duster!

Not all filter feeders are small. Three of the biggest and most spectacular creatures of the sea are filter feeders—the *blue whale,* the *whale shark,* and the *basking shark.*

School of herring

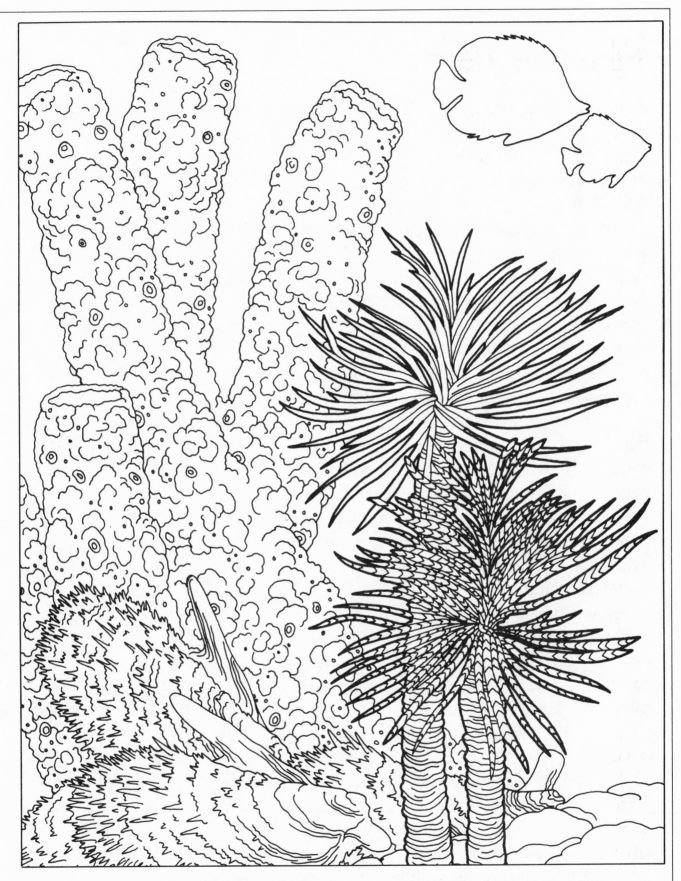

Filter feeders such as tube sponges (top left), oysters (bottom left), and tube worms (right) filter food from the water that surrounds them.

Scavenger Hunters

Some ocean animals eat things that sound disgusting. They eat the waste products of other animals, and the rotting parts of dead plants and animals called *detritus* (de-TRY-tus). It's not a fancy diet. But it is a way of life for many creatures, and it helps recycle nutrients back into the sea.

Sea cucumbers plow along the ocean floor, gobbling up sand and mud at one end, digesting anything contained in it, and expelling it from the other end. Other detritus feeders are marine catfishes and sturgeons, mud snails, many marine worms that burrow in soft ocean bottoms, and fiddler crabs on the shore.

Animals that feed on the dead bodies of other animals are called *scavengers*. Some fishes, such as nurse sharks, and some types of eels, are scavengers. Many shore crabs spend their lives in a constant scavenger hunt.

Many animals eat whatever comes their way—be it plant or animal. Hermit crabs and many shrimps feed this way. So does the pinfish, one of the most common fishes along the Atlantic coast.

Some animals feed in more than one way. The sea fan, a soft-bodied coral, sways in the current, filtering little animals through its lacy fan. Then, like a meat eater, it stuns the tiny animals with its stinging cells and eats them.

Some scavengers and detritus feeders: 1. *Hermit crabs (upper left);* 2. *pea crabs (upper middle);* 3. *edible crabs (middle left and lower right);* 4. *masked crabs (middle right);* 5. *pin fish (middle);* 6. *sea cucumbers (lower left);* and 7. *sea slaters (lower middle). All these animals feed on dead animals or waste products.*

Armor

You may have seen pictures of medieval knights who protected themselves in battle by wearing heavy metal armor. Many slow-moving sea creatures have a kind of armor, too. The shells that surround mollusks and the tough hides of starfish give important protection to these animals.

Once many fishes had this type of armor. About 500 million years ago, there were two groups of slow-moving, heavily-armored fishes, called *placoderms* (PLAK-o-dermz) and *ostracoderms* (os-TRAK-o-dermz). Their armor protected them from enemies, but it could not protect them from changes in the ocean around them. Both kinds of fishes became extinct millions of years ago.

Today, only a few types of armored fish remain. Tropical fishes called *trunk fishes* or *box fishes* live near coral reefs. These fishes have a body almost entirely encased in a hard, thick, continuous shell of plate-like scales. This armor is not just for show—it really works. Only rarely can an adult trunk fish be eaten by anything else. (However, every once in a while, a big shark may swallow one whole!)

Sturgeon fishes have several rows of armor plates on the sides of their bodies. These plates help protect them from their enemies. Sturgeons grow to more than 10 feet in length. The eggs of female sturgeons are valued as the delicacy called *caviar.* (The most expensive caviar comes from sturgeons caught in Russia and Iran.)

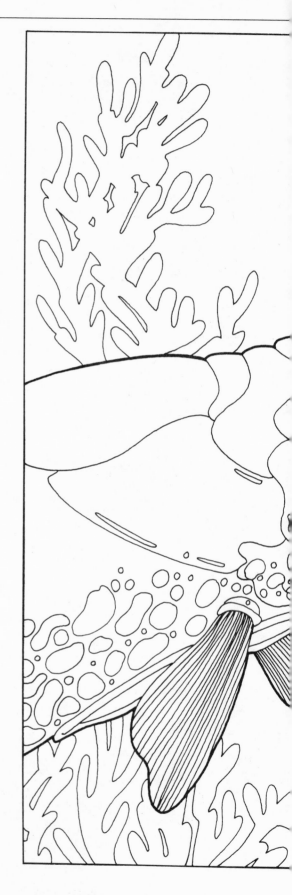

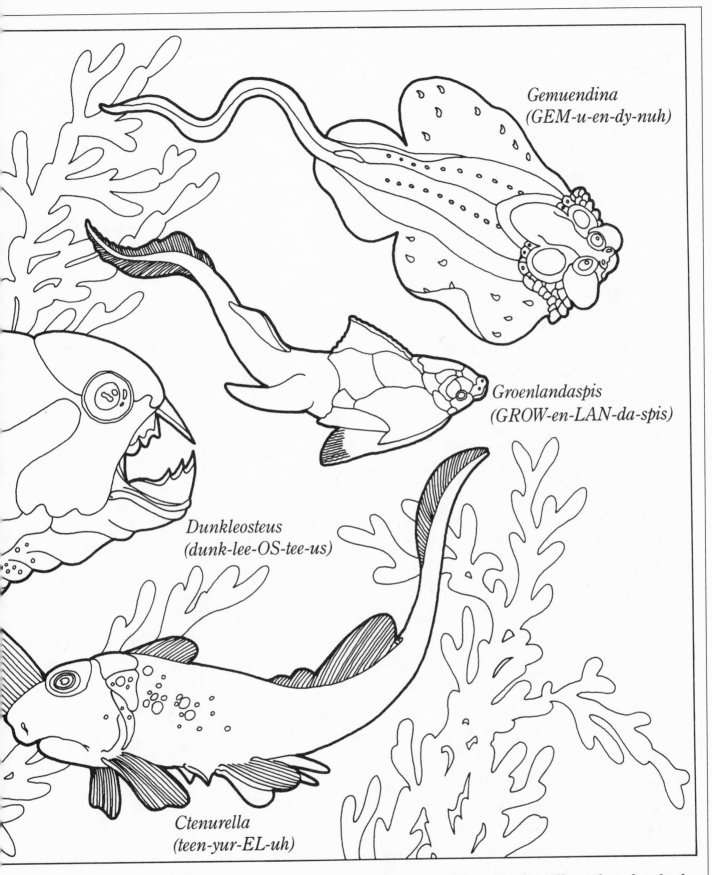

Gemuendina
(GEM-u-en-dy-nuh)

Groenlandaspis
(GROW-en-LAN-da-spis)

Dunkleosteus
(dunk-lee-OS-tee-us)

Ctenurella
(teen-yur-EL-uh)

These fishes lived millions of years ago. Their fossils tell us that they had plates of armor to protect them from larger, meat-eating fishes.

Fishes that Inflate

Imagine that, out of the corner of your eye, you spy your worst enemy sneaking up on you. Imagine that you could suddenly inflate your body until you were twice your normal size. Your enemy would scurry away in terror! Some sea animals can do this.

When a fish swells to twice its normal size, it often becomes too big for an enemy to swallow. The quick swelling-up also may help scare away the predator.

Two very different types of fishes that can inflate are *puffer fishes* and *swell sharks*. Many different types of puffer fishes can be found throughout the world. Most puffers are between two inches and one foot long. They live close to shore in the shallow waters of the continental shelf. If threatened, a puffer gulps large amounts of water into a pouch of its stomach. Its body swells into a nearly perfect ball and it becomes several times larger than its usual size.

Most kinds of puffer fishes have spines that stand straight up when the body inflates. So the puffer fish becomes a firm round ball with spines sticking out all over it—not a very appetizing meal!

Puffers usually feed on crabs, mollusks, and other hard-shelled animals. Puffers will nibble at almost any kind of bait, so they are easy to catch by anyone fishing along the shore.

There are seven types of swell sharks. All of them live in the Indian or Pacific Oceans. Swell sharks grow to be about three feet long. Like puffers, they have an area in their stomachs that they can fill with water to greatly increase their size. During the day, swell sharks stay hidden around rocks and coral reefs. They come out at night to feed on small fishes and other animals, using their many small, pointed teeth.

Both puffers and swell sharks normally inflate with water, but if they are disturbed while they are at the surface, they can swallow air. Then they bob along like corks until they expel the air and sink back down below the surface of the ocean.

A swell shark puffs up to scare away its enemies.

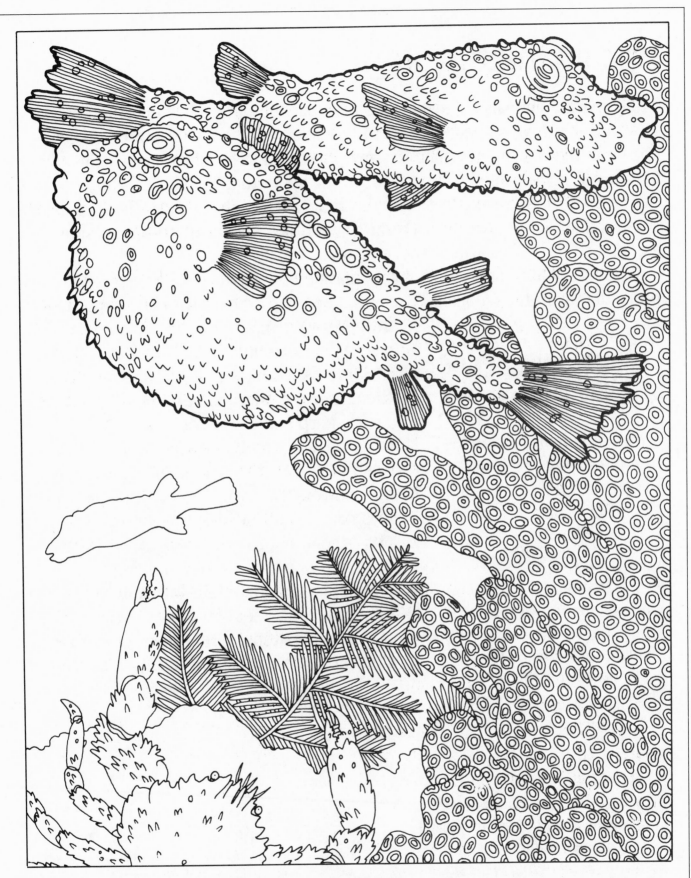

Puffer fishes protect themselves from larger, meat-eating fishes by swallowing water and swelling up.

Spiny Creatures

Many marine animals have sharp spines that they use to defend themselves.

The black, *long-spined sea urchin* has one of the best sets of defensive spines in the ocean. Anything (or any person) that brushes against this sea urchin will get a painful wound from every spine that pricks the skin.

The *crown-of-thorns starfish* of the Indo-Pacific (the Indian Ocean and tropical and warmer western Pacific Ocean) has short, sharp-tipped spines along each of its five arms. These also can cause a painful wound.

When they are very young, many marine animals have sharp spines projecting from their bodies. These spines help protect them from predators in the ocean. In some cases, these spines also help them float.

Some fishes have spines that help defend them in other ways. A *surgeon fish* has razor-sharp spines on each side of the base of its tail. It uses these spines to lash and slash at a predator. The long tails of *sting rays* have spines with notched edges. Sting rays can thrash these spines into the body of a predator (or a foot, if someone is unlucky enough to step on a sting ray!).

When you wade in shallow water, it's best to shuffle your feet along the bottom instead of taking big steps. Otherwise, you might step on something spiny. That's a step you would regret.

BIOLUMINESCENCE

Sometimes, at night, when a wave crashes against the shore, the water seems to glow. The glow is light, called bioluminescence *(by-oh-loo-mi-NES-sense), produced by millions of microscopic creatures.*

Many animals capable of bio-luminescence, such as lantern fishes and viper fishes, live in the middle depths and deeper areas of the ocean. These creatures have organs called photophores *that produce light. Many kinds of squids and octopuses also are luminescent.*

So if you're out at sea, just remember that there are as many lights glowing in the depths of the ocean at night as there are stars you can see twinkling in the sky.

In just a few inches of water, you may be able to see 1. a purple sea urchin (bottom center and left center); 2. a thorny sea star (lower left); 3. a blue crab (lower left); 4. mussels (middle, center); and 5. barnacles (bottom left and right).

Poisonous Animals

Most animals in the sea won't hurt you. But there are some dangerous marine animals, and it's good to know which they are, especially when swimming or wading in tropical seas.

The *scorpion fishes* are well-named. Most members of this family of bottom-dwelling fishes have poisonous spines in their dorsal (top) fins. These spines can cause a painful and sometimes fatal wound. Scorpion fishes that live off the coasts of North America are not deadly, but they can give a painful wound.

The most deadly of the scorpion fishes is the *stone fish*. It lives in the Indo–Pacific. Each of its 13 dorsal spines has a sac at its base that produces a poison. The poison flows to the tip of the hollow spine.

The stone fish looks just like a rock sitting on the ocean floor. Anyone who steps on a stone fish will immediately have one of the worst pains imaginable. Anyone unlucky enough to get a full dose of the poison will die in great pain in about 15 minutes.

The beautiful, frilly *lion-fish* is another member of the scorpion fish family. Its red and orange colors warn other fishes to stay away. But its bright colors are just right to help it blend into the red and orange of the coral reefs where it lives. The poison from its spines can kill other fishes.

Sea snakes live only in the Indo–Pacific. They look like big eels, but they are true snakes. Like land snakes, some sea snakes are poisonous. They are found far at sea, around coral reefs, and in the mouths of some rivers. A sea snake's teeth have glands that produce strong poisons. The sea snake uses these poisons to kill its food, usually fishes. Sea snakes are normally sluggish and docile. But when aroused they can be fierce. Anyone who disturbs a sea snake may get bitten and possibly die.

The bold colors of the frilly lion-fish warn other fish to stay away. This fish blends in well with the colors of the coral found where it lives.

Creatures that Sting

Drifting silently in the ocean, often near the surface, are *jellyfishes*. Moved by the currents, these pale, delicate creatures look defenseless. But jellyfishes and their relatives have a hidden weapon.

A typical jellyfish has a large, squashy, umbrella-like body. Dangling from the body are thread-like tentacles. Each tentacle has structures called *nematocysts* (NEM-a-to-sists). At the tip of each nematocyst is an arrow-shaped barb. These barbs contain poison.

When a jellyfish brushes against an animal floating by, the barbed nematocysts shoot out and stun the victim. Even though these poison arrows are so small that we need a microscope to see them, they are deadly effective when fired off by the hundreds and thousands. The jellyfish then pulls its tentacles, with the dead or stunned prey, up to its mouth on the underside of its umbrella-shaped body and digests its meal.

Usually, if a jellyfish stings you, it can only give you a mild sting. Even so, the burning feeling may last several hours. But several kinds of jellyfishes have poison so strong that they can kill humans. The large *Portuguese man-of-war* jellyfish that lives in the Atlantic Ocean usually feeds on small, surface-swimming fishes. But a swimmer who brushes against its tentacles will get a very painful burning rash that lasts for days. If someone is stung by too many tentacles, the shock to the body can be so strong that the swimmer may drown. In the Indo–Pacific, the *sea-wasp* jellyfish is even more venomous, and its sting can kill a person in less than half an hour.

Sea anemones are relatives of the jellyfishes that attach themselves to corals, rocks, mangrove roots, and other firm surfaces. They have fleshy bodies and tentacles with nematocysts to stun little animals that touch them.

The orange or yellowish-tan *fire coral* also is related to the jellyfishes. When touched it fires off poisonous darts. The pain of its sting can last many days.

The *fire worm* is another stinging creature that deserves its name. A fire worm has rows or bunches of hair-like bristles along the sides of its body. These become erect when it bends. The erect bristles are hollow and full of a poison that the fire worm injects into anything that touches it, whether a hungry fish or a curious human. Its painful, fiery sting repels most things that bother it.

A large jellyfish called a Portuguese Man-o-War uses its stinging tentacles to capture a fish.

Protective Coloration

Whenever you wear a piece of very brightly-colored clothing, you stand out in a crowd! Some sea creatures have bright colors and bold patterns that help them stand out in their own world. Many of these animals are poisonous, and their bright colors and patterns warn predators away.

However, other animals seek safety by hiding. Their colors let them blend into the background, wherever they live.

The best color-changer in the sea is the octopus. An octopus can change its appearance instantly as it swims from one place to another. In the dark crevice of its home, the octopus is dark, too. But when it travels to a white sand bottom to feed on a clam, it turns a pale color. When it moves onto rocks covered with seaweed, its body immediately takes on a blotched pattern that blends in perfectly with the background. And when it moves through several kinds of backgrounds, an octopus can change its color so rapidly that it is very hard to keep it in sight. What a magician!

Other creatures have unchanging color patterns that let them blend in.

Perhaps the most beautifully colored and patterned coral reef creature is the *harlequin* (or clown) *dragonette*. This fish grows to several inches long. Its greenish body is covered with yellowish and reddish lines and spots that are outlined by darker rings. This bright and dramatic color pattern blends in surprisingly well with the reef where the harlequin fish lives. Even if you swim right over a reef, this fish is very hard to see.

HIDE & SEEK

The peacock flounder *has a tan body with light blue rings and pale spots. This coloration makes the fish nearly invisible when it is partly buried in sand. Other kinds of flounders can slowly change their colors. But no fish can do so as rapidly as an octopus.*

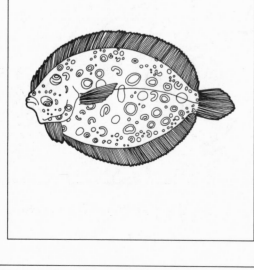

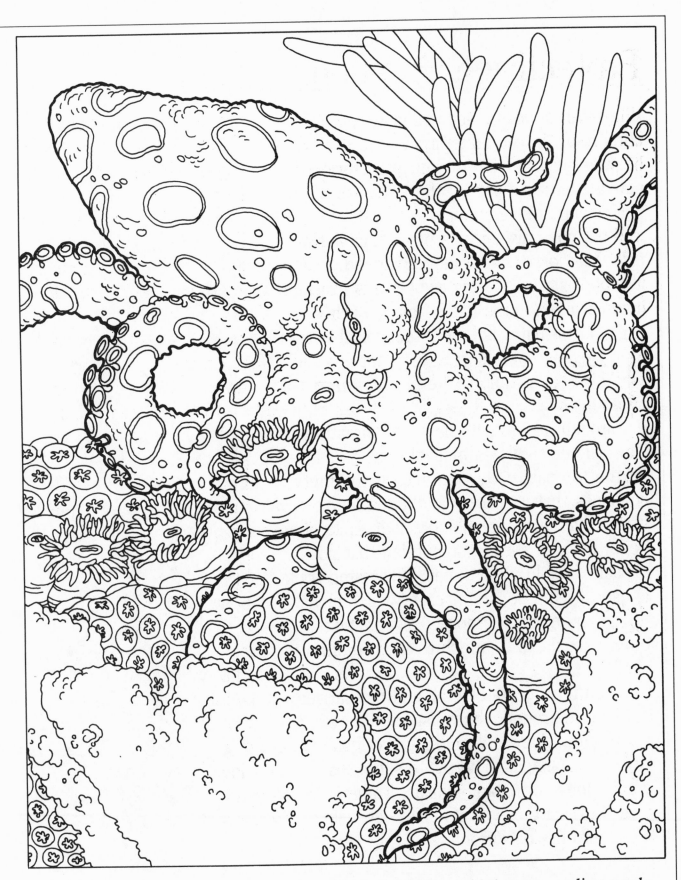

An octopus is almost invisible amid the surrounding corals.

Camouflage

Imagine that you're scuba diving near a coral reef. As you stare at a clump of seaweed just in front of you, you may be startled to see a part of the "seaweed" swim away!

What you have seen is not a plant—it's a *frilly sea horse*, with many branched, leaf-like body parts growing right out of its skin. The frilly sea horse has so many of these body parts that it is barely recognizable as a fish. Because of this, it is very hard to see when it nestles among the plants where it lives.

Camouflage protects many sea creatures. The *carrier shell* is a mollusk that dresses up the top part of its own shell with empty seashells that it collects and glues onto itself. The carrier shell looks like a pile of dead, useless shells—something that no predator would want to eat. This same trick is used by the *decorator crab*, which picks up live sponges, anemones, algae, and empty seashells to attach to the top of its shell.

When the decorator crab and the carrier shell move around, their disguises move with them. They look nothing like living crabs or seashells. The white *spiny sea urchin* does something similar: it puts pieces of sea grass on its spines to help it blend into the background.

1

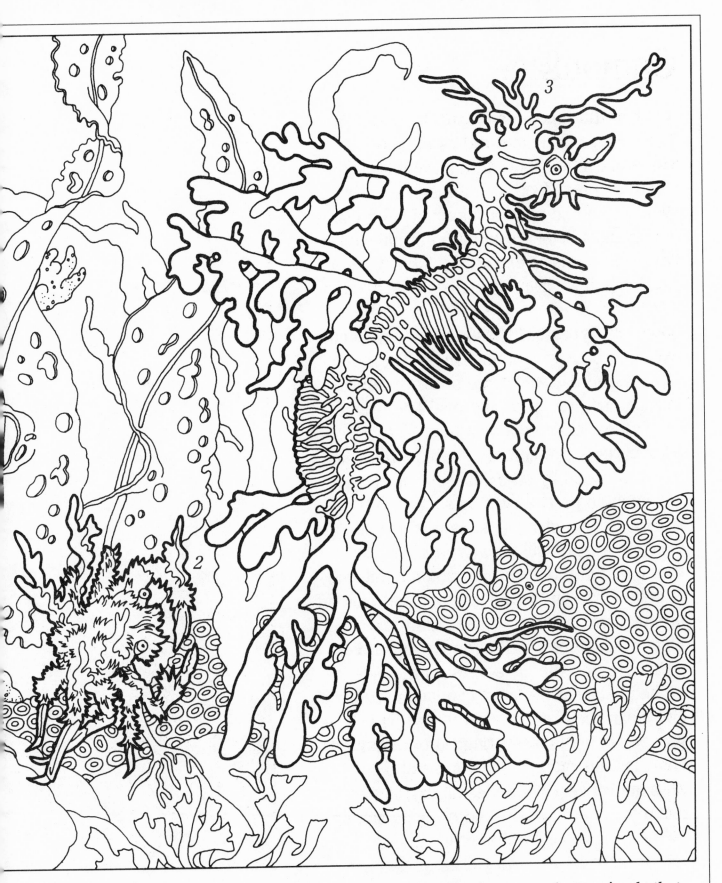

Now you see them, now you don't! Hidden in this picture are three animals that protect themselves with camouflage: 1. at left, a carrier shell; 2. at center, a decorator crab; 3. at right, a frilly sea horse (or leafy sea dragon).

Partners

Most of the time, sea creatures view other living things in their world as either predators (enemies that might eat or injure them) or prey (food for themselves). But there are some relationships between plants and animals or between different animals in which both creatures benefit. This type of relationship is called *symbiosis* (sim-bye-O-sis).

Several types of fishes feed on parasites from the bodies of other fishes. The most famous and easiest to see are the *cleaning gobies* that live on coral reefs. The bright blue, one-inch-long gobies tend to swim over parts of the coral reef where they can be easily seen by other fishes. Scientists call such an area a *cleaning station*.

How does a cleaning station work? Imagine a fish, such as a *grouper*, swimming in the waters around a coral reef. A goby darts out to the grouper and nips off crustaceans, worms, or dead skin from the bigger fish's body. The grouper may open its mouth and the gill covers on the side of its head so that the goby can swim inside and clean the grouper's teeth and gills. The grouper benefits by getting rid of unwanted animals, and the goby gets a meal! This cleaning process continues all day as one fish after another visits the cleaning station.

Some types of shrimp clean fishes. They, too, tend to have bright colors or patterns as if to advertise their services.

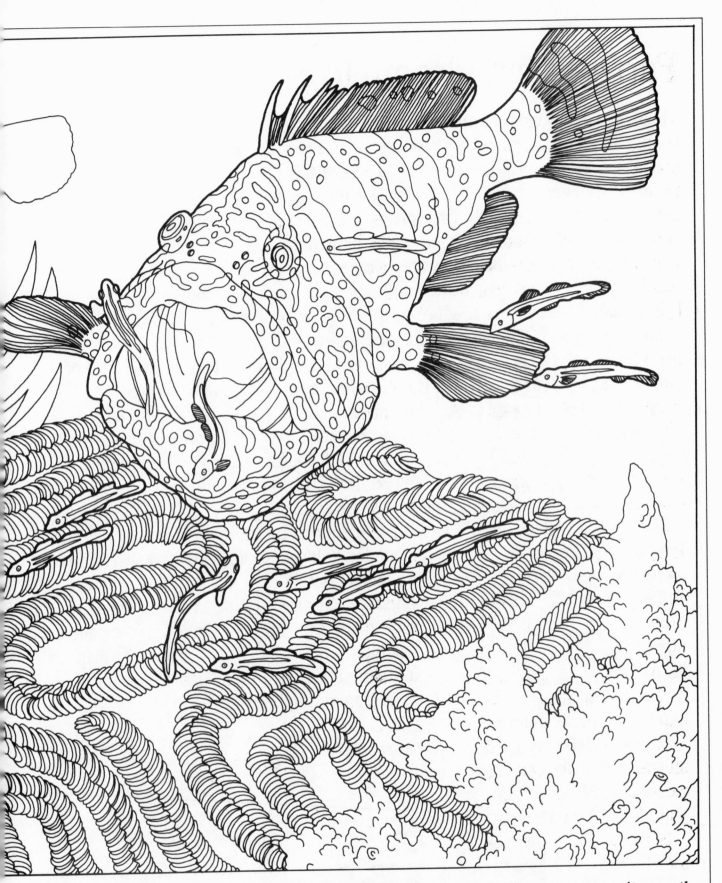

Gobies at their cleaning station above brain coral. A grouper opens its mouth
so the little gobies can swim inside and clean its teeth.

Sponges with Room to Spare

Most of the sponges in our kitchens are factory-made sponges. But living sponges can be found in all of the oceans. Their bodies have many different shapes, depending on the conditions where they live.

Large sponges several feet wide, like the *manjack* and the *loggerhead*, have enormous numbers of irregularly winding tubes or canals throughout their bodies. The sponges suck water into these tubes, remove food particles, and then expel the water through a central opening. Dozens of different kinds of worms, brittle starfishes, crustaceans, mollusks, and even fishes live in these canals. More than 35 kinds of fishes are known to live inside sponges.

Some fishes and invertebrates live all of their adult lives inside their sponge. One common sponge inhabitant is the *pistol shrimp*, which makes a popping sound with its claws. A marine biologist once counted more than 16,000 pistol shrimps living inside one large sponge.

Sponges can be nearly any color, and one lavender-colored sponge even glows! Some sponges contain chemicals that keep away enemies. Some of these sponges smell so foul to the human nose that they are called "stinker" sponges. But a "stinker" attracts as many roomers to its "apartment house" as any non-smelly loggerhead.

DIVING FOR SPONGES

Once, there was a thriving industry for sponges in the Gulf of Mexico but they were killed by disease. Sponges were collected by divers wearing steel helmets into which air was pumped through a hose from a boat on the surface. The sponges were brought to the surface, put in the sun to dry, and then washed in the seawater to remove all the living tissue. Only the squashy skeletons remained, and these were sponges that were used in kitchens and baths.

An old-fashioned diving helmet. Air was pumped from the surface and through a valve on the side of the helmet.

Tube sponges make good homes for shrimps and gobies.

Fishes that Talk with Sounds and Signals

The sea can be a noisy place. Porpoises chirp. Whales make sounds that may pass information from one individual to another. But most sounds in the sea are made by fishes.

Fishes cannot talk, of course. But some can communicate with each other with sounds or signals. One common family of fishes makes so much noise that its members are called *grunts*. Members of another common family are called *croakers* or *drums*. Scientists believe that fishes make these sounds so that some members of a school can tell others what is happening. For example, one member of a school of fish may alert others to a predator lurking nearby.

Another family of fishes that make noises are the *toad fishes*. The sounds they make are very useful to them because they live in murky water, where it is hard for them to see one another. (They are also helped by round, light-producing organs along the sides of their bodies.)

Many fishes communicate by signaling with their fins or by making twisting movements of their bodies. The common *butterfly fishes* on coral reefs often live as mated pairs (one male and one female) where there are hundreds of others of the same kind of fish around the same reef. Since these fishes spend a lot of time poking around the bottom, browsing on algae and coral polyps, members of a pair may lose sight of each other from time to time. When that happens, one of them may rise above the reef and swim in a dancing motion that its mate will recognize. Then the pair gets back together again.

Another fish that signals with its fins is the *flagfin blenny*. It has a large dorsal fin that it can wave rapidly back and forth like a flag. The flagfin blenny lives in holes in coral rocks. Males have especially large dorsal fins. A male flagfin blenny comes out of his burrow several hundred times a day to hover, vigorously flagging his dorsal fin to warn other males to stay away from his territory, and probably to encourage females to come to his burrow to lay eggs. Once a female has laid eggs in his burrow, he guards the eggs and flags all the more to defend his nursery.

French grunts communicate with each other by making grunting sounds.

The Smallest Creatures of the Sea

Just for fun, imagine that your science class is taking a field trip to the seashore. Your teacher dips a bucket into the salty water and pulls it out.

"But there's nothing in it," someone complains.

Ah, but look closely—that bucket of seawater contains billions of tiny sea creatures we call *plankton*. Some are plants, or *phytoplankton* (FY-toe-plank-ton). Some plankton are animals, or *zooplankton* (ZOE-plank-ton). Most of these creatures are much too small to see without a microscope. If you put a couple of drops of seawater on a glass slide and look at it under a microscope, you'll see some of the most common—and most important—sea life of all.

In some areas of the ocean there may be as many as several thousand *bacteria* (microscopic organisms) in one cubic inch of seawater. Because bacteria are neither plants nor animals, they are placed in a special group called *microbes*. Bacteria measure less than eight ten thousandths (0.0008) of an inch across, but they are very important. They decompose, or break down, dead plants and animals into nutrients that living organisms can use. In this way nutrients in the ocean are constantly recycled.

Specialized bacteria have recently been found living in the Gulf of Mexico at places where oil and gas seep through the ocean floor. These bacteria break down the oil and gas into food that colonies of clams, mussels, worms, and crabs can eat. Without the bacteria these colonies would not be able to exist. Bacteria themselves are an important source of food for other microscopic animals.

Diatoms are one type of phytoplankton. They are probably the most important plants in the ocean, because so many animals feed on them. Some diatoms have only one cell; others may have a chain of cells. Diatoms are only about four to eight thousandths (0.004 to 0.008) of an inch. They live near the surface of the oceans and are most plentiful in colder water.

Another kind of phytoplankton are *dinoflagellates* (dI-no-FLAJ-el-lets). They usually have one or two whip-like filaments that propel them through the water. Sometimes dinoflagellates have huge population bursts that turn the water red. This is called a *red tide*. Clams and oysters that eat red-tide dinoflagellates may not be harmed. But people have become very sick from eating shellfish that have fed on red-tide dinoflagellates.

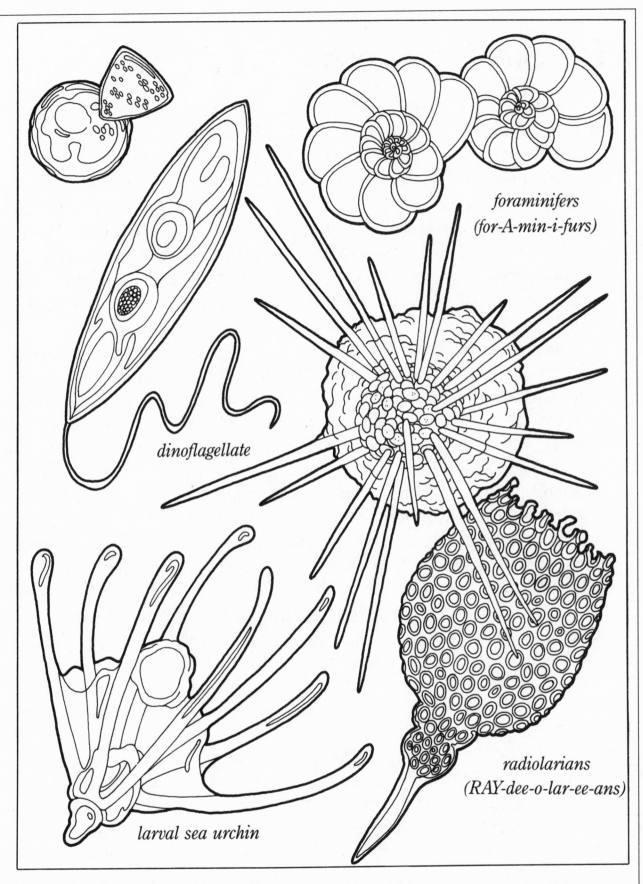

foraminifers
(for-A-min-i-furs)

dinoflagellate

radiolarians
(RAY-dee-o-lar-ee-ans)

larval sea urchin

The smallest sea life: Most of these creatures cannot be seen without a microscope.

The Smallest Creatures of the Sea

Blue-green algae are a third kind of phytoplankton. Most live in warmer surface waters.

Many different kinds of tiny marine animals make up the *zooplankton*. Some have only a single cell. They feed on phytoplankton. Other zooplankton that feed on phytoplankton are larger and much more complex. They include animals like *copepods*, which may be the most numerous animals in the sea, and *krill*, which are relatives of shrimp. Krill are one of the most important sources of food, especially in polar regions, for some of the largest animals on Earth, such as baleen whales.

Some zooplankton feed on other zooplankton. *Comb-jellies*, or *ctenophores* (TENA-fors) are transparent jellylike creatures. They have hairs, called *cilia* (SILL-ee-uh), that help them "swim" through the water. Some have long tentacles to capture other zooplankton.

Invertebrates and fishes often release their eggs and sperm into the seawater, where they combine. The fertilized eggs drift in the water until they hatch into the form called a larva. The eggs and larvae also are part of the zooplankton. They are important as food for many small fishes. Some larvae, called *free-swimming larvae*, are able to somewhat control where they are swimming. Other larvae simply drift with the currents. When larvae find a good place to live, they settle down out of the water and they grow into juveniles and adults.

If you live near the ocean, ask if you can take some seawater to school and look at it under a microscope. You and your classmates may be able to see some of these tiny creatures!

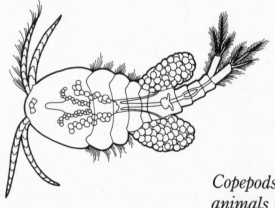

Copepods may be the most numerous animals in the sea.

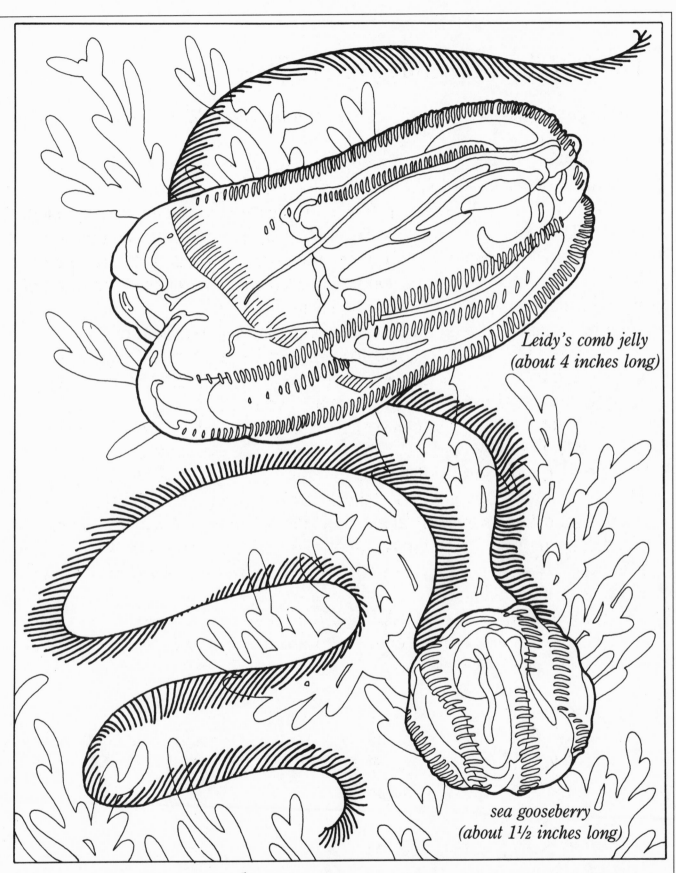

Leidy's comb jelly
(about 4 inches long)

sea gooseberry
(about 1½ inches long)

The hairs of these ctenophores help them to swim. Some of these animals use their tentacles to capture other zooplankton.

PART FOUR

GIANTS OF THE OCEAN

Whales, Dolphins, and Porpoises

Whales, dolphins, and porpoises belong to a group of animals called *cetaceans* (si-TAY-shuns). These marine mammals had land-dwelling ancestors that millions of years ago returned to the sea to live. Life in the oceans freed the cetaceans from the effects of gravity on land, where it was harder to move around. The ocean's salt water helped them to float. Some species took advantage of that to grow to very large sizes.

A cetacean breathes through a "blowhole" on the top of its head. When it breathes out, compressed air is forced out the blowhole in a spray of air and water called a *spume*. A careful observer can often identify the type of whale from far away by studying the height and direction of its spume.

Whales can dive to great depths of the ocean and stay there a long time. The deepest divers are the *sperm* and *bottle-nosed whales*, which regularly dive to 1,500 feet. Some whales can dive even deeper. Although some types of whales can stay underwater for only 5 to 15 minutes, the deep-divers can remain underwater for up to two hours! Some whales can launch themselves part way out of the water in a spectacular display called *breaching*.

Cetaceans can make a variety of sounds. It's believed that some kinds of whales, dolphins, and porpoises use these sounds to communicate with others of their kind. The *humpback whale* makes an eerie "song" of deep "groans."

Cetaceans also use sounds to find their way through the dark ocean depths. Such cetaceans can measure the distance between themselves and an object (such as the ocean floor or a squid) by bouncing sound waves off the object and measuring the amount of time it takes for the sound to return. This ability is called *echolocation* (ek-o-lo-KAY-shun).

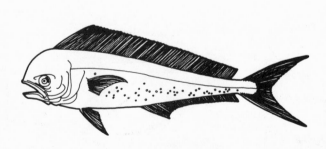

This tasty fish, called a dolphin fish, grows to about six feet long. It is often called Mahi Mahi in the islands of the Pacific. Because of its name it is sometimes confused with cetacean dolphins like the ones shown at right.

Dolphins are highly intelligent social animals that can communicate with one another through a complex system of whistles and clicks.

Baleen Whales

Scientists separate whales into two groups, the *baleen whales* and the *toothed whales*. All baleen whales have horny triangular plates (called *baleen*) that hang from their upper jaws. On the sides of these plates are hairs. As a baleen whale swims through the ocean, it opens its mouth and the hairs on the baleen plates filter the water to trap the whale's food. Baleen whales eat *krill* (tiny, shrimp-like animals), small fishes, and *zooplankton* (microscopic animals). A baleen whale's lower jaw is much larger than the upper jaw, and has no baleen. Baleen whales have two blowholes.

One baleen whale, the *blue whale*, is the largest mammal ever to live on the earth. It is found in almost all of the oceans. The average adult blue whale is 80 feet long and weighs about 150,000 pounds. The longest blue whale ever recorded measured 98 feet long!

In the North Pacific, blue whales migrate from their summer feeding grounds off the coasts of the Aleutian Islands, Alaska, western Canada, and central California to their winter grounds near Mexico and Central America, where they mate and give birth. At birth, a blue whale calf weighs 5,500 pounds and is 20 to 25 feet long. The calf feeds on its mother's milk. A blue whale's milk contains so much fat that a calf may gain 200 pounds in one day.

It is estimated that there were once several hundred thousand blue whales. But because so many blue whales have been killed by the whaling industry, especially in the 1930s, and because female blue whales give birth to only one calf every two or three years, there may be fewer than 5,000 blue whales alive today.

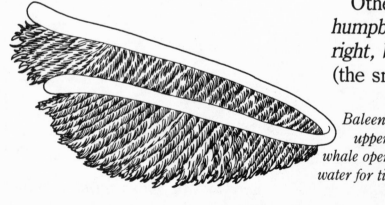

Other baleen whales include the *humpback, fin, sei, Bryde's, gray, right, bowhead,* and the *Minke whale* (the smallest).

Baleen plates like this one hang from the upper jaw of a baleen whale. When the whale opens its mouth, these plates filter the water for tiny plants and animals.

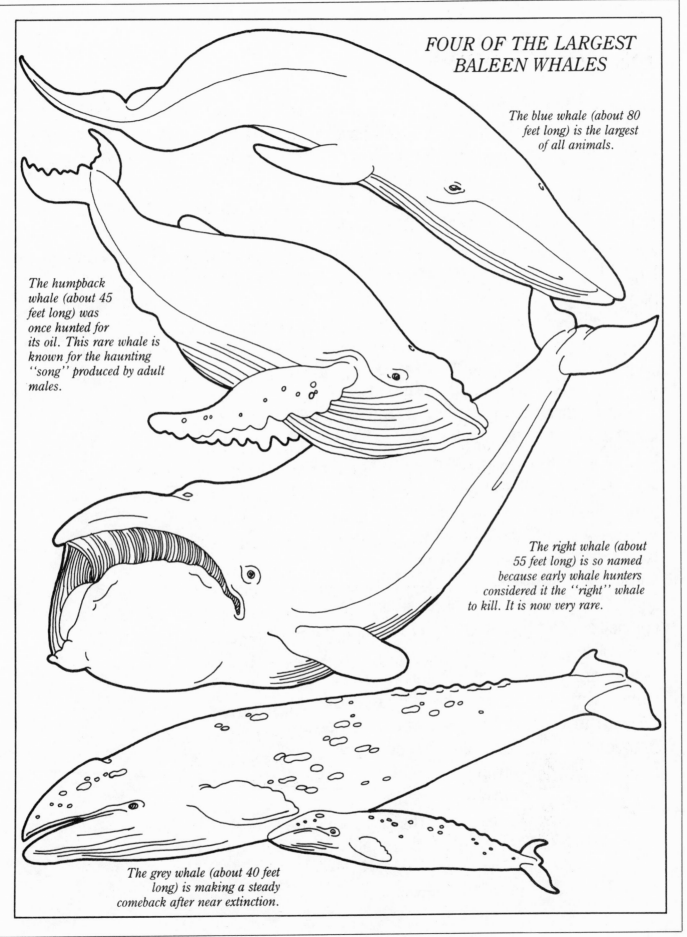

FOUR OF THE LARGEST BALEEN WHALES

The blue whale (about 80 feet long) is the largest of all animals.

The humpback whale (about 45 feet long) was once hunted for its oil. This rare whale is known for the haunting "song" produced by adult males.

The right whale (about 55 feet long) is so named because early whale hunters considered it the "right" whale to kill. It is now very rare.

The grey whale (about 40 feet long) is making a steady comeback after near extinction.

Toothed Whales

The most famous toothed whale is the *killer whale*. Like all toothed whales, killer whales have simple cone-shaped teeth and one blowhole.

Their diet is partly made up of warm-blooded marine mammals such as seals, porpoises, and even other whales. A killer whale is easy to recognize by its black back and sides, its white throat and belly, and the white patch behind its eyes.

Killer whales live in all the oceans, especially in colder waters, often in groups called ''pods.'' In 1964, the Vancouver Public Aquarium in Canada became the first aquarium to exhibit a killer whale. Since then, many aquariums have captured and trained killer whales to perform tricks upon command by animal trainers.

Probably the most unusual-looking toothed whale is the *narwhal*. The male has a spiral-shaped tusk that extends from the front of its head. The tusk is actually a specialized tooth, but how the narwhal uses it is not known. When narwhals die, their tusks sometimes break off and wash ashore. Before the narwhal was discovered in the 1600s, these tusks were thought to be proof of unicorns. The narwhal is a relatively small whale, measuring about 15 feet long. It lives only in the Arctic Ocean.

Other toothed whales are the *bottle-nosed whales*, *beaked whales,* the all-white *beluga whale,* and the *sperm whale* (the largest).

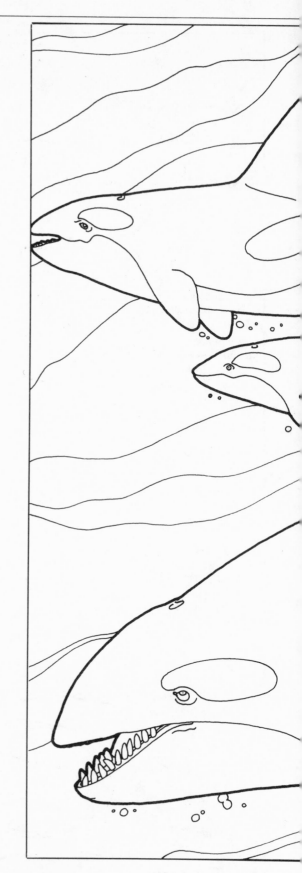

Killer whales live in groups called pods.

Giant Squids

For hundreds of years, sailors told tales of monsters of the deep—including giant squids that rose from the depths of the ocean to attack ships and gobble up their sailors. Today scientists know these stories are not true.

Giant squids are members of a group of animals without backbones called *cephalopods* (SEF-a-lo-podz). *Octopus, nautilus,* and *cuttlefishes* also are cephalopods. Each has a head with an extension of arms and tentacles. Like other squids, giant squids have four pairs of arms and one pair of tentacles. The inner surface of the arms and tentacles have cup-shaped discs that work like suction cups. The tentacles are much longer than the arms and are used to grasp fishes and other food. The arms help to hold the prey as it is brought to the squid's mouth.

Very little is known about giant squids. Most of what we know has come from animals that have died and washed ashore on the coasts of Newfoundland and Great Britain. The largest known squid was 55 feet long. Its tentacles alone were 35 feet long, and its body was 12 feet around. The giant squid's eyes, the biggest eyes known in nature, are about 10 inches across—about the size of an automobile headlight.

Scientists believe that giant squids live near the rocks of continental shelves at about 900 to 2,000 feet deep. The only known enemy of the giant squid is another giant of the deep, the sperm whale. Many sperm whales have disc-shaped scars on their heads left by the suckers of giant squids that fought being eaten.

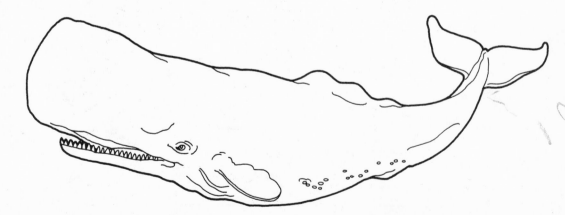

An adult sperm whale is 35 to 50 feet long.

Although no one knows for sure, giant squids may live along rocky areas of the continental shelf.

Giant Fishes

The world's largest fish is the *whale shark*. In fact, it is the largest fish ever known to have lived. It usually grows to about 36 feet long, though the longest one ever measured was 59 feet long. Even though this fish is a shark, it's quite gentle. A few divers have even ridden on its back!

Like baleen whales, the whale shark is a filter feeder. A whale shark has no baleen; instead it filters plankton, shrimp, and small fishes by straining the seawater through its gills. The whale shark's back is gray with white stripes and spots, and its belly is white.

Another very large shark is the *great white shark*. This shark is a meat eater. Its large, triangle-shaped teeth have edges as jagged as a saw. It eats many types of marine creatures, including fish, dead whales, other sharks, and marine mammals such as dolphins, porpoises, seals, and sea lions. Great white sharks have attacked humans many times, especially near Australia, South Africa, and off the coast of California. Some people suspect that the sharks mistake divers in black wetsuits and people on surfboards for seals or sea lions.

Other giant fishes include *marlins* and *tunas*. Both of these types of fishes can swim very fast for long periods of time. Because of this, they are very popular catches among sport fishermen. Tuna fishes are very important food for humans.

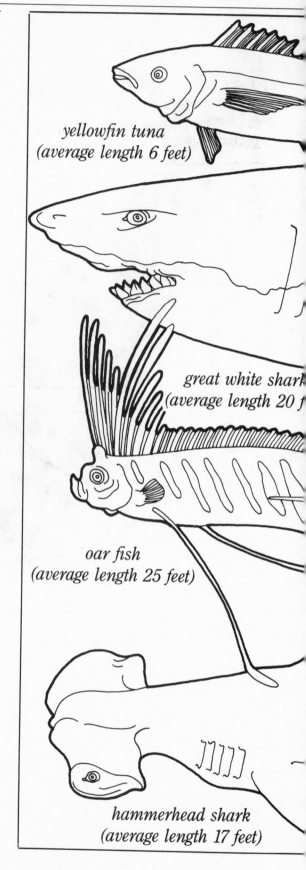

yellowfin tuna
(average length 6 feet)

great white shark
(average length 20 f[eet])

oar fish
(average length 25 feet)

hammerhead shark
(average length 17 feet)

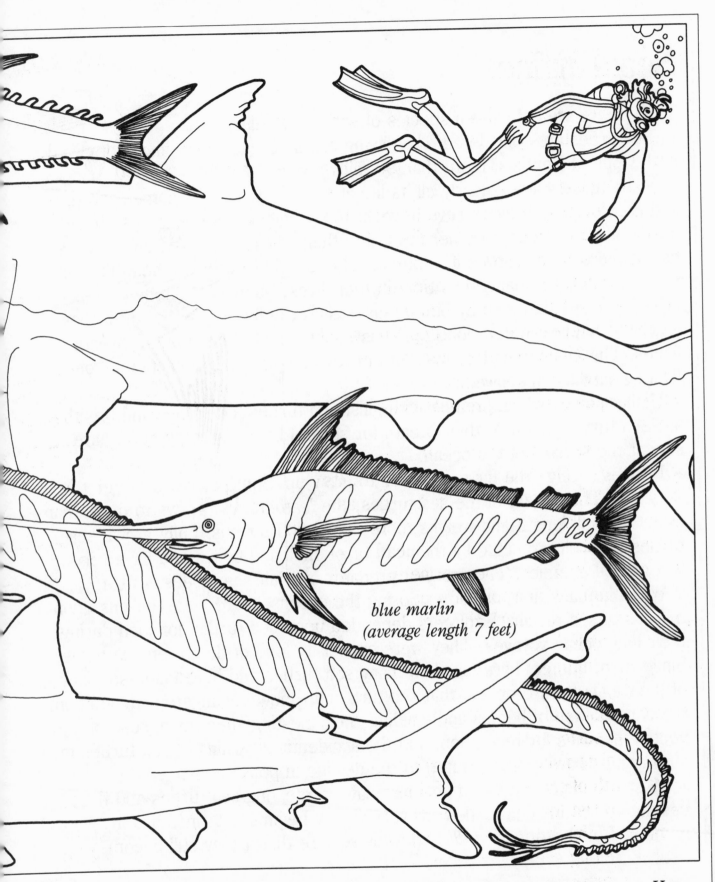

blue marlin
(average length 7 feet)

As you can see, giant fishes can be quite a bit larger than humans. How much larger than you are these fish?

Sea Turtles

Today there are only seven species of sea turtles alive.

Sea turtles are considered to be living relics because their ancestors lived in the Age of Reptiles, more than 90 million years ago.

A sea turtle spends nearly all its life at sea. Only females come ashore, and then only once every several years to lay eggs on the beach. A female digs a pit in the sand, lays her eggs, and then covers them. When the eggs hatch, the tiny sea turtles instantly crawl out and head for the sea. This is probably the most dangerous time in their lives. Many of them never reach the sea. They are eaten by birds, mammals, or crabs on the beach; if they reach the shallow water along the coast, they may be eaten by meat-eating fishes. The lucky ones that make it out to sea often find protection among floating sargassum seaweed.

Unlike fishes, which breathe with gills, sea turtles have lungs and breathe air. Sea turtles can hold their breath for several hours, so they don't have to stay at the surface of the ocean.

It takes a long time for sea turtles to grow up. Some may live longer than 30 years. The largest of the sea turtles, the *leatherback*, grows to more than 6 feet in shell length and weighs more than 1,000 pounds. Fully-grown sea turtles are well protected by their armor of shell and bones and have very few natural enemies. The greatest predator of adult sea turtles is man.

When humans first started exploring the oceans, there were millions upon millions of sea turtles. Explorers depended upon sea turtles for food during their long ocean voyages. They were especially fond of the *green sea turtle*. Since then, hunters have killed so many sea turtles and have taken so many of their eggs from beaches, that sea turtles are now endangered. In addition, the construction of homes and buildings near nesting sites, man's use of nesting beaches for recreation, and the accidental drowning of sea turtles in shrimp nets have all contributed to the decline in populations.

Most nations of the world now have laws protecting sea turtles and their nesting areas, and sea turtles are very slowly beginning to increase in number. But the *Atlantic ridley* turtle is so rare that it may still become extinct.

A leatherback turtle lays her eggs on a sandy beach.

PART FIVE

RICHES FROM THE OCEANS

Hook and Line

A girl sits on a riverbank on a summer afternoon dangling a fishing pole into the slow-moving river. Suddenly her line jerks, and she sits up straight. "I caught a fish!" she shouts, reeling in her line. She's caught a three-pound catfish.

Far out at sea, professional fishermen use the same general method to catch fishes that may weigh as much as 50 pounds or more. Much of the fish that we eat is caught in this way, even though the deep-sea fishermen's equipment is a little more complicated than a fishing pole.

On a commercial fishing boat, crew members sometimes still stand along the railings of the ship with strong poles in hand. They fish over the side, their heavy lines baited with anchovies or sardines. This is one way that *skipjack* and *albacore* tuna are caught. Two strong people may be needed, pulling on two poles attached to a single line, to pull in a tuna weighing 30 to 50 pounds. *Salmon* also are caught on a hook and line, often as they travel from the sea to breed in freshwater rivers and streams.

Long-line fishing is another hook-and-line method. A very long line, often more than one mile long, is attached to floats called buoys. The buoys keep the line floating at the surface. From this surface line, other lines are tied a few feet apart. These lines hang down in the water, and at the end of each one is a hook baited with a small fish. Larger fishes that try to eat the bait are caught by the hooks. Swordfishes and many kinds of tunas and sharks are caught this way. A good catch from one of these long lines, which the Japanese have taught the world to use, will bring up thousands of big fishes in a single day.

You may not think of shark as a food fish. Not many Americans go to the market to buy shark (although *mako* shark is especially tasty). However, shark meat is becoming more popular in the United States, as it has been for years in Europe and Asia. So one day you may enjoy a shark sandwich or a charcoal-broiled shark steak just as much as a tuna-fish sandwich or a grilled filet of salmon.

Fishermen haul in a large tuna that they have caught with a rod and reel.

Nets

One way to catch fishes from a boat is to drag a net along the ocean floor to catch fishes and shellfishes that live on the bottom. This is called *trawling*. One large trawl net can be let out behind a boat and dragged along the bottom for several hours before being pulled in.

To keep the mouth of the sack-like net open, large wooden doors are attached to either side of the net. As water flows against the doors, they spread apart and stretch out the front end of the net. The lower edge of the net rides along the ocean floor, sweeping anything in its path up and back into the net. Everything is washed to the back of the net, called the *cod end*. The boat pulls the net slowly, at only one or two miles per hour. Faster-swimming fishes can avoid being captured. But many creatures can't swim away fast enough. Bottom trawls bring in most of our codfish, hake, pollock, flounder, and shrimp.

Fishermen also use nets near the surface of the ocean to catch fishes. Sometimes long, delicate nets are floated down from the surface. Fishes that swim into these nets can become caught by the gill covers on the sides of their heads. For that reason, these nets are called gill nets. Conservationists do not like the use of long gill nets because they not only capture edible fishes, but they also kill fishes we do not eat, as well as mammals such as seals and dolphins.

The *purse seine* is another net used by many fishermen. This is a long net which is let out as a boat circles a large school of fishes. After the fishes are surrounded, the net is pulled together, just as you might close a purse. This traps the fishes.

FOR DOLPHINS

A tuna fisherman always keeps an eye out for a school of dolphins, for there are often yellowfin tuna swimming beneath them. When he finds such a school, he will surround it with a net called a purse seine in order to catch the tunas. The fishermen have to be very careful to let the dolphins escape from the circling net, but unfortunately, when the tunas are caught, some dolphins may also be caught. No one knows why yellowfin tunas like to swim under schools of dolphins, but we all wish we could separate them so that the tunas could be caught, but not the dolphins.

114

A purse seine can catch large numbers of tuna.

More Ways to Get Food from the Sea

There are many ways to get food from the sea. Some fishermen harpoon big fishes that come to the surface. Shell fishermen use long-handled poles with claws or rakes at the ends to scoop up shellfishes from the bottom of the sea. Each of these methods is thousands of years old.

Fishermen who use harpoons hunt schools of swordfish or giant bluefin tuna. The fisherman must be patient in trying to find a school. But the rewards can be great. A fisherman who harpoons a 2,000-pound bluefin tuna that can be sold at the dock for even $1.00 a pound will have a very profitable day. After the bluefin is sold at the dock, it is immediately gutted, cleaned, and put on ice. Most bluefins will then be put in big wooden crates and flown the same evening to Tokyo. The Japanese love to eat the raw, fresh meat of the bluefin tuna. There is a saying in Japan that one giant bluefin tuna is worth the price of a small Japanese car.

Another ancient method of fishing involves gathering up oysters and clams with long poles called *tongs*. The tongs are fastened together near the bottom end, just above the rakes, or grasping claws. The fisherman opens and closes the bottom raker basket by moving the ends of his poles back and forth, scooping the shellfish into the basket and then lifting them up to the boat.

*You can dig for clams on beaches
and in shallow waters.*

Farming the Sea

Thousands of years ago, humans found food by hunting with spears, or by gathering plants, fruits, and nuts. Later, people began to raise cattle and chickens and to grow grain and fruit. Finding food in the wild no longer filled all of the days. In a similar way, until fairly recently, most food taken from the sea was discovered by chance and by luck—by people who searched the sea, armed with hooks, poles, and nets.

Just as people have practiced agriculture for thousands of years, now some people practice *mariculture* (MAYR-uh-cul-chur).

People raise oysters, clams, shrimps, and edible seaweeds in protected bays. In the simplest form of mariculture, a marine farmer provides a safe and food-filled home in which plants and young animals can grow quickly. This is very much like the way farmers fatten calves and pigs for market.

An oyster farmer spreads a layer of old, broken oyster shells on the bottom of a sheltered nursery area. There the farmer adds live oysters. As one oyster can make millions of eggs, it takes only a small number of oysters to provide enough eggs to start a new colony. Soon after the eggs hatch, the young attach themselves to pieces of old shell on the nursery floor and soon become little oysters, called "spat." (They got this name because people used to think that the babies were simply spat out by other oysters.)

Within two to four years, the spat grow into adult oysters that the sea farmer can easily harvest, and the farmer is spared the trouble of having to travel in a boat to many spots, hoping to find oysters.

Pearl oysters are grown in farms, too. A tiny, round piece of shell is placed between each oyster's shell and its soft body. Then each oyster is hung in the sea on a thread. The bead irritates the oyster's body—so, to protect itself, the oyster begins to surround it with a smooth coating. This coating hardens into *mother-of-pearl*. In this way, layer by layer, cultured pearls are slowly made as the oysters hang suspended in the ocean.

Seaweed, a very popular food in Asia, also is grown by mariculture. Like oysters, seaweed is grown on racks in shallow water.

The culturing of pearls is an important industry in Japan,
the Philippines, and other countries in the Pacific.
Can you find the pearl in this oyster?

Oil and Gas

We use two of the most valuable resources of the ocean every day. Much of the oil and natural gas we use is pumped from the ocean floors of the continental shelf.

Oil and gas were formed millions of years ago from the decayed bodies of dead plants and animals. After they died, these creatures settled to the bottom of the sea. Sand and soil washed from the land into the sea and settled over them. Over millions of years, as they became buried deeper and deeper, the pressure and heat of the earth around them changed their remains into oil and gas.

Offshore oil drilling began off the coast of California in 1896. Since then, oil drilling has become common in the Gulf of Mexico, the Persian Gulf, the North Sea, and the northern shores of Alaska.

Drilling an offshore well is very difficult. First, drilling ships dig test wells. Drilling ships have propellers around their hulls to help the ships stay in one place on the surface, even in bad weather when the winds are strong and the waves are rough. When a drilling ship finds oil, a production crew builds a platform. That platform is used to pump up the oil, and the drilling ship leaves to drill new test wells elsewhere.

Oil is a limited resource. It is not being replaced nearly as fast as we are using it. Many people are working to find new energy sources. Some people are making solar energy cells to help us store the energy of the sun. Other people are developing nuclear energy. Others study wind power. And some researchers are even trying to find ways to harness the power of the ocean's tides and currents.

Until these other energy sources are cheap and easy to use, we will need to depend on oil and gas for our cars, diesel fuel for our trucks, and oil for our furnaces. Oil also runs many of the generators we use to make electricity to light our homes and power our telephones and computers.

While we look for substitutes for oil, our need to drill in the oceans means that we continue to run the risk of oil spills which pollute our coasts and harm our marine life.

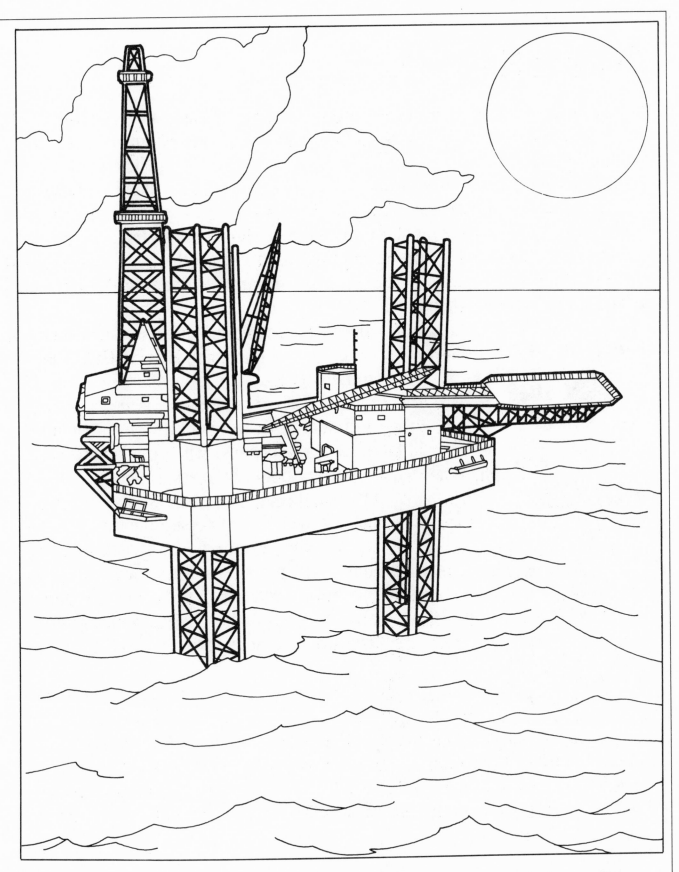

Oil wells are drilled from platforms offshore.
The oil is pumped through pipes or shipped
to the mainland.

Minerals

Seawater contains valuable minerals other than salt. The most valuable mineral taken from seawater today is *magnesium*. Magnesium is used in making metal and in photography. It also is used to make milk of magnesia, a medicine that settles upset stomachs, and in Epsom salts, used to soothe swollen or sprained joints.

A third important mineral taken from the sea is *bromine*. Bromine is added to gasoline to help cars' engines run more smoothly.

Other valuable minerals, including gold, are found in seawater. But these minerals are found in such small amounts that it costs too much to take them out of the water.

One metal that many scientists think will some day be mined from the sea is *manganese*. Manganese is a metal that occurs as rock-like nodules on the sea floors of all of the oceans. The nodules are important not only for the manganese, but also for the other valuable metals such as copper, nickel, and cobalt found with it.

Sand and gravel are also common, but important, resources of the ocean. Because much sand and gravel is found near land, it can be dredged up in huge amounts and used to build houses and roads.

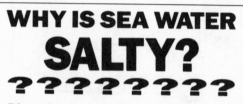

WHY IS SEA WATER SALTY? ????????

If you've ever tasted seawater, you know that it's salty! About three percent of seawater is salt.

The oceans have been forming since the origin of the Earth, about 5 million years ago. Over the course of time, freshwater rain that falls on land washed salt from the soil and carried it to the sea.

Since the earliest times, people have removed salt from seawater. This is still done today on many tropical islands. To do this, people build shallow ponds and flood them with seawater. The sun dries up the water, leaving behind a layer of salt.

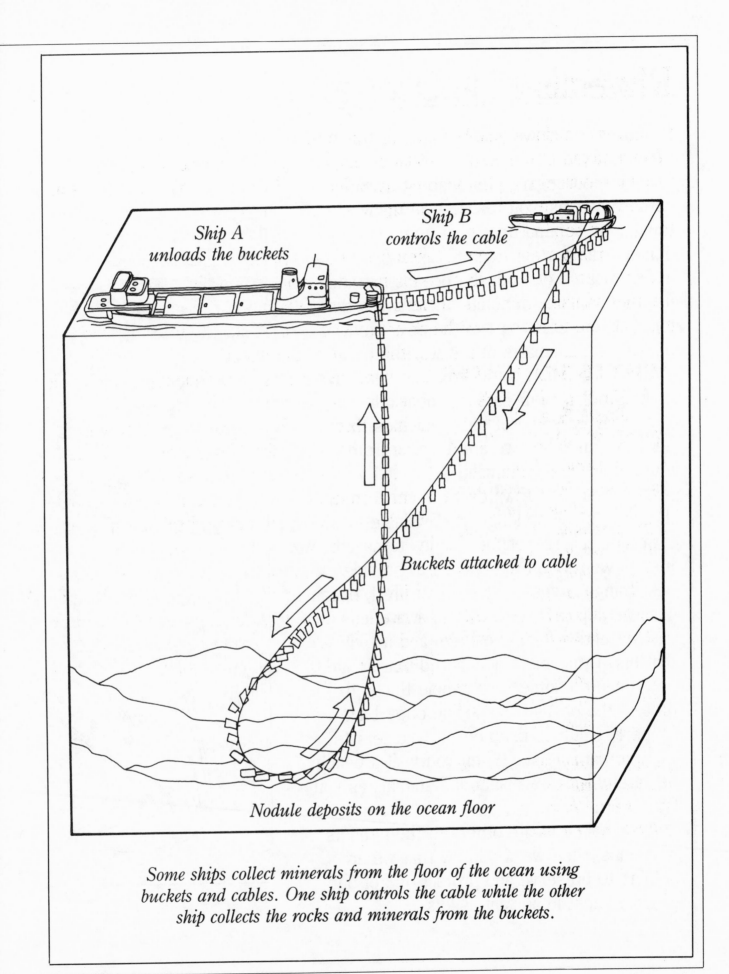

Ship A
unloads the buckets

Ship B
controls the cable

Buckets attached to cable

Nodule deposits on the ocean floor

Some ships collect minerals from the floor of the ocean using
buckets and cables. One ship controls the cable while the other
ship collects the rocks and minerals from the buckets.

Protecting the Oceans

Imagine if there were no oceans on Earth. What would life be like?

When you begin to think about a world without oceans, you realize how many things you depend upon that come from beneath the waves.

As a source of food, the oceans provide us with a variety of plants and animals that form an important part of the daily diets of people in many parts of the world.

Oil and gas that come from the seas give us fuel to drive our cars and heat our homes. Even some of the medicines that help cure us when we are ill come from marine plants and animals.

Of course, the rewards we receive from the oceans will no longer be available to us if we neglect our responsibilities to nature. Just as we rely on the oceans to provide us with things necessary to our survival, ocean survival depends upon human awareness of, and protection from, pollution and activities that harm valuable, endangered marine life.

You can do some very simple things to protect the oceans. Disposing of garbage properly will help keep ocean wildlife safe from contamination. When you visit a beach, be careful to leave plants and animals as you find them.

If we help educate others to the benefits of oceans, then we will know that we are helping to preserve and protect one of our planet's most important assets.

If we each do our part to protect the ocean, it will always be alive for all of us to enjoy.

FOR FURTHER READING

The Hidden Sea. A Studio Book. Douglas Faulkner and C. Lavett Smith. New York: Viking Press, 1970. 148 pages.

Kingdom of the Seashell. R. Tucker Abbott. New York: Crown Publishers, Inc., 1979. 256 pages.

The Ocean World. Jacques Yves Cousteau. New York: H. N. Abrams, 1989. 446 pages.

Ranger Rick Presents Amazing Creatures of the Sea. Edited by Victor H. Waldrop. Vienna, Virginia: National Wildlife Federation, 1987. 96 pages.

Seashells of the World. Revised edition. A Golden Guide. Herbert S. Zim and R. Tucker Abbott. New York: Golden Press, 1985.

Seashores, a Guide to Animals and Plants Along the Beaches. A Golden Guide. Herbert S. Zim and Lester Ingle. New York: Golden Press, 1955. 160 pages.

The World's Whales. Stanley M. Minasian, Kenneth C. Balcomb, III, and Larry Foster. Washington, D.C.: Smithsonian Books. Distributed by W. W. Norton and Company, New York, 1947. 224 pages.

JAMESTOWN  EDUCATION

Literature

An Adapted Reader

Grade 6

 **Glencoe**

New York, New York   Columbus, Ohio   Chicago, Illinois   Peoria, Illinois   Woodland Hills, California

W9-BOM-038

JAMESTOWN ⛵ EDUCATION

 **Glencoe**

The *McGraw·Hill* Companies

ACKNOWLEDGMENTS
Grateful acknowledgment is given authors, publishers, photographers,
museums, and agents for permission to reprint the following copyrighted
material. Every effort has been made to determine copyright owners. In
case of any omissions, the Publisher will be pleased to make suitable
acknowledgments in future editions.
Acknowledgments continued on p. 252.

Copyright © 2007 by The McGraw-Hill Companies, Inc. All rights reserved.
Except as permitted under the United States Copyright Act, no part of this
publication may be reproduced or distributed in any form or by any means,
or stored in a database or retrieval system, without prior written
permission of the publisher.

Send all inquiries to:
Glencoe/McGraw-Hill
8787 Orion Place
Columbus, OH 43240-4027

ISBN-13: 978-0-07-874313-9 (Student Edition)
ISBN-10: 0-07-874313-3 (Student Edition)

ISBN-13: 978-0-07-874326-9 (Annotated Teacher Edition)
ISBN-10: 0-07-874326-5 (Annotated Teacher Edition)

Printed in the United States of America
1 2 3 4 5 6 7 8 9 10 079 11 10 09 08 07 06

Contents

Why Use This Book?

Read a Variety of Texts

The notes and features of *Jamestown Literature* guide you through the process of reading and understanding each literature selection. As you use these notes and features, you practice the skills and strategies that good readers use whenever they read.

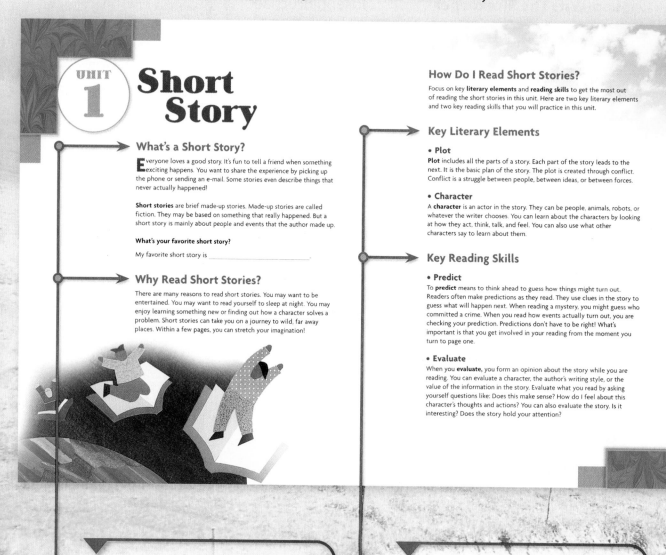

UNIT 1 Short Story

What's a Short Story?

Everyone loves a good story. It's fun to tell a friend when something exciting happens. You want to share the experience by picking up the phone or sending an e-mail. Some stories even describe things that never actually happened!

Short stories are brief made-up stories. Made-up stories are called fiction. They may be based on something that really happened. But a short story is mainly about people and events that the author made up.

What's your favorite short story?

My favorite short story is _____

Why Read Short Stories?

There are many reasons to read short stories. You may want to be entertained. You may want to read yourself to sleep at night. You may enjoy learning something new or finding out how a character solves a problem. Short stories can take you on a journey to wild, far away places. Within a few pages, you can stretch your imagination!

How Do I Read Short Stories?

Focus on key **literary elements** and **reading skills** to get the most out of reading the short stories in this unit. Here are two key literary elements and two key reading skills that you will practice in this unit.

Key Literary Elements

• Plot

Plot includes all the parts of a story. Each part of the story leads to the next. It is the basic plan of the story. The plot is created through conflict. Conflict is a struggle between people, between ideas, or between forces.

• Character

A **character** is an actor in the story. They can be people, animals, robots, or whatever the writer chooses. You can learn about the characters by looking at how they act, think, talk, and feel. You can also use what other characters say to learn about them.

Key Reading Skills

• Predict

To **predict** means to think ahead to guess how things might turn out. Readers often make predictions as they read. They use clues in the story to guess what will happen next. When reading a mystery, you might guess who committed a crime. When you read how events actually turn out, you are checking your prediction. Predictions don't have to be right! What's important is that you get involved in your reading from the moment you turn to page one.

• Evaluate

When you **evaluate,** you form an opinion about the story while you are reading. You can evaluate a character, the author's writing style, or the value of the information in the story. Evaluate what you read by asking yourself questions like: Does this make sense? How do I feel about this character's thoughts and actions? You can also evaluate the story. Is it interesting? Does the story hold your attention?

What Is It? Why Read?

The genre, or type of writing, is defined for you at the beginning of the unit. Learn why a particular genre offers important and entertaining reading.

Literary Elements and Reading Skills

New literary elements and reading skills are introduced in each unit opener. Use these elements and skills to get the most out of your reading.

UNIT 2 — Short Story

How is a short story organized?

Now that you have read a few short stories, let's [...] to take a closer look at how a short story is pu[...]

A short story always has a **beginning, middle,** and [...]

Short stories also include a **conflict**. A conflict is [...] characters or a struggle between a character and [...] outside force.

What's the Plan?

Within the three parts of the story [...]

Exposition: The story is set up. Ch[...] introduced.
Rising Action: Conflicts or probl[...]
Climax: The turning point in the [...] greatest interest or excitement.
Falling Action: The events follo[...]
Resolution: How things turn o[...]

exposition

beginning

As you read the next four [...] stages in each story. In th[...] stage happens.

Understanding the parts [...] better reader.

UNIT 3 — Drama

What's Drama?

Drama is all around you. Television shows—from daytim[...] cartoons—are drama. Movies are drama. Skits and pla[...] **Drama** is a story that is meant to be performed for an au[...] stage, in a movie or TV show, or on the radio.

What kinds of drama do you know? What kinds do you [...] **check next to the kinds of drama you have seen or he[...] Then describe your favorite kind on the lines that fol[...]

____ television comedy
____ serious television story
____ made-for-TV movie
____ soap opera
____ movie at the theater
____ stage play
____ radio broadcast of a play or show

Why Read Dra[...]

People read drama to hav[...] people. Drama can take y[...] you new experiences, an[...] about new ideas. Drama[...] people talk. Reading dra[...] the play ought to look [...] screen. Who should pla[...] would the characters [...] drama lets you stage t[...]

126

UNIT 4 — Folklore

What's Folklore?

If you have ever read a story about Paul Bunyan, Anansi, or Hercules, then you have read some folklore! These stories are not only fun to read, but they also teach you about the cultures they come from.

Every culture has its own **folklore**. Folklore includes information about a group's customs, songs, dances, and beliefs that have been passed down from one generation to the next. Before written language was invented, folklore was passed down by word of mouth, with one person telling these stories to another.

> **Think about some of the folklore you have read. Write the title of the story you liked the most.**

Why Read Folklore?

People read folklore for fun. These stories have unusual characters and exciting plots. But reading folklore can do more than entertain. Folklore can teach you about beliefs that people had long ago. Folklore can also tell how people who lived long ago explained natural events and how things came to be.

UNIT 5 — Nonfiction

What's Nonfiction?

Nonfiction is the name for writing that is about real events and real people. Articles in most newspapers and magazines are nonfiction. This kind of writing tells the facts. Nonfiction writing includes biographies, autobiographies, and essays.

A **biography** is the story of a person's life written by someone other than that person. An **autobiography** is the story of a person's life written by that person. An **essay** is a short piece of nonfiction about a single topic.

Nonfiction can deal with many topics—the lives of famous people, historical events, or facts about nature.

Write a nonfiction subject that you would like to read about.

Why Read Nonfiction?

Read nonfiction to learn about yourself and the world around you. Nonfiction can help you think about the details of people's lives and understand the past. It can introduce you to new ideas and opinions too.

Explore Literature

Your book features several of the most popular types of writing. Find out what makes each genre unique. Discover new and exciting types of writing.

Get Set!

The first page of each lesson helps you get ready to read. It sets the stage for your reading. The more you know about the reading up front, the more meaning it will have for you.

Get Ready to Read!

Madam C.J. Walker

Meet Jim Haskins

In the small Alabama town where Jim Haskins grew up, African Americans were not allowed to use the public library. Now his books fill libraries all over the country. He wrote more than one hundred books. Many of his books tell the stories of successful African Americans. Jim Haskins was born in 1941 and died in 2005. This selection was first published in 1992.

What You Know

A millionaire! Many people dream about being that rich. Do you? What are some ways people become millionaires?

Reason to Read

As you read, ask yourself why the author wrote this story. Does the author want to teach you how to get rich or does he have another purpose in writing?

Background Info

Most African Americans who lived in the United States before the Civil War were enslaved people. They worked very hard every day, but they earned nothing for their work. After the Civil War, when slavery ended, African Americans still lived very hard lives. Although it was difficult for any American to become rich, it was most difficult for African Americans. In spite of hard work and good ideas, they were often not allowed a chance to succeed.

What You Know

Think about your own experience and share your knowledge and opinions. Then, build on what you know as you read the lesson.

Reason to Read

Set a purpose for reading. Having a reason to read helps you get involved in what you read.

Background Info

Get a deeper insight into the reading. Knowing some background information helps you gain a greater appreciation and understanding of what you read.

Meet the Author

Meet the authors to get to know where they come from, what or who inspires them, and why they write.

Build Vocabulary

Each lesson introduces you to words that help build your vocabulary. You'll find these words in the reading. Understanding these words before you read makes reading easier.

Word Power

In an after-reading activity, you practice the vocabulary words you learned in the lesson.

Word Power

hesitated (hez′ ə tāt′ id) v. stopped for a minute; paused; p. 50
The swimmer *hesitated* before she dove into the cold water.

defeated (di fēt′ id) adj. disappointed; not successful; p. 50
The farmer felt *defeated* when all of his crops died.

restrained (ri strānd′) v. held back from acting; p. 51
I *restrained* my desire to buy a chocolate milkshake.

impulse (im′ puls) n. a sudden desire to act; p. 51
Following an *impulse*, the girl ran across the park.

transformed (trans fôrmd′) v. changed in form, appearance, or use; p. 51
A group of students *transformed* several big boxes into a fort.

expression (iks presh′ ən) n. a look on the face that shows feeling; p. 52
Everyone laughed at their friend's surprised *expression*.

Answer the following questions, using one of the new words above. Write your answers in the spaces provided.

1. Which word goes with "an urge"? _____

2. Which word goes with "showing emotion"? _____

3. Which word goes with "waited"? _____

4. Which word goes with "changed"? _____

5. Which word goes with "disappointed"? _____

6. Which word goes with "kept from happening"? _____

My Workspace

Have you ever had a friend from a different background?

"Bet he won't," Johnny said, attacking his scrambled
"Boyd wants to grow up and be a big strong man s
work hard," Mrs. Wilson said. "I'll bet Boyd's father ea
tomatoes."

"My father eats anything he wants to," Boyd said.

"So does mine," Johnny said. "Sometimes he doe
anything. He's a little guy, though. Wouldn't hurt
"Mine's a little guy too," Boyd said.

"I'll bet he's strong, though," Mrs. Wilson said
"Does he . . . work?"

"Sure," Johnny said. "Boyd's father works ir
"There, you see?" Mrs. Wilson said. "And h
strong to do that—all that lifting and carry

"Boyd's father doesn't have to," Johnny
Mrs. Wilson felt **defeated**. "What does
"My mother?" Boyd was surprised. "Sh
"Oh. She doesn't work, then?"

"Why should she?" Johnny said thre
"You don't work."

Literary Element
Character Reread the highlighted passage. What do you learn about Mrs. Wilson's character from this passage?

_____
_____
_____
_____
_____
_____

Word Power
hesitated (hez′ ə tāt′ id) v. stopped
defeated (di fēt′ id) adj. disappointe

50

Respond to Literature

C Word Power

Complete each sentence below, using one of the words in the box.

hesitated	defeated	restrained	impulse
	transformed	expression	

1. After their team lost, the _____ players were quiet in the locker room.

2. As time went by, the caterpillars _____ into butterflies.

3. The girl barely _____ her excitement at winning the contest.

4. The woman decided on an _____ to cut her long hair very short.

5. I could tell by his _____ that the boy was angry.

6. All of us _____ before we went through the door of the spooky house.

55

Word Power

Before you read, you learn key vocabulary words and their definitions. The definitions and sample sentences help you complete the questions that follow.

Word Power Footnotes

Look for pronunciations and definitions of vocabulary words at the bottom of pages throughout the reading. Vocabulary words appear in dark type in the text.

My Personal Dictionary

_____
_____
_____
_____
_____

My Personal Dictionary

As you read, jot down words in your personal dictionary that you want to learn more about. Later, ask a classmate or your teacher what they mean, or look them up in a dictionary.

Read, Respond, Interact

Notes in "My Workspace" support and guide you through the reading process. Interact with and respond to the text by answering the questions or following the directions in the workspace notes.

My Workspace

They were doing exactly what we were doing, just shooting a few lay-ups and waiting for the game to begin. They got the first tap and started passing the ball around. I mean they really started passing the ball around faster than anything I had ever seen. Zip! Zip! Zip! Two points! I didn't even know how they could see the ball, let alone get it inside to their big man. We brought the ball down and one of their players stole the ball from Sam. We got back on defense but they weren't in a hurry. The same old thing. Zip! Zip! Zip! Two points! They could pass the ball better than anybody I ever saw. Then we brought the ball down again and Chalky missed a jump shot. He missed the backboard, the rim, everything. One of their players caught the ball and then brought it down and a few seconds later the score was 6–0. We couldn't even get close enough to foul them. Chalky brought the ball down again, passed to Sam cutting across the lane, and Sam walked. They brought the ball down and it was 8–0.

They were really enjoying the game. You could see. Every time they scored they'd slap hands and carry on. Also, they had some cheerleaders. They had about five girls with little pink skirts on and white sweaters cheering for them.

Clyde brought the ball down this time, passed into our center, a guy named Leon, and Leon turned and missed a hook. They got the rebound and came down, and Chalky missed a steal and fouled his man. That's when Mr. Reese called time out.

"Okay, now, just trade basket for basket. They make a basket, you take your time and you make a basket—don't rush it." Mr. Reese looked at his starting five. "Okay, now, every once in a while take a look over at me and I'll let you know when I want you to make your move. If I put my hands palm down, just keep on playing cool. If I stand up and put my hands up like this"—he put both hands up near his face—"that means to make your move. You understand that?"

Literary Element

Setting Reread the passage highlighted in blue. What is the setting in this part of the story? Underline the details in the passage that help you picture the setting.

Reading Skill

Paraphrase Reread the sentence highlighted in green and the rest of the paragraph. What does Mr. Reese tell his players? Choose the sentence that **best** paraphrases this paragraph. Check the correct response.
- ☐ Mr. Reese tells his players to rush the game and play fast.
- ☐ Mr. Reese tells his players to watch his hand signals to know what to do.
- ☐ Mr. Reese tells his players to ignore him and keep scoring points.

Literary Element notes help you understand important features of literature. Whenever you read text that is highlighted in blue, look for a Literary Element note in your workspace.

Reading Skill notes let you practice active reading strategies that help good readers think as they read. Whenever you read text that is highlighted in green, look for a Reading Skill note in your workspace.

My Workspace

English Coach

Part means "to separate" in this sentence. In which of the following phrases does *part* have the same meaning as the highlighted text? Check the correct response.
- ☐ a part in a play
- ☐ a part in your hair
- ☐ a part of a store

Comprehension Check

Reread the boxed passage. Why does Mr. Roybal jump out onto the stage? Check the correct response.
- ☐ to introduce the next act to the audience
- ☐ to keep the tooth from falling off the stage
- ☐ to make the act more funny

"Tonight we bring you the best John Burroughs Elementary has to offer, and I'm sure that you'll be both pleased and amazed that our little school houses so much talent. And now, without further ado, let's get on with the show." He turned and, with a swish of his hand, commanded, "Part the curtain." The curtains parted in jerks. A girl dressed as a toothbrush and a boy dressed as a dirty gray tooth walked onto the stage and sang:

Brush, brush, brush
Floss, floss, floss
Gargle the germs away—
hey! hey! hey!

After they finished singing, they turned to Mr. Roybal, who dropped his hand. The toothbrush dashed around the stage after the dirty tooth, which was laughing and having a great time until it slipped and nearly rolled off the stage.

Mr. Roybal jumped out and caught it just in time. "Are you OK?"

The dirty tooth answered, "Ask my dentist," which drew laughter and applause from the audience.

The violin duo played next, and except for one time when the girl got lost, they sounded fine. People applauded, and some even stood up. Then the first-grade girls **maneuvered** onto the stage while jumping rope. They were all smiles and bouncing ponytails as a hundred cameras flashed at once. Mothers "aahed" and fathers sat up proudly.

The karate kid was next. He did a few kicks, yells, and chops, and finally, when his father held up a board, punched it in two. The audience clapped and looked at each other, wide-eyed with respect. The boy bowed to the audience, and father and son ran off the stage.

Word Power
maneuvered (mə nōō´ vərd) v. moved in a skillful or planned way

36

English Coach notes explain difficult or unusual words and cultural references. Whenever you read text that is highlighted in red, look for an English Coach note in your workspace.

Comprehension Check notes help you understand what you're reading. Whenever you read text that is boxed in green, look for a Comprehension Check note in your workspace.

The margin notes let you interact with what you're reading in several ways. Some notes ask you to write out your response. Other notes may ask you to draw a picture, underline answers in the text, or interact in some other way.

My Workspace

"Tell us the truth," the man who had given him the four hundred dollars said. "You used that money to set up this business."

The miller swore he hadn't, and he told them how he had given the piece of lead to his neighbor and how the fisherman had in return given him a fish with a very large diamond in its stomach. And he told them how he had sold the diamond.

"And that's how I **acquired** this business and many other things I want to show you," he said. "But, let's eat first."

So they ate and then the miller had three horses saddled and they rode out to see his summer home. The cabin was on the other side of the river where the mountains were cool and beautiful. During their ride they came upon a tall pine tree.

"What is on top of the tree?" one of them asked.

"That's the nest of a hawk," the miller replied.

"I would like to take a closer look at it!"

"Of course," the miller said, and he ordered a servant to climb the tree and bring down the nest so his friend could see how it was built.

Have you ever seen a hawk's nest? How do you think hawks build their nests?

Word Power
acquired (ə kwīrd´) v. got as one's own

161

Reading Skill
Cause & Effect Reread the highlighted passage. Read the cause boxes, then fill in the effect boxes below.

Cause
The miller gives the neighbor a piece of lead.

⬇

Effect

⬇

Cause
The fish contains a diamond.

⬇

Effect

My Workspace

Reading Skill
Visualize Reread the sentence highlighted in green. What do you imagine the golden ticket looks like? Draw a picture in the box below.

Your sketch

Literary Element
Dialogue Reread the text highlighted in blue. What do you learn about Charlie and his grandfather's relationship from this dialogue?

Have you ever won a great prize? What was it?

ALL. *You what?*

CHARLIE. I did! I did! I really did! I found the fifth Golden Ticket!!

ALL. [*Everyone yelling and dancing around.*] Hurray! Hurray! Hurray! Yipppppppeeeeeeeeeeee! It's off to the chocolate factory!!!

[*End of Scene 3.*]

SCENE 4
[*In front of the Chocolate Factory. CHARLIE and GRANDPA JOE enter together as scene opens.*]

CHARLIE. Boy, Grandpa Joe, I sure am glad that Dad let you take me today.

GRANDPA JOE. Well, Charlie, I guess he just feels that we understand each other.

CHARLIE. Speaking of the Golden Ticket, Grandpa Joe, could I read it one more time? I know it sounds silly, but the whole thing seems so magical.

140

Background Info notes give information about a particular event, time, person, or place mentioned in the reading. Whenever you read text that is boxed in orange, look for a Background Info note in your workspace.

Connect to the Text notes help you connect what you're reading to something in your own life. Whenever you read text that is boxed in purple, look for a Connect to the Text note in your workspace.

My Workspace

SCENE 1
[*NARRATOR enters in front of curtain.*]

NARRATOR. Welcome to the tale of a delicious adventure in a wonderful land. You can tell it will be delicious—can't you smell it already? [*Sniffs.*] Oh, how I love that gorgeous smell! You've all heard of Kraft, Neilson, Hershey, Nestles, Wonka— what's that? You say, what's Wonka? You mean you don't know what Wonka is? Why . . . Wonka Chocolate . . . of course! I admit that Willy Wonka's Chocolate is fairly new but it's also the greatest chocolate ever invented. Why, Willy Wonka himself is the most amazing, the most fantastic, the most extraordinary chocolate maker the world has ever seen. He's invented things like . . . say . . . why . . . I'm not going to tell you what he's invented. You came to see yourself! So I'll let you do just that . . . Mr. Willy Wonka, in order to sell a lot of candy once again, was running a contest. Yes sir, that's right . . . a contest! He had secretly wrapped a Golden Ticket under ordinary wrapping paper in five ordinary candy bars. The five winners will tour Mr. Wonka's new factory and take home enough chocolate for the rest of their lives. Now *that*, my friends, is where our story begins. Four of the tickets have already been found. Oh, by the way, would you like to meet the four lucky people? All right, listen and watch carefully! I think they're here somewhere. [*Looks out over audience.*] Let's see . . . Augustus Gloop! Where are you, Augustus Gloop!

Did You Know?
Cocoa and chocolate are the two main products made from *cacao beans*.

Background Info
Some words in a play are printed in italics (or slanted type) and set inside brackets. Those words are the stage directions. They are instructions telling the actors when to enter or exit the stage and how to stand, move, or speak. They also describe what the scene looks like. So *Sniffs* tells the actor playing the narrator to sniff after asking, ". . . can't you smell it already?"

Connect to the Text
Reread the sentence in the purple box. Imagine that you found the winning ticket. What would be the best part of winning a contest like this?

131

Use the **Did You Know?** feature to get a clear picture of something interesting in the text.

xi

Wrap It Up!

The Break Time, Respond to Literature, and Compare and Contrast pages help you focus your understanding of the text. You apply the skills and strategies you've practiced during reading.

Literary Element

In this activity, use the lesson's literary element to help you understand passages from the reading.

Respond to Literature

The All-American SLURP

A Comprehension Check

Answer the following questions in the spaces provided.

1. What "mistakes" do the Lins make at the Gleasons' dinner party?

2. What happens to upset the narrator at the Lakeview restaurant?

3. What does Mr. Gleason do at the Lin's party that shocks the narrator?

B Reading Skills

Complete the following activities in the spaces provided.

1. **Paraphrase** The Lins finally start to fit into life in America. Paraphrase the narrator's description of what they do to fit in.

2. **Infer** What does the narrator learn from seeing the table manners of the Gleason family?

3. **Infer** At the end of the story, how do you think the narrator feels about living in America?

120

Respond to Literature

D Literary Element: Conflict

Read the passage below from "The All-American Slurp." As you read, think about the conflict the sentences describe. Then answer the questions that follow.

> But I had another worry, and that was my appearance. My brother didn't have to worry, since Mother bought him blue jeans for school, and he dressed like all the other boys. But she insisted that girls had to wear skirts. By the time she saw that Meg and the other girls were wearing jeans, it was too late.

1. In the passage the narrator is one of the opposing forces in this conflict. Who or what is the other force? Is this an example of an internal or external conflict?

2. What is the conflict in this passage?

Comprehension Check and Reading Skills

In the Comprehension Check activity, you recall events and facts from the text. In the Reading Skills activity, you apply the reading skills you practiced while reading.

Break Time

The Break Time page helps you organize your thoughts about the text.

Break Time

The Lin family is facing a **problem** with language. What does each family member do about it? First read the problem that is in the box on the left below. Then in the boxes on the right, write each family member's **solution** to the problem.

The narrator's brother

The narrator

Problem:
The family is trying to learn English.

Father

Mother

GO Continue reading on the next page.

112

Respond to Literature

E "Missing" Poster

Imagine that you have been asked to create a "Missing" poster—for Aaron and Zlateh. Draw the characters, using details from the text to help you. Complete the written description of the missing characters, and identify the person people should contact if anyone sees them.

Description: Aaron is _____
Zlateh is _____

Information: They were las...

Aaron's family needed mon...

They are probably lost beca...

Aaron is smart; he and Zlat...

Contact: If you have seen A...
contact _____

90

Writing Activity

Develop your writing skills by completing various types of activities. Here's your chance to be creative!

Respond to Literature

Assessment

Fill in the circle next to each correct answer.

1. What do the scientists find out by studying the mummy's teeth?
   - ○ A. how the girl lost her legs
   - ○ B. the girl's age at the time of her death
   - ○ C. what part of Egypt the girl lived in
   - ○ D. why the organs are missing

2. In order to find more information about the girl's life, what is the **best** question to ask after reading the article?
   - ○ A. Why weren't the scientists' names mentioned in the article?
   - ○ B. What will the scientists work on next?
   - ○ C. What was daily life like in ancient Egypt?
   - ○ D. Where is the Manchester Museum?

3. Which of the following **best** states the main idea of the selection?
   - ○ A. Scientists were given a mummy to study and learned many details about the person's life.
   - ○ B. Scientists can date mummies using the carbon-14 dating process.
   - ○ C. It's important to have a dentist on a scientific team to determine the age of the mummy.
   - ○ D. The mummy had been wrapped twice.

4. Which of the following choices **best** describes how the information is presented in the selection?
   - ○ A. from most interesting details to least interesting details
   - ○ B. from least interesting details to most interesting details
   - ○ ... the author
   - ○ ... what the scientists did and discovered

   ... "delicate and easy to break"?

217

Assessment

The lesson assessment helps you evaluate what you learned in the lesson.

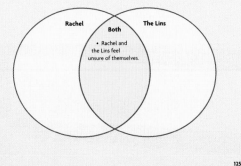

UNIT 2 **Wrap-up**

Compare and Contrast

Conflict is an important literary element in "Eleven" and "The All-American Slurp." Although the characters in these stories face very different situations, their conflicts share some similarities. Think about the conflicts that Rachel faces in "Eleven" and the conflicts that the Lin family (especially the narrator) faces in "The All-American Slurp." Think about how these conflicts affect how the characters feel and act.

Complete the Venn diagram below. In the outer parts of the circles, describe the different conflicts that the characters face. In the section where the circles overlap, tell how their conflicts are similar.

Rachel · Both · The Lins
• Rachel and the Lins feel unsure of themselves.

125

Compare and Contrast

The Compare and Contrast activity helps you see how two texts are alike and different.

xiii

The What, Why, and How of Reading

LITERARY ELEMENTS

Each lesson focuses on one literary element. Before you begin a lesson, read carefully the explanations of the literary elements found at the beginning of the unit. You can refer to this chart for an overview. The more familiar you become with these important features, the more you will understand and appreciate each reading.

Unit 1	What Is It?	Example
	Plot Plot is the basic structure of the story. It is the order of events in a story. Each event leads to the next. The plot is created through conflict—a struggle between people, between ideas, or between other forces.	In "The King of Mazy May," the plot follows the series of events as Walt tries to warn Loren Hall about the stampeders trying to steal his land.
	Character Characters are the actors in the story. You can learn about the characters by looking at how they act, think, talk, and feel. You can also use what other characters say to learn more about them.	In "La Bamba," you learn that the main character, Manuel, really wants to impress people. You learn about his character through the things he says and does to be popular.
Unit 2	**Setting** The setting is the time and place of a story. The setting connects you to other things you may know about that time and that place. Setting can also include customs, values, and beliefs of a place or time.	The setting of "The Game" is a basketball court during a championship game. The author provides details about the court, the players, and the game to help you to picture the setting.
	Conflict A conflict is a struggle between two forces in a story. There are two types of conflict. An external conflict occurs when a character has a conflict with another character or another outside force. An internal conflict is a struggle within the mind of a character.	In "Eleven," Rachel has an external conflict with her teacher about a red sweater. She has an internal conflict with herself about how it feels to be eleven years old.

Unit 3	What Is It?	Example
	Dialogue Dialogue is the words that characters say. Dialogue reveals the characters' personalities, gives information to the audience, and moves the story forward.	*Charlie and the Chocolate Factory* is a play, so all the characters speak in dialogue. You get a clear picture of the characters through what they say and how they say it.
Unit 4	**Folktales** Folktales come from different regions and cultures. They include fairy tales, legends, and tall tales. Folktales are often used to teach lessons about proper behavior.	"The Force of Luck" is a folktale from the Hispanic tradition. It questions whether it is wealth or luck that makes a man successful.
	Myths Myths are stories handed down from ancient cultures to explain how things came about. Myths explain events in nature or the beginnings of certain beliefs and customs.	"Loo-Wit: The Firekeeper" is a Native American myth that explains how the Creator, a god, creates Mt. St. Helens, Mt. Adams, and Mt. Hood.
Unit 5	**Informational Text** Informational text gives more than just facts. It might explain why something happened or how something works.	"Mummy No. 1770" explains how a team of scientists discover facts about a girl who lived more than 3,000 years ago.
	Author's Purpose The author's purpose is his or her reason for writing. An author's purpose can be to inform, to persuade, to describe, or to entertain—or a combination of several purposes.	The author's purpose in writing "Madam C.J. Walker" is to inform the reader about the first self-made African American female millionaire.

READING SKILLS

You will use reading skills to respond to questions in the lessons. Before you begin a lesson, read carefully the explanations of the reading skills found at the beginning of the unit. You can refer to this chart for an overview. The more you practice the skills in the chart, the more these active reading strategies will become a natural part of the way you read.

Unit 1	What Is It?	Why It's Important	How To Do It
	Predict Predicting means thinking ahead to guess how things might turn out.	Predicting gives you a reason to read. It helps you get involved in your reading.	Combine what you already know with clues in the text to guess what will happen next.
	Evaluate Evaluating is forming opinions about what you are reading as you read.	Evaluating can help you better understand a text and determine how well the text works.	As you read, ask yourself questions like: Does this make sense? What do I think about this character's thoughts and actions? Is the story interesting?
Unit 2	**Infer** Inferring is making a reasonable guess using the clues and details that the author gives you.	Inferring helps you figure out what the author is trying to suggest.	Combine clues and details from the story with what you already know to figure out what is not stated directly.
	Paraphrase Paraphrasing is putting a story or part of a story into your own words.	When you use your own words to paraphrase what you have read, you understand the author's meaning better.	Think about the characters and events in the story. Then describe the characters and events in your own words.

Unit 3	What Is It?	Why It's Important	How To Do It
	Visualize Visualizing is picturing in your mind what you are reading.	Visualizing is one of the best ways to understand and remember ideas, characters, and other details in a text.	Carefully read how the writer describes something. Use the details and exact words to help you create mental pictures.
	Sequence Sequence is the order in which events take place in a text.	Following the sequence of events helps you see how a text is organized and how events are related.	As you read, look for words like *first*, *then*, *meanwhile*, *eventually*, and *later*. These words can help you figure out the order in which things happen.
Unit 4	**Cause and Effect** A cause is something that happens that sets something else in motion. An effect is the result or outcome of that cause.	Understanding cause and effect helps you make connections between the events in a story.	Ask yourself: Did this happen because of something else? Sometimes clue words, such as *because, therefore, since,* and *so,* let you know of a cause-and-effect relationship.
	Respond Responding is thinking about what you are reading and how you feel about it.	The more you respond, the more you will understand what you are reading.	As you read, think about how you feel about the characters and events.
Unit 5	**Question** Questioning is asking questions to make sense of the information in a text.	When you ask yourself questions as you read, you are making sure that you understand what you are reading.	As you read, ask yourself *who, what, where, when, why,* and *how* questions about the text.
	Main Idea and Details The main idea is the topic of a text. Details are facts, examples, or quotations that explain and support the main idea.	Knowing the main idea helps you understand what a text is about. Finding details helps you see how the author supports the main points.	Look for the one idea that all of the sentences in a paragraph or in a text are about. Then look for smaller pieces of information that support that main idea.

UNIT 1 Short Story

What's a Short Story?

Everyone loves a good story. It's fun to tell a friend when something exciting happens. You want to share the experience by picking up the phone or sending an e-mail. Some stories even describe things that never actually happened!

Short stories are brief made-up stories. Made-up stories are called fiction. They may be based on something that really happened. But a short story is mainly about people and events that the author made up.

What's your favorite short story?

My favorite short story is _____.

Why Read Short Stories?

There are many reasons to read short stories. You may want to be entertained. You may want to read yourself to sleep at night. You may enjoy learning something new or finding out how a character solves a problem. Short stories can take you on a journey to wild, far away places. Within a few pages, you can stretch your imagination!

How Do I Read Short Stories?

Focus on key **literary elements** and **reading skills** to get the most out of reading the short stories in this unit. Here are two key literary elements and two key reading skills that you will practice in this unit.

Key Literary Elements

• Plot

Plot includes all the parts of a story. Each part of the story leads to the next. It is the basic plan of the story. The plot is created through conflict. Conflict is a struggle between people, between ideas, or between forces.

• Character

A **character** is an actor in the story. They can be people, animals, robots, or whatever the writer chooses. You can learn about the characters by looking at how they act, think, talk, and feel. You can also use what other characters say to learn about them.

Key Reading Skills

• Predict

To **predict** means to think ahead to guess how things might turn out. Readers often make predictions as they read. They use clues in the story to guess what will happen next. When reading a mystery, you might guess who committed a crime. When you read how events actually turn out, you are checking your prediction. Predictions don't have to be right! What's important is that you get involved in your reading from the moment you turn to page one.

• Evaluate

When you **evaluate,** you form an opinion about the story while you are reading. You can evaluate a character, the author's writing style, or the value of the information in the story. Evaluate what you read by asking yourself questions like: Does this make sense? How do I feel about this character's thoughts and actions? You can also evaluate the story. Is it interesting? Does the story hold your attention?

Meet Richard Peck

Richard Peck says that he tries to give readers "leading characters they can look up to and reasons to believe that problems can be solved." When Peck began writing as a full-time career, he wrote about problems he had seen as a high school teacher. He has written more than fifteen novels for teenagers.

Richard Peck was born in 1934. "Priscilla and the Wimps" was first published in 1984.

What You Know

Have you, or has anyone you know, ever had an experience with a school bully? How did the situation turn out? What do you think is the best way to deal with bullies?

Reason to Read

Read to enjoy a funny story about a bully who meets his match.

Background Info

Although their exact ages are never given, the characters in "Priscilla and the Wimps" are probably somewhere between middle school and early high school. There are plenty of individual differences among young people as they grow into teenagers. However, girls between the ages of ten and fourteen are often taller than boys of the same age. By the end of high school, many boys have grown taller than their female classmates.

Word Power

subtle (sut′əl) *adj.* not easily seen; p. 4
I like pastel colors because they are more *subtle* than bright ones.

lacerations (las′ə rā′ shəns) *n.* cuts; wounds; p. 5
When I got up from my bike accident, I noticed *lacerations* all over my knees.

pun (pun) *n.* a joke in which a word has two meanings; p. 6
My favorite *pun* is "Math teachers have a lot of problems!"

swaggers (swag′ərz) *v.* walks or behaves in a bold, rude, or proud way; p. 6
My big brother *swaggers* around the house like he owns the place.

immense (i mens′) *adj.* of great size; huge; p. 8
Our history textbook is so *immense* that I don't know how we'll ever finish it.

stragglers (strag′lərz) *n.* those who stay behind or stray from the main group; p. 8
A few *stragglers* finally left the party when the hosts started to clean up.

fate (fāt) *n.* a power that determines how things will turn out; p. 8
When my grandmother sent me a baseball mitt, I knew it was *fate* that I'd make the team.

**Answer the following questions, using one of the new words above.
Write your answers in the spaces provided.**

1. Which word goes with "a joke with a double meaning"? _____

2. Which word goes with "something you get when you skin your knee"? _____

3. Which word goes with "walks around proudly"? _____

4. Which word goes with "people apart from the rest of the group"? _____

5. Which word goes with "very large"? _____

6. Which word goes with "something that decides what will happen"? _____

7. Which word goes with "not easily noticed"? _____

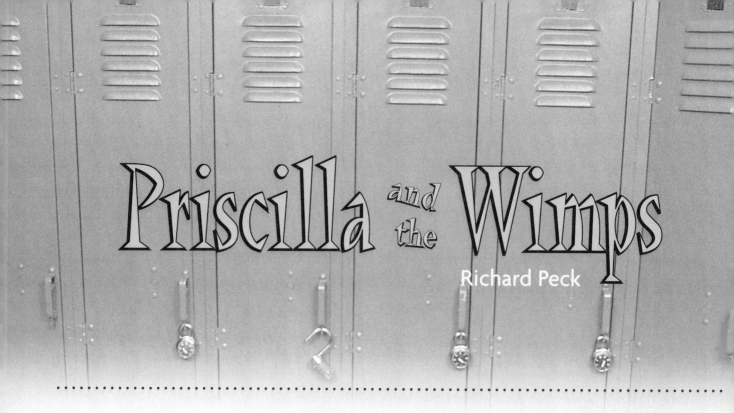

Priscilla and the Wimps

Richard Peck

Reading Skill

Evaluate When you evaluate, you form an opinion about what you are reading. Reread the highlighted passage. Evaluate the description of Monk. Do you think this is a good description of a school bully? Why?

_____

_____

_____

Listen, there was a time when you couldn't even go to the rest room around this school without a pass. And I'm not talking about those little pink tickets made out by some teacher. I'm talking about a pass that could cost anywhere up to a buck, sold by Monk Klutter.

Not that mighty Monk ever touched money, not in public. The gang he ran, which ran the school for him, was his collection agency. They were Klutter's Kobras, a name spelled out in nailheads on six well-known black plastic windbreakers.

Monk's threads were more . . . **subtle.** A pile-lined suede battle jacket with lizard-skin flaps over tailored Levis and a pair of ostrich-skin boots, brassed-toed and suitable for kicking people around. One of his Kobras did nothing all day but walk a half step behind Monk, carrying a fitted bag with Monk's gym shoes, a roll of restroom passes, a cashbox, and a switchblade that Monk gave himself manicures with at lunch over at the Kobras' table.

Word Power
subtle (sut ´ əl) *adj.* not easily seen

4

Speaking of lunch, there were a few cases of advanced malnutrition among the newer kids. The ones who were a little slow in handing over a cut of their lunch money and were therefore barred from the cafeteria. Monk ran a tight ship.

I admit it. I'm five foot five, and when the Kobras slithered by, with or without Monk, I shrank. And I admit this, too: I paid up on a regular basis. And I might add: so would you.

This school was old Monk's Garden of Eden. Unfortunately for him, there was a serpent in it. The reason Monk didn't recognize trouble when it was staring him in the face is that the serpent in the Kobras' Eden was a girl.

Practically every guy in school could show you his scars. Fang marks from Kobras, you might say. And they were all highly visible in the shower room: lumps, **lacerations,** blue bruises, you name it. But girls usually got off with a warning.

Except there was this one girl named Priscilla Roseberry. Picture a girl named Priscilla Roseberry, and you'll be light years off. Priscilla was, hands down, the largest student in our particular institution of learning. I'm not talking fat. I'm talking big. Even beautiful, in a bionic way. Priscilla wasn't inclined toward organized crime. Otherwise, she could have put together a gang that would turn Klutter's Kobras into garter snakes.

Priscilla was basically a loner except she had one friend. A little guy named Melvin Detweiler. You talk about The Odd Couple. Melvin's one of the smallest guys above midget status ever seen. A really nice guy, but, you know—little. They even had lockers next to each other, in the same bank as mine. I don't know what they had going. I'm not saying this was a romance. After all, people deserve their privacy.

Word Power

lacerations (las ´ ə rā´ shəns) *n.* cuts; wounds

Literary Element

Plot Reread the passage highlighted in blue. The plot of a story is created through conflict. In this passage, whom is the conflict between? Check the correct response.
- ☐ between the Kobras and the rest of the students
- ☐ between the new kids and the cafeteria workers
- ☐ between the narrator and the new kids

Reading Skill

Predict When you predict, you make a guess about what will happen. Reread the passage highlighted in green. What do you think Priscilla will do?

_____

_____

_____

English Coach

The suffix -*est* means "the most." The narrator is saying that Melvin is really short. Write the word that means "the most smart."

_____

What are the students at your school like? How are they similar to the students in this photo? How are they different?

Reading Skill

Evaluate Reread the highlighted passage. In this passage the narrator is saying that when someone joins a gang, he or she is no longer an individual. Do you agree? Why or why not?

_____

_____

_____

_____

Priscilla was sort of above everything, if you'll pardon a **pun.** And very calm, as only the very big can be. If there was anybody who didn't notice Klutter's Kobras, it was Priscilla.

Until one winter day after school when we were all grabbing our coats out of our lockers. And hurrying, since Klutter's Kobras made sweeps of the halls for after-school shakedowns.

Anyway, up to Melvin's locker **swaggers** one of the Kobras. Never mind his name. Gang members don't need names. They've got group identity. He reaches down and grabs little Melvin by the neck and slams his head against his locker door. The sound of skull against steel rippled all the way down the locker row, speeding the crowds on their way.

"Okay, let's see your pass," snarls the Kobra.

"A pass for what this time?" Melvin asks, probably still dazed.

Word Power

pun (pun) *n.* a joke in which a word has two meanings
swaggers (swag´ ərz) *v.* walks or behaves in a bold, rude, or proud way

6

"Let's call it a pass for very short people," says the Kobra, "a dwarf tax." He wheezes a little Kobra chuckle at his own wittiness. And already he's reaching for Melvin's wallet with the hand that isn't circling Melvin's windpipe. All this time, of course, Melvin and the Kobra are standing in Priscilla's big shadow.

She's taking her time shoving her books into her locker and pulling on a very large-size coat. Then, quicker than the eye, she brings the side of her enormous hand down in a chop that breaks the Kobra's hold on Melvin's throat. You could hear a pin drop in that hallway. Nobody'd ever laid a finger on a Kobra, let alone a hand the size of Priscilla's.

Then Priscilla, who hardly ever says anything to anybody except to Melvin, says to the Kobra, "Who's your leader, wimp?"

This practically blows the Kobra away. First he's chopped by a girl, and now she's acting like she doesn't know Monk Klutter, the Head Honcho of the World. He's so amazed, he tells her. "Monk Klutter."

"Never heard of him," Priscilla mentions. "Send him to see me." The Kobra just backs away from her like the whole situation is too big for him, which it is.

Pretty soon Monk himself slides up. He jerks his head once, and his Kobras slither off down the hall. He's going to handle this interesting case personally. "Who is it around here doesn't know Monk Klutter?"

He's standing inches from Priscilla, but since he'd have to look up at her, he doesn't. "Never heard of him," says Priscilla.

Monk's not happy with this answer, but by now he's spotted Melvin, who's grown smaller in spite of himself. Monk breaks his own rule by reaching for Melvin with his own hands. "Kid," he says, "you're going to have to educate your girlfriend."

Reading Skill

Predict Reread the passage highlighted in green. Now think back to the prediction you made earlier in the story. It's okay if it does not match— a prediction is a guess! What do you think the Kobras will do to Priscilla?

_____

_____

_____

_____

_____

Literary Element

Plot Reread the paragraph highlighted in blue. What series of events leads to this point in the story's plot? Check the **best** response.

☐ a Kobra threatens Melvin; Melvin fights back; Priscilla breaks it up

☐ a Kobra threatens Priscilla; Melvin runs away; Priscilla runs after him

☐ a Kobra threatens Melvin; Priscilla stands up to him; she claims not to know Monk

Background Info

To *frog-march* means to grab someone from behind and force him or her to march in front of you.

Comprehension Check

Reread the boxed paragraph. What happens after Monk is put into the locker?

_____

_____

_____

_____

His hands never quite make it to Melvin. In a move of pure poetry Priscilla has Monk in a hammerlock. His neck's popping like gunfire, and his head's bowed under the **immense** weight of her forearm. His suede jacket's peeling back, showing pile.

Priscilla's behind him in another easy motion. And with a single mighty thrust forward, frog-marches Monk into her own locker. It's incredible. His ostrich-skin boots click once in the air. And suddenly he's gone, neatly wedged into the locker, a perfect fit. Priscilla bangs the door shut, twirls the lock, and strolls out of school. Melvin goes with her, of course, trotting along below her shoulder. The last **stragglers** leave quietly.

Did You Know?

In wrestling, a *hammerlock* is a hold in which one person twists the opponent's arm behind his or her back.

....

Well, this is where **fate,** an even bigger force than Priscilla, steps in. It snows all that night, a blizzard. The whole town ices up. And school closes for a week.

What would you do if your school was closed for a week?

Word Power

immense (i mens´) *adj.* of great size; huge

stragglers (strag´ lərz) *n.* those who stay behind or stray from the main group

fate (fāt) *n.* a power that determines how things will turn out

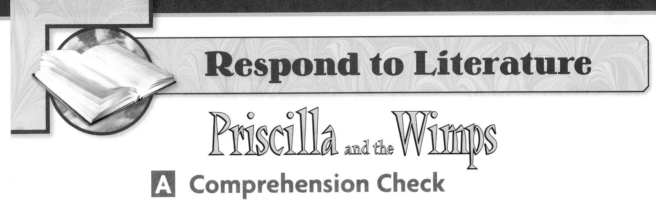

Respond to Literature

Priscilla and the Wimps

A Comprehension Check

Answer the following questions in the spaces provided.

1. What words are spelled out on the jackets worn by Monk's gang?

   _____

2. What kind of "pass" does the Kobra demand from Melvin after school?

   _____

B Reading Skills

Answer the following questions in the spaces provided.

1. **Predict** What do you think will happen after Monk gets out of the locker? Do you think the Kobra gang will continue to bully the other students? Why or why not?

   _____

   _____

   _____

2. **Evaluate** Think about how the author slowly introduces each character: the narrator, Monk the bully, Priscilla the tall girl, and Melvin her short friend. Do you think this helps the reader understand the conflict? Does it make the story more interesting? Why or why not?

   _____

   _____

   _____

Background Info

The words *gee* and *haw* are commands used to direct dogs, horses, and some other animals. *Gee* is "to the right," and *haw* is "to the left."

Connect to the Text

Reread the text in the purple box. How would you feel if you were in Walt's situation?

_____

_____

_____

No snow had fallen for several weeks, and the traffic had packed the main river trail till it was hard and glassy as ice. Over this the sled flew along, and the dogs kept the trail fairly well, although Walt quickly discovered that he had made a mistake in choosing the leader. He had to guide them by his voice and it was clear that the head dog had never learned the meaning of "gee" and "haw." He hugged the inside of the curves too closely, often forcing the other dogs behind him into the soft snow, while several times he overturned the sled.

Looking back, Walt could see the sled of his pursuers, rising and falling over the ice like a boat in the sea. The Irishman and the black-bearded leader were with it, taking turns in running and riding.

Night fell, and in the blackness of the first hour or so Walt struggled desperately with his dogs. On account of the poor lead dog, they were continually going off the beaten track into the soft snow. The sled was as often riding on its side or top as it was in the proper way. This work and strain tried Walt's strength greatly. Had he not been in such a hurry he could have avoided much of it, but he feared the stampeders would creep up in the darkness and overtake him. However, he could hear them yelling to their dogs, and knew from the sounds they were coming up very slowly.

When the moon rose, Dawson was only fifty miles away. He was almost exhausted. Looking back, he saw his enemies had crawled up within four hundred yards. At this space they remained, a black speck of motion on the white river. Try as they would, they could not shorten this distance, and try as he would, he could not increase it.

When he was near the mouth of Rosebud Creek, the sound of a gun and the ping of a bullet on the ice beside him told him that they were this time shooting at him with a rifle. And from then on as he cleared the top of each ice jam, he stretched flat on the leaping sled till the rifle shot from the rear warned him that he was safe till the next ice jam was reached.

Now it is very hard to lie on a moving sled, jumping and plunging and swaying like a boat in the wind, and so is shooting through the moonlight at an object four hundred yards away on another moving sled. So it is not a surprise that the black-bearded leader did not hit him.

After several hours of this, their bullets began to give out and their shooting decreased. They took greater care, and shot at him only at the best opportunities. He was also leaving them behind, the distance slowly increasing to six hundred yards.

Near Indian River, Walt Masters had his first accident. A bullet flew past his ears, and struck the bad lead dog.

The poor animal plunged in a heap, with the rest of the dogs on top of him.

Like a flash, Walt was by the leader. He dragged the dying animal to one side and straightened out the team.

How is this photo similar to what is happening in the story?
_____

Literary Element

Plot Reread the highlighted passage. What event occurs at this point of the story?

_____

_____

_____

Reading Skill

Predict Reread the paragraph highlighted in green. What do you predict will happen next?

_____

_____

_____

_____

Literary Element

Plot Reread the passage highlighted in blue. How is the problem in the story solved?

_____

_____

_____

He glanced back. The other sled was coming up quickly. He cried "Mush on!" and leaped upon the sled just as the pursuers came alongside him.

The Irishman was preparing to spring for him—they were so sure they had him that they did not shoot—when Walt turned fiercely upon them with his whip.

He struck at their faces, and the men protected their faces with their hands. So there was no shooting just then. Before they could recover, Walt reached out from his sled, catching one of their dogs by the front legs in midspring, and throwing him heavily. This snarled the dogs, overturning the sled and tangling his enemies up beautifully.

Away Walt flew, his sled screaming as it leaped over the frozen surface. And what had seemed an accident proved to be a blessing in disguise.

The proper lead dog was now in front. He stretched low and cried with joy as he jerked his **comrades** along.

By the time he reached Ainslie's Creek, seventeen miles from Dawson, Walt had left his pursuers, a tiny speck, far behind. At Monte Cristo Island he could no longer see them. And at Swede Creek, just as daylight was lighting up the pines, he ran right into the camp of old Loren Hall.

Almost as quick as it takes to tell it, Loren had his sleeping furs rolled up, and had joined Walt on the sled. They allowed the dogs to travel more slowly, as there was no sign of the chase in the rear. Just as they pulled up at the gold commissioner's office in Dawson, Walt, who had kept his eyes open to the last, fell asleep.

And because of what Walt Masters did on this night, the men of the Yukon have become proud of him, and speak of him now as the King of Mazy May.

Word Power

comrades (kom´radz) _n._ fellow members of a group

Respond to Literature

The King of Mazy May

A Comprehension Check

Answer the following questions in the spaces provided.

1. What are Walt Masters and his father doing in the Klondike?

   _____

2. What does Walt do to protect his neighbor's claim?

   _____

   _____

B Reading Skills

Answer the following questions in the spaces provided.

1. **Evaluate** The author uses the word "manliness" to describe Walt. What details support this description?

   _____

   _____

2. **Evaluate** Which part of the story did you find the most exciting? Explain.

   _____

3. **Predict** Did you correctly predict what the story would be about? Explain.

   _____

   _____

C Word Power

Complete each sentence below, using one of the words in the box.

| claims | injustice | suspense |
| pursuers | comrades | |

1. The scary movie kept us in _____.

2. The _____ chased the dog, but they could not catch it.

3. Soldiers in the same unit are _____.

4. Prospectors hoped there would be gold on their _____.

5. Stealing is an example of an _____.

Circle the word that best completes each sentence.

6. Ten **(pursuers, claims)** finally caught the animal that escaped.

7. The **(comrades, suspense)** enjoy working together.

8. A map showed the location of several **(claims, pursuers)** in the Klondike.

9. Treating others unfairly is an **(comrades, injustice)**.

10. Dion was in **(suspense, injustice)** while he waited for his report card.

D Literary Element: Plot

Read the passages below from "The King of Mazy May." As you read, think about the action and events of the plot. Then answer the questions that follow.

Walt lay in the snow, thinking rapidly.[1] He was only a boy, but in the face of the threatened injustice to old Loren Hall he felt that he must do something.[2] He broke into a run for the camp of the stampeders.[3]

By the time he reached Ainslie's Creek, seventeen miles from Dawson, Walt had left his pursuers, a tiny speck, far behind.[4] At Monte Cristo Island he could no longer see them.[5] And at Swede Creek, just as daylight was lighting up the pines, he ran right into the camp of old Loren Hall.[6]

1. In sentences 1–3, what conflict or problem does Walt have to face? What action does he take?

   _____

   _____

   _____

   _____

2. In sentences 4–6, how is the problem that Walt faced resolved?

   _____

   _____

   _____

   _____

E Newspaper Article

Suppose that Walt's adventure was a true story. Imagine that you are a newspaper reporter in the late 1800s in the Klondike. Write a newspaper article about this exciting event.

DAILY NEWS

WALT SAVES THE DAY

Walt Masters was in the Klondike _____

_____

He was also looking after the claim of Loren Hall because

_____

He noticed five strange men. He followed them _____

_____

_____

Walt prepared a dog sled and _____

_____

_____

_____

After a seventy-mile trip, Walt _____

_____

_____

Assessment

Fill in the circle next to each correct answer.

1. What does Walt do when his lead dog is shot?
   - ○ A. He drags it aside and keeps going.
   - ○ B. He throws things off the sled to make it lighter.
   - ○ C. He stops to bury the dog.
   - ○ D. He gets off the sled and runs behind it.

2. What is the main conflict, or problem, that Walt had to face?
   - ○ A. how to drive a team of dogs
   - ○ B. how to warn Loren Hall about the claim jumpers
   - ○ C. how to pan for gold
   - ○ D. how to find his way to Dawson in the dark

3. Which detail **best** helped you predict that Walt would go to warn Loren Hall?
   - ○ A. Walt had nothing to fear now that his father had gone on a short trip up the White River.
   - ○ B. Walt can go to the Indian camps and "talk big" with the men, and trade with them for their precious furs.
   - ○ C. Although Walt does not know a great deal that most boys know, he knows much that other boys do not know.
   - ○ D. In the face of the threatened injustice to old Loren Hall, Walt felt that he must do something.

4. When settlers on Mazy May Creek lost their *claims*, it meant they lost their
   - ○ A. cabins.
   - ○ B. dogs.
   - ○ C. land.
   - ○ D. sleds.

5. Which word means "unfairness"?
   - ○ A. injustice
   - ○ B. prospectors
   - ○ C. suspense
   - ○ D. comrades

Meet
Gary Soto

"There are a lot of people who never discover what their talent is. . . . I am very lucky to have found mine." Gary Soto published several books of poetry and a book of stories about his life before he tried writing fiction. In his stories, Soto says, he tries to recreate the friends and Mexican American neighborhood of his early years.
Gary Soto was born in 1952. "La Bamba" was first published in 1990.

What You Know

Have you ever performed in public? How did you feel while you were performing? How did you feel after the performance?

Reason to Read

Read "La Bamba" to find out how a boy handles an exciting experience.

Background Info

Ritchie Valens, a singer mentioned in the story, was a teenage singer in the 1950s. He was one of the first Mexican American rock-and-roll stars. "La Bamba" was one of his biggest hits. Valens died in an airplane crash when he was only seventeen years old.

Word Power

pantomime (pan´ tə mīm´) *n.* the use of gestures only, without words, to tell something; p. 33
Because Aubra did not speak English, she used *pantomime* to tell the clerk what she wanted to buy.

debut (dā bū´) *n.* first public appearance; p. 33
My cousin made his *debut* as a dancer in the high school play.

coordinator (kō ôr´ də nā´ tər) *n.* one who organizes an event; p. 33
My teacher asked me to be the *coordinator* of this year's science fair.

confident (kon´ fə dənt) *adj.* certain; full of belief in oneself; p. 34
After studying for three hours, I was *confident* that I would get an A on my test.

commotion (kə mō´ shən) *n.* noisy confusion; p. 35
When the cat ran past the six dogs, it caused a great *commotion* on the street.

maneuvered (mə nōō´ vərd) *v.* moved in a skillful or planned way; p. 36
I carefully *maneuvered* my way past the crowd of people and got in the car.

jargon (jär´ gən) *n.* terms used in a particular field that may not be understood by outsiders; p. 40
The computer programmer uses *jargon* when she talks about computers.

**Answer the following questions, using one of the new words above.
Write your answers in the spaces provided.**

1. Which word goes with "telling without speaking"? _____

2. Which word goes with "a noisy uproar"? _____

3. Which word goes with "vocabulary only certain people understand"? _____

4. Which word goes with "feeling sure of yourself"? _____

5. Which word goes with "moved carefully"? _____

6. Which word goes with "a first appearance"? _____

7. Which word goes with "someone who puts things in order"? _____

La Bamba

Gary Soto

Reading Skill

Predict Reread the passage highlighted in green. When you predict, you make a guess about what might happen. Predict what will happen to Manuel at the talent show.

_____

_____

_____

_____

English Coach

Here, the phrase *that was bad* is slang and means that something was really good. Which of the following sentences is another way to say "that concert was bad," if the word *bad* has the same meaning as it does in the highlighted sentence?

☐ I really liked the concert.

☐ I hated the concert.

☐ I didn't go to the concert.

Manuel was the fourth of seven children and looked like a lot of kids in his neighborhood: black hair, brown face, and skinny legs scuffed from summer play. But summer was giving way to fall: the trees were turning red, the lawns brown, and the pomegranate trees were heavy with fruit. Manuel walked to school in the frosty morning, kicking leaves and thinking of tomorrow's talent show. He was still amazed that he had volunteered. He was going to pretend to sing Ritchie Valens's "La Bamba" before the entire school.

Why did I raise my hand? he asked himself, but in his heart he knew the answer. He yearned for the limelight. He wanted applause as loud as a thunderstorm, and to hear his friends say, "Man, that was bad!" And he wanted to impress the girls, especially Petra Lopez, the second-prettiest girl in his class. The prettiest was already taken by his friend Ernie. Manuel knew he should be reasonable, since he himself was not great-looking, just average.

Manuel kicked through the fresh-fallen leaves. When he got to school he realized he had forgotten his math workbook. If his teacher found out, he would have to stay after school and miss practice for the talent show. But fortunately for him, they did drills that morning.

During lunch Manuel hung around with Benny, who was also in the talent show. Benny was going to play the trumpet in spite of the fat lip he had gotten playing football.

"How do I look?" Manuel asked. He cleared his throat and started moving his lips in **pantomime.** No words came out, just a hiss that sounded like a snake. Manuel tried to look emotional, flailing his arms on the high notes and opening his eyes and mouth as wide as he could when he came to "*Para bailar* la baaaaammmba."

After Manuel finished, Benny said it looked all right, but suggested Manuel dance while he sang. Manuel thought for a moment and decided it was a good idea.

"Yeah, just think you're like Michael Jackson or someone like that," Benny suggested. "But don't get carried away."

During rehearsal, Mr. Roybal, nervous about his **debut** as the school's talent **coordinator,** cursed under his breath when the lever that controlled the speed of the record player jammed.

"Darn," he growled, trying to force the lever. "What's wrong with you?"

"Is it broken?" Manuel asked, bending over for a closer look. It looked all right to him.

Mr. Roybal assured Manuel that he would have a good record player at the talent show, even if it meant bringing his own stereo from home.

Manuel sat in a folding chair, twirling his record on his thumb. He watched a skit about personal hygiene, a mother-and-daughter violin duo, five first-grade girls jumping rope, a karate kid breaking boards, three girls singing "Like a Virgin," and a skit about the pilgrims. If the record player hadn't been broken, he would have gone after the karate kid, an easy act to follow, he told himself.

Word Power

pantomime (panʹ tə mīmʹ) *n.* the use of gestures only, without words, to tell something

debut (dā būʹ) *n.* first public appearance

coordinator (kō ôrʹ də nāʹ tər) *n.* one who organizes an event

Background Info

The Spanish phrase *para bailar* (pärʹə bī lärʹ) is repeated often during the song "La Bamba." *Bailar* means "to dance" in Spanish. The words to the song are all in Spanish.

Reading Skill

Predict Reread the highlighted passage. Think about the last prediction you made. Based on what happens at rehearsal, what do you predict will happen during the performance?

_____

_____

_____

_____

_____

My Workspace

Connect to the Text

Reread the boxed paragraph. What event at your school have you taken part in? Describe your experience below.

_____

_____

_____

_____

_____

Reading Skill

Evaluate Reread the highlighted sentence. Why might practicing in the shower not be as useful as practicing in some other part of the house, where Manuel could use a record player?

_____

_____

_____

_____

_____

Did You Know?

Before compact discs, music was recorded on records and played on record players. Record players have different rates of speed. A *forty-five record* makes 45 complete turns each minute.

· · · · · · · · · · · · · · · · · · · ·

As he twirled his forty-five record, Manuel thought they had a great talent show. The entire school would be amazed. His mother and father would be proud, and his brother and sisters would be jealous and pout. It would be a night to remember.

Benny walked onto the stage, raised his trumpet to his mouth, and waited for his cue. Mr. Roybal raised his hand like a symphony conductor and let it fall dramatically. Benny inhaled and blew so loud that Manuel dropped his record, which rolled across the cafeteria floor until it hit a wall. Manuel raced after it, picked it up, and wiped it clean.

"Boy, I'm glad it didn't break," he said with a sigh.

That night Manuel had to do the dishes and a lot of homework, so he could only practice in the shower. In bed he prayed that he wouldn't mess up. He prayed that it wouldn't be like when he was a first-grader. For Science Week he had wired together a C battery and a bulb, and told everyone he had discovered how a flashlight worked. He was so pleased with himself that he practiced for hours pressing the wire to the battery, making the bulb wink a dim, orangish light. He showed it to so many kids in his neighborhood that when it was time to show his class how a flashlight worked, the battery was dead. He pressed the wire to the battery, but the bulb didn't respond. He pressed until his thumb hurt and some kids in the back started snickering.

But Manuel fell asleep **confident** that nothing would go wrong this time.

The next morning his father and mother beamed at him. They were proud that he was going to be in the talent show.

Word Power

confident (kon´ fə dənt) *adj.* certain; full of belief in oneself

34

What would you do if you had to perform for an audience?

"I wish you would tell us what you're doing," his mother said. His father, a pharmacist who wore a blue smock with his name on a plastic rectangle, looked up from the newspaper and sided with his wife. "Yes, what are you doing in the talent show?"

"You'll see," Manuel said with his mouth full of Cheerios.

The day whizzed by, and so did his afternoon chores and dinner. Suddenly he was dressed in his best clothes and standing next to Benny backstage, listening to the **commotion** as the cafeteria filled with school kids and parents. The lights dimmed, and Mr. Roybal, sweaty in a tight suit and a necktie with a large knot, wet his lips and parted the stage curtains.

"Good evening, everyone," the kids behind the curtain heard him say. "Good evening to you," some of the smart-alecky kids said back to him.

Literary Element

Character Reread the highlighted sentence. Mr. Roybal is nervous about the show. Underline the words or phrases that tell you he is nervous.

Word Power

commotion (kə mō′ shən) *n.* noisy confusion

35

My Workspace

English Coach

Part means "to separate" in this sentence. In which of the following phrases does *part* have the same meaning as the highlighted text? Check the correct response.

☐ a part in a play
☐ a part in your hair
☐ a part of a store

Comprehension Check

Reread the boxed passage. Why does Mr. Roybal jump out onto the stage? Check the correct response.

☐ to introduce the next act to the audience
☐ to keep the tooth from falling off the stage
☐ to make the act more funny

"Tonight we bring you the best John Burroughs Elementary has to offer, and I'm sure that you'll be both pleased and amazed that our little school houses so much talent. And now, without further ado, let's get on with the show." He turned and, with a swish of his hand, commanded, "Part the curtain." The curtains parted in jerks. A girl dressed as a toothbrush and a boy dressed as a dirty gray tooth walked onto the stage and sang:

> *Brush, brush, brush*
> *Floss, floss, floss*
> *Gargle the germs away—*
> *hey! hey! hey!*

After they finished singing, they turned to Mr. Roybal, who dropped his hand. The toothbrush dashed around the stage after the dirty tooth, which was laughing and having a great time until it slipped and nearly rolled off the stage.

Mr. Roybal jumped out and caught it just in time. "Are you OK?"

The dirty tooth answered, "Ask my dentist," which drew laughter and applause from the audience.

The violin duo played next, and except for one time when the girl got lost, they sounded fine. People applauded, and some even stood up. Then the first-grade girls **maneuvered** onto the stage while jumping rope. They were all smiles and bouncing ponytails as a hundred cameras flashed at once. Mothers "aahed" and fathers sat up proudly.

The karate kid was next. He did a few kicks, yells, and chops, and finally, when his father held up a board, punched it in two. The audience clapped and looked at each other, wide-eyed with respect. The boy bowed to the audience, and father and son ran off the stage.

Word Power
maneuvered (mə nōō′ vərd) *v.* moved in a skillful or planned way

Manuel remained behind the stage shivering with fear. He mouthed the words to "La Bamba" and swayed from left to right. Why did he raise his hand and volunteer? Why couldn't he have just sat there like the rest of the kids and not said anything? While the karate kid was on stage, Mr. Roybal, more sweaty than before, took Manuel's forty-five record and placed it on the new record player.

"You ready?" Mr. Roybal asked. "Yeah . . ."

Mr. Roybal walked back on stage and announced that Manuel Gomez, a fifth-grader in Mrs. Knight's class, was going to pantomime Ritchie Valens's classic hit "La Bamba."

The cafeteria roared with applause. Manuel was nervous but loved the noisy crowd. He pictured his mother and father applauding loudly and his brother and sisters also clapping, though not as energetically.

Manuel walked on stage and the song started immediately. Glassy-eyed from the shock of being in front of so many people, Manuel moved his lips and swayed in a made-up dance step. He couldn't see his parents, but he could see his brother Mario, who was a year younger, thumb-wrestling with a friend. Mario was wearing Manuel's favorite shirt; he would deal with Mario later. He saw some other kids get up and head for the drinking fountain, and a baby sitting in the middle of an aisle sucking her thumb and watching him intently.

What am I doing here? thought Manuel. This is no fun at all. Everyone was just sitting there. Some people were moving to the beat, but most were just watching him, like they would a monkey at the zoo.

Literary Element

Character Reread the paragraph highlighted in blue. What does this paragraph tell you about how Manuel feels before he goes onstage? Check the **best** response.

☐ Manuel feels scared and angry.

☐ Manuel feels tired and confident.

☐ Manuel feels nervous and excited.

English Coach

Manuel compares himself to a monkey at the zoo. This is called a *simile*. A simile is a comparison that uses the words *like* or *as*. Write another simile to describe how Manuel might feel as people watch him perform.

_____

_____

_____

Seabreeze. Gil Mayers (b. 1947). Private collection.
What musical instruments do you see in this painting?

Reading Skill

Predict Reread the highlighted text and the rest of the paragraph. The record gets stuck. Does it match the last prediction you made? Don't worry if it doesn't match! How do you think Manuel will handle this situation?

_____

_____

_____

Connect to the Text

Reread the boxed passage. Have you ever been in an embarrassing situation? How did you handle it?

_____

_____

_____

But when Manuel did a fancy dance step, there was a burst of applause and some girls screamed. Manuel tried another dance step. He heard more applause and screams and started getting into the groove as he shivered and snaked like Michael Jackson around the stage. But the record got stuck, and he had to sing

Para bailar la bamba
Para bailar la bamba
Para bailar la bamba
Para bailar la bamba

again and again.

Manuel couldn't believe his bad luck. The audience began to laugh and stand up in their chairs. Manuel remembered how the forty-five record had dropped from his hand and rolled across the cafeteria floor. It probably got scratched, he thought, and now it was stuck, and he was stuck dancing and moving his lips to the same words over and over. He had never been so embarrassed. He would have to ask his parents to move the family out of town.

After Mr. Roybal ripped the needle across the record, Manuel slowed his dance steps to a halt. He didn't know what to do except bow to the audience, which applauded wildly, and scoot off the stage, on the verge of tears. This was worse than the homemade flashlight. At least no one laughed then, they just snickered.

Manuel stood alone, trying hard to hold back the tears as Benny, center stage, played his trumpet. Manuel was jealous because he sounded great, then mad as he recalled that it was Benny's loud trumpet playing that made the forty-five record fly out of his hands. But when the entire cast lined up for a curtain call, Manuel received a burst of applause that was so loud it shook the walls of the cafeteria. Later, as he mingled with the kids and parents, everyone patted him on the shoulder and told him, "Way to go. You were really funny."

Funny? Manuel thought. Did he do something funny?

Funny. Crazy. Hilarious. These were the words people said to him. He was confused, but beyond caring. All he knew was that people were paying attention to him, and his brother and sisters looked at him with a mixture of jealousy and awe. He was going to pull Mario aside and punch him in the arm for wearing his shirt, but he cooled it. He was enjoying the limelight. A teacher brought him cookies and punch, and the popular kids who had never before given him the time of day now clustered around him. Ricardo, the editor of the school bulletin, asked him how he made the needle stick.

"It just happened," Manuel said, crunching on a star-shaped cookie.

At home that night his father, eager to undo the buttons on his shirt and ease into his La-Z-Boy recliner, asked Manuel the same thing, how he managed to make the song stick on the words *"Para bailar la bamba."*

Comprehension Check

Reread the boxed passage. What does the audience think about Manuel's performance?

_____

_____

_____

Reading Skill

Predict Reread the highlighted passage. Does this match the last prediction you made? How did things turn out for Manuel? Revise your prediction as needed.

_____

_____

_____

Background Info

Que niños tan truchas (kā nēn´yos tän trŌo´chəs) is Spanish for "These kids are so sharp!"

Manuel thought quickly and reached for scientific **jargon** he had read in magazines. "Easy, Dad. I used laser tracking with high optics and low functional decibels per channel." His proud but confused father told him to be quiet and go to bed. "Ah, que niños tan truchas," he said as he walked to the kitchen for a glass of milk. "I don't know how you kids nowadays get so smart."

Manuel, feeling happy, went to his bedroom, undressed, and slipped into his pajamas. He looked in the mirror and began to pantomime "La Bamba," but stopped because he was tired of the song. He crawled into bed. The sheets were as cold as the moon that stood over the peach tree in their backyard.

He was relieved that the day was over. Next year, when they asked for volunteers for the talent show, he wouldn't raise his hand. Probably.

What musical instrument would you like to learn to play? Why?

_____

_____

Word Power

jargon (jär´ gən) *n.* terms used in a particular field that may not be understood by outsiders

Respond to Literature

La Bamba

A Comprehension Check

Answer the following questions in the spaces provided.

1. What does Manuel volunteer to do? Why?

_____

_____

2. What happens during the performance?

_____

_____

B Reading Skills

Answer the following questions in the spaces provided.

1. **Predict** At the end of the story, the narrator states that Manuel will probably not raise his hand to volunteer in next year's talent show. Do you think Manuel will volunteer next year? Why or why not?

_____

_____

2. **Evaluate** The author gives details about the other acts in the show. Does this make the story more interesting? Why or why not?

_____

_____

C Word Power

Complete each sentence below, using one of the words in the box.

pantomime	debut	coordinator
confident	commotion	maneuvered	jargon

1. Charise was so _____ that she would win the election that she wrote her thank you speech before the votes were counted.

2. In the quiet classroom, Jamie used _____ to tell me where to meet her after school.

3. The driver carefully _____ his car into the parking space.

4. The lightning set off all the car alarms in the parking lot and caused a great _____.

5. Angela had a wonderful _____ as an artist and sold her first painting.

6. Hilary and Matthew use _____ when they talk about science.

7. Ahmed's job as the _____ of the festival was to keep track of all the activities.

D Literary Element: Character

Read the passage below from "La Bamba." As you read, think about what the sentences reveal about Manuel. Then answer the questions that follow.

> What am I doing here? thought Manuel.[1] This is no fun at all.[2] Everyone was just sitting there.[3] Some people were moving to the beat, but most were just watching him, like they would a monkey at the zoo.[4]
>
> But when Manuel did a fancy dance step, there was a burst of applause and some girls screamed.[5] Manuel tried another dance step.[6] He heard more applause and screams and started getting into the groove as he shivered and snaked like Michael Jackson around the stage.[7]

1. What do sentences 1–4 reveal about Manuel?

   _____

   _____

   _____

2. Reread sentences 5–7. How does Manuel react when the audience applauds? What do his actions tell you about him?

   _____

   _____

   _____

E A Review

Imagine that you are writing a review about the talent show for your school newspaper. Describe some of the other performances, but be sure to focus on Manuel's performance. Rate the performances, from 1 to 4 stars.

John Burroughs Elementary Gazette

Last Friday night, we were treated to a great talent show at John Burroughs Elementary School.

The show began with a skit about a toothbrush and a tooth. The skit was _____

_____

I give it _____ stars.

Manuel Gomez was the star of the show. I have never seen "La Bamba" performed quite this way! Manuel excited the crowd with _____

_____

The crowd went crazy when Manuel _____

_____

His performance was the best of the night, with _____ stars!

At the curtain call, Manuel _____

_____

Mr. Roybal put together a great show!

Way to go, John Burroughs Elementary!

Assessment

Fill in the circle next to each correct answer.

1. Why does Manuel volunteer to enter the talent show?
   - ○ A. He has a great voice.
   - ○ B. He wants to be the center of attention.
   - ○ C. He thinks he is a great dancer.
   - ○ D. He doesn't want Benny to get all the attention.

2. Which sentence from the story helps you predict that Manuel's performance will not go as planned?
   - ○ A. No words came out, just a hiss that sounded like a snake.
   - ○ B. The next morning his father and mother beamed at him.
   - ○ C. Manuel was nervous but loved the noisy crowd.
   - ○ D. The lever that controlled the speed of the record player jammed.

3. When Manuel hurries off the stage, he is on the verge of tears. What does his reaction tell you about his character?
   - ○ A. He cares about what people think of him.
   - ○ B. He is afraid of success.
   - ○ C. He doesn't like to get a lot of attention.
   - ○ D. He isn't used to making mistakes.

4. What does the audience think about Manuel's performance?
   - ○ A. They enjoyed his great singing.
   - ○ B. They think he made a fool of himself.
   - ○ C. They think he was funny on purpose.
   - ○ D. They did not like his performance at all.

5. Which of the following words means "first public appearance"?
   - ○ A. debut
   - ○ B. maneuvered
   - ○ C. pantomime
   - ○ D. confident

Get Ready to Read!

After you, My Dear Alphonse

Meet Shirley Jackson

Shirley Jackson was a popular author during her lifetime. Many of her stories are filled with strange twists and turns, often exploring the darker side of life. However, she also wrote funny stories about family life. Most of her short stories were published in magazines. Shirley Jackson was born in 1916 and died in 1965.

"After You, My Dear Alphonse" was first printed in *The New Yorker* magazine in 1943.

What You Know

Think about the first time you met a person. What did you think of this person? Did your ideas about this person change after you got to know him or her? How?

Reason to Read

Read "After You, My Dear Alphonse" to find out how a woman reacts to someone she meets for the first time.

Background Info

"After You, My Dear Alphonse" was written in the 1940s. During this time in the United States, laws in some parts of the country separated African American people from white people. These laws kept African Americans out of many public places. African Americans did not have the same opportunities as whites in voting, education, and jobs. As a result, many African Americans were poor. It was common for whites to believe that all African Americans were poor and uneducated.

Word Power

hesitated (hez′ ə tāt′ id) *v.* stopped for a minute; paused; p. 50
The swimmer *hesitated* before she dove into the cold water.

defeated (di fēt′ id) *adj.* disappointed; not successful; p. 50
The farmer felt *defeated* when all of his crops died.

restrained (ri strānd′) *v.* held back from acting; p. 51
I *restrained* my desire to buy a chocolate milkshake.

impulse (im′ puls) *n.* a sudden desire to act; p. 51
Following an *impulse*, the girl ran across the park.

transformed (trans fôrmd′) *v.* changed in form, appearance, or use; p. 51
A group of students *transformed* several big boxes into a fort.

expression (iks presh′ ən) *n.* a look on the face that shows feeling; p. 52
Everyone laughed at their friend's surprised *expression*.

**Answer the following questions, using one of the new words above.
Write your answers in the spaces provided.**

1. Which word goes with "an urge"? _____

2. Which word goes with "showing emotion"? _____

3. Which word goes with "waited"? _____

4. Which word goes with "changed"? _____

5. Which word goes with "disappointed"? _____

6. Which word goes with "kept from happening"? _____

After you, My Dear Alphonse

Shirley Jackson

Background Info

This phrase was spoken by a cartoon character, Gaston, who was popular many years ago. In the comic, he and his friend Alphonse were extremely polite to each other. They would say, "After you," back and forth over and over again.

English Coach

The word *mother'll* is a contraction. A contraction is a shortening of a word or words. *Mother'll* is a shortened way to say *mother will*. The word *will* is shortened to *'ll*. What is the contraction for *you will*?

Mrs. Wilson was just taking the gingerbread out of the oven when she heard Johnny outside talking to someone.

"Johnny," she called, "you're late. Come in and get your lunch."

"Just a minute, Mother," Johnny said. "After you, my dear Alphonse."

"After *you*, my dear Alphonse," another voice said.

"No, after *you*, my dear Alphonse," Johnny said.

Mrs. Wilson opened the door. "Johnny," she said, "you come in this minute and get your lunch. You can play after you've eaten."

Johnny came in after her, slowly. "Mother," he said, "I brought Boyd home for lunch with me."

"Boyd?" Mrs. Wilson thought for a moment. "I don't believe I've met Boyd. Bring him in, dear, since you've invited him. Lunch is ready."

"Boyd!" Johnny yelled. "Hey, Boyd, come on in!"

"I'm coming. Just got to unload this stuff."

"Well, hurry, or my mother'll be sore."

"Johnny, that's not very polite to either your friend or your mother," Mrs. Wilson said. "Come sit down, Boyd."

As she turned to show Boyd where to sit, she saw he was a Negro boy, smaller than Johnny but about the same age. His arms were loaded with split kindling wood. "Where'll I put this stuff, Johnny?" he asked.

Mrs. Wilson turned to Johnny. "Johnny," she said, "what did you make Boyd do? What is that wood?"

"Dead Japanese," Johnny said mildly. "We stand them in the ground and run over them with tanks."

"How do you do, Mrs. Wilson?" Boyd said.

"How do you do, Boyd? You shouldn't let Johnny make you carry all that wood. Sit down now and eat lunch, both of you."

"Why shouldn't he carry the wood, Mother? It's his wood. We got it at his place."

"Johnny," Mrs. Wilson said, "go on and eat your lunch."

"Sure," Johnny said. He held out the dish of scrambled eggs to Boyd. "After you, my dear Alphonse."

"After *you*, my dear Alphonse," Boyd said.

"After *you*, my dear Alphonse," Johnny said. They began to giggle.

"Are you hungry, Boyd?" Mrs. Wilson asked.

"Yes, Mrs. Wilson."

"Well, don't you let Johnny stop you. He always fusses about eating, so you just see that you get a good lunch. There's plenty of food here for you to have all you want."

"Thank you, Mrs. Wilson."

"Come on, Alphonse," Johnny said. He pushed half the scrambled eggs on to Boyd's plate. Boyd watched while Mrs. Wilson put a dish of stewed tomatoes beside his plate.

"Boyd don't eat tomatoes, do you Boyd?" Johnny said.

"*Doesn't* eat tomatoes, Johnny. And just because you don't like them, don't say that about Boyd. Boyd will eat *anything*."

Literary Element

Character Reread the highlighted sentence. We learn about characters from the way they talk. What do you learn about Boyd from this sentence?

_____
_____
_____
_____
_____

Comprehension Check

Reread the boxed text. What does Mrs. Wilson serve to Boyd? Why doesn't she serve the same thing to Johnny?

_____
_____
_____
_____

49

Have you ever had a friend that came from a different background?

Literary Element

Character Reread the highlighted passage. What do you learn about Mrs. Wilson's character from this passage?

_____

_____

_____

_____

_____

_____

_____

"Bet he won't," Johnny said, attacking his scrambled eggs.

"Boyd wants to grow up and be a big strong man so he can work hard," Mrs. Wilson said. "I'll bet Boyd's father eats stewed tomatoes."

"My father eats anything he wants to," Boyd said.

"So does mine," Johnny said. "Sometimes he doesn't eat hardly anything. He's a little guy, though. Wouldn't hurt a flea."

"Mine's a little guy too," Boyd said.

"I'll bet he's strong, though," Mrs. Wilson said. She **hesitated.** "Does he . . . work?"

"Sure," Johnny said. "Boyd's father works in a factory."

"There, you see?" Mrs. Wilson said. "And he certainly has to be strong to do that—all that lifting and carrying at a factory."

"Boyd's father doesn't have to," Johnny said. "He's a foreman."

Mrs. Wilson felt **defeated.** "What does your mother do, Boyd?"

"My mother?" Boyd was surprised. "She takes care of us kids."

"Oh. She doesn't work, then?"

"Why should she?" Johnny said through a mouthful of eggs. "You don't work."

Word Power

hesitated (hez´ ə tāt´ id) *v.* stopped for a minute; paused

defeated (di fēt´ id) *adj.* disappointed; not successful

"You really don't want any stewed tomatoes, Boyd?"

"No, thank you, Mrs. Wilson," Boyd said.

"No, thank you, Mrs. Wilson, no, thank you, Mrs. Wilson, no, thank you, Mrs. Wilson," Johnny said. "Boyd's sister's going to work, though. She's going to be a teacher."

"That's a fine attitude for her to have, Boyd." Mrs. Wilson **restrained** an **impulse** to pat Boyd on the head. "I imagine you're all very proud of her?"

"I guess so," Boyd said.

"What about all your other brothers and sisters? I guess all of you want to make just as much of yourselves as you can."

"There's only me and Jean," Boyd said. "I don't know yet what I want to be when I grow up."

"We're going to be tank drivers, Boyd and me," Johnny said.

"Zoom." Mrs. Wilson caught Boyd's glass of milk as Johnny's napkin ring, suddenly **transformed** into a tank, plowed heavily across the table.

"Look, Johnny," Boyd said. "Here's a foxhole. I'm shooting at you."

Mrs. Wilson, with the speed born of long experience, took the gingerbread off the shelf and placed it carefully between the tank and the foxhole.

"Now eat as much as you want to, Boyd," she said. "I want to see you get filled up."

"Boyd eats a lot, but not as much as I do," Johnny said. "I'm bigger than he is."

"You're not much bigger," Boyd said. "I can beat you running."

Reading Skill

Predict Reread the highlighted paragraph. Based on what you already know about Mrs. Wilson, do you think she will ever have one correct idea about Boyd's family? Why?

_____

_____

_____

_____

_____

English Coach

The word *foxhole* is a compound word. It is made by joining the two smaller words *fox* and *hole*. Soldiers dig *foxholes* to protect themselves. What two words make up the compound word *gingerbread*?

_____

Word Power

restrained (ri strānd´) *v.* held back from acting

impulse (im´puls) *n.* a sudden desire to act

transformed (trans fôrmd´) *v.* changed in form, appearance, or use

51

Do you and your friends like the same foods? What foods do you eat?

Reading Skill

Evaluate Reread the highlighted sentence and the rest of the paragraph. Do you think Mrs. Wilson is being kind when she offers Boyd the clothes? Why?

_____

_____

_____

_____

_____

_____

Mrs. Wilson took a deep breath. "Boyd," she said. Both boys turned to her. "Boyd, Johnny has some suits that are a little too small for him, and a winter coat. It's not new, of course, but there's lots of wear in it still. And I have a few dresses that your mother or sister could probably use. Your mother can make them over into lots of things for all of you, and I'd be very happy to give them to you. Suppose before you leave I make up a big bundle and then you and Johnny can take it over to your mother right away . . ." Her voice trailed off as she saw Boyd's puzzled **expression.**

"But I have plenty of clothes, thank you," he said. "And I don't think my mother knows how to sew very well, and anyway I guess we buy about everything we need. Thank you very much, though."

"We don't have time to carry that old stuff around, Mother," Johnny said. "We got to play tanks with the kids today."

Word Power

expression (iks presh´ ən) _n._ a look on the face that shows feeling

Mrs. Wilson lifted the plate of gingerbread off the table as Boyd was about to take another piece. "There are many little boys like you, Boyd, who would be very grateful for the clothes someone was kind enough to give them."

"Boyd will take them if you want him to, Mother," Johnny said.

"I didn't mean to make you mad, Mrs. Wilson," Boyd said.

"Don't think I'm angry, Boyd. I'm just disappointed in you, that's all. Now let's not say anything more about it."

She began clearing the plates off the table, and Johnny took Boyd's hand and pulled him to the door. "'Bye, Mother," Johnny said. Boyd stood for a minute, staring at Mrs. Wilson's back.

"After you, my dear Alphonse," Johnny said, holding the door open.

"Is your mother still mad?" Mrs. Wilson heard Boyd ask in a low voice.

"I don't know," Johnny said. "She's screwy sometimes."

"So's mine," Boyd said. He hesitated.

"After *you*, my dear Alphonse."

Literary Element

Character Reread the sentence highlighted in blue. What does this action tell you about how Mrs. Wilson is feeling? Check the correct response.

- [ ] She is happy because Boyd ate so well.
- [ ] She is angry because Boyd refused to take the clothes.
- [ ] She is tired and ready for the boys to leave.

Reading Skill

Predict Reread the text highlighted in green. Do you think Mrs. Wilson will learn anything from her lunch with Boyd and Johnny? Why?

_____
_____
_____
_____
_____
_____

Respond to Literature

After you, My Dear Alphonse

A Comprehension Check

Answer the following questions in the spaces provided.

1. What does Boyd's father do for a living? _____

_____

2. Why doesn't Boyd want to take home the clothes Mrs. Wilson wants to

give him? _____

_____

B Reading Skills

Answer the following questions in the spaces provided.

1. **Evaluate** Boyd and Johnny use the phrase *After you, my dear Alphonse*
throughout the story. Do you think this phrase adds humor to the story?

Why? _____

_____

2. **Evaluate** How well does the author show that Mrs. Wilson is set in her way

of thinking? Why do you think so? _____

_____

_____

3. **Predict** Do you think that Mrs. Wilson's beliefs about African American

people will ever change? Explain. _____

_____

_____

C Word Power

Complete each sentence below, using one of the words in the box.

hesitated	defeated	restrained	impulse
	transformed	expression	

1. After their team lost, the _____ players were quiet in the locker room.

2. As time went by, the caterpillars _____ into butterflies.

3. The girl barely _____ her excitement at winning the contest.

4. The woman decided on an _____ to cut her long hair very short.

5. I could tell by his _____ that the boy was angry.

6. All of us _____ before we went through the door of the spooky house.

D Literary Element: Character

Read the passage below from "After You, My Dear Alphonse." As you read, think about what the sentences tell you about the characters. Then answer the questions that follow.

> Mrs. Wilson lifted the plate of gingerbread off the table as Boyd was about to take another piece.[1] "There are many little boys like you, Boyd, who would be very grateful for the clothes someone was kind enough to give them."[2]
>
> "Boyd will take them if you want him to, Mother," Johnny said.[3]
>
> "I didn't mean to make you mad, Mrs. Wilson," Boyd said.[4]

1. Read sentences 1 and 2. Why is Mrs. Wilson being rude to Boyd? What do you learn about her from sentences 1 and 2?

_____

_____

_____

_____

_____

2. In sentences 3 and 4, how do the two boys try to stop Mrs. Wilson from being angry? What does this tell you about their characters?

_____

_____

_____

_____

E A Conversation

Imagine that you are Boyd. You are telling your mother about your visit to Johnny's house. Write a conversation that you and your mother might have.

Mother: Did you have fun today with Johnny, Boyd?

Boyd: Yes, we played _____

_____

Mother: What was Mrs. Wilson like?

Boyd: She was _____ She asked me

_____

_____

She offered to give me some old clothes, but _____

_____

Mother: Would you like to play at Johnny's house again?

Boyd: _____

_____

Assessment

Fill in the circle next to each correct answer.

1. When Mrs. Wilson asks Boyd about his mother, he reacts with
   - ○ A. anger.
   - ○ B. amusement.
   - ○ C. surprise.
   - ○ D. fear.

2. What will Johnny and Boyd do when they finish eating lunch?
   - ○ A. clear plates off the table
   - ○ B. collect more kindling wood
   - ○ C. play tanks with some kids
   - ○ D. take clothes to Boyd's house

3. What clue shows that Mrs. Wilson is angry?
   - ○ A. She mentions that Johnny fusses about eating.
   - ○ B. She wants to pat Boyd on the head.
   - ○ C. She corrects the way Johnny speaks.
   - ○ D. She doesn't let Boyd have more gingerbread.

4. Which sentence from the story **best** helps you predict that Mrs. Wilson may have negative opinions of African Americans?
   - ○ A. "Johnny, that's not very polite to either your friend or your mother."
   - ○ B. As she turned to show Boyd where to sit, she saw that he was a Negro boy.
   - ○ C. Mrs. Wilson caught Boyd's glass of milk.
   - ○ D. "Is your mother still mad?" Mrs. Wilson heard Boyd ask in a low voice.

5. If you had a sudden desire to do something, you would
   - ○ A. have an impulse.
   - ○ B. be defeated.
   - ○ C. have an expression.
   - ○ D. be restrained.

Wrap-up

Compare and Contrast

Character is an important literary element in "La Bamba" and "After You, My Dear Alphonse." In "La Bamba," the main character Manuel has a performance in the school talent show. In "After You, My Dear Alphonse," one main character, Mrs. Wilson, meets a boy and expresses her beliefs about African Americans. Think about these two characters. Think about what they do and say and how they feel.

Complete the chart below. In the column labeled **Alike at the Beginning,** tell how Manuel and Mrs. Wilson are alike at the beginning of the stories. In the column labeled **Different at the End,** tell how Manuel and Mrs. Wilson are different at the end of the stories.

Alike at the Beginning	Different at the End
Both characters want to impress other people.	Manuel comes to understand why people respond to him the way they do.

Short Story

How is a short story organized?

Now that you have read a few short stories, let's stop for a moment to take a closer look at how a short story is put together.

A short story always has a **beginning, middle,** and **end.**

Short stories also include a **conflict.** A conflict is a struggle between characters or a struggle between a character and nature or another outside force.

What's the Plan?

Within the three parts of the story, there are five stages:

Exposition: The story is set up. Characters and places are introduced.
Rising Action: Conflicts or problems happen in the story.
Climax: The turning point in the story. This is the point of greatest interest or excitement.
Falling Action: The events following the climax.
Resolution: How things turn out.

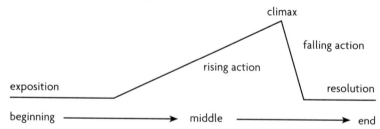

As you read the next four short stories, try to find the five stages in each story. In the text, mark the places where each stage happens.

Understanding the parts of a story can help you become a better reader.

How Do I Read Short Stories?

Focus on key **literary elements** and **reading skills** to get the most out of reading the short stories in this unit. Here are two key literary elements and two key reading skills that you will practice in this unit.

Key Literary Elements

• Setting

The **setting** is the time and place in which a story takes place. Knowing the setting helps you understand a story. It connects you to other things you may know about that time and that place. Setting can also include the customs, values, and beliefs of a place or time. A story that takes place in a village in Russia in the 1800s would be very different from a story that takes place in the United States today.

• Conflict

A **conflict** is a struggle between two opposing forces in a story. There are two types of conflict: external and internal. An **external conflict** occurs when a character has a conflict with another character or an outside force, like nature. An **internal conflict** is a struggle within the mind of a character.

Key Reading Skills

• Infer

Authors do not always directly state what they want you to get out of a story. Instead, they give clues and interesting details to suggest certain things. Combine those clues and details with what you already know to **infer,** or figure out, what is not stated directly. When you infer you are making an educated guess about what is happening in the story.

• Paraphrase

When you **paraphrase** part or all of a story, you are putting it into your own words. Paraphrasing helps you understand what you have read. When you use your own words to restate what you have read, you understand the author's meaning better.

Get Ready to Read!

Meet Walter Dean Myers

Walter Dean Myers was born in 1937. He has written more than thirty books for young people. His goal is to provide good literature about African American children. "I feel the need to show them the possibilities that exist for them that were never revealed to me as a youngster."

"The Game" is from the book *Fast Sam, Cool Clyde, and Stuff*, which was first published in 1988.

What You Know

Have you ever had to do something under pressure? How did you handle it?

Reason to Read

Read "The Game" to find out how a basketball player and his teammates deal with pressure.

Background Info

A basketball game is played between two teams of five players. The five best players, the starters, play most of the game. When these players need to rest, there are other players on the team who are ready to take their place. A basketball game is divided into four 12-minute quarters. The object of the game is to score points by throwing a basketball through a raised hoop. The two teams play against each other, trying to score points and to keep the other team from scoring points. The team with the most points at the end of the game wins.

Word Power

underneath (un´dər nēth´) *adv.* down below; p. 66
The road continued *underneath* the bridge.

palms (päms) *n.* the underside of hands between fingers and wrists; p. 66
In the cold room, I rubbed my *palms* together to warm my hands.

defensive (di fen´siv) *adj.* ready to guard or protect; p. 67
In soccer, the goalkeeper is a *defensive* player who tries to keep the other team from scoring.

controlled (kən trōld´) *v.* had power over; p. 67
The police *controlled* the crowd at the outdoor concert.

ridiculous (ri dik´yə ləs) *adj.* funny; foolish; p. 70
The *ridiculous* tricks of the clown made everyone laugh.

Answer the following questions, using one of the new words above.
Write your answers in the spaces provided.

1. Which word goes with "the underside of your hands"? _____

2. Which word goes with "took charge"? _____

3. Which word goes with "silly"?_____

4. Which word goes with "down below"? _____

5. Which word goes with "to protect"? _____

Adapted from

the Game

Walter Dean Myers

Literary Element

Setting Reread the highlighted sentence and the rest of the paragraph. Where are the characters at the beginning of the story? What are they getting ready for?

_____

_____

_____

_____

_____

_____

Did You Know?
A *basketball court* is 84 feet long and 50 feet wide. The hoop is 10 feet above the court.

We had practiced and practiced until it ran out of our ears. Every guy on the team knew every play. We were ready. It meant the championship. Everybody was there. I never saw so many people at the center at one time. We had never seen the other team play but Sam said that he knew some of the players and that they were good. Mr. Reese told us to go out and play as hard as we could every moment we were on the floor. We all shook hands in the locker room and then went out. Mostly we tried to ignore them warming up at the other end of the court but we couldn't help but look a few times.

They were doing exactly what we were doing, just shooting a few lay-ups and waiting for the game to begin. They got the first tap and started passing the ball around. I mean they really started passing the ball around faster than anything I had ever seen. Zip! Zip! Zip! Two points! I didn't even know how they could see the ball, let alone get it inside to their big man. We brought the ball down and one of their players stole the ball from Sam. We got back on defense but they weren't in a hurry. The same old thing. Zip! Zip! Zip! Two points! They could pass the ball better than anybody I ever saw. Then we brought the ball down again and Chalky missed a jump shot. He missed the backboard, the rim, everything. One of their players caught the ball and then brought it down and a few seconds later the score was 6-0. We couldn't even get close enough to foul them. Chalky brought the ball down again, passed to Sam cutting across the lane, and Sam walked. They brought the ball down and it was 8-0.

They were really enjoying the game. You could see. Every time they scored they'd slap hands and carry on. Also, they had some cheerleaders. They had about five girls with little pink skirts on and white sweaters cheering for them.

Clyde brought the ball down this time, passed into our center, a guy named Leon, and Leon turned and missed a hook. They got the rebound and came down, and Chalky missed a steal and fouled his man. That's when Mr. Reese called time out.

"Okay, now, just trade basket for basket. They make a basket, you take your time and you make a basket—don't rush it." Mr. Reese looked at his starting five. "Okay, now, every once in a while take a look over at me and I'll let you know when I want you to make your move. If I put my hands palm down, just keep on playing cool. If I stand up and put my hands up like this"—he put both hands up near his face—"that means to make your move. You understand that?"

Literary Element

Setting Reread the passage highlighted in blue. What is the setting in this part of the story? Underline the details in the passage that help you picture the setting.

_____

_____

Reading Skill

Paraphrase Reread the sentence highlighted in green and the rest of the paragraph. What does Mr. Reese tell his players? Choose the sentence that **best** paraphrases this paragraph. Check the correct response.

☐ Mr. Reese tells his players to rush the game and play fast.

☐ Mr. Reese tells his players to watch his hand signals to know what to do.

☐ Mr. Reese tells his players to ignore him and keep scoring points.

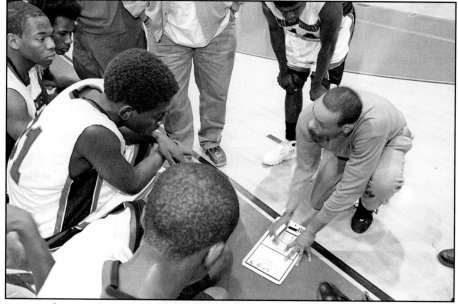

Do you play any sports? What's your favorite sport?

English Coach

In a basketball game, a *break* occurs when a player gets a ball and makes a fast move down the court. What is another meaning of the word *break*?

_____

_____

_____

Reading Skill

Infer Reread the highlighted passage. How do you think the narrator feels about being put into the game? How do you know?

_____

_____

_____

_____

Everyone said that they understood. When the ball was back in play Chalky and Sam and Leon started setting picks from the outside and then passed to Clyde for our first two points. They got the ball and started passing around again. Zip! Zip! Zip! But this time we were just waiting for that pass **underneath** and they knew it. Finally they tried a shot from outside and Chalky slapped it away to Sam on the break. We came down real quick and scored. On the way back Mr. Reese showed everybody that his **palms** were down. To keep playing cool.

They missed their next shot and fouled Chalky. They called time out and, much to my surprise, Mr. Reese put me in. My heart was beating so fast I thought I was going to have a heart attack. Chalky missed the foul shot but Leon slapped the ball out to Clyde, who passed it to me. I dribbled about two steps and threw it back to Leon in the bucket. Then I didn't know what to do so I did what Mr. Reese always told us.

Word Power

underneath (un´dər nēth´) *adv.* down below
palms (päms) *n.* the underside of hands between fingers and wrists

If you don't know what to do then, just move around. I started moving toward the corner and then I ran quickly toward the basket. I saw Sam coming at me from the other direction and it was a play. Two guards cutting past and one of the **defensive** men gets picked off. I ran as close as I could to Sam, and his man got picked off. Chalky threw the ball into him for an easy lay-up. They came down and missed again but one of their men got the rebound in. We brought the ball down and Sam went along the base line for a jump shot, but their center knocked the ball away. I caught it just before it went out at the corner and shot the ball. I remembered what Mr. Reese had said about following your shot in, and I started in after the ball but it went right in. It didn't touch the rim or anything. Swish!

One of their players said to watch out for 17—that was me. I played about two minutes more, then Mr. Reese took me out. But I had scored another basket on a lay-up. We were coming back. Chalky and Sam were knocking away just about anything their guards were throwing up, and Leon, Chalky, and Sam **controlled** the defensive backboard. Mr. Reese brought in Cap, and Cap got fouled two times in two plays. At the end of the half, when I thought we were doing pretty well, I found out the score was 36–29. They were beating us by seven points. Mr. Reese didn't seem worried, though.

"Okay, everybody, stay cool. No sweat. Just keep it nice and easy."

We came out in the second half and played it pretty cool. Once we came within one point, but then they ran it up to five again. We kept looking over to Mr. Reese to see what he wanted us to do and he would just put his palms down and nod his head for us to play cool.

Connect to the Text

Reread the passage in the purple box. Have you ever followed someone's advice? How did the advice help or not help you?

_____

_____

_____

Comprehension Check

Reread the passage in the green box. What is the score at the end of the first half? Which team is winning?

_____

_____

_____

Word Power

defensive (di fen´siv) *adj.* ready to guard or protect
controlled (kən trōld´) *v.* had power over

Have you ever been to a sporting event? What event would you like to see live? Why?

Reading Skill

Infer Reread the highlighted passage. Why do you think Mr. Reese puts the narrator and Turk in the game? Do you think it has anything to do with the way they played before?

_____

_____

_____

_____

_____

_____

Comprehension Check

Reread the boxed passage. Why is the narrator surprised when Turk makes the lay-up? Check the correct response.

☐ Turk only shoots free throws.

☐ Turk is not in the game.

☐ Turk usually misses lay-ups.

There were six minutes to go when Mr. Reese put me and another guy named Turk in. Now I didn't really understand why he did this because I know I'm not the best basketball player in the world, although I'm not bad, and I know Turk is worse than me. Also, he took out both Sam and Chalky, our two best players.

We were still losing by five points, too. And they weren't doing anything wrong. There was a jump ball between Leon and their center when all of a sudden this big cheer goes up and everybody looks over to the sidelines. Well, there was Gloria, BB, Maria, Sharon, Kitty, and about four other girls, all dressed in white blouses and black skirts and with big T's on their blouses and they were our cheerleaders. One of their players said something stupid about them but I liked them. They looked real good to me.

We controlled the jump and Turk drove right down the lane and made a lay-up. Turk actually made the lay-up. Turk once missed seven lay-ups in a row in practice and no one was even guarding him. But this one he made. Then one of their men double-dribbled and we got the ball and I passed it to Leon, who threw up a shot and got fouled. The shot went in and when he made the foul shot it added up to a three-point play. They started down court and Mr. Reese started yelling for us to give a foul.

"Foul him! Foul him!" he yelled from the sidelines.

Now this was something we had worked on in practice and that Mr. Reese had told us would only work once in a game. Anybody who plays basketball knows that if you're fouled while shooting the ball you get two foul shots and if you're fouled while not shooting the ball you only get one. So when a guy knows you're going to foul him he'll try to get off a quick shot. At least that's what we hoped. When their guard came across the mid-court line, I ran at him as if I was going to foul him. Then, just as I was going to touch him, I stopped short and moved around him without touching him. Sure enough, he threw the ball wildly toward the basket. It went over the base line and it was our ball. Mr. Reese took me out and Turk and put Sam and Chalky back in. And the game was just about over.

We hadn't realized it but in the two minutes that me and Turk played the score had been tied. When Sam and Chalky came back in they outscored the other team by four points in the last four minutes. We were the champs. We got the first-place trophies and we were so happy we were all jumping around and slapping each other on the back. Gloria and the other girls were just as happy as we were, and when we found that we had an extra trophy we gave it to them. Then Mr. Reese took us all in the locker room and shook each guy's hand and then went out and invited the parents and the girls in. He made a little speech about how he was proud of us and all, and not just because we won tonight but because we had worked so hard to win. When he finished everybody started clapping for us and, as usual, I started boo-hooing. But it wasn't so bad this time because Leon started boo-hooing worse than me.

Comprehension Check

Reread the boxed passage. Why does the narrator pretend that he is going to foul the other player? What does he think will happen?

_____

_____

_____

_____

_____

_____

English Coach

Boo-hooing means "crying loudly." When you say *boo* and *hoo* together, they almost sound like crying. There are other words that imitate sounds too. Which word imitates a sound: *buzz* or *jump*?

_____

Connect to the Text

How do you think it feels to win a championship game?

_____

_____

_____

_____

_____

_____

_____

_____

You know what high is? We felt so good the next couple of days that it was **ridiculous.** We'd see someone in the street and we'd just walk up and be happy. Really.

Word Power

ridiculous (ri dik´ yə ləs) *adj.* funny; foolish

Respond to Literature

the Game

A Comprehension Check

Answer the following questions in the spaces provided.

1. What are the players supposed to do when Mr. Reese puts his hands palm down?

    _____

    _____

2. How does a group of girls help Mr. Reese's team?

    _____

    _____

B Reading Skills

Complete the following activities in the spaces provided.

1. **Paraphrase** Paraphrase Mr. Reese's advice: "Okay, everybody, stay cool. No sweat. Just keep it nice and easy." _____

    _____

2. **Infer** Why does Mr. Reese say that pretending to try to foul someone would work only once in a game? _____

    _____

3. **Infer** Why does the team give the other championship trophy to the cheerleaders? _____

    _____

C Word Power

Complete each sentence below, using one of the words in the box.

underneath	palms	defensive
controlled	ridiculous	

1. The security guard _____ the excited group of students.

2. The words to the silly poem were _____.

3. The dog buried the bone _____ the dirt.

4. Some children were holding ladybugs in their _____.

5. The _____ bear was the mother of the cubs.

Circle the word that best completes each sentence.

6. The woman's **(defensive, ridiculous)** hat had real bananas on it.

7. Snakes slither **(underneath, controlled)** rocks to get out of the hot sun.

8. The theater owner **(defensive, controlled)** the number of tickets sold.

9. The baby put both of his **(palms, underneath)** on the cake.

10. Covering your eyes against blowing sand is a **(ridiculous, defensive)** action.

D Literary Element: Setting

Read the passages below from "The Game." As you read, think about the setting and how it affects the story. Then answer the questions that follow.

> Then we brought the ball down again and Chalky missed a jump shot.[1] He missed the backboard, the rim, everything.[2] One of their players caught the ball and then brought it down and a few seconds later the score was 6-0.[3] We couldn't even get close enough to foul them.[4] Chalky brought the ball down again, passed to Sam cutting across the lane, and Sam walked.[5]
>
> Then Mr. Reese took us all in the locker room and shook each guy's hand and then went out and invited the parents and the girls in.[6] He made a little speech about how he was proud of us and all, and not just because we won tonight but because we had worked so hard to win.[7]

1. What details in sentences 1–5 tell you that this story takes place on a basketball court?

_____

_____

2. Where does the scene described in sentences 6 and 7 take place?

_____

_____

_____

E School Announcement

Imagine that you are writing an announcement to tell your school about the championship basketball game. Complete the sentences by writing details about the game.

Attention basketball fans! Listen up!

Last night our basketball team _____

_____

At first the other team _____

_____

But our guys _____

_____

Our girls _____

_____

At the end of the game, everyone gathered in the locker

room and _____

_____

Some of the players were _____

We are the champions!

Assessment

Fill in the circle next to each correct answer.

1. Why does Mr. Reese's team try not to look at the other team while warming up?
   - ○ A. Mr. Reese tells his players to ignore the other team.
   - ○ B. They need to spend the time talking to each other.
   - ○ C. They are afraid the other team will yell at them.
   - ○ D. They are nervous about how good the other team is.

2. Why does Mr. Reese want his players to pretend to foul a player on the other team?
   - ○ A. He hopes the player will throw the ball wildly.
   - ○ B. He wants an opportunity to rest his best players.
   - ○ C. It was a way for him to call time out.
   - ○ D. The other players are pushing one of his players.

3. Where does Mr. Reese make his speech congratulating the team on their victory?
   - ○ A. on the benches
   - ○ B. on the basketball court
   - ○ C. on the sidelines
   - ○ D. in the locker room

4. Which sentence **best** paraphrases the story's ending?
   - ○ A. The narrator starts boo-hooing by himself.
   - ○ B. The cheerleaders give Mr. Reese a speech.
   - ○ C. The champs celebrate with their families and friends.
   - ○ D. The team goes out to dinner to celebrate their win.

5. Which word means "funny" or "foolish"?
   - ○ A. controlled
   - ○ B. ridiculous
   - ○ C. defensive
   - ○ D. underneath

Reading Skill

Paraphrase Reread the highlighted sentences. The author is describing the storm. Which sentence **best** paraphrases the author's description? Check the correct response.

☐ The wind was quiet and the snow was melting.

☐ The wind was loud and it blew the snow around.

☐ The wind was gentle and it didn't move the snow.

Background Info

A *blizzard* is a very heavy snowstorm with high winds.

At first Zlateh didn't seem to mind the change in weather. She, too, was twelve years old and knew what winter meant. But when her legs sank deeper and deeper into the snow, she began to turn her head and look at Aaron in wonderment. Her mild eyes seemed to ask, "Why are we out in such a storm?" Aaron hoped that a peasant would come along with his cart, but no one passed by.

The snow grew thicker, falling to the ground in large, whirling flakes. Beneath it Aaron's boots touched the softness of a plowed field. He realized that he was no longer on the road. He had gone **astray.** He could no longer figure out which was east or west, which way was the village, the town. The wind whistled, howled, whirled the snow about in eddies. It looked as if white imps were playing tag on the fields. A white dust rose above the ground. Zlateh stopped. She could walk no longer. Stubbornly she anchored her cleft hooves in the earth and bleated as if pleading to be taken home. Icicles hung from her white beard, and her horns were glazed with frost.

Aaron did not want to admit the danger, but he knew just the same that if they did not find shelter they would freeze to death. This was no ordinary storm. It was a mighty blizzard. The snowfall had reached his knees. His hands were numb, and he could no longer feel his toes. He choked when he breathed. His nose felt like wood, and he rubbed it with snow. Zlateh's bleating began to sound like crying. Those humans in whom she had so much confidence had dragged her into a trap. Aaron began to pray to God for himself and for the innocent animal.

Word Power
astray (ə strāʹ) *adv.* off the right path

Have you ever been on a long journey? Where did you go? What did you do?

Suddenly he made out the shape of a hill. He wondered what it could be. Who had piled snow into such a huge heap? He moved toward it, dragging Zlateh after him. When he came near it, he realized that it was a large haystack which the snow had blanketed.

Aaron realized immediately that they were saved. With great effort he dug his way through the snow. He was a village boy and knew what to do. When he reached the hay, he hollowed out a nest for himself and the goat. No matter how cold it may be outside, in the hay it is always warm. And hay was food for Zlateh. The moment she smelled it she became contented and began to eat. Outside, the snow continued to fall. It quickly covered the passageway Aaron had dug. But a boy and an animal need to breathe, and there was hardly any air in their hideout. Aaron bored a kind of a window through the hay and snow and carefully kept the passage clear.

Comprehension Check

Reread the boxed paragraph. What does Aaron do to get the goat and himself out of the storm?

_____

_____

_____

_____

_____

English Coach

On the contrary means "quite the opposite." It is used to show how two situations or events are different. Write another pair of sentences using this phrase.

_____

_____

_____

_____

Literary Element

Setting Reread the highlighted passage. How is the setting inside the haystack different from the setting outside?

_____

_____

_____

_____

_____

Zlateh, having eaten her fill, sat down on her hind legs and seemed to have regained her confidence in man. Aaron ate his two slices of bread and cheese, but after the difficult journey he was still hungry. He looked at Zlateh and noticed her udders were full. He lay down next to her, placing himself so that when he milked her he could squirt the milk into his mouth. It was rich and sweet. Zlateh was not **accustomed** to being milked that way, but she did not resist. On the contrary, she seemed eager to reward Aaron for bringing her to a shelter whose very walls, floor, and ceiling were made of food.

Through the window Aaron could catch a glimpse of the **chaos** outside. The wind carried before it whole drifts of snow. It was completely dark, and he did not know whether night had already come or whether it was the darkness of the storm. Thank God that in the hay it was not cold. The dried hay, grass, and field flowers **exuded** the warmth of the summer sun. Zlateh ate frequently; she nibbled from above, below, from the left and right. Her body gave forth an animal warmth, and Aaron cuddled up to her. He had always loved Zlateh, but now she was like a sister. He was alone, cut off from his family, and wanted to talk. He began to talk to Zlateh. "Zlateh, what do you think about what has happened to us?" he asked.

"Maaaa," Zlateh answered.

"If we hadn't found this stack of hay, we would both be frozen stiff by now," Aaron said.

"Maaaa," was the goat's reply.

"If the snow keeps on falling like this, we may have to stay here for days," Aaron explained.

"Maaaa," Zlateh bleated.

Word Power

accustomed (ə kus´ təmd) *adj.* used to; in the habit of

chaos (kā´ os) *n.* extreme confusion

exuded (ig zōōd´ id) *v.* gave off; released

"What does 'maaaa' mean?" Aaron asked. "You'd better speak up clearly."

"Maaaa, maaaa," Zlateh tried.

"Well, let it be 'maaaa' then," Aaron said patiently. "You can't speak, but I know you understand. I need you and you need me. Isn't that right?"

"Maaaa."

Aaron became sleepy. He made a pillow out of some hay, leaned his head on it, and dozed off. Zlateh, too, fell asleep.

When Aaron opened his eyes, he didn't know whether it was morning or night. The snow had blocked up his window. He tried to clear it, but when he had bored through to the length of his arm, he still hadn't reached the outside. Luckily he had his stick with him and was able to break through to the open air. It was still dark outside. The snow continued to fall and the wind wailed, first with one voice and then with many. Sometimes it had the sound of devilish laughter. Zlateh, too, awoke, and when Aaron greeted her, she answered, "Maaaa." Yes, Zlateh's language **consisted** of only one word, but it meant many things. Now she was saying, "We must accept all that God gives us—heat, cold, hunger, satisfaction, light, and darkness."

Aaron had awakened hungry. He had eaten up his food, but Zlateh had plenty of milk.

For three days Aaron and Zlateh stayed in the haystack. Aaron had always loved Zlateh, but in these three days he loved her more and more. She fed him with her milk and helped him keep warm. She comforted him with her patience. He told her many stories, and she always cocked her ears and listened. When he patted her, she licked his hand and his face. Then she said, "Maaaa," and he knew it meant, I love you, too.

Word Power

consisted (kən sist′ id) *v.* made up (of); contained

Reading Skill

Infer Reread the first highlighted passage. Why do Aaron and Zlateh need each other? Check all the responses that apply.
- [ ] to keep each other awake
- [ ] for food and warmth
- [ ] for friendship and conversation

Reading Skill

Paraphrase Reread the second highlighted passage. Which sentence **best** paraphrases what Zlateh seems to mean? Check the correct response.
- [ ] Everything in life is bad.
- [ ] Only accept the good things in life.
- [ ] Accept all the good and bad things in life.

What would you have done in a situation similar to Aaron's?

Literary Element

Setting Reread the highlighted passage. Which words would you use to describe the setting after the storm? Check the **best** response.
☐ powerful and strong
☐ angry and forceful
☐ calm and peaceful

The snow fell for three days, though after the first day it was not as thick and the wind quieted down. Sometimes Aaron felt that there could never have been a summer, that the snow had always fallen, ever since he could remember. He, Aaron, never had a father or mother or sisters. He was a snow child, born of the snow, and so was Zlateh. It was so quiet in the hay that his ears rang in the stillness. Aaron and Zlateh slept all night and a good part of the day. As for Aaron's dreams, they were all about warm weather. He dreamed of green fields, trees covered with blossoms, clear brooks, and singing birds. By the third night the snow had stopped, but Aaron did not dare to find his way home in the darkness. The sky became clear and the moon shone, casting silvery nets on the snow. Aaron dug his way out and looked at the world. It was all white, quiet, dreaming dreams of heavenly splendor. The stars were large and close. The moon swam in the sky as in a sea.

On the morning of the fourth day Aaron heard the ringing of sleigh bells. The haystack was not far from the road. The peasant who drove the sleigh pointed out the way to him—not to the town and Feivel the butcher, but home to the village. Aaron had decided in the haystack that he would never part with Zlateh.

Aaron's family and their neighbors had searched for the boy and the goat but had found no trace of them during the storm. They feared they were lost. Aaron's mother and sisters cried for him; his father remained silent and gloomy. Suddenly one of the neighbors came running to their house with the news that Aaron and Zlateh were coming up the road.

There was great joy in the family. Aaron told them how he had found the stack of hay and how Zlateh had fed him with her milk. Aaron's sisters kissed and hugged Zlateh and gave her a special treat of chopped carrots and potato peels, which Zlateh gobbled up hungrily.

Nobody ever again thought of selling Zlateh, and now that the cold weather had finally set in, the villagers needed the services of Reuven the furrier once more. When Hanukkah came, Aaron's mother was able to fry pancakes every evening, and Zlateh got her portion, too. Even though Zlateh had her own pen, she often came to the kitchen, knocking on the door with her horns to **indicate** that she was ready to visit, and she was always admitted. In the evening Aaron, Miriam, and Anna played dreidel. Zlateh sat near the stove watching the children and the flickering of the Hanukkah candles.

Did You Know?

Similar to a spinning top, the *dreidel* (drād´ əl) is a toy used in a game played during Hanukkah.

······················

Comprehension Check

Reread the boxed paragraph. How does Aaron find the way home? What does he decide to do?

_____

_____

_____

_____

Reading Skill

Infer Reread the highlighted paragraph. What do the sisters' actions tell you about how they feel about Zlateh?

_____

_____

_____

_____

Word Power

indicate (in´ di kāt´) *v.* to show; to be a sign of

85

Once in a while Aaron would ask her, "Zlateh, do you remember the three days we spent together?"

And Zlateh would scratch her neck with a horn, shake her white bearded head, and come out with the single sound which expressed all her thoughts, and all her love.

Connect to the Text

If you could talk to an animal, what would you say?

_____

_____

_____

_____

_____

Respond to Literature

Zlateh the Goat

A Comprehension Check

Answer the following questions in the spaces provided.

1. How does Zlateh save Aaron during the snowstorm?

_____

_____

2. What does the family decide to do with Zlateh?

_____

_____

B Reading Skills

Answer the following questions in the spaces provided.

1. **Infer** What can you infer about Aaron from the way he makes a safe place in the haystack and keeps a passage open to get air?

_____

_____

_____

2. **Paraphrase** In your own words, tell how Aaron found shelter for Zlateh and himself.

_____

_____

_____

C Word Power

Complete each sentence below, using one of the words in the box.

penetrated	astray	accustomed	chaos
exuded	consisted	indicate	

1. The science project _____ of a short report and a small display of rocks.

2. Ken wandered _____ and then could not find his way back to the campsite.

3. The flowers _____ a sweet scent throughout the neighborhood.

4. The drill _____ the wood and made a deep hole.

5. Alberto raised his hand to _____ that he had a question.

6. My bossy brother is _____ to getting his way all the time.

7. The fire alarm created confusion and _____ among the students.

D Literary Element: Setting

Read the two passages below from "Zlateh the Goat." As you read, think about how the description of the setting helps you visualize where the characters are and what they are doing. Then answer the questions that follow.

He realized that he was no longer on the road.[1] He had gone astray.[2] He could no longer figure out which was east or west, which way was the village, the town.[3] The wind whistled, howled, whirled the snow about in eddies.[4] It looked as if white imps were playing tag on the fields.[5]

Even though Zlateh had her own pen, she often came to the kitchen, knocking on the door with her horns to indicate that she was ready to visit, and she was always admitted.[6] In the evening Aaron, Miriam, and Anna played dreidel.[7] Zlateh sat near the stove watching the children and the flickering of the Hanukkah candles.[8]

1. How do sentences 1–5 show that Aaron and Zlateh are in a bad storm that could be dangerous?

_____

_____

_____

2. Sentences 6–8 describe the setting of Aaron's home. What do the details in this setting tell you about Aaron's family life?

_____

_____

_____

E "Missing" Poster

Imagine that you have been asked to create a "Missing" poster—for Aaron and Zlateh. Draw the characters, using details from the text to help you. Complete the written description of the missing characters, and identify the person people should contact if anyone sees them.

Description: Aaron is _____

Zlateh is _____

Information: They were last seen _____

_____

Aaron's family needed money to _____

They are probably lost because of the _____

_____

Aaron is smart; he and Zlateh _____

_____

Contact: If you have seen Aaron and Zlateh, please
contact _____

Assessment

Fill in the circle next to each correct answer.

1. How do Aaron and his family feel about Zlateh?
   - ○ A. They are very fond of her.
   - ○ B. They feel she is too much trouble.
   - ○ C. They see her as just another farm animal.
   - ○ D. At first, they think she is too old to keep.

2. What is one thing Aaron believes Zlateh means when she says, "Maaaa"?
   - ○ A. Give me some more carrots.
   - ○ B. Don't take me to the butcher.
   - ○ C. Let's play in the snow.
   - ○ D. I love you, too.

3. Which sentence **best** paraphrases this sentence: "The dried hay, grass, and field flowers exuded the warmth of the summer sun"?
   - ○ A. The hay, grass, and flowers grew in the sun.
   - ○ B. The hay, grass, and flowers were warm and dry.
   - ○ C. The hay, grass, and flowers were cold and had no heat.
   - ○ D. The hay, grass, and flowers smelled like the sun.

4. Where and when does the story take place?
   - ○ A. in a village, during the spring
   - ○ B. in a city, close to Hanukkah
   - ○ C. on a village road, close to Hanukkah
   - ○ D. on a farm, during harvest

5. Which of the following words means "extreme confusion"?
   - ○ A. chaos
   - ○ B. astray
   - ○ C. penetrated
   - ○ D. accustomed

Get Ready to Read!

Meet Sandra Cisneros

Sandra Cisneros (sēs nā´ rōs) grew up in a family with six brothers. She learned to speak up to get noticed. "You had to be fast and you had to be funny—you had to be a *storyteller*," she says. Her family moved often between Chicago and Mexico City. She often writes about Latino children living in the United States.

Sandra Cisneros was born in 1954. This story was first published in 1991.

What You Know

What were you like five years ago? What did you like to do? What made you laugh?

Reason to Read

Read to find out how a young girl feels at different ages.

Background Info

You remember things through your senses. When you hear a song, you might think of the time you last heard it. The song can remind you of what you were thinking and feeling at that time. A smell can bring you back to a time and place too. Smells may help you remember things even more than seeing or hearing them.

Word Power

rattling (rat´ ling) *v.* making repeated quick, sharp sounds; p. 95
The tree branch was *rattling* against the windows of the house.

raggedy (rag´ id ē) *adj.* torn or worn-out; p. 95
She put on *raggedy* pants with holes in them.

schoolyard (skool´ yärd´) *n.* an area around a school used for play; p. 96
Some boys were playing ball at one end of the *schoolyard*.

waterfall (wô´ tər fôl´) *n.* a stream of water that falls from a high place; p. 96
The *waterfall* flowed down the sides of the rocks.

nonsense (non´ sens) *n.* foolish actions or words; p. 96
Putting mittens on kittens is *nonsense*.

**Answer the following questions using one of the new words above.
Write your answers in the spaces provided.**

1. Which word goes with "a place to play with friends"? _____

2. Which word goes with "being silly and eating peas with a knife"? _____

3. Which word goes with "shaking rocks in a can"? _____

4. Which word goes with "a coat that is worn out"? _____

5. Which word goes with "water flowing over an edge"? _____

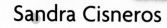

ELEVEN

Sandra Cisneros

Connect to the Text

Reread the boxed paragraph. The narrator says that sometimes you feel much younger than your real age. Tell about a time when you felt like you were younger than your real age.

_____

_____

_____

_____

_____

_____

What they don't understand about birthdays and what they never tell you is that when you're eleven, you're also ten, and nine, and eight, and seven, and six, and five, and four, and three, and two, and one. And when you wake up on your eleventh birthday you expect to feel eleven, but you don't. You open your eyes and everything's just like yesterday, only it's today. And you don't feel eleven at all. You feel like you're still ten. And you are—underneath the year that makes you eleven.

Like some days you might say something stupid, and that's the part of you that's still ten. Or maybe some days you might need to sit on your mama's lap because you're scared, and that's the part of you that's five. And maybe one day when you're all grown up maybe you will need to cry like if you're three, and that's okay. That's what I tell Mama when she's sad and needs to cry. Maybe she's feeling three.

Because the way you grow old is kind of like an onion or like the rings inside a tree trunk or like my little wooden dolls that fit one inside the other, each year inside the next one. That's how being eleven years old is.

You don't feel eleven. Not right away. It takes a few days, weeks even, sometimes even months before you say Eleven when they ask you. And you don't feel smart eleven, not until you're almost twelve. That's the way it is.

Only today I wish I didn't have only eleven years **rattling** inside me like pennies in a tin Band-Aid box. Today I wish I was one hundred and two instead of eleven because if I was one hundred and two I'd have known what to say when Mrs. Price put the red sweater on my desk. I would've known how to tell her it wasn't mine instead of just sitting there with that look on my face and nothing coming out of my mouth.

"Whose is this?" Mrs. Price says, and she holds the red sweater up in the air for all the class to see. "Whose? It's been sitting in the coatroom for a month."

"Not mine," says everybody. "Not me." "It has to belong to somebody," Mrs. Price keeps saying, but nobody can remember. It's an ugly sweater with red plastic buttons and a collar and sleeves all stretched out like you could use it for a jump rope. It's maybe a thousand years old and even if it belonged to me I wouldn't say so.

Maybe because I'm skinny, maybe because she doesn't like me, that stupid Sylvia Saldívar says, "I think it belongs to Rachel." An ugly sweater like that, all **raggedy** and old, but Mrs. Price believes her. Mrs. Price takes the sweater and puts it right on my desk, but when I open my mouth nothing comes out.

"That's not, I don't, you're not … Not mine," I finally say in a little voice that was maybe me when I was four.

"Of course it's yours," Mrs. Price says. "I remember you wearing it once." Because she's older and the teacher, she's right and I'm not.

English Coach

Band-Aid is the name of a company that makes bandages. Why do you think the company uses *Band* and *Aid* in its name?

_____

_____

_____

_____

Reading Skill

Infer Reread the highlighted sentences. How does the narrator feel about the possibility of the sweater belonging to her? Check the correct response.

☐ proud
☐ ashamed
☐ neutral

What phrases show how the narrator feels?

_____

_____

_____

_____

Word Power

rattling (rat´ ling) *v.* making repeated quick, sharp sounds
raggedy (rag´ id ē) *adj.* torn or worn-out

Literary Element

Conflict Reread the first highlighted passage. Describe the conflict Rachel is struggling with. How do you know it's an internal conflict?

_____

_____

_____

_____

_____

_____

Literary Element

Conflict Reread the second highlighted passage. What is the conflict between Rachel and Mrs. Price? How do you know it's an external conflict?

_____

_____

_____

_____

_____

_____

_____

Not mine, not mine, not mine, but Mrs. Price is already turning to page thirty-two, and math problem number four. I don't know why but all of a sudden I'm feeling sick inside, like the part of me that's three wants to come out of my eyes, only I squeeze them shut tight and bite down on my teeth real hard and try to remember today I am eleven, eleven. Mama is making a cake for me for tonight, and when Papa comes home everybody will sing Happy birthday, happy birthday to you.

But when the sick feeling goes away and I open my eyes, the red sweater's still sitting there like a big red mountain. I move the red sweater to the corner of my desk with my ruler. I move my pencil and books and eraser as far from it as possible. I even move my chair a little to the right. Not mine, not mine, not mine.

In my head I'm thinking how long till lunchtime, how long till I can take the red sweater and throw it over the **schoolyard** fence, or leave it hanging on a parking meter, or bunch it up into a little ball and toss it in the alley. Except when math period ends Mrs. Price says loud and in front of everybody, "Now, Rachel, that's enough," because she sees I've shoved the red sweater to the tippy-tip corner of my desk and it's hanging all over the edge like a **waterfall,** but I don't care.

"Rachel," Mrs. Price says. She says it like she's getting mad. "You put that sweater on right now and no more **nonsense.**"

"But it's not—"

"Now!" Mrs. Price says.

Word Power

schoolyard (skool´ yärd´) *n.* an area around a school used for play
waterfall (wô´ tər fôl´) *n.* a stream of water that falls from a high place
nonsense (non´ sens) *n.* foolish actions or words

This is when I wish I wasn't eleven, because all the years inside of me—ten, nine, eight, seven, six, five, four, three, two, and one—are pushing at the back of my eyes when I put one arm through one sleeve of the sweater that smells like cottage cheese, and then the other arm through the other and stand there with my arms apart like if the sweater hurts me and it does, all itchy and full of germs that aren't even mine.

That's when everything I've been holding in since this morning, since when Mrs. Price put the sweater on my desk, finally lets go, and all of a sudden I'm crying in front of everybody. I wish I was invisible but I'm not. I'm eleven and it's my birthday today and I'm crying like I'm three in front of everybody. I put my head down on the desk and bury my face in my stupid clown-sweater arms. My face all hot and spit coming out of my mouth because I can't stop the little animal noises from coming out of me, until there aren't any more tears left in my eyes, and it's just my body shaking like when you have the hiccups, and my whole head hurts like when you drink milk too fast.

Carmela Bertagna, c. 1880. John Singer Sargent. Oil on canvas, 23½ x 19½ in. Columbus Museum of Art, OH. Bequest of Frederick W. Schumacher.

How is the girl in this painting like the narrator of "Eleven"?

Reading Skill

Paraphrase Reread the highlighted paragraph. In your own words, tell what is happening to Rachel at this point in the story.

_____

_____

_____

_____

_____

_____

Reading Skill

Infer Reread the highlighted paragraph. Why does Rachel think that the worst part of the day is when Phyllis admits to owning the sweater? Check the correct response.

☐ Mrs. Price acts like nothing is wrong.

☐ Rachel is unhappy that the sweater belongs to Phyllis.

☐ Rachel wants to keep the sweater.

But the worst part is right before the bell rings for lunch. That stupid Phyllis Lopez, who is even dumber than Sylvia Saldívar, says she remembers the red sweater is hers! I take it off right away and give it to her, only Mrs. Price pretends like everything's okay.

Today I'm eleven. There's a cake Mama's making for tonight, and when Papa comes home from work we'll eat it. There'll be candles and presents and everybody will sing Happy birthday, happy birthday to you, Rachel, only it's too late.

I'm eleven today. I'm eleven, ten, nine, eight, seven, six, five, four, three, two, and one, but I wish I was one hundred and two. I wish I was anything but eleven, because I want today to be far away already, far away like a runaway balloon, like a tiny o in the sky, so tiny-tiny you have to close your eyes to see it.

Respond to Literature

ELEVEN

A Comprehension Check

Answer the following questions in the spaces provided.

1. Why does Mrs. Price think the red sweater belongs to Rachel?

    _____

    _____

2. What does Mrs. Price make Rachel do with the sweater?

    _____

    _____

B Reading Skills

Complete the following activities in the spaces provided.

1. **Paraphrase** Paraphrase Rachel's description of the sweater.

    _____

    _____

2. **Infer** What does Rachel mean when she says that her birthday party at home will be too late?

    _____

    _____

C Word Power

Complete each sentence below, using one of the words in the box.

rattling	raggedy	schoolyard
waterfall	nonsense	

1. The farmer put _____ clothes on the scarecrow.

2. I rode in a boat at the bottom of a _____.

3. She told a silly story filled with _____ words.

4. Yesterday my gym class ran around the _____.

5. The cook was _____ pots and pans in the kitchen.

Circle the word that best completes each sentence.

6. They swam under the **(waterfall, schoolyard)**.

7. The monkey was **(raggedy, rattling)** the cage door.

8. Stop your **(nonsense, raggedy)** and do not laugh.

9. We played soccer in the **(waterfall, schoolyard)**.

10. The old doll wore a **(rattling, raggedy)** dress.

D Literary Element: Conflict

Read the passage below from "Eleven." As you read, think about the conflict the sentences describe. Then answer the questions that follow.

> And when you wake up on your eleventh birthday you expect to feel eleven, but you don't. You open your eyes and everything's just like yesterday, only it's today. And you don't feel eleven at all. You feel like you're still ten. And you are—underneath the year that makes you eleven.
>
> Like some days you might say something stupid, and that's the part of you that's still ten. Or maybe some days you might need to sit on your mama's lap because you're scared, and that's the part of you that's five. And maybe one day when you're all grown up maybe you will need to cry like if you're three, and that's okay.

1. What conflict is Rachel struggling with in this passage?

_____

_____

_____

_____

_____

2. Is her conflict internal or external? How do you know?

_____

_____

_____

_____

E Instant Message

Imagine you could send an instant message to Rachel. You want to write a message that will make her feel better on her birthday. Tell her your thoughts about her bad day. Share a personal experience that is similar to hers. Send her happy birthday wishes.

■ □ ✖

Hi Rachel,

I read about your bad day, and I think _____

_____

_____

Once I had a bad day. I _____

_____

_____

I hope you and your family _____

_____

_____

Your friend,

_____

| | Send |

Assessment

Fill in the circle next to each correct answer.

1. What does Rachel compare getting older to?
   - ○ A. a parking meter
   - ○ B. pennies in a Band-Aid box
   - ○ C. rings in a tree trunk
   - ○ D. a balloon in the sky

2. Rachel's external conflict is with
   - ○ A. herself.
   - ○ B. her school.
   - ○ C. her teacher.
   - ○ D. her best friends.

3. Rachel speaks to Mrs. Price in a little voice because she is
   - ○ A. excited.
   - ○ B. upset.
   - ○ C. sick.
   - ○ D. bored.

4. Which statement **best** paraphrases how Rachel feels about turning eleven?
   - ○ She doesn't feel any older than she did the day before.
   - ○ She feels much older than eleven.
   - ○ She is very happy because she feels older and smarter.
   - ○ She is excited about her party.

5. Which of the following words means "worn-out"?
   - ○ A. rattling
   - ○ B. nonsense
   - ○ C. schoolyard
   - ○ D. raggedy

Get Ready to Read!

The All-American SLURP

Meet Lensey Namioka

Lensey Namioka (len′ še nä mē′ ō kä) and her family moved several times within China before coming to the United States. Because they moved so often, Namioka and her sisters had few toys. So for fun, they made up stories. Namioka became quite good at telling stories. Many of her books are adventure stories that take place in Japan and China hundreds of years ago.

Lensey Namioka was born in 1929. This story was first published in 1987.

What You Know

Have you ever moved to a new city or a new school? What things surprised you? What things did you like?

Reason to Read

Read "The All-American Slurp" to find out how a family learns about a new culture.

Background Info

Immigrants are people who come to live in a country where they were not born. Sometimes they leave their cultures and customs behind and learn the ways of their new country. Sometimes they keep their traditions while learning new customs. Many thousands of people immigrate to the United States every year. During one year in the 1990s, about 54,000 people from China came to the United States.

Word Power

disgraced (dis grāsd´) *v.* brought shame to; p. 106
The pupil *disgraced* his family by cheating.

disinfect (dis´in fekt´) *v.* to rid a surface of germs; p. 106
Some soaps can help you *disinfect* your hands.

mortified (môr´ tə fīd´) *adj.* very embarrassed; p. 108
The singer was *mortified* when she forgot the words to the song.

acquainted (əkwān´ tid) *adj.* having knowledge of something; familiar with; p. 109
Football players must be *acquainted* with the rules of the game.

promotion (prə mō shən) *n.* to move up in position or grade; p. 113
The writer received a *promotion* at work.

systematic (sis´ tə mat´ ik) *adj.* well organized; doing things a certain way; p. 113
He had a *systematic* way of doing homework.

etiquette (et´ i ket´) *n.* rules of proper social behavior; p. 114
We studied a book on dining *etiquette*.

consumption (kən sump´ shən) *n.* the act of eating, drinking, or using; p. 115
We packed food for *consumption* on our picnic.

**Answer the following questions, using one of the new words above.
Write your answers in the spaces provided.**

1. Which word goes with "doing things in an orderly fashion"? _____

2. Which word goes with "eating something"? _____

3. Which word goes with "good table manners"? _____

4. Which word goes with "having known an old neighbor"? _____

5. Which word goes with "being very embarrassed"? _____

6. Which word goes with "getting a better job"? _____

7. Which word goes with "brought shame to yourself"? _____

8. Which word goes with "cleaning a sink to get rid of germs"? _____

The All-American SLURP

Lensey Namioka

Background Info

Emigrated means "moved from one country or place to settle in another." People who emigrate are called emigrants.

Reading Skill

Paraphrase When you paraphrase, you retell something in your own words. Paraphrase the highlighted paragraph.

_____

_____

_____

_____

_____

The first time our family was invited out to dinner in America, we **disgraced** ourselves while eating celery. We had emigrated to this country from China, and during our early days here, we had a hard time with American table manners.

In China we never ate celery raw, or any other kind of vegetable raw. We always had to **disinfect** the vegetables in boiling water first. When we were presented with our first relish tray, the raw celery caught us unprepared.

We had been invited to dinner by our neighbors, the Gleasons. After arriving at the house, we shook hands with our hosts and packed ourselves into a sofa. As our family of four sat stiffly in a row, my younger brother and I stole glances at our parents for a clue as to what to do next.

Mrs. Gleason offered the relish tray to Mother. The tray looked pretty, with its tiny red radishes, curly sticks of carrots, and long, slender stalks of pale green celery. "Do try some of the celery, Mrs. Lin," she said. "It's from a local farmer, and it's sweet."

Word Power

disgraced (dis grāsd´) *v.* brought shame to
disinfect (dis´ in fekt´) *v.* to rid a surface of germs

Mother picked up one of the green stalks, and Father followed suit. Then I picked up a stalk, and my brother did too. So there we sat, each with a stalk of celery in our right hand.

Mrs. Gleason kept smiling. "Would you like to try some of the dip, Mrs. Lin? It's my own recipe: sour cream and onion flakes, with a dash of Tabasco sauce."

Most Chinese don't care for dairy products, and in those days I wasn't even ready to drink fresh milk. Sour cream sounded perfectly revolting. Our family shook our heads in unison.

Mrs. Gleason went off with the relish tray to the other guests, and we carefully watched to see what they did. Everyone seemed to eat the raw vegetables quite happily.

Mother took a bite of her celery. Crunch. "It's not bad!" she whispered.

Father took a bite of his celery. Crunch. "Yes, it is good," he said, looking surprised.

I took a bite, and then my brother. Crunch, crunch. It was more than good; it was delicious. Raw celery has a slight sparkle, a zingy taste that you don't get in cooked celery. When Mrs. Gleason came around with the relish tray, we each took another stalk of celery, except my brother. He took two.

There was only one problem: long strings ran through the length of the stalk, and they got caught in my teeth. When I help my mother in the kitchen, I always pull the strings out before slicing celery.

I pulled the strings out of my stalk. *Z-z-zip, z-z-zip.* My brother followed suit.

Z-z-zip, z-z-zip, z-z-zip. To my left, my parents were taking care of their own stalks.

Z-z-zip, z-z-zip, z-z-zip.

English Coach

The author uses the word *crunch* to help the reader hear the sound of someone chewing a stalk of raw celery. As you read the rest of the page, underline other examples of words that imitate sounds.

Reading Skill

Infer Reread the highlighted paragraph. What do you suppose the neighbors are thinking when they see the Lins pull the strings out of their celery?

_____

_____

_____

_____

English Coach

To _nurse_ food means to eat it slowly so it will last longer. If you nursed a piece of pie, would you take big or little bites of it?

_____

_____

_____

_____

Suddenly I realized that there was dead silence except for our zipping. Looking up, I saw that the eyes of everyone in the room were on our family. Mr. and Mrs. Gleason, their daughter Meg, who was my friend, and their neighbors the Badels—they were all staring at us as we busily pulled the strings of our celery.

That wasn't the end of it. Mrs. Gleason announced that dinner was served and invited us to the dining table. It was lavishly covered with platters of food, but we couldn't see any chairs around the table. So we helpfully carried over some dining chairs and sat down. All the other guests just stood there.

Mrs. Gleason bent down and whispered to us, "This is a buffet dinner. You help yourselves to some food and eat it in the living room."

Our family beat a retreat back to the sofa as if chased by enemy soldiers. For the rest of the evening, too **mortified** to go back to the dining table, I nursed a bit of potato salad on my plate.

Next day Meg and I got on the school bus together. I wasn't sure how she would feel about me after the spectacle our family made at the party. But she was just the same as usual, and the only reference she made to the party was, "Hope you and your folks got enough to eat last night. You certainly didn't take very much. Mom never tries to figure out how much food to prepare. She just puts everything on the table and hopes for the best."

Word Power
mortified (môr´ tə fīd´) _adj._ very embarrassed

I began to relax. The Gleasons' dinner party wasn't so different from a Chinese meal after all. My mother also puts everything on the table and hopes for the best.

Meg was the first friend I had made after we came to America. I eventually got **acquainted** with a few other kids in school, but Meg was still the only real friend I had. My brother didn't have any problems making friends. He spent all his time with some boys who were teaching him baseball, and in no time he could speak English much faster than I could—not better, but faster.

I worried more about making mistakes, and I spoke carefully, making sure I could say everything right before opening my mouth. At least I had a better accent than my parents, who never really got rid of their Chinese accent, even years later. My parents had both studied English in school before coming to America, but what they had studied was mostly written English, not spoken.

Father's approach to English was a scientific one. Since Chinese verbs have no tense, he was fascinated by the way English verbs changed form according to whether they were in the present, past imperfect, perfect, pluperfect, future, or future perfect tense. He was always making diagrams of verbs and their inflections, and he looked for opportunities to show off his mastery of the pluperfect and future perfect tenses, his two favorites. "I shall have finished my project by Monday," he would say smugly.

Mother's approach was to memorize lists of polite phrases that would cover all possible social situations. She was constantly muttering things like "I'm fine, thank you. And you?" Once she accidentally stepped on someone's foot, and hurriedly blurted, "Oh, that's quite all right!" Embarrassed by her slip, she resolved to do better next time. So when someone stepped on her foot, she cried, "You're welcome!"

Connect to the Text

Reread the boxed sentence. How do you make new friends?

_____

_____

_____

_____

Reading Skill

Infer Reread the highlighted sentences. What words describe what the father is like? Check the responses that describe the father.

☐ careful
☐ messy
☐ organized

Word Power

acquainted (ə kwān′ tid) *adj.* having knowledge of something; familiar with

My Workspace

Literary Element

Conflict Reread the highlighted passage. Describe the conflict the narrator is having with her mother. How do you know it's an external conflict?

_____

_____

_____

_____

_____

_____

Connect to the Text

Reread the boxed sentence. The narrator tells about how kids at school stared at her clothes. Think about a time when you felt like you weren't wearing the "right" clothes. How did it make you feel?

_____

_____

_____

_____

_____

_____

In our own different ways, we made progress in learning English. But I had another worry, and that was my appearance. My brother didn't have to worry, since Mother bought him blue jeans for school, and he dressed like all the other boys. But she insisted that girls had to wear skirts. By the time she saw that Meg and the other girls were wearing jeans, it was too late. My school clothes were bought already, and we didn't have money left to buy new outfits for me. We had too many other things to buy first, like furniture, pots, and pans.

The first time I visited Meg's house, she took me upstairs to her room, and I wound up trying on her clothes. We were pretty much the same size, since Meg was shorter and thinner than average. Maybe that's how we became friends in the first place. Wearing Meg's jeans and T-shirt, I looked at myself in the mirror. I could almost pass for an American—from the back, anyway.

At least the kids in school wouldn't stop and stare at me in the hallways, which was what they did when they saw me in my white blouse and navy blue skirt that went a couple of inches below the knees.

When Meg came to my house, I invited her to try on my Chinese dresses, the ones with a high collar and slits up the sides. Meg's eyes were bright as she looked at herself in the mirror. She struck several sultry poses, and we nearly fell over laughing.

The dinner party at the Gleasons' didn't stop my growing friendship with Meg. Things were getting better for me in other ways too. Mother finally bought me some jeans at the end of the month, when Father got his paycheck. She wasn't in any hurry about buying them at first, until I worked on her. This is what I did. Since we didn't have a car in those days, I often ran down to the neighborhood store to pick up things for her. The groceries cost less at a big supermarket, but the closest one was many blocks away. One day, when she ran out of flour, I offered to borrow a bike from our neighbor's son and buy a ten-pound bag of flour at the big supermarket. I mounted the boy's bike and waved to Mother. "I'll be back in five minutes!"

Before I started pedaling, I heard her voice behind me. "You can't go out in public like that! People can see all the way up to your thighs!"

Did You Know?
A *pot-sticker* is a pouch of dough stuffed with meat and vegetables and then steamed or fried.

"I'm sorry," I said innocently. "I thought you were in a hurry to get the flour." For dinner we were going to have pot-stickers (fried Chinese dumplings), and we needed a lot of flour.

"Couldn't you borrow a girl's bicycle?" complained Mother. "That way your skirt won't be pushed up."

"There aren't too many of those around," I said. "Almost all the girls wear jeans while riding a bike, so they don't see any point buying a girl's bike."

We didn't eat pot-stickers that evening, and Mother was thoughtful. Next day we took the bus downtown and she bought me a pair of jeans. In the same week, my brother made the baseball team of his junior high school, Father started taking driving lessons, and Mother discovered rummage sales. We soon got all the furniture we needed, plus a dart board and a 1,000-piece jigsaw puzzle (fourteen hours later, we discovered that it was a 999-piece jigsaw puzzle). There was hope that the Lins might become a normal American family after all.

Reading Skill

Paraphrase Paraphrase the highlighted paragraph. Explain how everyone in the family is starting to fit in.

_____

_____

_____

_____

_____

_____

_____

STOP Stop here for **Break Time** on the next page.

Break Time

The Lin family is facing a **problem** with language. What does each family member do about it? First read the problem that is in the box on the left below. Then in the boxes on the right, write each family member's **solution** to the problem.

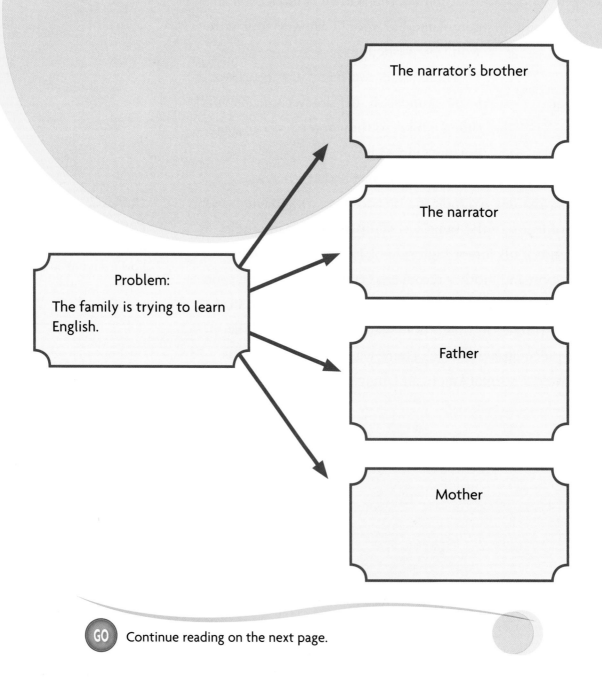

The narrator's brother

The narrator

Problem:

The family is trying to learn English.

Father

Mother

GO   Continue reading on the next page.

Then came our dinner at the Lakeview restaurant.

The Lakeview was an expensive restaurant, one of those places where a head-waiter dressed in tails conducted you to your seat, and the only light came from candles and flaming desserts. In one corner of the room a lady harpist played tinkling melodies.

Father wanted to celebrate, because he had just been promoted. He worked for an electronics company, and after his English started improving, his superiors decided to appoint him to a position more suited to his training. The **promotion** not only brought a higher salary but was also a tremendous boost to his pride.

Up to then we had eaten only in Chinese restaurants. Although my brother and I were becoming fond of hamburgers, my parents didn't care much for western food, other than chow mein.

But this was a special occasion, and Father asked his coworkers to recommend a really elegant restaurant. So there we were at the Lakeview, stumbling after the head-waiter in the murky dining room.

At our table we were handed our menus, and they were so big that to read mine I almost had to stand up again. But why bother? It was mostly in French, anyway.

Father, being an engineer, was always **systematic.** He took out a pocket French dictionary. "They told me that most of the items would be in French, so I came prepared." He even had a pocket flashlight, the size of a marking pen. While Mother held the flashlight over the menu, he looked up the items that were in French.

"*Pâté en croûte,*" he muttered. "Let's see . . . *pâté* is paste . . . *croûte* is crust . . . hmm . . . a paste in crust."

The waiter stood looking patient. I squirmed and died at least fifty times.

At long last Father gave up. "Why don't we just order four complete dinners at random?" he suggested.

Background Info

The head waiter is wearing a fancy suit with a jacket that has a long back. The back is split into two parts. This kind of suit is called *tails* because the parts look like the tail of a bird.

Comprehension Check

Reread the boxed paragraph. How does Father decide what to order?

_____

_____

_____

Word Power

promotion (prə mō shən) *n.* to move up in position or grade

systematic (sis ´ tə mat ´ ik) *adj.* well-organized; doing things a certain way

"Isn't that risky?" asked Mother. "The French eat some rather peculiar things, I've heard."

"A Chinese can eat anything a Frenchman can eat," Father declared.

The soup arrived in a plate. How do you get soup up from a plate? I glanced at the other diners, but the ones at the nearby tables were not on their soup course, while the more distant ones were invisible in the darkness.

Comprehension Check

Reread the boxed paragraph. How did the Lin family learn to eat soup from a plate?

_____

_____

_____

_____

Fortunately my parents had studied books on western **etiquette** before they came to America. "Tilt your plate," whispered my mother. "It's easier to spoon the soup up that way."

She was right. Tilting the plate did the trick. But the etiquette book didn't say anything about what you did after the soup reached your lips. As any respectable Chinese knows, the correct way to eat your soup is to slurp. This helps to cool the liquid and prevent you from burning your lips. It also shows your appreciation.

Have you ever eaten in a fancy restaurant? What was it like? Were you afraid to make mistakes?

_____

_____

Word Power

etiquette (et´ i ket´) *n.* rules of proper social behavior

114

We showed our appreciation. *Shloop*, went my father. *Shloop*, went my mother. *Shloop, shloop*, went my brother, who was the hungriest.

The lady harpist stopped playing to take a rest. And in the silence, our family's **consumption** of soup suddenly seemed unnaturally loud. You know how it sounds on a rocky beach when the tide goes out and the water drains from all those little pools? They go *shloop, shloop, shloop*. That was the Lin family, eating soup.

At the next table a waiter was pouring wine. When a large shloop reached him, he froze. The bottle continued to pour, and red wine flooded the tabletop and into the lap of a customer. Even the customer didn't notice anything at first, being also hypnotized by the *shloop, shloop, shloop*.

It was too much. "I need to go to the toilet," I mumbled, jumping to my feet. A waiter, sensing my urgency, quickly directed me to the ladies' room.

I splashed cold water on my burning face, and as I dried myself with a paper towel, I stared into the mirror. In this perfumed ladies' room, with its pink-and-silver wallpaper and marbled sinks, I looked completely out of place. What was I doing here? What was our family doing in the Lakeview restaurant? In America?

The door to the ladies' room opened. A woman came in and glanced curiously at me. I retreated into one of the toilet cubicles and latched the door.

Time passed—maybe half an hour, maybe an hour. Then I heard the door open again, and my mother's voice. "Are you in there? You're not sick, are you?"

Reading Skill

Infer Reread the paragraph highlighted in green. The narrator describes the sounds her family makes when they eat soup. How do the other people in the restaurant react? Check the responses which might explain how the other people felt.

☐ shocked
☐ excited
☐ embarrassed

Literary Element

Conflict Reread the paragraph highlighted in blue. What internal conflict is the narrator struggling with as she stares into the mirror?

_____

_____

_____

_____

Word Power

consumption (kən sump´ shən) *n.* the act of eating, drinking, or using

115

There was real concern in her voice. A girl can't leave her family just because they slurp their soup. Besides, the toilet cubicle had a few drawbacks as a permanent residence. "I'm all right," I said, undoing the latch.

Mother didn't tell me how the rest of the dinner went, and I didn't want to know. In the weeks following, I managed to push the whole thing into the back of my mind, where it jumped out at me only a few times a day. Even now, I turn hot all over when I think of the Lakeview restaurant.

> But by the time we had been in this country for three months, our family was definitely making progress toward becoming Americanized. I remember my parents' first PTA meeting. Father wore a neat suit and tie, and Mother put on her first pair of high heels. She stumbled only once. They met my homeroom teacher and beamed as she told them that I would make honor roll soon at the rate I was going. Of course Chinese etiquette forced Father to say that I was a very stupid girl and Mother to protest that the teacher was showing favoritism toward me. But I could tell they were both very proud.

The day came when my parents announced that they wanted to give a dinner party. We had invited Chinese friends to eat with us before, but this dinner was going to be different. In addition to a Chinese-American family, we were going to invite the Gleasons.

"Gee, I can hardly wait to have dinner at your house," Meg said to me. "I just *love* Chinese food."

That was a relief. Mother was a good cook, but I wasn't sure if people who ate sour cream would also eat chicken gizzards stewed in soy sauce.

> Mother decided not to take a chance with chicken gizzards. Since we had western guests, she set the table with large dinner plates, which we never used in Chinese meals. In fact we didn't use individual plates at all, but picked up food from the platters in the middle of the table and brought it directly to our rice bowls.

Comprehension Check

Reread the first boxed paragraph. Underline one detail in the boxed paragraph that shows how the Lin family is beginning to fit into life in America.

Comprehension Check

Reread the second boxed paragraph. What does the Lin family usually eat their food from? Check the correct response.
- ☐ individual plates
- ☐ rice bowls
- ☐ large platters

Following the practice of Chinese-American restaurants, Mother also placed large serving spoons on the platters.

The dinner started well. Mrs. Gleason exclaimed at the beautifully arranged dishes of food: the colorful candied fruit in the sweet-and-sour pork dish, the noodle-thin shreds of chicken meat stir-fried with tiny peas, and the glistening pink prawns in a ginger sauce.

At first I was too busy enjoying my food to notice how the guests were doing. But soon I remembered my duties. Sometimes guests were too polite to help themselves and you had to serve them with more food.

Did You Know?
Prawns are large shrimp.
....

I glanced at Meg, to see if she needed more food, and my eyes nearly popped out at the sight of her plate. It was piled with food: the sweet-and-sour meat pushed right against the chicken shreds, and the chicken sauce ran into the prawns. She had been taking food from a second dish before she finished eating her helping from the first!

Horrified, I turned to look at Mrs. Gleason. She was dumping rice out of her bowl and putting it on her dinner plate. Then she ladled prawns and gravy on top of the rice and mixed everything together, the way you mix sand, gravel, and cement to make concrete.

I couldn't bear to look any longer, and I turned to Mr. Gleason. He was chasing a pea around his plate. Several times he got it to the edge, but when he tried to pick it up with his chopsticks, it rolled back toward the center of the plate again. Finally he put down his chopsticks and picked up the pea with his fingers. He really did! A grown man!

Reading Skill

Paraphrase Paraphrase the highlighted paragraph. Tell why Meg's plate looked the way it did.

_____

_____

_____

_____

_____

_____

_____

English Coach

Mr. Gleason wasn't really chasing a pea around his plate. He was trying to pick up a pea with his chopsticks. Was Mr. Gleason having an easy time or a difficult time picking up the pea?

_____

_____

_____

117

All of us, our family and the Chinese guests, stopped eating to watch the activities of the Gleasons. I wanted to giggle. Then I caught my mother's eyes on me. She frowned and shook her head slightly, and I understood the message: the Gleasons were not used to Chinese ways, and they were just coping the best they could. For some reason I thought of celery strings.

When the main courses were finished, Mother brought out a platter of fruit. "I hope you weren't expecting a sweet dessert," she said. "Since the Chinese don't eat dessert, I didn't think to prepare any."

"Oh, I couldn't possibly eat dessert!" cried Mrs. Gleason. "I'm simply stuffed!"

Meg had different ideas. When the table was cleared, she announced that she and I were going for a walk. "I don't know about you, but I feel like dessert," she told me, when we were outside. "Come on, there's a Dairy Queen down the street. I could use a big chocolate milkshake!"

Although I didn't really want anything more to eat, I insisted on paying for the milkshakes. After all, I was still hostess.

Meg got her large chocolate milkshake and I had a small one. Even so, she was finishing hers while I was only half done. Toward the end she pulled hard on her straws and went *shloop, shloop*.

"Do you always slurp when you eat a milkshake?" I asked, before I could stop myself.

Meg grinned. "Sure. All Americans slurp."

Reading Skill

Infer Reread the highlighted paragraph. How do you suppose the narrator felt when Meg went *shloop, shloop*? Check the response that might explain how the narrator felt.

- ☐ upset
- ☐ disgusted
- ☐ surprised

Connect to the Text

Do you have a best friend? What types of things do you like to do together?

_____

_____

_____

Respond to Literature

The All-American SLURP

A Comprehension Check

Answer the following questions in the spaces provided.

1. What "mistakes" do the Lins make at the Gleasons' dinner party?

   _____

2. What happens to upset the narrator at the Lakeview restaurant?

   _____

3. What does Mr. Gleason do at the Lin's party that shocks the narrator?

   _____

B Reading Skills

Complete the following activities in the spaces provided.

1. **Paraphrase** The Lins finally start to fit into life in America. Paraphrase the narrator's description of what they do to fit in.

   _____

   _____

2. **Infer** What does the narrator learn from seeing the table manners of the Gleason family?_____

   _____

3. **Infer** At the end of the story, how do you think the narrator feels about living in America?_____

   _____

C Word Power

Complete each sentence below, using one of the words in the box.

disgraced	systematic	disinfect	etiquette
mortified	acquainted	consumption	promotion

1. Washing bottles in boiling water can _____ them.

2. Because very little rain fell, people limited their _____ of water.

3. I spilled juice on the carpet. I felt _____ when everyone laughed.

4. We found the wallet after a _____ search of the house.

5. Proper table _____ shows good manners.

6. After he got a _____, he earned more money.

7. The player _____ her team by cheating.

8. I am _____ with my neighbors.

D Literary Element: Conflict

Read the passage below from "The All-American Slurp." As you read, think about the conflict the sentences describe. Then answer the questions that follow.

But I had another worry, and that was my appearance. My brother didn't have to worry, since Mother bought him blue jeans for school, and he dressed like all the other boys. But she insisted that girls had to wear skirts. By the time she saw that Meg and the other girls were wearing jeans, it was too late.

1. In the passage the narrator is one of the opposing forces in this conflict. Who or what is the other force? Is this an example of an internal or external conflict?

_____

_____

_____

_____

_____

2. What is the conflict in this passage?

_____

_____

_____

_____

_____

E Postcard

Imagine you are the narrator in the story. You are writing a postcard to send to a cousin in China. Tell your cousin what surprises you about America. Explain what you like best about living in America.

Hello from America!

Some things that surprise me here are what Americans eat. They eat _____

_____

But Americans don't eat soup the way we do. I found out when we went out to dinner. We all _____

_____

Then we invited our American friends to dinner. They

_____

The thing I like best about living in America is wearing jeans. I have a good friend now. We went out for a milkshake. She

_____

_____

Love from your cousin, _____

To:
My Family

At:
My Home

Assessment

Fill in the circle next to each correct answer.

1. Which statement **best** paraphrases this sentence: "Our family beat a retreat back to the sofa as if chased by enemy soldiers."?
   - ○ A. We were being chased by enemy soldiers.
   - ○ B. Our family had to run away from the sofa.
   - ○ C. Our family quickly went to sit down on the sofa.
   - ○ D. Our family got up from the sofa.

2. Mrs. Gleason whispers to the Lins about the buffet because she
   - ○ A. does not want to embarrass the Lins.
   - ○ B. always speaks in a soft voice.
   - ○ C. wants the Lins to sit on the sofa.
   - ○ D. needs help carrying chairs.

3. What conflict does the narrator have with her mother?
   - ○ A. The narrator wants her mother to teach her how to cook.
   - ○ B. The narrator wants her mother to buy her jeans.
   - ○ C. Mrs. Lin does not want her daughter to be friends with Meg.
   - ○ D. Mrs. Lin wants her daughter to study harder.

4. What upsets the narrator at the restaurant?
   - ○ A. Her brother tells jokes.
   - ○ B. Her family arrives late.
   - ○ C. Her father yells at the waiter.
   - ○ D. Her family slurps soup.

5. The act of eating dinner is called
   - ○ A. promotion.
   - ○ B. mortified.
   - ○ C. consumption.
   - ○ D. acquainted.

Wrap-up

Compare and Contrast

Conflict is an important literary element in "Eleven" and "The All-American Slurp." Although the characters in these stories face very different situations, their conflicts share some similarities. Think about the conflicts that Rachel faces in "Eleven" and the conflicts that the Lin family (especially the narrator) faces in "The All-American Slurp." Think about how these conflicts affect how the characters feel and act.

Complete the Venn diagram below. In the outer parts of the circles, describe the different conflicts that the characters face. In the section where the circles overlap, tell how their conflicts are similar.

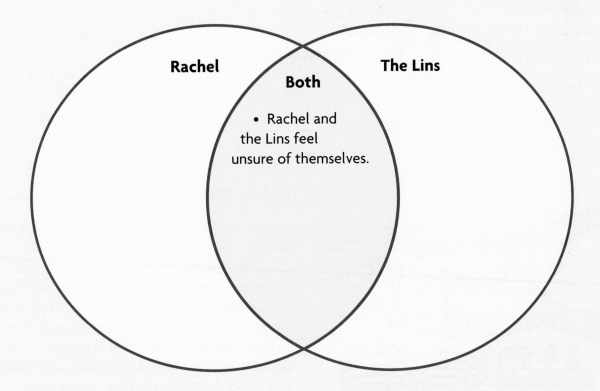

Rachel

Both

The Lins

• Rachel and the Lins feel unsure of themselves.

Drama

What's Drama?

Drama is all around you. Television shows—from daytime series to cartoons—are drama. Movies are drama. Skits and plays are drama. **Drama** is a story that is meant to be performed for an audience—on stage, in a movie or TV show, or on the radio.

What kinds of drama do you know? What kinds do you like? **Put a check next to the kinds of drama you have seen or heard before. Then describe your favorite kind on the lines that follow.**

_____television comedy
_____serious television story
_____made-for-TV movie
_____soap opera
_____movie at the theater
_____stage play
_____radio broadcast of a play or show

_____

_____

Why Read Drama?

People read drama to have fun and to learn about people. Drama can take you to new places, give you new experiences, and let you get to know about new ideas. Drama also lets you hear how people talk. Reading drama lets you imagine how the play ought to look on the stage or on the screen. Who should play that character? How would the characters move in this scene? Reading drama lets you stage the play in your mind.

How Do I Read Drama?

Focus on the key **literary element** and **reading skills** to get the most out of reading the drama in this unit. Here are one key literary element and two key reading skills that you will practice in this unit.

Key Literary Element

Dialogue

Dialogue is the words that characters say. A play is a story that is told almost entirely through dialogue. The audience learns about what is happening and how the characters think and feel through dialogue. Dialogue reveals the characters' personalities, gives information to the audience, and moves the story forward.

Key Reading Skills

• Visualize

When you **visualize,** you picture in your mind what you are reading. As you read, use the details and exact words to help you create mental pictures. Visualize the characters and events in your mind. For example, if a character is described as having a face full of gum, you would picture someone who is chewing a big wad of gum. Use your own experiences to help you understand as well as imagine the scene.

• Sequence

The order in which ideas or events take place is called the **sequence.** Many stories tell the events in the order in which they happen. The story begins at the beginning and ends at the end. As you read, look for clue words like *first, then, meanwhile, eventually*, and *later*. These words can help you figure out when things happen.

Get Ready to Read!

Charlie and the Chocolate Factory

Meet Roald Dahl

Roald Dahl was born in 1916. In World War II, he became a fighter pilot in the Royal Air Force. Later he married and had five children. He once said, "Had I not had children of my own, I would never have written books for children, nor would I have been capable of doing so."

Richard R. George adapted Dahl's popular book into a play for his sixth-grade class. The book has also been made into two feature films.

Roald Dahl died in 1990. The book *Charlie and the Chocolate Factory* was first published in 1964. The play was published in 1976.

What You Know

Have you ever imagined yourself in a chocolate factory? What might it be like?

Reason to Read

Read "Charlie and the Chocolate Factory" to find out what happens when a boy gets the chance to visit a chocolate factory.

Background Info

This play takes place in a chocolate factory. Chocolate is made from cacao (kə ka´ ō) beans, which are seeds that grow on the cacao tree. First, the seeds are picked and dried out. Then, they are taken to a chocolate factory, where they are cleaned, roasted, and taken out of their shells. Finally, the seeds are ground down and added to a liquid mixture of cocoa, butter, sugar, and milk to make the final product—chocolate.

Word Power

possession (pə zesh′ ən) *n.* a thing owned; p. 132
Terrell's favorite *possession* is his telescope.

extremely (iks trēm′ lē) *adv.* much more than usual; p. 134
All winter long, the weather has been *extremely* cold.

repulsive (ri pul′ siv) *adj.* causing dislike; disgusting; p. 135
Rotten food stinks and is *repulsive* to most people.

tremendous (tri men′ dəs) *adj.* wonderful; p. 141
We had a *tremendous* vacation in Grand Canyon National Park.

procession (prə sesh′ ən) *n.* a march; people or things moving forward
in an orderly way; p. 141
A *procession* of students walked across the stage.

proceedings (prə sē′ dingz) *n.* actions or events; p. 143
The *proceedings* taking place in the gym are noisy.

**Answer the following questions that contain the new words above.
Write your answers in the spaces provided.**

1. Which is *extremely* hot, boiling water or an ice cube? _____

2. Do most school *proceedings* take place during the week or on weekends?

   _____

3. Would a *tremendous* movie be boring or wonderful? _____

4. If a book is your *possession*, does it belong to you or a library? _____

5. Would a *procession* of ducks swim across a pond or stand at the edge?

   _____

6. Would a *repulsive* odor smell good or bad? _____

Adapted from

Charlie and the Chocolate Factory

Roald Dahl

English Coach

Sometimes you can tell what a character is like from his or her name. The word *gloop* probably came from *glop*, which is a mess of thick, sticky, sloppy food. Do you think Augustus Gloop will be a neat, clean boy, or a sloppy, messy boy?

_____

_____

_____

CHARACTERS
(in order of appearance)

NARRATOR

AUGUSTUS GLOOP

VIOLET BEAUREGARDE

VERUCA SALT

MIKE TEAVEE

MR. BUCKET

GRANDMA JOSEPHINE

GRANDPA GEORGE

GRANDMA GEORGINA

MRS. BUCKET

GRANDPA JOE

CHARLIE BUCKET

MRS. GLOOP

WILLY WONKA

MRS. TEAVEE

MR. SALT

MRS. SALT

MRS. BEAUREGARDE

MR. TEAVEE

SCENE 1

[NARRATOR enters in front of curtain.]

NARRATOR. Welcome to the tale of a delicious adventure in a wonderful land. You can tell it will be delicious—can't you smell it already? [*Sniffs.*] Oh, how I love that gorgeous smell! You've all heard of Kraft, Neilson, Hershey, Nestles, Wonka— what's that? You say, what's Wonka? You mean you don't know what Wonka is? Why...Wonka Chocolate...of course! I admit that Willy Wonka's Chocolate is fairly new but it's also the greatest chocolate ever invented. Why, Willy Wonka himself is the most amazing, the most fantastic, the most extraordinary chocolate maker the world has ever seen. He's invented things like...say...why...I'm not going to tell you what he's invented. You came to see yourself! So I'll let you do just that....Mr. Willy Wonka, in order to sell a lot of candy once again, was running a contest. Yes sir, that's right...a contest! He had secretly wrapped a Golden Ticket under ordinary wrapping paper in five ordinary candy bars. The five winners will tour Mr. Wonka's new factory and take home enough chocolate for the rest of their lives. Now *that*, my friends, is where our story begins. Four of the tickets have already been found. Oh, by the way, would you like to meet the four lucky people? All right, listen and watch carefully! I think they're here somewhere. [*Looks out over audience.*] Let's see...Augustus Gloop! Where are you, Augustus Gloop?

Did You Know?
Cocoa and chocolate are the two main products made from *cacao beans*.

· ·

Background Info

Some words in a play are printed in italics (or slanted type) and set inside brackets. Those words are the stage directions. They are instructions telling the actors when to enter or exit the stage and how to stand, move, or speak. They also describe what the scene looks like. So *Sniffs* tells the actor playing the narrator to sniff after asking, "...can't you smell it already?"

Connect to the Text

Reread the sentence in the purple box. Imagine that you found the winning ticket. What would be the best part of winning a contest like this?

_____

_____

_____

_____

_____

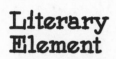

AUGUSTUS GLOOP. *[From somewhere in audience.]*
Chocolate . . . chocolate . . . chocolate . . .CHOCOLATE!!! I . . .
LOVE . . . CHOCOLATE! Ummmmmmmmmmmmmmmm . . . food
. . . FOOD! *[Smacks lips repeatedly.]* Ummmmmmmmmmmmm
mmmmmmmmmmmmm-mm . . . I MUST EAT ALL THE TIME . . .

NARRATOR. Well, uh, friends, that was our first Golden Ticket
finder—Augustus Gloop. Let's see now if the lucky girl who
found our second Golden Ticket is here. Oh Violet . . . Violet
Beauregarde?

VIOLET BEAUREGARDE. *[Chewing ferociously on gum,
waving arms excitedly, talking in a rapid and loud manner,
from somewhere in audience.]* I'm a gum-chewer normally,
but when I heard about these ticket things of Mr. Wonka's, I
laid off the gum and switched to candy bars in the hope of
striking it lucky. *Now*, of course, I'm right back on gum. I just
adore gum. I can't do without it. I munch it all day long
except for a few minutes at mealtimes when I take it out and
stick it behind my ear for safekeeping. To tell you the honest
truth, I simply wouldn't feel *comfortable* if I didn't have that
little wedge of gum to chew on every moment of the day. And
now, it may interest you to know that this piece of gum I'm
chewing right at this moment is one I've been working on for
over *three months solid*. That's a record, that is. It's my most
treasured **possession** now, this piece of gum is.

Literary Element

Dialogue Reread the
highlighted sentence and the
rest of Violet's lines. Dialogue
is the words characters say
in a play. What can you tell
about Violet from what she
says?

_____

_____

_____

_____

_____

Word Power

possession (pə zesh´ ən) *n.* a thing owned

132

NARRATOR.   Such a, uh, lucky, uh, girl. Isn't she, uh, uh, wonderful? The third Golden Ticket was found by another lucky girl. Her name is Veruca Salt. *Is Veruca here now?*

VERUCA SALT.   [*From somewhere in audience.*] As soon as I told my father that I simply had to have one of those Golden Tickets, he went out into the town and started buying up all the Wonka candy bars he could lay his hands on. He's in the peanut business, you see, and he's got about a hundred women working for him over at his joint, shelling peanuts for roasting and salting. That's what they do all day long, those women . . . they just sit there shelling peanuts. So he says to them, "Okay, girls," he says, "from now on, you can stop shelling peanuts and start shelling the wrappers off these crazy candy bars instead!" And they did. But three days went by, and we had no luck. Oh . . . it was terrible! I got more and more upset each day, and every time he came home I would scream at him, "Where's my Golden Ticket! I want my Golden Ticket!" And I would lie for hours on the floor, kicking and yelling in the most disturbing way. Then suddenly, on the evening of the fourth day, one of his workers yelled, "I've got it! A Golden Ticket!" And my father said, "Give it to me, quick!" And she did. And he rushed it home and gave it to me, and now . . . I'm all smiles . . . and we have a happy home . . . once again.

NARRATOR.   Thank you, Veruca. Isn't she a lovely girl? Now the fourth and last ticket was found by a boy named Mike Teavee. I wonder if Mike's got his ticket with him? *Where are you, Mike?*

Reading Skill

Visualize Reread the highlighted passage. As you read, picture what Veruca looks like in your mind. What do you think Veruca looks like when she acts this way?

_____

_____

_____

_____

_____

Literary Element

Dialogue Reread the highlighted paragraph. What can you tell about Charlie from the things he says here? Check the correct responses.

☐ Charlie loves Willy Wonka chocolate.

☐ Charlie does not think he can win the ticket.

☐ Charlie takes the bus to school.

Background Info

Plays are usually divided into acts. Acts are then divided into scenes. Each scene takes place in a specific place and time.

MR. BUCKET. [*Looking up from his paper.*] It makes you wonder if all children behave like this nowadays . . . like these brats we've been hearing about.

GRANDPA JOE. Of course not! Some do, of course. In fact, quite a lot of them do. But not all.

MRS. BUCKET. And now there's only one ticket left.

GRANDPA JOE. I bet I know somebody who'd like to find that Golden Ticket. How about it, Charlie? You love chocolate more than anyone I ever saw!

CHARLIE. Yes, I sure would, Grandpa Joe! You know . . . it just about makes me faint when I have to pass Mr. Wonka's Chocolate Factory every day as I go to school. The smell of that wonderful chocolate makes me so dreamy that I often fall asleep and bump into Mr. Wonka's fence. But I guess I should realize that dreams don't come true. Just imagine! Me imagining that I could win the fifth Golden Ticket. Why, it's . . . it's . . . it's pure imagination.

GRANDPA JOE. Well my boy, it may be pure imagination, but I've heard tell that what you imagine sometimes comes true.

CHARLIE. Gee, you really think so, Grandpa Joe? Gee . . . I wonder. . . .

[*End of Scene 2.*]

 Stop here for **Break Time** on the next page.

Break Time

When you **visualize,** you picture in your mind what is described by the words in a story. So far you've read dialogue from the four Golden Ticket winners. In the picture frames below, draw what you think each character looks like based on what you've read. Next to each picture write a caption that describes the character.

Augustus Gloop

_____
_____
_____

Violet Beauregarde

_____
_____
_____

Veruca Salt

_____
_____
_____

Mike Teavee

_____
_____
_____

GO Turn the page to continue reading.

English Coach

The author makes jokes with the characters' names. *Beauregarde* means "beautiful look" in French. Why do you think Dahl uses this name for Violet? Remember, she has a face that is always full of gum.

_____

_____

_____

_____

Background Info

Before the refrigerator was invented, people used salt to keep meat from spoiling. Dahl may be creating a joke with the Salts' last name because Mr. and Mrs. Salt keep "spoiling" Veruca.

GRANDPA JOE.   And today is the first of February, and say, Charlie—look, we're here already . . . and I guess everyone else is arriving together.

[*AUGUSTUS GLOOP, VIOLET BEAUREGARDE, VERUCA SALT, MIKE TEAVEE, MRS. GLOOP, MR. and MRS. TEAVEE, MR. and MRS. SALT, MRS. BEAUREGARDE enter. WILLY WONKA enters from opposite side.*]

MRS. GLOOP.   There he is! That's him! It's Willy Wonka!

WILLY WONKA.   Welcome! Welcome! Welcome! Hello, everyone! Let's see now. I wonder if I can recognize all of you by the pictures of you in the newspaper. Let's see. [*Pause.*] You're Augustus Gloop.

AUGUSTUS GLOOP.   Uhhhhh . . . y—e—a—hhhhh and this is . . . uhh . . . my mother.

WILLY WONKA.   Delighted to meet you both! Delighted! Delighted! [*Turns to VIOLET.*] You're Violet Beauregarde.

VIOLET BEAUREGARDE.   So what if I am—let's just get on with the whole thing, huh?

WILLY WONKA.   And you must be Mrs. Beauregarde. Very happy to meet you! Very happy! [*Turns to VERUCA.*] I think you are . . . yes . . . you're Veruca Salt. And you must be Mr. and Mrs. Salt.

VERUCA SALT. Don't shake his hand, Daddy—it's probably all sticky and chocolatey from working in the factory. After all, he does only run a silly little factory. He's not important enough for you to bother shaking hands with, anyway!

WILLY WONKA. You're Mike Teavee. Enchanted to meet you! Yes . . . enchanted.

MIKE TEAVEE. [*Blasting his guns.*] Come on! I'm missing all my favorite TV shows!

MR. AND MRS. TEAVEE. And we're the Teavees. Pleased to meet you.

WILLY WONKA. Overjoyed! Overjoyed! [*Turns to CHARLIE.*] And you must be the boy who just found the ticket yesterday. Congratulations! You're . . . Charlie Bucket—aren't you?

CHARLIE. Yes sir, thank you. And this, sir, is my Grandpa Joe.

GRANDPA JOE. Howdy, Mr. Wonka. I'm real pleased to meet you!

WILLY WONKA. How do you do, Mr. Grandpa Joe. How do you do! Well now, is that everybody? Hmmmmmm . . . why . . . I guess it is! Good! Now will you please follow me! Our tour is about to begin! But do keep together! Please don't wander off by yourselves! I shouldn't like to lose any of you at this stage of the **proceedings**! Oh, dear me, no! Here we are! Through this big red door, please. That's right! It's nice and warm inside! I have to keep it warm inside the factory because of the workers!

Literary Element

Dialogue Reread the highlighted passage. What words would you use to describe Veruca? Check the boxes next to the words you would use to describe Veruca.

☐ rude
☐ mean
☐ polite

Comprehension Check

Reread the boxed paragraph. How is the way Charlie behaves different from the way the other children behave?

_____

_____

_____

Word Power

proceedings (prə sēʹdingz) *n.* actions or events

143

What would you do if you were invited to Willy Wonka's factory?

Reading Skill

Visualize What do you think Willy Wonka's factory looks like? Draw a picture of the factory in the frame below.

Your Sketch

AUGUSTUS GLOOP. But...who...are these...uhh...workers?

WILLY WONKA. All in good time, my dear boy! Be patient! You shall see everything as we go along! [*All exit with WILLY WONKA remaining alone.*] Are all of you inside? Good! Would you mind closing the door? Thank you!

[*Exit.*]

[*End of Scene 4.*]

Respond to Literature

Charlie and the Chocolate Factory

A Comprehension Check

Answer the following questions in the spaces provided.

1. How does Charlie get the winning ticket?

   _____

   _____

2. What is the reward for the winners of the Golden Ticket?

   _____

B Reading Skills

Answer the following questions in the spaces provided.

1. **Visualize** From the author's description, how do you picture Augustus Gloop in your mind?

   _____

   _____

   _____

2. **Visualize** How do you picture Violet Beauregarde?

   _____

   _____

3. **Sequence** In Scene 4, all the winners arrive at Willy Wonka's factory. Number the following events from that scene in the order in which they happen._____ They all go into the factory. _____ The four other winners arrive. _____ They meet Willy Wonka. _____ Charlie and Grandpa Joe go to the factory.

C Word Power

Complete each sentence below, using one of the words in the box.

possession	extremely	repulsive
tremendous	procession	proceedings

1. The garbage can was full of rotting fish and other _____ things.

2. We marched in front of a _____ of bands.

3. The doctor was _____ concerned about Ana's high fever.

4. The _____ will take place in the mayor's office.

5. A suitcase is an important _____ to a traveler.

6. The circus performers put on a _____ show!

D Literary Element: Dialogue

Read the passage below from "Charlie and the Chocolate Factory." As you read, think about what you learn from the dialogue. Then answer the questions that follow.

These trucks, I can promise you, will be loaded with enough delicious eatables to last you and your entire household for many years.[1] If, at any time thereafter, you should run out of supplies, you have only to come back to the factory and show this Golden Ticket, and I shall be happy to refill your cabinet with whatever you want.[2] And now, here are your instructions: the day I have chosen for the visit is the first day in the month of February.[3] On this day, and on no other, you must come to the factory gates at ten o'clock sharp in the morning.[4] Don't be late![5]

1. What do sentences 1 and 2 tell you about Willy Wonka? Is he selfish or generous? Explain.

   _____

   _____

   _____

   _____

2. What information in sentences 3–5 tells you that Willy Wonka is used to being in charge?

   _____

   _____

   _____

   _____

E A Journal Entry

Imagine that you are Charlie Bucket. Write a journal entry about the contest.

January 25

I FOUND THE GOLDEN TICKET! This is how it happened. I
was _____

_____

_____

I feel so _____

The other ticket winners _____

_____

There's Augustus Gloop, _____

Violet Beauregarde, who _____

Veruca Salt, who _____ *Mike Teavee,*

who _____

I am so excited because _____

_____

_____

I can't wait to meet Willy Wonka!

Assessment

Fill in the circle next to each correct answer.

1 Willy Wonka is running a contest because he wants to
   ○ A. give away extra candy.
   ○ B. show off his new candy inventions.
   ○ C. meet the children from the town.
   ○ D. sell a lot of his candy.

2 Who finds a Golden Ticket first?
   ○ A. Violet Beauregarde
   ○ B. Charlie Bucket
   ○ C. Augustus Gloop
   ○ D. Veruca Salt

3 The narrator says, "Such a, uh, lucky, uh, girl. Isn't she, uh, uh, wonderful?" This dialogue shows that the narrator
   ○ A. thinks Veruca Salt is a wonderful girl.
   ○ B. is a slow talker who pauses between words.
   ○ C. is trying to think of something nice to say.
   ○ D. has trouble speaking because he has a cough.

4 What information **best** helps you picture what the Bucket home looks like?
   ○ A. This is the home of Charlie Bucket.
   ○ B. The house has two rooms and only one bed.
   ○ C. Mr. Bucket lost his job a few weeks ago.
   ○ D. Charlie's grandparents are very old people.

5 When Willy Wonka promises *tremendous* surprises, he means they will be
   ○ A. wonderful.
   ○ B. colorful.
   ○ C. noisy.
   ○ D. scary.

Folklore

What's Folklore?

If you have ever read a story about Paul Bunyan, Anansi, or Hercules, then you have read some folklore! These stories are not only fun to read, but they also teach you about the cultures they come from.

Every culture has its own **folklore.** Folklore includes information about a group's customs, songs, dances, and beliefs that have been passed down from one generation to the next. Before written language was invented, folklore was passed down by word of mouth, with one person telling these stories to another.

Think about some of the folklore you have read. Write the title of the story you liked the most.

Why Read Folklore?

People read folklore for fun. These stories have unusual characters and exciting plots. But reading folklore can do more than entertain. Folklore can teach you about beliefs that people had long ago. Folklore can also tell how people who lived long ago explained natural events and how things came to be.

How Do I Read Folklore?

Focus on key **literary elements** and **reading skills** to get the most out of reading the folklore in this unit. Here are two key literary elements and two key reading skills that you will practice in this unit.

Key Literary Elements

• Folktale

Folktales come from different regions and cultures. They include fairy tales, legends, and tall tales. Folktales are often used to teach lessons about proper behavior. The characters in folktales often include animals, people with special powers, animals that act like humans, or ordinary people who experience extraordinary events.

• Myth

Myths are stories handed down from ancient cultures to explain how things came about. Myths explain events in nature or the beginnings of certain beliefs and customs. The characters in myths are usually gods, magical creatures, and people with superhuman powers.

Key Reading Skills

• Cause and Effect

A **cause** is something that happens that sets something else in motion. An **effect** is the result or outcome. To find a cause-and-effect relationship, ask yourself: Did this happen because of something else? For example, a character may go for a walk in the rain, causing his clothes to get wet. Sometimes clue words, such as *because*, *as a result*, *therefore*, *since*, and *so*, let you know of a cause-and-effect relationship.

• Respond

When you **respond,** you think about what you have read and how you feel about it. Have you ever laughed at something you read? Were you interested in reading more? Did you ever think that a character was just like you? If so, you were responding to what you read. Share your thoughts and feelings. The more you respond, the more you will understand what you have read.

The Force of Luck

Meet
Rudolfo A. Anaya

The land and culture of New Mexico have inspired Rudolfo A. Anaya (rōō dôl´ fō ä nā´ yä) since he was a child. Anaya, born in 1937, has written that "the most important elements of my childhood are the people of those villages and the wide open plains." In his short stories, novels, and plays, Anaya draws upon Mexican legends, myths, and symbolism to offer insight into the Mexican American community.

What You Know

Do you believe good fortune comes to those who are hardworking and honest or to those who are simply lucky?

Reason to Read

Read "The Force of Luck" to find out what roles hard work and luck play in the life of one character.

Background Info

"The Force of Luck" is part of the oral tradition of the Hispanic people who lived in the American Southwest. This story, like many folktales, takes place in a small village a long time ago, when people ground wheat into flour by hand at a mill. It was the miller's job to grind, or mill, the wheat grain into a fine powder to make flour. The flour was then passed on to the baker, who used it to make bread.

Word Power

prosperous (pros′ pər əs) *adj.* having wealth or good fortune; p. 154
The *prosperous* rancher lived in a grand house.

modestly (mod′ ist lē) *adv.* in a humble manner; p. 154
The shopkeeper lived *modestly* in a small cottage.

poverty (pov′ ər tē) *n.* condition of being poor; p. 155
Poverty is often the result of having no work.

accuse (ə kūz′) *v.* to blame or state that someone has done something wrong; p. 157
Did the coach *accuse* the player of cheating?

illuminate (i lōō′ mə nāt) *v.* to light up; p. 158
Sometimes moonlight will *illuminate* the road at night.

novelty (nov′ əl tē) *n.* anything new and unusual; p. 158
Cars that give the driver directions are a *novelty*.

consulting (kən sul′ ting) *v.* getting advice or information from; p. 160
After *consulting* a vet, she knew what to feed her dog.

acquired (ə kwīrd′) *v.* got as one's own; p. 161
He *acquired* the old chest at an antique store.

Answer the following questions, using one of the new words above.
Write your answers in the spaces provided.

1. Which word goes with "using a lamp to see in the dark"? _____

2. Which word goes with "a new kind of toy"? _____

3. Which word goes with "having a lot of money"? _____

4. Which word goes with "having no money"? _____

5. Which word goes with "saying that someone has done something wrong"? _____

6. Which word goes with "asking an expert for information"? _____

7. Which word goes with "got something you wanted"? _____

8. Which word goes with "not bragging or boasting about your skills"? _____

Adapted from

The Force of Luck

Rudolfo A. Anaya

Farmers (Agricultores), 1935. Antonio Gattorno. Gouache and ink on paper laid down on board, 17 ½ x 19 ½ in. Private Collection.

Connect to the Text

Reread the boxed paragraph. Think about a time when you and someone else had different ideas about something. How did you settle the argument?

_____

_____

_____

_____

_____

Once two wealthy friends got into a heated argument. One said that it was money which made a man **prosperous,** and the other maintained that it wasn't money, but luck, which made the man. They finally decided that if only they could find an honorable man then perhaps they could prove their different points of view.

One day they came upon a miller who was grinding corn and wheat. They paused to ask the man how he ran his business. The miller replied that he worked for a master and that he earned only four bits a day, and with that he had to support a family of five.

"Do you mean to tell us you can support a family of five on only fifteen dollars a month?" one asked.

"I live **modestly** to make ends meet," the humble miller replied.

One of them said to the miller, "I will give you two hundred dollars and you may do whatever you want with the money."

"But why would you give me this money when you've just met me?" the miller asked.

Word Power

prosperous (pros´ pər əs) *adj.* having wealth or good fortune
modestly (mod´ ist lē) *adv.* in a humble manner

Well, my good man, my friend contends that it is luck which raises a man to a high position, and I say it is money. By giving you this money perhaps we can settle our argument."

So the poor miller took the money and spent the rest of the day thinking what could he possibly do with all this money? The miller decided the first thing he would do would be to buy food for his family. He took out ten dollars and wrapped the rest of the money in a cloth and put the bundle in his bag. Then he went to the market and bought supplies and a good piece of meat.

On the way home he was attacked by a hawk that had smelled the meat. The miller fought off the bird, but it grabbed the bag and flew away.

"Ah," he moaned, "now I'm in the same **poverty** as before! And worse, because now those two men will say I am a thief! I should have gone straight home and this wouldn't have happened!"

So he gathered what was left of his supplies and continued home, and when he arrived he told his family the entire story.

When he was finished telling his story his wife said, "It has been our destiny to be poor, but have faith in God and maybe someday our luck will change."

Three months after he had lost the money to the hawk, the two wealthy men returned to the village. When the miller saw them he felt ashamed and afraid that they would think that he had wasted the money on worthless things. But he decided to tell them the truth and as soon as they had greeted each other he told his story. The one who insisted that it was money and not luck which made a man prosper took out another two hundred dollars and gave it to the miller.

Word Power

poverty (pov′ ər tē) *n.* condition of being poor

Comprehension Check

Reread the boxed paragraph. What does the miller do with the money he is given?

_____

_____

_____

Background Info

Hawks mostly eat birds and small mammals. When hunting, hawks usually sit in a hidden location and watch for small animals. When they see something to eat, they quickly swoop down and grab it.

Literary Element

Folktale Reread the highlighted paragraph. Folktales often involve extraordinary events. What two extraordinary events does the ordinary miller experience in this part of the folktale? Check the correct responses.

☐ A hawk flies away with the bag of money.

☐ He went to work at the mill.

☐ One of the wealthy men gives him another two hundred dollars.

155

"Let's try again," he said, "and let's see what happens this time."

"Kind sir, maybe it would be better if you put this money in the hands of another man?"

"No," the man insisted, "I want to give it to you because you are an honest man, and if we are going to settle our argument you have to take the money!"

The miller thanked them. Then as soon as the two men left he began to think what to do with the money so that it wouldn't disappear as it had the first time. He took out ten dollars, wrapped the rest in a cloth, and headed home.

When he arrived his wife wasn't at home. He went to the pantry where he had stored a large jar filled with bran. He emptied out the grain and put the bundle of money at the bottom of the jar, then covered it up with the grain.

That afternoon when he arrived home from work he was greeted by his wife.

"Look, my husband, today I bought some good clay to whitewash the entire house."

"And how did you buy the clay if we don't have any money?" he asked.

"Well, the man who was selling the clay was willing to trade for anything of value," she said. "The only thing we had of value was the jar full of bran, so I traded it for the clay."

Background Info

To *whitewash* means "to cover something, usually walls, with whitewash." Whitewash is a white, liquid mixture used like paint.

Reading Skill

Cause and Effect Reread the highlighted paragraph. The miller's wife wanted to get some clay. What happens as a result?

_____

_____

_____

La Molendera I, 1924. Diego Rivera. *Encaustica sobre tela,* 90 x 117 cm. Museo de Arte Moderno, Bosque de Chapultepec, Mexico.

Which character in the story is most like this woman?

_____

The man groaned and pulled his hair.

"What have you done? We're ruined again!"

"But why?" she asked.

"Today I met the same two friends who gave me the two hundred dollars three months ago," he explained. "And after I told them how I lost the money they gave me another two hundred. And I came home and hid it inside the jar of bran—the same jar you have traded for dirt! Now we're as poor as we were before! And what am I going to tell the two men? They'll think I'm a liar and a thief for sure!"

"Let them think what they want," his wife said calmly. "We will be poor until God wills it otherwise."

Time came and went, and one day the two wealthy friends returned to ask the miller how he had done with the second two hundred dollars. He was afraid they would **accuse** him of being a liar, but he decided to be truthful and as soon as they had greeted each other he told them what had happened to the money.

"That is why poor men remain honest," the man who had given him the money said. "Because they don't have money they can't get into trouble. But I think you gambled and lost the money."

"Either way," he continued, "I still believe that it is money and not luck which makes a man prosper."

"Well, you certainly didn't prove your point by giving the money to this poor miller," his friend reminded him. "Good evening, you unlucky man," he said to the miller.

"Oh, by the way, here is a worthless piece of lead I've been carrying around. Maybe you can use it for something," said the man who believed in luck.

Reading Skill

Respond Reread the highlighted paragraph. Do you agree with the man who says that people without money cannot get into trouble? Explain.

_____

_____

_____

_____

English Coach

The suffix -*less* means "without." Something that is *worthless* is without worth. What word would you use to describe something that is without use?

_____

Word Power

accuse (ə kūz´) *v.* to blame or state that someone has done something wrong

The miller put it in his jacket pocket. He forgot all about it until he arrived home. When he threw his jacket on a chair he heard a thump and he remembered the piece of lead. He took it out of the pocket and threw it under the table. Later that night after the family had gone to bed, they heard a knock at the door.

"Who is it?" the miller asked.

"It's me, your neighbor," a voice answered. "My husband sent me to ask you if you have any lead you can spare. He is going fishing tomorrow and he needs the lead to weight down the nets."

The miller remembered the lead he had thrown under the table. He found it and gave it to the woman.

"Thank you very much, neighbor," the woman said. "I promise you the first fish my husband catches will be yours."

The miller returned to bed. The next day he got up and went to work. In the afternoon when he returned home he found his wife cooking a big fish for dinner.

"Since when are we so rich that we can afford fish for supper?" he asked his wife.

"Don't you remember that our neighbor promised us the first fish her husband caught?" his wife reminded him. "Well this was the fish he caught the first time he threw his net. It's a beauty. But you should have been here when I gutted him! I found a large piece of glass in his stomach!"

"And what did you do with it?"

"Oh, I gave it to the children to play with," she shrugged.

When the miller saw the piece of glass he noticed it shone so brightly it appeared to **illuminate** the room, but he didn't realize its value and left it to the children. The bright glass was such a **novelty** that the children were soon fighting over it and raising a terrible fuss.

Comprehension Check

Reread the boxed paragraph. How did the miller's wife get the fish? Check the correct response.

☐ She caught the fish herself.

☐ She got the fish from the neighbor.

☐ She bought the fish at the store.

Word Power

illuminate (i lōō′ mə nāt) *v.* to light up

novelty (nov′ əl tē) *n.* anything new and unusual

Now it so happened that the miller and his wife had other neighbors who were jewelers. The following morning the jeweler's wife visited the miller's wife to complain about all the noise her children had made.

"You know how it is with a large family," the miller's wife explained. "Yesterday we found a beautiful piece of glass and I gave it to my youngest one to play with and when the others tried to take it from him he raised a storm."

"Won't you show me that piece of glass?" she asked.

"But of course. Here it is."

"Ah, yes, it's a pretty piece of glass."

"Why don't you let me take it home for just a moment. You see, I have one just like it and I want to compare them."

"Yes, why not?" answered the miller's wife.

When the jeweler saw the glass he instantly knew it was one of the finest diamonds he had ever seen.

"Go tell the neighbor we'll give her fifty dollars for it, but don't tell her it's a diamond!"

"No, no," his wife chuckled, "of course not." She ran to her neighbor's house. "My husband is willing to buy it for fifty dollars—so we can have a pair."

"I can't sell it," the miller's wife answered. "You will have to wait until my husband comes home."

That evening when the miller came home his wife told him about the offer the jeweler had made.

"But why would they offer fifty dollars for a worthless piece of glass?" the miller wondered aloud. They were interrupted by the jeweler's wife.

English Coach

The author uses the phrase *raised a storm* to mean "got very angry." How might the boy's actions have been like a storm?

_____

_____

_____

Reading Skill

Respond Reread the highlighted passage. How do you feel about the jeweler's wife? Check the boxes with the words that you would use to describe her.

☐ selfish
☐ honest
☐ clever
☐ greedy

Literary Element

Folktale Reread the highlighted passage. In folktales, unusual things happen that may not happen in real life. How is this conversation between the jeweler's wife and the miller different from what might happen in real life?

_____

_____

_____

_____

_____

English Coach

The phrase *fair and square* means "with justice and honesty." Can someone who cheats win a game fair and square? Explain.

_____

_____

_____

"What do you say, neighbor, will you take fifty dollars for the glass?" she asked.

"No, that's not enough," the miller said cautiously. "Offer more."

"I'll give you fifty thousand!" the jeweler's wife blurted out.

"A little bit more," the miller replied.

"Impossible!" the jeweler's wife cried, "I can't offer any more without **consulting** my husband." She ran off to her husband, and he told her he was prepared to pay a hundred thousand dollars.

He handed her seventy-five thousand dollars and said, "Take this and tell him that tomorrow, he'll have the rest."

When the miller heard the offer and saw the money he couldn't believe his eyes.

"I don't know about this money," he told his wife. "Maybe the jeweler plans to accuse us of robbing him and take it back."

"Oh no," his wife said, "the money is ours. We sold the diamond fair and square."

"I think I'll still go to work tomorrow," the miller said. "Something might happen and the money will disappear. So he went to work the next day, and all day he thought about how he could use the money. When he returned home that afternoon his wife asked him what he had decided to do with their new fortune.

"I think I will start my own mill," he answered. "Once I set up my business we'll see how our luck changes."

The next day he set about buying everything he needed to start his mill and to build a new home. Soon he had everything going.

Time passed and the miller prospered. His business grew and he even built a summer cottage. He had many employees. One day while he was at his store he saw the two wealthy men riding by. He rushed out to greet them and ask them to come in. He was overjoyed to see them, and he was happy to see that they admired his store.

Word Power

consulting (kən sul´ting) *v.* getting advice or information from

"Tell us the truth," the man who had given him the four hundred dollars said. "You used that money to set up this business."

The miller swore he hadn't, and he told them how he had given the piece of lead to his neighbor and how the fisherman had in return given him a fish with a very large diamond in its stomach. And he told them how he had sold the diamond.

"And that's how I **acquired** this business and many other things I want to show you," he said. "But, let's eat first."

So they ate and then the miller had three horses saddled and they rode out to see his summer home. The cabin was on the other side of the river where the mountains were cool and beautiful. During their ride they came upon a tall pine tree.

"What is that on top of the tree?" one of them asked.

"That's the nest of a hawk," the miller replied.

"I would like to take a closer look at it!"

"Of course," the miller said, and he ordered a servant to climb the tree and bring down the nest so his friend could see how it was built.

Have you ever seen a hawk's nest? How do you think hawks build their nests?

Reading Skill

Cause & Effect Reread the highlighted passage. Read the cause boxes, then fill in the effect boxes below.

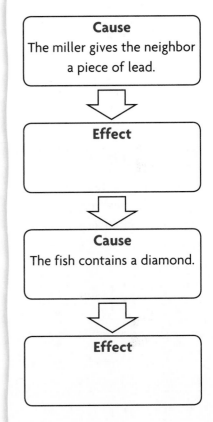

> **Cause**
> The miller gives the neighbor a piece of lead.
>
> ⬇
>
> **Effect**
>
> ⬇
>
> **Cause**
> The fish contains a diamond.
>
> ⬇
>
> **Effect**

Word Power

acquired (ə kwīrd´) v. got as one's own

161

Literary Element

Folktale Reread the paragraphs highlighted in blue. Identify one feature of a folktale in this passage.

_____

_____

_____

_____

Reading Skill

Respond Reread the sentence highlighted in green. Which do you believe makes the miller rich: luck or money? Why?

_____

_____

_____

_____

_____

_____

_____

_____

_____

They noticed that there was a cloth bag at the bottom of the nest.

"You won't believe me, friends, but this is the very same bag in which I put the first two hundred dollars you gave me," he told them.

"If it's the same bag," the man who had doubted him said, "then the money you said the hawk took should be there."

The miller said. "Let's see what we find."

The three of them examined the old bag. When they tore it apart they found the money. The two men remembered what the miller had told them, and they agreed he was an honest and honorable man. Still, the man who had given him the money wondered what had really happened to the second two hundred.

They spent the rest of the day riding in the mountains and returned very late to the house.

As he unsaddled their horses, the servant in charge of the horses suddenly realized that he had no grain for them. So he ran to the neighbor's and bought a large clay jar of bran. He carried the jar home and emptied the bran into a bucket to wet it before he fed it to the horses. When he got to the bottom of the jar he noticed a large lump which turned out to be a rag covered package. He immediately went to give it to his master.

"Master," he said, "look at this package which I found in a jar of grain which I just bought from our neighbor!"

The three men carefully unraveled the cloth and found the other one hundred and ninety dollars which the miller had told them he had lost. That is how the miller proved to his friends that he was truly an honest man.

And they had to decide for themselves whether it had been luck or money which had made the miller a wealthy man!

The Force of Luck

A Comprehension Check

Answer the following questions in the spaces provided.

1. What are the two wealthy men trying to prove?

   _____

2. How does the miller get money to start his own business?

   _____

B Reading Skills

Answer the following questions in the spaces provided.

1. **Respond** Do you think that either of the wealthy men proved his argument? Explain.

   _____

   _____

2. **Cause and Effect** The servant has no grain to feed the horses. Write one effect that happens as a result of this situation, or cause.

   _____

   _____

3. **Respond** When the miller tells his wife that he has lost his money, she responds calmly. How would you have responded if you were the miller's wife?

   _____

   _____

C Word Power

Complete each sentence below, using one of the words in the box.

prosperous	modestly	poverty	accuse
illuminate	novelty	consulting	acquired

1. The girl used a flashlight to _____ the path.

2. He decided what to wear after _____ his friends.

3. The family decorated their simple house _____.

4. Governments are trying to help homeless people living

   in _____.

5. The _____ woman gave money to help others.

6. I _____ several books at a library sale.

7. Why did the boy _____ his sister of breaking the toy?

8. When it was invented, television was a _____.

D Literary Element: Folktale

Read the passage below from "The Force of Luck." As you read, think about the characteristics of a folktale. Then answer the questions that follow.

Three months after he had lost the money to the hawk, the two wealthy men returned to the village.[1] When the miller saw them he felt ashamed and afraid that they would think that he had wasted the money on worthless things.[2] But he decided to tell them the truth and as soon as they had greeted each other he told his story.[3] The one who insisted that it was money and not luck which made a man prosper took out another two hundred dollars and gave it to the miller.[4]

1. In sentences 1–4, what are two things that happen to the miller that would not occur in a more realistic story?

   _____

   _____

   _____

   _____

2. The main character in this folktale is an honest and hardworking person who deserves good fortune. How does sentence 3 show that the miller deserves the money?

   _____

   _____

   _____

   _____

E A Diary Entry

Imagine that you are the miller. Write a diary entry about the last day of this story.

Dear Diary,

I had a great day!

The men and I saw a pine tree. This was _____

_____

_____

Then my servant brought me a jar. I found _____

_____

I proved to the men that

_____

_____

The men still did not agree about luck or money, but I proved to them that _____

_____

Assessment

Fill in the circle next to each correct answer.

1 How does the miller lose the second package of money?
- ○ A. A hawk steals it.
- ○ B. A fish swallows it.
- ○ C. His wife trades it away.
- ○ D. The jeweler's wife takes it.

2 Which of the following describes the characters in the folktale "The Force of Luck"?
- ○ A. people who have special powers
- ○ B. animals with extraordinary powers
- ○ C. animals that speak to people
- ○ D. people who have unusual experiences

3 The neighbor gave the miller's wife a fish because
- ○ A. the miller had given the neighbor a piece of lead.
- ○ B. the miller's wife had given the neighbor some bran.
- ○ C. the miller's wife cooked dinner for the neighbors.
- ○ D. the neighbor had caught a lot of fish that day.

4 Why do the two men choose the miller to settle their argument?
- ○ A. He was working at a mill.
- ○ B. They think he is honorable.
- ○ C. They think he is friendly and generous.
- ○ D. He looks like he has good fortune.

5 Which of the following means "to blame"?
- ○ A. accuse
- ○ B. acquired
- ○ C. consulting
- ○ D. illuminate

Connect to the Text

Reread the boxed paragraph. The myth says that humans must treat the land with respect. Check the boxes below that show ways to respect the land.

☐ recycle cans, paper, and plastic
☐ throw trash on the ground
☐ plant trees and flowers

Me
Jos

Josep
smal
Adir
ance
Aber
this,
to sh
share
Nati
Ame
abou
best
care
Jose

Though she was asleep, Loo-Wit was still aware, the people said. The Creator had placed her between the two quarreling mountains to keep the peace, and it was **intended** that humans, too, should look at her beauty and remember to keep their hearts good, to share the land and treat it well. If we human beings do not treat the land with respect, the people said, Loo-Wit will wake up and let us know how unhappy she and the Creator have become again. So they said, long before the day in the 1980s when Mount St. Helens woke again.

Have you ever seen a movie or TV show about a volcano erupting? Describe what happened.

Word Power

intended (in ten´did) *v.* to have planned, meant

174

Respond to Literature

Loo-Wit: THE FIREKEEPER

A Comprehension Check

Answer the following questions in the spaces provided.

1. Why does the Creator go to Loo-Wit's lodge?

   _____

   _____

   _____

2. What does the Creator change the two chiefs and Loo-Wit into?

   _____

   _____

B Reading Skills

Answer the following questions in the spaces provided.

1. **Respond** How do you feel about the way the brothers behave in the story?

   _____

   _____

   _____

2. **Cause and Effect** What is the cause of this effect: "the Creator took fire away"?

   _____

   _____

C Word Power

Complete each sentence below, using one of the words in the box.

quarrel	suffered	lodge
heartbroken	intended	

1. There were four rooms in the _____ .

2. The brothers had a _____ over the toys.

3. We had _____ to have a picnic at the beach, but it rained.

4. The poor girl _____ a great loss.

5. People were _____ over the bad news.

Circle the word that best completes each sentence.

6. Did the two boys (**quarrel**, **lodge**) over who would go first?

7. They (**intended**, **suffered**) to be on time but they were very late.

8. Pam was (**heartbroken**, **intended**) when her dog ran away.

9. The (**quarrel**, **lodge**) was built from big logs.

10. Tim (**heartbroken**, **suffered**) from a bad cold and stayed in bed.

D Literary Element: Myth

Read the passage below from "Loo-Wit: The Firekeeper." As you read, think about the kinds of things a myth explains. Then answer the questions that follow.

> When the Creator saw the fighting, he became angry. [1] He broke down the Great Stone Bridge. [2] He took the two chiefs and changed them into mountains. [3] The chief of the Klickitats became the mountain we now know as Mount Adams. [4] The chief of the Multnomahs became the mountain we now know as Mount Hood. [5] Even as mountains, they continued to quarrel, throwing flames and stones at each other. [6] In some places, the stones they threw almost blocked the river between them. [7] That is why the Columbia River is so narrow in the place called the Dalles today. [8]

1. In sentences 1–5 what natural feature does the myth explain?

   _____

   _____

   _____

2. Reread sentences 6–8. How does this myth explain why the Columbia River is so narrow?

   _____

   _____

   _____

E Rules to Live By

Imagine that the Creator has asked you to make a list of rules that people should follow to keep peace. Write the rules, and tell why they are important. Write your own rule for Rule #4.

Rule 1: Be happy with the land you have. Do not think that another land is better than yours because

_____

_____

Rule 2: Do not be greedy. If you are greedy, you will

_____

_____

Rule 3: Share what you have with others. When you share, you will _____

_____

Rule 4: _____

_____

Assessment

Fill in the circle next to each correct answer.

1. The cause of the brothers' quarrel over Loo-Wit is her
   - ○ A. fire.
   - ○ B. beauty.
   - ○ C. lodge.
   - ○ D. land.

2. What does Loo-Wit become?
   - ○ A. Mount Adams
   - ○ B. Mount Hood
   - ○ C. Mount St. Helens
   - ○ D. Columbia River

3. One message of this myth is that people should
   - ○ A. treat the land with respect.
   - ○ B. want what others have.
   - ○ C. live near volcanoes.
   - ○ D. quarrel with each other.

4. In this myth the Creator is
   - ○ A. an ordinary person.
   - ○ B. a mountain.
   - ○ C. a chief.
   - ○ D. a superhuman god.

5. Which of the following words means "planned"?
   - ○ A. intended
   - ○ B. suffered
   - ○ C. lodge
   - ○ D. heartbroken

Get Ready to Read!

The End of the World

Meet Jenny Leading Cloud

Jenny Leading Cloud was born in South Dakota in the late 1800s and died sometime around 1980. She was a Native American who retold many legends and stories from her Sioux background. Leading Cloud spent her life in White River, a town in South Dakota. This story was first published in 1984.

What You Know

Have you ever read or heard a story that explains why something happens, such as why you hear thunder after you see lightning? Share your story with a classmate.

Reason to Read

Read "The End of the World" to learn about Sioux culture and how they believed the world could end.

Background Info

Long ago the Sioux and other Plains Indians began to use porcupine quills for decoration. Quills are needlelike spikes that protect a porcupine's body. The plucked quills were dyed, and then folded, twisted, wrapped, braided, and sewn to decorate clothing, bags, knife holders, baskets, wooden handles, and pipe stems. Around 1850 people started to use glass beads to create the same designs used in quillwork. Beads were available in more colors. Today some Native Americans continue to use quillwork as well as glass beads to decorate things.

Word Power

generations (jen′ ə rā′ shəns) *n.* steps in the history of a family; p. 182
This picture shows three *generations* of my family: my grandmother, my father, and my sister.

ancestors (an′ ses′ tərs) *n.* people from whom someone is descended, especially from the distant past; p. 182
My grandfather told me that our *ancestors* came to the United States by boat.

continent (kont′ ən ənt) *n.* one of the seven large land areas on Earth; p. 182
There were no horses in North America before Europeans brought them to the *continent*.

feeble (fē′ bəl) *adj.* not strong; weak; p. 183
The newborn lamb was so *feeble* that I had to feed it from a baby bottle.

hobble (hob′ əl) *v.* to walk with a limp or in a clumsy way; p. 183
When I broke my leg, I had to *hobble* around on crutches.

**Answer the following questions, using one of the new words above.
Write your answers in the spaces provided.**

1. Which word goes with "limping"? _____

2. Which word goes with "daughter, mother, and grandmother"? _____

3. Which word goes with "a big area of land"? _____

4. Which word goes with "not having strength"? _____

5. Which word goes with "family members who lived many years ago"? _____

The End of the World

Jenny Leading Cloud

Reading Skill

Respond Reread the description of the old woman in the highlighted passage. Would you want to get to know her? Why?

_____

_____

_____

_____

English Coach

Here, the suffix *-less* means "not able to." *Numberless* means "not able to be counted." What does the word *measureless* mean?

_____

_____

_____

Somewhere, at a place where the prairie and the Mako Sica, the badlands, meet, there is a hidden cave. Not for many **generations** has anyone been able to find it. Even now, with so many cars and highways and tourists, no one has found this cave.

In the cave lives an old woman. She is so old that her face looks like a shriveled-up walnut. She is dressed in rawhide, the way people used to go around before the white people came to this country. She is sitting there—has been sitting there for a thousand years or more—working on a blanket strip for her buffalo robe. She is making that blanket strip out of dyed porcupine quills, the way our **ancestors** did before white traders brought glass beads to this turtle **continent.** Resting beside her, licking his paws, watching her all the time, is a Shunka Sapa, a huge black dog. His eyes never wander from the old woman whose teeth are worn flat, worn down to little stumps from using them to flatten numberless porcupine quills.

Did You Know?
Badlands National Park is a dry region of South Dakota that has many ridges and peaks cut by the wind, but little plant life.

Word Power

generations (jen´ ə rā´ shəns) *n.* steps in the history of a family

ancestors (an´ ses´ tərs) *n.* people from whom someone is descended, especially from the distant past

continent (kont´ ən ənt) *n.* one of the seven large land areas on Earth

What has been in your family for several generations?

A few steps from where the old woman sits working on her blanket strip, a big fire is kept going. She lit this fire a thousand or more years ago and has kept it alive ever since. Over the fire hangs a big earthenware pot, the kind some Indian people used to make before the white man came with his kettles of iron. Inside the big pot, wojapi is boiling and bubbling. Wojapi is berry soup. It is good and sweet and red. That wojapi has been boiling in that pot for a long time, ever since the fire was lit.

Every now and then the old woman gets up to stir the wojapi in the huge earthenware pot. She is so old and **feeble** that it takes her a while to get up and **hobble** over to the fire. The moment the old woman's back is turned, the huge, black dog starts pulling out the porcupine quills from her blanket strip. This way, she never makes any progress, and her quillwork remains forever half finished. The Sioux people used to say that if the woman ever finished her blanket strip, in the very moment that she would thread the last porcupine quill to complete her design, the world would come to an end.

Word Power

feeble (fē′ bəl) *adj.* not strong; weak
hobble (hob′ əl) *v.* to walk with a limp or in a clumsy way

Literary Element

Myth Characters in myths often have superhuman powers. Reread the sentences highlighted in blue. What is superhuman about the old woman? Check the correct response.

☐ She is working on a blanket strip.

☐ She is cooking soup in a big pot.

☐ She has been alive for over a thousand years.

Reading Skills

Cause and Effect Reread the sentence highlighted in green and the rest of the paragraph. Why does the world never end? Read the effect box. Then fill in the cause box above it.

Cause

⬇

Effect
The blanket is never finished, so the world never ends.

183

Respond to Literature

The End of the World

A Comprehension Check

Answer the following questions in the spaces provided.

1. What does the old woman do all day?

   _____

   _____

2. What keeps the old woman from finishing her work?

   _____

   _____

B Reading Skills

Answer the following questions in the spaces provided.

1. **Respond** If you were in the cave with the old woman and the dog, would you try to help the dog? Why? _____

   _____

   _____

   _____

2. **Cause and Effect** What would happen if the old woman completed her design? _____

   _____

   _____

C Word Power

Complete each sentence below, using one of the words in the box.

generations   ancestors   continent

feeble   hobble

1. My new shoes hurt my feet so much that I had to _____ home and put on an old pair of sneakers.

2. I learned that my _____ were from Africa and Spain.

3. The _____ of Australia is surrounded by water on all sides.

4. The knight was too sick and _____ to fight the mighty dragon.

5. The jeweled crown has been in my family for five _____.

Circle the word that best completes each sentence.

6. This recipe has been in our family for several (**continent, generations**).

7. When I saw my dog (**hobble, generations**), I told my mom we should take him to the vet.

8. My grandmother, who is very old and (**ancestors, feeble**), needs help with her household chores.

9. Did I ever tell you that my (**hobble, ancestors**) used to live in a castle?

10. Asia is the largest (**continent, feeble**) in the world.

D Literary Element: Myth

Read the two passages below from "The End of the World." Myths often show customs and beliefs that are important to a group. As you read, think about what the passages reveal about the Sioux and their beliefs. Then answer the questions that follow.

She is dressed in rawhide, the way people used to go around before the white people came to this country.[1] She is sitting there—has been sitting there for a thousand years or more—working on a blanket strip for her buffalo robe.[2] She is making that blanket strip out of dyed porcupine quills, the way our ancestors did before white traders brought glass beads to this turtle continent.[3]

The Sioux people used to say that if the woman ever finished her blanket strip, in the very moment that she would thread the last porcupine quill to complete her design, the world would come to an end.[4]

1. Reread sentences 1–3. What Sioux customs are described in this passage?

_____

_____

_____

2. Reread sentence 4. The old woman continues to create an object that has always been important to the Sioux people. This is the reason the world doesn't end. What is the message of this myth?

_____

_____

_____

E A Sioux Design

Imagine that you are creating a photo-essay of the Sioux woman and her blanket strip. Based on the story, draw a design for a blanket strip. Underneath the drawing, complete a paragraph that explains your picture.

This is a design for a blanket strip that has been in the making for 1,000 years. It is true. An old Sioux woman has been making it with

_____

She lives with her dog in _____

In the cave, she _____

_____

Each time she turns her back to stir the wojapi, _____

_____

If the woman were ever to complete her design, _____

_____

Assessment

Fill in the circle next to each correct answer.

1. Why can no one find the woman and the dog?
   - ○ A. They live in the spirit world.
   - ○ B. They live in a hidden cave.
   - ○ C. They hide from other people.
   - ○ D. They do not live on the turtle continent.

2. What does the woman use to make her blanket strip?
   - ○ A. strips of rawhide
   - ○ B. strips of wool blanket
   - ○ C. porcupine quills
   - ○ D. glass beads

3. What happens when the woman gets up to stir the wojapi?
   - ○ A. The dog pulls the porcupine quills out of the blanket strip.
   - ○ B. The dog flattens the porcupine quills with its teeth.
   - ○ C. The dog digs a hole and hides the porcupine quills.
   - ○ D. The dog licks its paws and waits to get fed.

4. What does this story explain?
   - ○ A. how the dog rules the world
   - ○ B. how the Sioux got fire
   - ○ C. how the porcupine lost its quills
   - ○ D. why the world does not end

5. Which of the following words means the **opposite** of "strong and powerful"?
   - ○ A. generations
   - ○ B. ancestors
   - ○ C. feeble
   - ○ D. hobble

Wrap-up

Compare and Contrast

The stories "Loo-Wit: The Firekeeper" and "The End of the World" have many similarities because they are both myths. **Myths** share similar purposes. They can tell how things came to be, and they can tell about the cultures they came from. Many myths teach important lessons. Think about the literary element myth in these two selections. Think about what each myth explains.

Using the Venn diagram below, explain how the elements of myth in "Loo-Wit: The Firekeeper" and "The End of the World" are alike and how they are different. In the outer parts of the circles, write about the different things in each story that make it a myth. In the section where the circles overlap, write about how the two myths are similar.

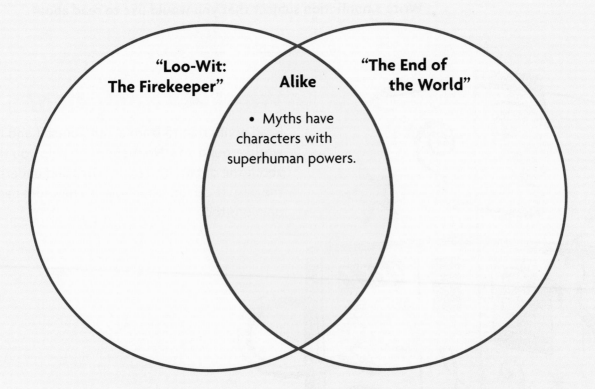

"Loo-Wit:
The Firekeeper"

Alike

"The End of
the World"

• Myths have characters with superhuman powers.

Nonfiction

What's Nonfiction?

Nonfiction is the name for writing that is about real events and real people. Articles in most newspapers and magazines are nonfiction. This kind of writing tells the facts. Nonfiction writing includes biographies, autobiographies, and essays.

A **biography** is the story of a person's life written by someone other than that person. An **autobiography** is the story of a person's life written by that person. An **essay** is a short piece of nonfiction about a single topic.

Nonfiction can deal with many topics—the lives of famous people, historical events, or facts about nature.

Write a nonfiction subject that you would like to read about.

Why Read Nonfiction?

Read nonfiction to learn about yourself and the world around you. Nonfiction can help you think about the details of people's lives and understand the past. It can introduce you to new ideas and opinions too.

How Do I Read Nonfiction?

Focus on key **literary elements** and **reading skills** to get the most out of reading the nonfiction selections in this unit. Here are two key literary elements and two key reading skills that you will practice in this unit.

Key Literary Elements

• Informational Text

Informational text gives more than just facts. It might explain why something happened or how something works. As the selection presents information, different statements tell where the article is headed and why. Most informational texts report events or processes in the order that they happen.

• Author's Purpose

The **author's purpose** is his or her reason for writing. An author's purpose can be to inform, to persuade, to describe, to entertain—or a combination of these things. Writers give facts when they want to inform. Writers who want to entertain may tell a story or describe something in detail. Writers who hope to persuade may present ideas to make readers believe something.

Key Reading Skills

• Question

Question yourself as you read. Ask yourself *who, what, where, when, why,* and *how* questions to make sure you understand what you are reading. Ask yourself questions like: Do I understand what is happening? Does this make sense based on what I have already read? What does this paragraph mean?

• Main Idea and Details

A piece of nonfiction writing has a topic, or **main idea.** Writers may state the main idea directly, or they may let readers figure it out for themselves. **Details** are facts, examples, or quotations that support the main idea.

Köko : Smart Signing Gorilla

Meet Jean Craighead George

When she was young, Jean Craighead George spent her summers on her family's farm in southern Pennsylvania, where she developed a genuine love of nature and its creatures. As a writer, George has combined her loves of nature and literature to create many popular books.

Jean Craighead George was born in 1919. "Koko" was first published in 1994.

What You Know

People talk to their pets all the time. What would you do if your pet or another animal talked back?

Reason to Read

Read "Koko: Smart Signing Gorilla" to find out how a special gorilla communicates.

Background Info

American Sign Language is a language that uses hand signs and gestures only. Some deaf people in North America use American Sign Language to communicate.

In the 1960s, researchers taught American Sign Language to a chimpanzee named Washoe. Around the same time, researchers taught a chimpanzee named Lana to communicate by using a computer. Scientists at Stanford University believed that gorillas could also learn human language.

Word Power

annoying (ə noi´ ing) *adj.* upsetting; disturbing; p. 194
Loud noises are *annoying* to my sister.

demonstrated (dem´ ən strāt id) *v.* showed; explained; p. 194
Our science experiment *demonstrated* how a magnet works.

expanded (iks pand´ id) *v.* increased in size; grew; p. 195
The library *expanded* from having 2,500 to 5,000 books.

stubborn (stub´ ərn) *adj.* not willing to give in or obey; p. 195
The girl's *stubborn* puppy will not come when called.

disciplined (dis´ ə plind) *v.* brought under control; punished; p. 196
The coach *disciplined* the player for missing practice.

expletive (eks´ plə tiv) *n.* an expression of anger, often a rude word or phrase; p. 196
My brother let out a sudden *expletive* when he stubbed his toe.

captivity (kap tiv´ ə tē) *n.* a state of being kept within bounds; p. 198
It is easier to observe animals in *captivity* than in the wild.

**Answer the following questions that contain the new words above.
Write your answers in the spaces provided.**

1. If you use an *expletive*, are you happy or angry? _____

2. If you *expanded* a card collection, were cards added or taken away? _____

3. Which is an *annoying* sound: nails on a chalkboard or your favorite song?

   _____

4. Would a bird in *captivity* be kept in or out of a cage? _____

5. How would you have *demonstrated* that you knew certain math skills: with a low or

   high test score? _____

6. When a child is *disciplined,* has she done something good or bad? _____

7. Would it be easy or difficult to change the mind of a *stubborn* person?

   _____

Adapted from

Koko:
Smart Signing Gorilla

Jean Craighead George

Reading Skill
Main Idea & Details Reread the highlighted sentence. This is the main idea of this paragraph. Underline one detail in this paragraph that supports or explains that gorillas can use language.

"Fine animal gorilla," said a young gorilla, Koko, in American Sign Language. A door to the silent world of the animals had been opened.

Using sign language and eventually a talking computer, Koko—under the teaching of her "mother," Francine (Penny) Patterson—has told us what it is like to be a gorilla. It is just as **annoying** and pleasant as being a human being.

Koko was born July 4, 1971, in the San Francisco Zoo. Penny saw the infant three months later and knew what she wanted to do for a graduate study: She would teach Koko to speak in sign language. After another month the zoo and Stanford University agreed to let her try, and a most remarkable experiment began. It **demonstrated** that gorillas, which have no vocal cords, can use language. With sign language Koko expressed her inner emotions. "This gentle animal," Penny wrote, "feels all the emotions you and I experience; grief, hope, greed, generosity, shame, love and hate."

Word Power
annoying (ə noi′ ing) *adj.* upsetting; disturbing
demonstrated (dem′ ən strāt id) *v.* showed; explained

194

Koko's first word was "drink," the hand made into a fist with the thumb up, then put to the mouth. When that got her a bottle of milk, she quickly learned more signs. One lesson later, she signed "food" and Penny fed her. Koko was so pleased that she put a bucket over her head and ran around wildly. Two months later, when her vocabulary had **expanded** to eight words and combinations of those words, Penny wrote that Koko did "something simple but somehow very touching." She took Penny gently by the hand and led her around her room, pausing to change the position of their hands.

Gorillas have long been known to be moody and Koko was no exception. She was a very **stubborn** youngster. It took her two long months to learn the word for "egg," which she disliked, and one minute to learn "berry." She loved to eat berries.

A sense of humor often rose out of her stubbornness. When asked the color of her white towel for a number of times, she signed "red." When asked twice again, she replied "red," then carefully picked a tiny speck of red lint off her towel. She chuckled, and again said "red."

Did You Know?

Gorillas are found only in tropical Africa. They are disappearing because they are being hunted and their forests are being destroyed.

Koko turned the pages of picture books and named the animals, recognized herself in photographs and in the mirror, carefully cleaned her room, and played with her pets. So deeply did she grieve when her cat died that she was allowed to choose a new kitten from a litter. She took care of it with gentleness and love.

Literary Element

Informational Text Reread the highlighted sentence and the rest of the paragraph. Informational text often explains how something happens. How does Koko sign *drink*, the first word she learns?

_____

_____

_____

Comprehension Check

Reread the boxed paragraph. Why does it take Koko only one minute to learn the word *berry*?

_____

_____

_____

_____

_____

Word Power

expanded (iks pand′ id) *v.* increased in size; grew

stubborn (stub′ ərn) *adj.* not willing to give in or obey

195

Reading Skill

Main Idea and Details Reread the highlighted sentence and the rest of the paragraph. The sentence, "Mike, her young gorilla friend, was 'Mike nut' when she felt jealous of him," is a detail. What is the main idea of this paragraph? Check the correct response.

☐ She hated the noisy blue jays at the zoo, so she called people who annoyed her "bird."

☐ As Koko learned more words, she was not only able to express her likes, but her dislikes.

☐ When truly angry she had a great insult, "rotten toilet," which she made up herself.

English Coach

Irony exists when someone says one thing and means the opposite. An ironic statement is often meant to be funny. If you hated oranges, which sentence would be ironic? Check the correct response.

☐ Eating oranges is disgusting.

☐ Oranges are the worst fruit ever.

☐ Eating an orange is my favorite thing to do.

Eventually Penny purchased Koko from the zoo and moved her and her trailer to the Stanford campus.

As Koko learned more words, she was able to express not only her likes, but her dislikes. She hated the noisy blue jays at the zoo, so she called people who annoyed her "bird." One day when Kate, an assistant, would not open the refrigerator, Koko signed, "Kate bird rotten." When truly angry she had a great insult, "rotten toilet," which she made up herself. Mike, her young gorilla friend, was "Mike nut" when she felt jealous of him. Ron Cohn, Penny's coworker and the person who **disciplined** Koko, came in for the worst cases. "Stupid devil devilhead" was an **expletive** for him. One day when a teacher asked Koko to tell her something funny, she did. "Koko love Ron," she signed, and kissed him on the cheek—then she chuckled. She liked the irony of her own jokes.

What do you think Koko is working on in this photo?

Word Power

disciplined (dis´ ə plind) *v.* brought under control; punished

expletive (eks´ plə tiv) *n.* an expression of anger, often a rude word or phrase

196

Koko could be moody, but she could also be sweet. When Mike was having his picture taken, she told him, "Smile."

Koko liked words. She caught on to pig Latin when workers used it to avoid words like "candy." She also rhymed words. Part of her training was hearing the spoken word when her teachers signed. Asked one day if she could sign a rhyme, she replied, "hair bear" and "all ball."

She was a wizard at making up new words. After drinking her juice through a long rubber tube one day, she called herself an "elephant gorilla." A lighter was a "bottle match," and a mask was an "eyehat." A ring was a "finger bracelet."

Several years ago Koko, Mike, Ron, and Penny moved to the country, where the gorillas could behave like gorillas. Today Koko and Mike climb fruit trees and eat the pears, plums, apples, and apricots. Each has a building, an outdoor play yard, and a computer that speaks. Here is a sign conversation between Penny and Koko after Koko had asked for more words on her computer:

Koko: Do bean.

Penny: Oh, she wants bean.

Koko: Bad fake bird fake bird bird. Apple. (Koko uses the sign "bird" for word.)

At this point Penny realized Koko didn't want a bean but a being, a human being. She asked Koko if that was what she wanted.

Koko: (excitedly) Do bean, do bean.

She was quite satisfied when the image for human being appeared.

Background Info

Pig Latin is a language used to tell secrets. The beginning consonant is moved to the end of the word, followed by the long *a* sound. For example, in pig Latin, *candy* would be pronounced "andy-kay."

Literary Element
Informational Text

Reread the highlighted paragraph. Informational texts often explain why something happens. Why do Penny, Ron, Mike, and Koko move to the country?

_____

_____

_____

_____

_____

What do you think Koko and Mike are talking about?

Reading Skill

Question Reread the highlighted paragraph. Which is the best question to ask yourself to better understand this paragraph? Check the correct response.

☐ What is the Gorilla Foundation?

☐ When will Koko have a baby?

☐ What type of computer does Koko use?

Koko is one of an endangered species. The foundation she inspired, The Gorilla Foundation, is dedicated to breeding gorillas in **captivity.** If all goes as planned, Koko will teach her own baby to sign, use a computer, and tell the "beans" more about themselves and gorillas.

Word Power

captivity (kap tiv′ ə tē) *n.* a state of being kept within bounds

Respond to Literature

Koko : Smart Signing Gorilla

A Comprehension Check

Answer the following questions in the spaces provided.

1. Which emotions does Penny say Koko is able to express through sign language? _____

_____

2. What is the purpose of The Gorilla Foundation? _____

_____

B Reading Skills

Answer the following questions in the spaces provided.

1. **Main Idea & Details** What is one detail that supports the main idea that Koko has a sense of humor? _____

_____

_____

2. **Question** Penny moves Koko from the zoo to a trailer. What questions could you ask to get more information about this move?

_____

_____

C Word Power

Complete each sentence below, using one of the words in the box.

annoying	demonstrated	expanded	stubborn
disciplined	expletive	captivity	

1. The store _____ the number of its parking spaces from thirty to fifty.

2. My _____ sister will not even taste a new kind of food!

3. Several students were _____ for being rude to their classmates.

4. It's _____ when my little brother pulls my hair.

5. In the story, beasts were kept in _____ in dungeons.

6. The rescue _____ that the firefighter was brave.

7. She was so angry when she heard the news that she said an

_____.

D Literary Element: Informational Text

Read the two passages below from "Koko: Smart Signing Gorilla." As you read this informational text, think about what you learn about Koko and her life. Then answer the questions that follow.

Koko liked words.[1] She caught on to pig Latin when workers used it to avoid words like "candy."[2] She also rhymed words.[3] Part of her training was hearing the spoken word when her teachers signed.[4] Asked one day if she could sign a rhyme, she replied, "hair bear" and "all ball."[5]

Several years ago Koko, Mike, Ron, and Penny moved to the country, where the gorillas could behave like gorillas.[6] Today Koko and Mike climb fruit trees and eat the pears, plums, apples, and apricots.[7]

1. In sentences 1–5, how does Koko develop her language skills?

_____

_____

_____

_____

2. In sentences 6–7, what do you learn about how gorillas naturally act?

_____

_____

_____

_____

MUMMY

No. 1770

Meet Patricia Lauber

Patricia Lauber was born in 1924 in New York City. She is the author of more than eighty children's books, many of which focus on nature and science. Some topics have been volcanoes, earthquakes, and the planets. "I was born wanting to write," the author has said. Her nonfiction books require a lot of research, but she says the work helps her learn new things.

"Mummy No. 1770" is from Lauber's book *Tales Mummies Tell*, published in 1985.

What You Know

Have you ever seen a mummy at a museum and wondered who the person was? Have you ever wondered what it would have been like to live thousands of years ago?

Reason to Read

Read to find out how scientists learned about a mysterious mummy's life.

Background Info

A mummy is a dead body that has been preserved with chemicals and special wrappings. The most famous mummies are those from ancient Egypt. The Egyptians believed in life after death, and they preserved their dead so that the bodies could live on. Mummies have also been found in China and other parts of the world. Today mummies can teach scientists a lot about what life was like in ancient times. As scientists study the bodies and look for clues, the mysteries of ancient peoples can be uncovered.

Word Power

amputated (am′ pyə tāt′ id) *v.* cut from the body; p. 208
The doctor was unable to cure the illness, so the patient's leg had to be *amputated*.

decay (di kā′) *n.* a rotting or breaking down of something; p. 209
We left the fruit out too long and found it in a state of *decay*.

collapse (kə laps′) *n.* a caving or falling in; p. 209
The old bridge needs to be repaired because it is in danger of *collapse*.

corpse (kôrps) *n.* a dead body; p. 210
Medical students can learn about the human body by studying a *corpse*.

irritated (ir′ ə tāt′ ed) *v.* made red, raw, or sore; p. 211
Brianna's gums became *irritated* because she brushed her teeth too hard.

fragile (fraj′ əl) *adj.* easily broken; delicate; p. 212
Handle the glass vase carefully because it is very *fragile*.

attractive (ə trak′ tiv) *adj.* pleasing; good-looking; p. 212
I made sure to wear an *attractive* outfit on the first day of school.

**Answer the following questions, using one of the new words above.
Write your answers in the spaces provided.**

1. Which word goes with "something that can break easily"? _____

2. Which word goes with "the body of someone who is no longer alive"? _____

3. Which word goes with "made sore"? _____

4. Which word goes with "something nice to look at"? _____

5. Which word goes with "cut off from the rest of the body"? _____

6. Which word goes with "rot and waste away"? _____

7. Which word goes with "a cave-in"? _____

Adapted from MUMMY
No. 1770
Patricia Lauber

Background Info

Autopsies take place when a doctor looks closely at a dead body to figure out what caused its death.

Reading Skill

Question Reread the highlighted passage. What is the **best** question to ask to understand what this selection is about? Check the correct response.

- ☐ What are the scientists' names?
- ☐ Where is the Manchester Museum located?
- ☐ What will the scientists learn about the mummy?

Museums have a limited number of mummies. Every time one is unwrapped, the number grows smaller, and so autopsies are not often performed. But sometimes a museum has a mummy that is not important to its collection. This is a mummy it does not want to display and a mummy about which almost nothing is known. As it happened, the Manchester Museum had just such a mummy. Its wrappings were in poor condition and no one knew what period it dated from, where it was found, or who the dead person was. The mummy was known only by its museum number, 1770. This was the mummy the museum made available to a team of scientists who wanted to study the wrappings and body in detail.

It was also a mummy with a mystery. X-rays taken years earlier had shown the mummy was that of a young person. The lower parts of the legs were missing, and close to the leg bones was a rounded object. The x-rays did not make clear what it was, but the shape was that of a baby's head. Was this the mummy of a mother and child? Had the mother died shortly after giving birth? Was she perhaps an unwed-mother who had been punished with a terrible death? Those were questions the scientists wondered about as they began their work.

After new x-rays were taken, the unwrapping began. Insect remains found in the bandages were carefully removed for later study. As pieces of cloth were lifted away, the lower part of the mask came into view. Beneath it were the bare bones of the neck and skull. These were in small pieces, but even so, once the pieces had been cleaned it was possible to see that the left side of the nose had been damaged by the iron hook the embalmers had used to remove the brain. The team was surprised to see red and blue paint on the skull bones. How and why had the bones been exposed?

Gently removing more cloth, the scientists found the mummy's arms were crossed on the chest and the hands had gold fingertip covers. The inner organs had been removed and the space filled with bandages and mud. The organs themselves were missing.

A small, hard object that had appeared in the x-rays proved to be a Guinea worm. Guinea worms are swallowed in drinking water. When they grow they may cause blisters and sores in the feet and legs.

Literary Element

Informational Text

Reread the highlighted passage. Informational text is used to explain things. What do the scientists' questions tell you about what you will learn in this article? Check the correct response.

☐ The article will explain how the people working on the mummy decided to become scientists.

☐ The article will explain how the scientists worked to find information about the mummy.

☐ The article will give a brief biography of each scientist who worked on the mummy.

English Coach

Embalmers are people who treat dead bodies with chemicals to protect them from decay. The suffix *-er* means "one who does something." What would you call someone who paints?

_____

_____

207

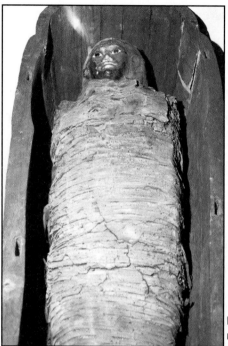

Have you ever seen a mummy in a museum? What was special about it?

Background Info

In ancient Egypt, plants called *papyrus reeds* grew along the Nile River. Egyptians used papyrus to make many things, including boats and baskets, and it was also used to make an early form of paper.

Reading Skill

Main Idea and Details Reread the highlighted sentence and the rest of the paragraph. Which of the following sentences states the main idea of the paragraph? Check the correct response.

☐ Mummy 1770 was very poorly preserved.

☐ The bones of the lower trunk were broken.

☐ Some of the scientists referred to the mummy as a female.

When the Manchester team unwrapped the legs of mummy 1770, they found, as the x-rays had shown, that both legs had been **amputated,** the left below the knee and the right above the knee. The mummy's right leg had been lengthened with a piece of wood to make it the same length as the left. The feet were man made and had gold toenail covers. The right foot was made of reeds and mud. The left foot was simply a mass of reeds and mud.

By now the scientists could see that there was no baby. The rounded shape that had shown in the x-rays was actually a pair of beautiful slippers that had been placed on the soles of the feet.

In one way mummy 1770 was disappointing—it was very poorly preserved. No one could even be certain of its sex, although members of the team came to feel that the young person had been a girl and spoke of the mummy as female. Very little skin, muscle, or soft tissue were left, and the bones of the skull and lower trunk were broken. The scientists could not tell whether the breaks occurred after death or shortly before.

Word Power
amputated (am´ pyə tāt´ id) *v.* cut from the body

208

In other ways, mummy 1770 was both interesting and puzzling. There were signs that the body had been in a state of **decay** when the embalmers worked on it. The wooden leg was attached to bone. All the internal organs were missing and so was the left kneecap. The red and blue paint on the skull bones was a sign that the hair and scalp had been missing.

Why had the body decayed? Why were the legs amputated?

Perhaps infections caused by the Guinea worms had cut off the flow of blood to the legs and feet. In an effort to save the girl's life, doctors had amputated her legs, but the patient died. But if that was the case, why hadn't she been promptly embalmed?

Or perhaps the legs had been cut off in an accident, such as the **collapse** of a building. If the girl had been buried and not found for some time, that might explain the decay.

Or suppose the girl had drowned in the Nile, where decay would set in quickly. The body might have been attacked by hippos or crocodiles.

As things turned out, there was another explanation for the state of the body and it took everyone by surprise. When carbon-14 dating was completed, it showed that the mummy was far older than its wrappings. They dated to a time when the Romans ruled Egypt, around A.D. 260. The mummy's bones dated to around 1000 B.C. This meant that 1770 was a mummy that had been wrapped twice. It had been preserved and wrapped after the girl died, then rewrapped more than a thousand years later. Now some pieces of the puzzle began to fall into place.

Reading Skill

Main Idea and Details Reread the highlighted sentence and the rest of the paragraph. Then read the statements below. One is the main idea and the other two are details. On the lines, write *M* for Main Idea, or *D* for Detail.

____ The wooden leg was attached to bone.

____ Mummy 1770 was both interesting and puzzling.

____ The left kneecap was missing.

Background Info

Carbon-14 dating is a scientific method of figuring out the age of carbon-based material. The method was discovered in 1949. It is often used by scientists who study bones.

English Coach

An abbreviation is a shortened word or phrase. *A.D.* and *B.C.* are abbreviations for time periods. What is the abbreviation for "compact disc"?

_____

Word Power

decay (di kā′) *n.* a rotting or breaking down of something

collapse (kə laps′) *n.* a caving or falling in

Reading Skill

Question Reread the highlighted paragraph. What is the **best** question to ask to understand this paragraph? Check the correct response.

☐ What are the wrappings made of?

☐ How was the mummy damaged?

☐ What color are the wrappings?

Comprehension Check

Reread the boxed passage. How does the dentist figure out the girl's age at the time of her death? What does he find out?

_____

_____

_____

_____

_____

There was no need to explain why the **corpse** had decayed, because it hadn't. Rather, it was the mummy that had been damaged by water and then had decayed. The soft tissues of the body were probably missing because they had stuck to the original wrappings.

The way the second embalmers had prepared the body made clear that they did not know whether they were dealing with a male or a female. This meant they did not know the mummy's identity. But the trouble they took shows that they thought they were dealing with someone of importance. The tomb from which the mummy came must have led them to that conclusion. At times in ancient Egypt royal mummies were moved to new tombs. If they had been damaged, they were repaired at the time of the move. Quite possibly 1770 was a person of royal or noble birth whose mummy was damaged when a tomb was flooded.

X-rays had shown that the mummy's wisdom teeth had not yet grown in, and so the girl must have been less than 20 years old. The dentist on the team now examined the roots of other teeth. Their stage of development told him that 1770 had been 13 to 14 years old. He was surprised to see that the teeth showed no sign of being worn down by the desert sand found in the bread of ancient Egypt. He also saw that two teeth in the upper jaw were oddly placed. A space between them near the gum formed a trap for food particles. Usually such a trap leads to infection, which damages the bone of the jaw. But this had not happened to 1770. The lack of wear and damage suggested that her diet was soft, perhaps mostly liquid. Or she may have swallowed food without trying to chew it much. Most likely she had not been very healthy.

Word Power

corpse (kôrps) *n.* a dead body

This photo represents a person who lived many years ago. What questions would you ask this person if she were alive?

She must also have breathed mainly through her mouth. The badly formed bones in the inner part of her nose would have made it almost impossible to breathe any other way. If a person always breathes through the mouth, the gums around the upper front teeth become **irritated** and the bone behind them pitted. Pits in the bones of 1770's mouth showed that she had indeed breathed through her mouth.

By this time the Manchester team had learned a great deal about 1770. She was a young person who had lived a short life with much suffering. She had had to breathe through her mouth, had sore gums, ate only liquid or soft food, and had been infected by Guinea worms, which cause fever and an itching rash as well as blisters. Finally, by means still not clear, she had lost her legs around the time she died.

Word Power

irritated (ir′ ə tāt′ ed) v. made red, raw, or sore

Literary Element

Informational Text Reread the paragraph highlighted in blue. Informational text can explain why something happens. What does this paragraph explain? Check the correct response.
- [ ] how bones are formed in the nose and other parts of the face
- [ ] what happens when a person can breathe only through the mouth
- [ ] how gums and teeth develop as a person continues to grow

Reading Skill

Main Idea and Details Reread the sentence highlighted in green and the rest of the paragraph. Underline the main idea of this paragraph.

My Workspace

Comprehension Check

Reread the paragraph boxed in green. What is the first thing the scientists have to do in order to find out what 1770 had looked like? Check the correct response.

☐ mix the bones with mud
☐ clean the bone pieces
☐ make a plaster cast

Connect to the Text

Reread the sentence boxed in purple. Think about a time when you saw a picture of someone who lived long ago, such as in a family album or in a museum. What things did you want to know about this person?

_____

_____

_____

One final step remained to be taken—to find out what 1770 had looked like. The skull had broken into about 30 pieces, some of them very small and **fragile.** The pieces lay in a jumbled heap and were mixed with mud and bandages. Once the pieces of bone had been cleaned, one member of the team made casts of them in plastic. When the plastic pieces were fitted together, much of the left side of the skull was still missing. A plaster cast was made to fill out the basic shape of the head. Now small pegs were placed in the plastic skull and cut to exact lengths. Each showed how thick the soft tissues of the face would be on a 13-year-old person. The face was then built up with modeling clay. First it took on a general human appearance. Then it took on an appearance of its own, shaped by the underlying bones. This model was used to cast the head in wax, so that changes could be made if more was learned about 1770. The wax head was painted, given glass eyes, a wig, and eyelashes. And there at last was 1770—an **attractive** teenager, perhaps of royal or noble birth, who had laughed, cried, and lived 3,000 years ago.

Word Power

fragile (fraj′ əl) *adj.* easily broken; delicate
attractive (ə trak′ tiv) *adj.* pleasing; good-looking

Respond to Literature

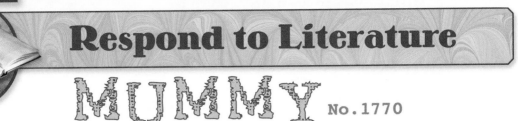

MUMMY No. 1770

A Comprehension Check

Answer the following questions in the spaces provided.

1. Why does the Manchester Museum give Mummy No. 1770 to scientists?

   _____

2. What do the scientists learn about what the girl ate?

   _____

B Reading Skills

Answer the following questions in the spaces provided.

1. **Question** Think about the point in the selection when the scientists discover the mummy's beautiful slippers. What is one question to ask yourself at this point in the article?

   _____

   _____

   _____

2. **Main Idea and Details** Think about the selection. If you were telling a friend about the article, how would you state its main idea?

   _____

   _____

   _____

C Word Power

Complete each sentence below, using one of the words in the box.

| amputated | decay | collapse | corpse |
| irritated | fragile | attractive |

1. The store display was so _____ that I went in to buy something.

2. When the bullet wound wouldn't heal, the soldier's leg had to be

   _____.

3. My grandmother's china is very _____, so she only uses it for special occasions.

4. If you don't pull out a splinter, the skin around it will get red and

   _____.

5. The tornado caused the _____ of several houses in our area.

6. If you don't brush your teeth after you eat sugary foods, you may get

   tooth _____.

7. The doctors examined the _____ to figure out the cause of death.

D Literary Element: Informational Text

Read the excerpts below from "Mummy No. 1770." As you read, think about the purposes of informational text. Then answer the questions that follow.

A small, hard object that had appeared in the x-rays proved to be a Guinea worm.[1] Guinea worms are swallowed in drinking water.[2] When they grow they may cause blisters and sores in the feet and legs.[3]

A plaster cast was made to fill out the basic shape of the head.[4] The face was then built up with modeling clay.[5] This model was used to cast the head in wax, so that changes could be made if more was learned about 1770.[6] The wax head was painted, given glass eyes, a wig, and eyelashes.[7]

1. What do you learn about Guinea worms in sentences 1–3?

_____

_____

_____

_____

2. Informational text can also explain how something works. What process is explained in sentences 4–7? In what order is the information given?

_____

_____

_____

_____

E Scientists Study Mummy No. 1770

Pretend you are a newspaper reporter writing about Mummy No. 1770. Complete the news story with details about what the scientists discovered.

A group of scientists was given a mummy to study. The mummy belonged to the _____

They gave the mummy to the scientist because _____

_____

First the scientists _____

Then they found out that _____

_____

_____

The scientists' most surprising discovery was that _____

_____

_____

The last thing the scientists had to do was _____

_____

After putting together her face bones and adding a wig, glass eyes, and eyelashes, they were able to see that _____

_____

Reported by _____

Assessment

Fill in the circle next to each correct answer.

1. What do the scientists find out by studying the mummy's teeth?
   - ○ A. how the girl lost her legs
   - ○ B. the girl's age at the time of her death
   - ○ C. what part of Egypt the girl lived in
   - ○ D. why the organs are missing

2. In order to find more information about the girl's life, what is the **best** question to ask after reading the article?
   - ○ A. Why weren't the scientists' names mentioned in the article?
   - ○ B. What will the scientists work on next?
   - ○ C. What was daily life like in ancient Egypt?
   - ○ D. Where is the Manchester Museum?

3. Which of the following **best** states the main idea of the selection?
   - ○ A. Scientists were given a mummy to study and learned many details about the person's life.
   - ○ B. Scientists can date mummies using the carbon-14 dating process.
   - ○ C. It's important to have a dentist on a scientific team to determine the age of the mummy.
   - ○ D. The mummy had been wrapped twice.

4. Which of the following choices **best** describes how the information is presented in the selection?
   - ○ A. from most interesting details to least interesting details
   - ○ B. from least interesting details to most interesting details
   - ○ C. in a random order chosen by the author
   - ○ D. step by step, in the order of what the scientists did and discovered

5. Which of the following words means "delicate and easy to break"?
   - ○ A. attractive
   - ○ B. fragile
   - ○ C. amputated
   - ○ D. irritated

Get Ready to Read!

The Land of Red Apples

Meet Zitkala-Ša

"As free as the wind that blew my hair, and no less spirited than a bounding deer." Zitkala-Ša (zēt kä´ lä shä), or Gertrude Bonnin, used these words to describe her Sioux childhood in South Dakota. At age eight, she was sent east to a school for Native American children in Indiana.

Bonnin took the name Zitkala-Ša—meaning Red Bird—and became an author and worker for Native American rights.

Zitkala-Ša was born in 1876 and died in 1938. This story was first published in 1900.

What You Know

Imagine that you are being sent far away from your family for several years. You are going somewhere where people speak another language and wear clothing different from yours.

Reason to Read

Read the autobiography "The Land of Red Apples" to discover what happens when Zitkala-Ša's life changes suddenly and completely.

Background Info

During the late 1800s and early 1900s, the U.S. government forced Native American children to be sent to schools far from their homes. At these schools, teachers did not allow children to speak their own languages or wear their own clothing. Children wore uniforms and were taught in English. Because the schools were so far from their homes, the children were away from their families for years at a time. The government wanted the children to "fit better" in white society. But most Native American children and their families felt like they were being punished and denied the right to practice their own customs.

Word Power

missionaries (mish′ ə ner′ ēz) *n.* people sent to spread a religion; p. 220
Missionaries teach the ways of their church.

horizon (hə rī′ zən) *n.* imaginary line where the earth meets the sky; p. 220
We watched the sun dip below the *horizon*.

verge (vurj) *n.* the point just before something begins; the edge; p. 221
The frightened animal was on the *verge* of running away.

incline (in′ klīn) *n.* a slope; slant; p. 223
We were tired after walking up the steep *incline*.

exhausted (ig zôst′ id) *v.* to make very weak or tired; p. 224
We *exhausted* ourselves by running for an hour.

**Answer the following questions, using one of the new words above.
Write your answers in the spaces provided.**

1. Which word goes with "a slope"? _____

2. Which word goes with "made very tired"? _____

3. Which word goes with "about to begin"? _____

4. Which word goes with "spreading religion"? _____

5. Which word goes with "an imaginary line"? _____

Adapted from

The Land of Red Apples

Zitkala-Ša

English Coach

The prefix *im-* means "not." Does the word *impatient* mean "not patient" or "being very patient"?

_____

_____

Background Info

"Palefaces" was what some Native Americans called white people.

There were eight in our group of copper-colored children who were going East with the **missionaries.** We were three young warriors, two tall girls, and three little ones, Judéwin, Thowin, and I.

We had been very impatient to start on our journey to the Red Apple Country. We were told it lay a little beyond the great circular **horizon** of the Western prairie. We dreamt of roaming as freely and happily under a sky of rosy apples there as we had chased the cloud shadows on the Dakota plains. We had looked forward to much pleasure from a ride on the iron horse, but the great crowds of staring palefaces disturbed and troubled us.

Did You Know?
Early trains were pulled by steam locomotives. This kind of locomotive was called the *iron horse*.

Word Power

missionaries (mish′ə ner′ ēz) *n.* people sent to spread a religion

horizon (hə rī′ zən) *n.* imaginary line where the earth meets the sky

On the train, light-skinned women, with babies on each arm, stopped and looked closely at us. We were children whose mothers were absent. Large men, with heavy bundles in their hands, stood nearby, and stared at us with their glassy blue eyes.

I sank deep into the corner of my seat, for I was annoyed at being watched. Directly in front of me, children who were no larger than I hung themselves upon the backs of their seats, with their bold white faces toward me. Sometimes they took their fingers out of their mouths and pointed at my moccasined feet.

Instead of scolding the children for being so rude, their mothers also studied me, and pointed out my blanket to their children. This embarrassed me, and kept me constantly on the **verge** of tears.

I sat perfectly still, with my eyes looking downward, daring only now and then to look around me. Turning to the window at my side, I was quite excited to see one familiar object. It was the telegraph pole which sped by one after another. Very near my mother's dwelling, along the edge of a road thickly bordered with wild sunflowers, some poles like these had been planted by white men. Often I had stopped, on my way down the road, to hold my ear against the pole. Hearing its low moaning, I used to wonder what the paleface had done to hurt it. Now I sat watching for each pole that glided by to be the last one. . . .

Did You Know?

Moccasins are soft shoes, often made from the skin of a deer. Moccasins were originally worn by North American Indians. The bottom and sides are stitched to the top with leather strips.
. . . .

Reading Skill
Main Idea & Details
Reread the highlighted sentence and the rest of the paragraph. The main idea is that people behaved rudely toward the narrator. Underline one detail that supports the main idea.

Comprehension Check

Reread the boxed passage. What is the narrator interested in looking at on her train ride? Why?

_____

_____

_____

_____

_____

Word Power
verge (vurj) *n.* the point just before something begins; the edge

221

What do the children in the photo have in common with the narrator?

Connect
to the Text

Reread the boxed sentence. Have you ever been in a frightening situation? What was it? How did you handle it?

It was night when we reached the school grounds. The lights from the windows of the large buildings fell upon some of the icicled trees that stood beneath them. We were led toward an open door. The brightness of the lights within flooded out over the heads of the excited palefaces who blocked the way. My body trembled more from fear than from the snow I walked upon.

Entering the house, I stood close against the wall. The strong glaring light in the large white room dazzled my eyes. The noisy hurrying of hard shoes upon a bare wooden floor increased the whirring in my ears. My only safety seemed to be in keeping next to the wall.

I was wondering in which direction to escape from all this confusion when two warm hands grasped me firmly. In the same moment I was tossed high in midair. A rosy-cheeked paleface woman caught me in her arms. I was both frightened and insulted by such treatment. I stared into her eyes, wishing her to let me stand on my own feet. But she only tossed me up and down with increasing energy. My mother had never made a plaything of her wee daughter. Remembering this I began to cry aloud.

They misunderstood the cause of my tears, and placed me at a white table loaded with food. There our group was united again. When I did not hush my crying, one of the older ones whispered to me, "Wait until you are alone in the night."

There was not much that I could swallow besides my sobs that evening.

"Oh, I want my mother and my brother Dawee! I want to go to my aunt!" I pleaded; but the ears of the palefaces could not hear me.

From the table we were taken along an upward **incline** of wooden boxes, which I learned afterward to call a stairway. At the top was a quiet hall, dimly lighted. Many narrow beds were in one straight line down the entire length of the wall. In them lay sleeping brown faces, which peeped just out of the coverings. I was tucked into bed with one of the tall girls, because she talked to me in my own language and seemed to soothe me.

Reading Skill

Question Reread the highlighted passage. What is the **best** question to ask while reading to get the most important information from this passage? Check the correct response.

- [ ] Why is the narrator crying?
- [ ] What are the children eating?
- [ ] What is the narrator wearing?

Word Power

incline (in′ klīn) *n.* a slope; slant

223

Literary Element

Author's Purpose

Reread the highlighted paragraph. The author is trying to inform the reader about how she felt during this time. Which emotions does the author express? Check the correct responses.

- ☐ fear
- ☐ excitement
- ☐ loneliness
- ☐ disappointment
- ☐ joy

I had arrived in the wonderful land of rosy skies. But I was not happy, as I had thought I should be. My long travel and the confusing sights had **exhausted** me. I fell asleep, heaving deep, tired sobs. My tears were left to dry themselves in streaks, because neither my aunt nor my mother was near to wipe them away.

Compare this photo with the photo on page 222. How have the girls changed?

_____

_____

Word Power

exhausted (ig zôst´ id) *v.* to make very weak or tired

Respond to Literature

The Land of Red Apples

A Comprehension Check

Answer the following questions in the spaces provided.

1. Where are the children on the train going, and with whom?

   _____

   _____

2. What do the children expect life in the Red Apple Country to be like?

   _____

   _____

B Reading Skills

Answer the following questions in the spaces provided.

1. **Question** Write one question you could ask yourself to understand what happens when the narrator arrives at the school.

   _____

   _____

2. **Main Idea & Details** What is one detail that supports the main idea that Zitkala-Ša is homesick?

   _____

   _____

   _____

C Word Power

Complete each sentence below, using one of the words in the box.

> missionaries   horizon
>
> verge   incline   exhausted

1. The runner was on the _____ of setting a world record.

2. The painter _____ himself after painting the whole house.

3. The house was built on a steep _____.

4. The _____ built a school and a hospital.

5. In the distance we saw ships sailing across the _____.

Circle the word that best completes each sentence.

6. The (**missionaries**, **incline**) wanted to help people.

7. We walked to the top of the (**incline**, **horizon**).

8. The broken tree branch was on the (**missionaries**, **verge**) of falling.

9. The sun set below the (**exhausted**, **horizon**).

10. The hikers (**incline**, **exhausted**) themselves during their long climb.

D Literary Element: Author's Purpose

Read the passages below from "The Land of Red Apples." As you read, think about why the author wrote this story. Then answer the questions that follow.

The lights from the windows of the large buildings fell upon some of the icicled trees that stood beneath them.[1] We were led toward an open door.[2] The brightness of the lights within flooded our over the heads of the excited palefaces who blocked the way.[3] My body trembled more from fear than from the snow I walked upon.[4]

I had arrived in the wonderful land of rosy skies.[5] But I was not happy, as I had thought I should be.[6] . . . I fell asleep, heaving deep, tired sobs.[7] My tears were left to dry themselves in streaks, because neither my aunt nor my mother was near to wipe them away.[8]

1. In sentences 1–4 the author gives us facts about when she arrives at school. What is the author's purpose?

_____

_____

_____

2. In sentences 6–8 the author tells how unhappy she is. What is the author trying to persuade us to believe?

_____

_____

_____

E A Postcard

Imagine that you are Zitkala-Ša. You have arrived at the school and want to send a postcard to your mother. Draw a picture of the school or your room. Then write a short message.

Dear Mother,

This is a picture of _____

This place is _____

_____

On my first night here _____

_____

Being here makes me feel _____

_____

I miss you very much.

Love,
Zitkala-Ša

To:
My Family

At:
My Home

Assessment

Fill in the circle next to each correct answer.

1. What does the narrator do when people stare at her on the train?
    ○ A. cover her eyes
    ○ B. hide under her blanket
    ○ C. look out a window
    ○ D. cry out loud

2. Which sentence is a detail that supports the main idea that Zitkala-Sa is excited about going to the Red Apple Country?
    ○ A. We had been very impatient to start on our journey.
    ○ B. I sank deep into the corner of my seat.
    ○ C. We were children whose mothers were absent.
    ○ D. Now I sat watching for each pole that glided by to be the last one.

3. Which is the **best** question that a reader might ask to understand the selection?
    ○ A. How much does it cost to ride the train?
    ○ B. What food do the children eat at the school?
    ○ C. Why does the school have whitewashed walls?
    ○ D. What happens when the narrator reaches the school?

4. Which of the following is **not** the author's purpose in writing "The Land of Red Apples"?
    ○ A. to describe
    ○ B. to entertain
    ○ C. to inform
    ○ D. to persuade

5. Which word means "a slope"?
    ○ A. incline
    ○ B. verge
    ○ C. missionaries
    ○ D. horizon

Respond to Literature

Madam C. J. Walker

A Comprehension Check

Answer the following questions in the spaces provided.

1. What problem leads Sarah to look for better hair products?

   _____

2. Who becomes the president of the company after Madam Walker dies?

   _____

B Reading Skills

Complete the following activities in the spaces provided.

1. **Main Idea and Details** Write two details that support this main idea: Madam C. J. Walker proved that women could earn their own money and run their own business.

   _____

   _____

   _____

2. **Question** Write one question that would help you understand what happens to Madam Walker's estate after she dies.

   _____

   _____

   _____

C Word Power

Complete each sentence below, using one of the words in the box.

inherited   determined   remedy   advertise
established   expectations

1. Chicken noodle soup is a good _____ for a cold.

2. I _____ some great baseball cards from my grandmother.

3. The coach had high _____ for the team.

4. We can _____ our car in the newspaper.

5. The fund was set up and _____ to help many people.

6. Val was _____ to learn how to swim.

Glossary

A

accuse (ə kūz´) v. to blame or state that someone has done something wrong; p. 157

accustomed (ə kus´ təmd) adj. used to; in the habit of; p. 82

acquainted (əkwān´ tid) adj. having knowledge of something; familiar with; p. 109

acquired (ə kwīrd´) v. got as one's own; p. 161

advertise (ad´ vər tīz) v. to tell the public about a product or event; p. 234

amputated (am´ pyə tāt´ id) v. cut from the body; p. 208

ancestors (an´ ses´ tərs) n. people from whom someone is descended, especially from the distant past; p. 182

annoying (ə noi´ ing) adj. upsetting; disturbing; p. 194

astray (ə strā´) adv. off the right path; p. 80

attractive (ə trak´ tiv) adj. pleasing; good-looking; p. 212

C

captivity (kap tiv´ ə tē) n. a state of being kept within bounds; p. 198

chaos (kā´ os) n. extreme confusion; p. 82

claims (klāmz) n. pieces of land that people, such as miners, say they have a right to; p. 17

collapse (kə laps´) n. a caving or falling in; p. 209

commotion (kə mō´ shən) n. noisy confusion; p. 35

comrades (kom´ radz) n. fellow members of a group; p. 24

confident (kon´ fə dənt) adj. certain; full of belief in oneself; p. 34

consisted (kən sist´ id) v. made up (of); contained; p. 83

consulting (kən sul´ ting) v. getting advice or information from; p. 160

consumption (kən sump´ shən) n. the act of eating, drinking, or using; p. 115

continent (kont´ ən ənt) n. one of the seven large land areas on Earth; p. 182

controlled (kən trōld´) v. had power over; p. 67

coordinator (kō ôr´ də nā´ tər) n. one who organizes an event; p. 33

corpse (kôrps) n. a dead body; p. 210

D

debut (dā bū´) n. first public appearance; p. 33

decay (di kā´) n. a rotting or breaking down of something; p. 209

defeated (di fēt´ id) adj. disappointed; not successful; p. 50

defensive (di fen´siv) adj. ready to guard or protect; p. 67

demonstrated (dem´ ən strāt id) v. showed; explained; p. 194

determined (di tur´ mind) adj. having a set purpose; p. 233

disciplined (dis´ ə plind) v. brought under control; punished; p. 196

disgraced (dis grāsd´) v. brought shame to; p. 106

disinfect (dis´in fekt´) v. to rid a surface of germs; p. 106

E

established (es tab´ lisht) v. set up something; brought about; p. 237

etiquette (et´ i ket´) n. rules of proper social behavior; p. 114

Glossary

exhausted (ig zôst´ id) *v.* to make very weak or tired; p. 224

expanded (iks pand´ id) *v.* increased in size; grew; p. 195

expectations (eks´ pek tā´ shənz) *n.* thinking that something will happen; p. 239

expletive (eks´ plə tiv) *n.* an expression of anger, often a rude word or phrase; p. 196

expression (iks presh´ ən) *n.* a look on the face that shows feeling; p. 52

extremely (iks trēm´ lē) *adv.* much more than usual; p. 134

exuded (ig zo͞od´ id) *v.* gave off; released; p. 82

F

fate (fāt) *n.* a power that determines how things will turn out; p. 8

feeble (fē´ bəl) *adj.* not strong; weak; p. 183

fragile (fraj´ əl) *adj.* easily broken; delicate; p. 212

G

generations (jen´ ə rā´ shəns) *n.* steps in the history of a family; p. 182

H

heartbroken (härt´ brō kən) *adj.* extremely sad; p. 173

hesitated (hez´ ə tāt´ id) *v.* stopped for a minute; paused; p. 50

hobble (hob´ əl) *v.* to walk with a limp or in a clumsy way; p. 183

horizon (hə rī´ zən) *n.* imaginary line where the earth meets the sky; p. 220

I

illuminate (i lo͞o´ mə nāt) *v.* to light up; p. 158

immense (i mens´) *adj.* of great size; huge; p. 8

impulse (im´ puls) *n.* a sudden desire to act; p. 51

incline (in´ klīn) *n.* a slope; slant; p. 223

indicate (in´ di kāt´) *v.* to show; to be a sign of; p. 85

inherited (in her´ it id) *v.* received something from someone who died; p. 232

injustice (in jus´ tis) *n.* unfairness; p. 19

intended (in ten´ did) *v.* to have planned; meant; p. 174

irritated (ir´ ə tāt´ ed) *v.* made red, raw, or sore; p. 211

J

jargon (jär´ gən) *n.* terms used in a particular field that may not be understood by outsiders; p. 40

L

lacerations (las´ ə rā´ shəns) *n.* cuts; wounds; p. 5

lodge (loj) *n.* a small house; p. 172

M

maneuvered (mə no͞o´ vərd) *v.* moved in a skillful or planned way; p. 36

missionaries (mish´ ə ner´ ēz) *n.* people sent to spread a religion; p. 220

modestly (mod´ ist lē) *adv.* in a humble manner; p. 154

Glossary

mortified (môr′ tə fīd′) *adj.* very embarrassed; p. 108

N

nonsense (non′ sens) *n.* foolish actions or words; p. 96

novelty (nov′ əl tē) *n.* anything new and unusual; p. 158

P

palms (päms) *n.* the underside of hands between fingers and wrists; p. 66

pantomime (pan′ tə mīm′) *n.* the use of gestures only, without words, to tell something; p. 33

penetrated (pen′ ə trāt′ id) *v.* passed into; forced a way through; p. 79

possession (pə zesh′ ən) *n.* a thing owned; p. 132

poverty (pov′ ər tē) *n.* condition of being poor; p. 155

proceedings (prə sē′dingz) *n.* actions or events; p. 143

procession (prə sesh′ ən) *n.* a march; people or things moving forward in an orderly way; p. 141

promotion (prə mō shən) *n.* to move up in position or grade; p. 113

prosperous (pros′ pər əs) *adj.* having wealth or good fortune; p. 154

pun (pun) *n.* a joke in which a word has two meanings; p. 6

pursuers (pər sōō′ ərs) *n.* people chasing someone or something; p. 21

Q

quarrel (kwôr′ əl) *v.* to disagree angrily; p. 170

R

raggedy (rag′ id ē) *adj.* torn or worn-out; p. 95

rattling (rat′ ling) *v.* making repeated quick, sharp sounds; p. 95

remedy (rem′ə dē) *n.* a cure for a problem; p. 233

repulsive (ri pul′siv) *adj.* causing dislike; disgusting; p. 135

restrained (ri strānd′) *v.* held back from acting; p. 51

ridiculous (ri dik′yə ləs) *adj.* funny; foolish; p. 70

S

schoolyard (skool′ yärd′) *n.* an area around a school used for play; p. 96

stragglers (strag′ lərz) *n.* those who stay behind or stray from the main group; p. 8

stubborn (stub′ ərn) *adj.* not willing to give in or obey; p. 195

subtle (sut′ əl) *adj.* not easily seen; p. 4

suffered (suf′ ərd) *v.* experienced pain or loss; p. 171

suspense (sə spens′) *n.* being anxious or unsure in a situation; p. 20

swaggers (swag′ ərz) *v.* walks or behaves in a bold, rude, or proud way; p. 6

systematic (sis′ tə mat′ ik) *adj.* well organized; doing things a certain way; p. 113

T

transformed (trans fôrmd′) *v.* changed in form, appearance, or use; p. 51

tremendous (tri men′dəs) *adj.* wonderful; p. 141

Glossary

U

underneath (un´dər nēth´) *adv.* down
below; p. 66

V

verge (vurj) *n.* the point just before
something begins; the edge; p. 221

W

waterfall (wô´ tər fôl´) *n.* a stream of water
that falls from a high place; p. 96

ACKNOWLEDGMENTS

LITERATURE

UNIT 1

"Priscilla and the Wimps" by Richard Peck, copyright © 1984 by Richard Peck, from *Sixteen: Short Stories* by Donald R. Gallo, ed. Used by permission of Random House Children's Books, a division of Random House, Inc.

"La Bamba" from *Baseball in April and Other Stories,* copyright © 1990 by Gary Soto, reprinted by permission of Harcourt, Inc.

"After You, My Dear Alphonse" from *The Lottery and Other Stories* by Shirley Jackson. Copyright © 1948, 1949 by Shirley Jackson. Copyright renewed 1976, 1977 by Laurence Hyman, Barry Hyman, Mrs. Sarah Webster and Mrs. Joanne Schnurer. Reprinted by permission of Farrar, Straus & Giroux, LLC.

UNIT 2

"The Game" by Walter Dean Myers. Copyright © 1975 by Walter Dean Myers. Reprinted by permission of Miriam Altshuler Literary Agency, on behalf of Walter Dean Myers.

"Zlateh the Goat" from *Zlateh the Goat and Other Stories* by Isaac Bashevis Singer. Text copyright © 1966 by Isaac Bashevis Singer, copyright renewed 1994 by Alma Singer. Used by permission of HarperCollins Publishers.

"Eleven" from *Woman Hollering Creek.* Copyright © 1991 by Sandra Cisneros. Published by Vintage Books, a division of Random House, Inc., and originally in hardcover by Random House Inc. Adapted and reprinted by permission of Susan Bergholz Literary Services, New York. All rights reserved.

"The All-American Slurp," by Lensey Namioka, copyright © 1987, from *Visions,* edited by Donald R. Gallo. Reprinted by permission of Lensey Namioka. All rights are reserved by the Author.

UNIT 3

Adapted from Roald Dahl's *Charlie & the Chocolate Factory,* adapted by Richard R. George. Copyright © 1976 by Roald Dahl and Richard R. George. Adapted and reprinted by permission of David Higham Associates.

UNIT 4

Adapted from "The Force of Luck" by Rudolfo A. Anaya, from *Cuentos.* Copyright © 1980 by the Museum of New Mexico Press. Adapted and reprinted by permission of the Museum of New Mexico Press.

"Loo-Wit: the Fire-Keeper" by Joseph Bruchac. Adapted and reprinted by permission of Barbara S. Kouts.

"The End of the World" by Jenny Leading Cloud, from *The Sound of Flutes and Other Indian Legends* by Richard Erdoes and Paul Goble, copyright © 1976 by Richard Erdoes. Illustrations copyright © 1976 by Paul Goble. Used by permission of Random House Children's Books, a division of Random House, Inc.

UNIT 5

Adapted from "Koko: Smart Signing Gorilla" copyright © 1994 by Jean Craighead George. Used by permission of HarperCollins Publishers.

Adapted from "Mummy No. 1770" from *Tales Mummies Tell,* by Patricia Lauber. Copyright © 1985 by Patricia G. Lauber.
Used by permission of HarperCollins Publishers.

Adaptation of "Madam C.J. Walker" from *One More River to Cross* by Jim Haskins. Copyright © 1992 by James Haskins. Adapted and reprinted by permission of Scholastic, Inc.

IMAGE CREDITS:

Cover Images.com/CORBIS; **iii** Getty Images; **iv** Owain Kirby/Getty Images; **vi–xiii** Goodshoot/
PunchStock; **xiv–xvii** Getty Images, **(bkgd)**CORBIS; **xviii** Getty Images; **2** courtesy Penguin Putnam;
4 Mark C. Burnett; **6** Dick Clintsman/Getty Images; **8 (t)**David Madison, **(b)**Alamy Images; **14** Hulton
Archive/Getty Images; **16** Paul Souders/Getty Images; **20** North Wind Picture Archives; **23** Kim
Heacox/Getty Images; **30** Carolyn Soto; **32 34** Aaron Haupt Photography; **35** Randy Faris/CORBIS;
38 Gilbert Mayers/SuperStock; **40** Richard Laird/Getty Images; **46** AP/Wide World Photos;
48 Matt Carr/Getty Images; **50** Lucien Aigner/CORBIS; **52** Chaloner Woods/Getty Images;
60 Images.com/CORBIS; **62** courtesy Scholastic, Inc.; **64 (t)**Steve Casimiro/Getty Images, **(b)**Getty
Images; **66** Jeff Greenberg/PhotoEdit; **68 70** Bob Daemmrich/PhotoEdit; **76** Susan Greenwood/
The Liaison Agency/Getty Images; **78** Orion Press/Natural Selection; **81 84** reprinted from
Harper-Collins, illustration by Maurice Sendak; **85** Doug Martin; **86** reprinted from Harper-Collins,
illustration by Maurice Sendak; **92** M. Toussant/The Liaison Agency/Getty Images; **94** Aaron Haupt
Photography; **97** Columbus Museum of Art, Ohio; bequest of Frederick W. Schumacher,Cat.#17
accession (57)43.11; **98** Guy Grenier/Masterfile; **104** Courtesy Lensey Namioka, photo by Don Perkins;
106 108 KS Studio/Bob Mullenix; **111** Doug Martin; **114** Johnér Bildbyrå; **117** Arthur Beck/CORBIS;
119 David Young-Wolff/Getty Images; **126** Owain Kirby/Getty Images; **128** Horst Tappe/Hulton
Archive/Getty Images; **30** Matt Meadows; **131** Kurt Scholz/SuperStock; **135** WARNER BROS./THE
KOBAL COLLECTION/MOUNTAIN, PETER; **140 144** Warner Bros/ZUMA/CORBIS; **150** Alamy Images;
152 Miriam Berkley; **154 156** Christie's Images/SuperStock; **161** Roger Tidman/CORBIS; **168** John Pflug;
170 CORBIS; **172** Pat O'Hara/CORBIS; **174** CORBIS; **180** Richard Erdoes; **182 (t)**Pat O'Hara/CORBIS,
(b) Layne Kennedy/CORBIS; **183** Christie's Images/CORBIS; **190** Images.com/CORBIS; **192** Ellan Young;
194–198 Dr. Ronald Cohn/Gorilla Foundation; **204** courtesy Scholastic, Inc.; **206** CORBIS;
208 Charles & Josette Lenars/CORBIS; **211** Sandro Vannini/CORBIS; **218** Dakota Indian Foundation;
220 (t) Getty Images, **(b)**Mark E. Gibson/Gibson Stock Photography; **221** David McGlynn/Getty
Images; **222 224** Pennsylvania State Archives; **230** University of Florida; **232 (t)**Bettmann/CORBIS,
(b) Library of Congress; **235** A'Lelia Bundles/Madam Walker Family Collection; **238** Getty Images,
(inset) Madam C.J. Walker Collection, Indiana Historical Society; **others** Getty Images.